FIERCE

ROSEWOOD HIGH #4

TRACY LORRAINE

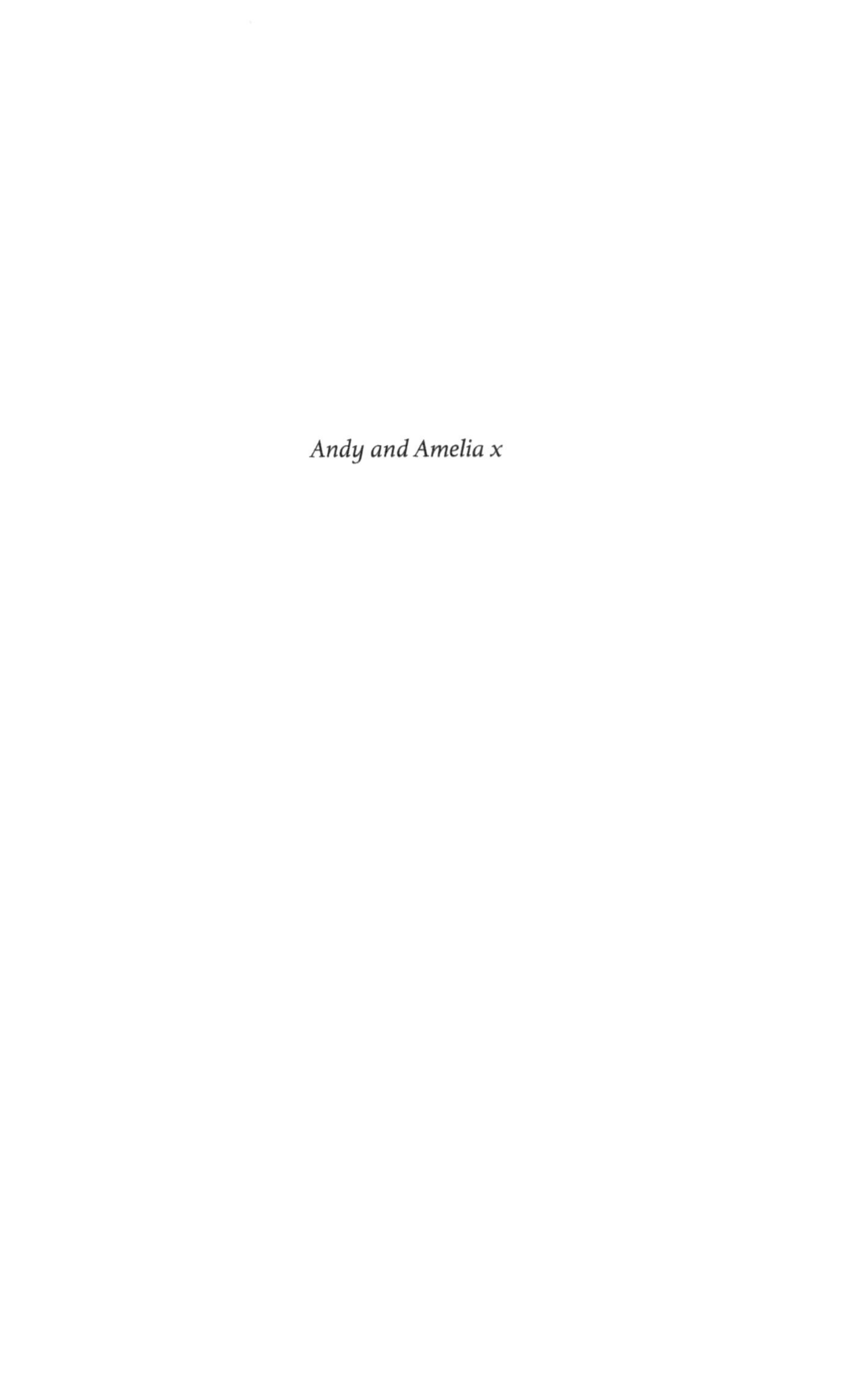

Andy and Amelia x

1

CHELSEA

I stare out the window at the building I've spent the past eight weeks of my life inside and as much as I hate the place, I can't help but crave being back inside. It's safe in there. People understand me. They don't look at me like I don't belong, like I'm a piece of shit on their shoe after all the mistakes I've made.

My hands tremble in my lap as the gray brick walls disappear in the distance as my driver heads toward my home.

Home. It's a funny word. It's meant to be a place where you feel safe, loved, protected. You're meant to feel like you belong.

I've never felt any of those things. Even before I was old enough to know things around me weren't right, I knew. Even now being somewhere where those feelings should come easily, they don't. My past is too ingrained. The fear too real after all these years.

I blow out a breath as anticipation races through me for what I'll find waiting for me. My parents have visited me weekly after they shipped me off to "have a breather" as they put it. They made it sound like they were doing me a favor, but after the drama I've brought down on them, I'm pretty sure the breather was more for them than me.

Derek and Honey are the perfect parents on paper. I guess that's why they signed up to foster broken kids all those years ago. Shame this broken teenager doesn't fit into their perfect life.

I've done everything I can to become a person people would want to spend time with, to want to be friends with. But I still end up as the outcast. Okay granted, most of that is my fault. I've spent the past eight weeks reflecting on all my mistakes, on my weaknesses. The counselors seem to think I've turned a corner and am strong enough to show my face in a place where everyone hates me. I, on the other hand, am not so sure.

I think back over what my senior year at Rosewood High has been like so far. I've lost the guy I've wanted for as long as I can remember to a freaking supermodel. I drugged said supermodel in my attempt at him noticing me once again like he did that one night in the summer. When that didn't work, I moved on to his best friend in the hope it would make him jealous. Wrong. All that resulted in was my parents sending me away for my breather.

Everyone hates me and I'm about to go walking back into that school like nothing happened. It has disaster written all over it. But what else am I supposed to do?

I refuse to cower down. I'm stronger than that.

I'm Chelsea fucking Fierce.

My parents must have been at the window waiting for my arrival. They wanted to come and get me themselves, but I refused, knowing that I'd need this time to try to adjust.

The smiles on their faces are wide, but I'm not stupid, they're just as worried about this as I am, if not more so.

They've done everything for me. I couldn't ask for better parents really, but their traditional views on things make my rule-breaking all the worse in their eyes. Just coming home drunk is a major sin, let alone some of the other things I've forced them to deal with.

Sucking in a huge lungful of air, I push the door open and step out.

"Chelsea, it's so good to have you home," Mom sings, rushing toward me with her arms out wide.

She engulfs me in her hug and for the first time since I watched that building disappear, a lump crawls up my throat and tears burn my eyes.

I was safe there. No one wanted to hurt me. No one wanted to make me an outcast for my mistakes like I'm sure this entire town does.

I'm not naïve enough to think what happened that final night stayed inside the walls of the Savage's house. I'm sure everyone knows what a disappointment I am, just how screwed up I am.

"Everything's going to be okay," she whispers in my ear, sounding a little emotional herself. She hands me off to my dad who gives me a much briefer one-armed hug. He's not really the touchy-feely type like Mom, so even this gesture is a lot for him.

"We've got a surprise for you inside."

I have a fleeting thought that they might have got some friends to come and meet me, but I push it away instantly. I lost my squad the moment I dropped that pill into Amalie's drink, let alone Mason's. It was stupid. I was desperate. I just wanted someone to want me.

I shake my head. My excuses mean shit. My behavior was inexcusable, which is why none of my squad will be here. They'll have turned their backs on me as fast as I ran from Ethan's house that night.

I might have spent my entire Rosewood High career trying to be the cheer squad captain, needing the title, the accolade to make me feel like I belong, but I'm not stupid enough to think that the rest of the girls weren't doing something similar.

Yes, we had each other's backs. We played the part of being best friends. But the reality was that we were all as fake as each other. None of them will have missed me. I don't need to look any farther than my cell phone to know that's the case. The only person who's bothered to reach out is Ethan. Guilt fills me that I mostly ignored his attempts to check that I was okay, but I wasn't in the right frame of mind to talk to anyone from Rosewood. I'm still not, but I seem to have little choice about it now.

I follow my parents up the steps onto the porch and into the house. They both look excited about whatever is inside for me. I, however, don't feel any of it. Dread is what fills my belly.

The downstairs appears empty—I was right about the squad then—so I expect them to turn toward the stairs. But when we don't do that, I'm thoroughly confused.

Dad steps out of the open back door, and Mom and I follow. I glance around, but everything is as I remember. That is until Dad opens the door to the pool house, it's then I see that things have changed.

So they've decorated the pool house. Am I really supposed to get excited about this?

"Um... I don't understand." My irritation levels are beginning to rise. All I want to do is fall onto my bed and forget that I'm back here. I really don't need to give my opinion on the shade of cream Mom chose for the walls.

"It's for you," Dad says, gesturing to the space beyond.

"You decorated it for me. Why?"

Mom takes my hand and leads me to the new couch in the center of the living area. With both my hands in hers, she blows out a breath.

"This is a fresh start, Chelsea. For all of us. We know we've been hard on you, had unrealistic expectations. We love you, but we also know that we've been a little overbearing in our need to protect you. We neglected to notice that you're a young woman now who's going to be embarking on her life without parents very soon. And as much as we hate that our time together is coming to an end, we know that we need to accept it. You're no longer our little bug, but a beautiful young woman who has the world at her feet.

"So this is for you. We've moved all of your stuff from your room. You've got your own front door key." Dad pulls it from his pocket and hands it over. "There's food and drinks in the fridge along with everything else you might need."

"I... um... I don't understand." I can't deny that this sounds freaking incredible, but I was expecting to come home and find myself locked in my bedroom and only allowed to attend school for classes for the foreseeable future.

"This is for you. We want you to be able to have your space to do as you wish. You're eighteen now, Chelsea," he says, reminding me that I was forced to celebrate my biggest birthday in that place. "We think taking control of your life will help you. We—"

"We'll only be in the house, and it's still your home, we're not kicking you out or anything," Mom adds, clearly not as on board with this plan as Dad.

"Of course. You're our daughter. We love you, but we came to the conclusion while you were away that we're smothering you. So we did this."

I look around, now seeing a few of my ornaments and picture frames that I didn't notice when I first entered.

A genuine smile creeps onto my face. It's an alien feeling as every one I've given for almost as long as I can remember has been fake.

All but that one night, a little voice chirps, but I shoot it down. I don't think about that night. Nothing good can come of what happened that night.

"Are you serious?"

"We are. We know things have been strained, but we hope that by giving you space you'll be able to continue with everything you've been working on without us breathing down your neck."

For the second time in less than fifteen minutes, tears burn my eyes. I'm not used to these overpowering emotions. I much prefer being the hard as nails girl everyone is scared of, not the weak emotional one I've turned into.

"T-thank you," I choke out.

"We'll leave you to get settled. We're both home all day if you need anything. I'll give you a shout when lunch is ready."

They both get up to leave, but Mom turns back before she gets to the door and pulls me into another hug.

"We're so proud of you, sweetie."

"Thanks, Mom."

"Are you going to the game tonight?"

I blow out a breath. Tonight is the final state championship game. Other than the cheer finals, it's the one day I've been looking forward to more than any other. I knew our boys could do it—or more so that Jake could do it—there was never any doubt in my mind, and I'd love nothing more than to watch them lift that trophy.

"I'm not sure."

"Your uniform is washed and pressed in your closet. It's time to restart your life again."

I nod against her, and she releases me to explore my new home.

I spin on the spot, a smile creeping onto my face, and excitement bubbling in my belly. I've basically got my own apartment; this couldn't be any more perfect. Well, actually that's not true, a lot of things could be a lot fucking better right now, but at least I've got some privacy while I try to figure my shit out.

I look around before walking toward the bedroom. They've painted it a deep purple, my favorite color. I run my hand over the comforter and push down on the luxury memory foam mattress. I think I'm going to like that.

Poking my head into the bathroom, I find the purple theme continues and that I've got a brand-new suite and what looks like a waterfall shower.

Maybe this homecoming isn't going to be so bad.

2

SHANE

I sit on the bench in the locker room before our final game. The other guys are pacing, looking nervous, but all I hear is my dad's words from earlier.

"This is the moment we've dreamed of, son. This is our night. Go out there and make me proud. Show those scouts what for."

Everything is about him. About his success and how he can look good. It's fucking exhausting.

I glance at all the others.

I want this as much as they do, of course I do. But the pressure to be the best, to continue the Dunn name, to go to an Ivy League college and then take the NFL by storm is too fucking much. Even if that was what I wanted it would be too much.

I want to go to college, sure. I wouldn't even mind playing college football, but it's not my future. No matter how Dad tries to ignore it, I'm not as much of a natural like him and my brothers.

"All right, ladies. Get in here," Coach calls, and everyone comes running. Some stare at the floor as the pressure of the night gets too much for them, others look pumped and ready for a fight. "This is it, boys. This is what you've worked all your life for. You will forever remember this night. Now, let's make sure it's for the right fucking reasons, shall we?"

The ones who aren't lost in their own heads reply, but that's not enough for Coach.

"I didn't fucking hear you, ladies. Are we going to fucking do this?"

"Yes, Coach."

"Come on, we can do better than that. We're the fucking Rosewood Bears," Jake shouts, coming back to life and spurring on his team the way he knows best. I stare at my captain, the one who's led us to this point, and like always my opinions of him duel. He's an asshole, no one would deny that, and other than always taking what I fucking want, I'm pretty sure there's a decent guy in there somewhere. Amalie seems to think so, and she's pretty awesome, so... "Now, are we going to do this?"

The noise from everyone around me is mind-blowing. The excitement is palpable, nerves are running rampant but over all of that is the belief that we can do this.

I can do this.

I can do this for me.

Not for my dad.

Not for the Dunn name or to prove I'm as good as them.

I can do this for me. After all, something's got to go my fucking way for once.

"Let's fucking do this," someone shouts as we move toward the doors that lead us out to the field for our final game together.

Some of us have played together since little league, it's been a long fucking time and we deserve this success.

The pounding of feet reverberates through me before the cheering of the crowd takes over. The guys continue forward, but I can't help slowing down to take in the moment. The stadium is full to the brim, most wearing Bears red but there is a significant mass of blue to the side of me.

Everyone is on their feet shouting and screaming for their team.

It's really quite sobering to be part of something this big.

"Dunn, what the fuck, man?" Zayn bumps into my shoulder as he passes me, forcing me to continue toward the huddle that's forming on our half of the field.

I'm almost there when our cheerleaders catch my eye. My stomach knots like it does every time I see them. But unlike before, now it's for a different reason. The person I look for is no longer there. Her squad has left her behind, most days it's like she never even existed.

Something uncomfortable tugs at my gut, but anger begins to burn through me. I have no idea if it's for the way they've allowed her to vanish like she was nothing, or for how she hurt those I care about, but it's there, nonetheless.

I'm just about to move to where the guys are waiting for me when the cheerleaders part and a familiar flash of dark hair catches my eye.

My breathing falters, and I stop dead in my tracks as I wait for her to turn to see me. But she never does.

"Everyone in," Jake shouts, dragging me from my daze.

I run over to join my team and huddle with them. Normally when we're like this before a game, we're the only people who exist, the outside world stops, the crowd disappears and we focus on the game, on our teammates, on our win. But that's far from how I'm feeling right now. My head's spinning with questions and my blood is boiling with anger. Everyone thinks I'm the quiet one, the calm one, and mostly that's true. But there's something about her that makes me forget all that and lose my goddamn mind.

"Champions on three. One. Two. Three."

I fight to pull my head out of my ass and focus on what I should be doing.

"CHAMPIONS."

We part, take our positions, listen to the sound of the whistle starting the game, but it's all a blur.

Every chance I get, I'm looking toward the squad, desperate to know if she's looking at me, although, I know she's not. I'd feel it if she were. What is obvious every time I glance over is the fact she's no longer front and center of her own squad, but more pushed to the sidelines. I see the way the other girls look at her. It seems they are less than impressed with their captain's reappearance, much like the rest of the school will be when they discover she's back, I would imagine.

A few weeks might have passed, but it hasn't been long enough for anyone to forget what she did. I'm not sure any amount of time will be enough for some.

I struggle to get into the game for the entire sixty minutes, thankfully my body does what it's supposed to be doing while my mind is back in my bedroom all those weeks ago. I told myself that I needed to forget it. That it was a moment of madness that we'd both regret, but I can't. No matter what I do, I can't fucking forget it.

The win is euphoric, especially after it looked like we were going to come away second at one point. The guilt was already beginning to build that it would have been my fault for not being fully focused, but how can I be with her right there?

Winning a game always feels incredible. But nothing can prepare me for the moment that final whistle blows announcing us the state champion winners. It's fucking mind-blowing.

Every single one of us turns and runs for Jake, needing to celebrate as one, as a team. I might have spent a lot of my time trying to separate myself from some of these guys, but right now. We are one. And we just fucking smashed it.

We're all grinning and laughing like idiots as we eventually stumble back into the locker room. We're sweaty, covered in mud, but no one gives a shit. All everyone wants to do is party. I don't blame them, if things were different, I'd want to celebrate in style too. But the euphoria of the win aside, the last thing I want to do is go home to watch my dad soak up the glory as if he just won our final game single-handedly.

So what, he's ex-NFL and might have been the one to first teach me to catch and throw a ball. He wasn't on the field tonight. I was. He shouldn't be soaking up the glory, lapping up the attention. I should. I mean, mostly it's the last thing I want, all attention on me, but still. If I wanted it, it should be mine.

We hit the showers, the excitement for what the rest of the night might hold vibrates around us, how the girls are going to hero-worship us the second we leave this room is all the guys can talk about. And while it might be an exciting prospect. I know that I'm going to have to deal with her. Or worse, she's going to ignore me like I don't exist. Don't get me wrong, it's fairly standard to be invisible. Most days I've thrived on it. But she's ignored me one too many times and made one too many mistakes.

Everyone else might be angry, but it's the quiet one she needs to be worried about.

The crowd erupts once again when the guys push open the double doors that take us out of the stadium. They immediately get swallowed up into the crowd, which unsurprisingly the cheer squad are front and center of.

Jake and Mason are immediately pounced on by their girls before Ethan parts the crowd and makes a beeline for his. Jealousy stirs in my belly. It's not just because I went after Amalie first, despite his asshole ways, even I can see that they're right together. I was just trying to convince myself that

I could want someone else. Something more... normal. But I guess that wasn't meant to be.

I'm just about to push my way through to find my parents who no doubt will be somewhere close, my dad most probably signing autographs like he just made the final play to win the game. I roll my eyes and grit my teeth. Nothing ever changes. I'd like to think that when I get out of here in a few months that I'll be able to live my own life, but that's not likely to happen with my dad already having colleges lined up for me. Him and football seem to control every part of my life. Just because my brothers have it flowing through their veins like he does and happily followed his advice to start at Maddison last year, it doesn't mean I want the same.

I step forward, ready to push away the roaming hands of any cheerleader who thinks they've got a chance with me tonight, but before I reach the crowd, warm fingers wrap around my wrist.

I know who it is immediately. I don't need to turn, the tingles that run up my arm are evidence enough.

She tugs and I stupidly follow. I should ignore her and walk on by like she's nothing to me. Only she's not. No matter how much she might deserve it. She's something. Always has been.

She pulls me into the shadows, away from prying eyes of the gathered crowd waiting for their heroes.

"Congrats, champ." Her voice flows over me like fucking silk and it makes my teeth clench. She should not have this effect on me.

I keep my eyes on the ground, afraid of what'll happen when I look into her large, chocolate ones.

"Shane?"

I take a step closer. If she thinks it's because I've missed her and want to be close, then she's wrong. This is nothing but a warning. She's messed with my head long enough. It's time for this bullshit between us to end.

I suck in a breath and prepare to look at her.

Lifting my head, my throat closes slightly when I take in her expression. Gone is the confident girl who thought she ran the school, and in her place is the girl I always knew was hiding beneath.

Where did she go and what exactly has happened to her in the past few weeks?

I push my concern aside. She doesn't deserve it.

"What the fuck are you doing here, Chelsea?"

3

CHELSEA

I knew returning without warning wasn't going to be easy, but I never could have imagined the looks on my squad's faces when I arrived to warm up before the game.

Shelly stood front and center leading the troops. I knew she'd step up, as my assistant captain she was always hungry for power. She was probably barking orders before I was even out of town.

Every single set of eyes stared me up and down, their lips curling in disgust that I dare turn up dressed in my uniform and expecting to join them.

This was my squad. So what I left? I never quit, I never officially handed things over to Shelly, I just had a... break.

They allowed me to cheer for the game, although none of them wanted me there. That was clear enough from the looks alone, but they had clearly put a lot of work into re-choreographing my routines so that I didn't exist. It was embarrassing, I could only hope that people were too excited about the game to notice me looking like a lost puppy while the entire squad appeared to be experts.

I was out of practice, I knew that, but it was even more horrific than I was expecting.

The eyes of the team drilled into me as each one noticed my sudden appearance. A few ran their eyes down my body in the way they do that makes my skin crawl with disgust. I know why they do it. It's my own fault. I know how I acted. What I made them all think of me.

It was stupid. *I'm* stupid.

Once the crowd started dispersing and the squad brings their routine to a close. Shelly turns to me, what was my loyal group of girls standing behind her like an army.

"You can go now. No one wants you here." She looks me up and down as she would one of the nerds we used to mock together and a lump the size of the ball the guys were just throwing around climbs up my throat.

"But—"

"No. You lost any right to this squad when you started drugging our players," Shelly spits, her hands on her hips. "You're nothing here. You. Are. Not. Welcome."

She nods her head to the squad and they immediately follow her lead. They all walk past me. Not one giving me a second glance as they make their way toward where the team will emerge from. A couple even go as far as slamming their shoulders into mine just to really nail the point home.

"Fuck," I bark once they're out of earshot. Tears burn the back of my eyes, but I refuse to cry. I am stronger than this.

They won't break me.

They might think they've dethroned me, but they need to realize that my crown is going nowhere, it's currently just a little crooked.

Sucking in a large breath, I straighten my uniform. It used to fit me like a second skin, but now... I just can't wait to get out of it and into something more comfortable. That's something I never thought I'd say.

I follow the way the squad left a few minutes ago. I might have been dreading seeing them, but their reaction was predictable. There's someone else whose opinion about me being back is a little more up in the air.

I know he's seen me. I felt his eyes drilling into me when he should have been focusing on the game. It was one of the reasons I nearly didn't come. I didn't want to take anyone's focus away from winning this for us, but equally, I wanted to be a part of it. I've worked tirelessly for years for this squad and supporting our team, I wanted to experience it too. Selfish? Yeah, probably after everything I've done, but I'm still a senior at this school. I want these memories too.

The crowd is already huge by the doors where the team will emerge from, so it takes me quite a while to fight my way through. I also successfully drag a few more students' attention my way that clearly weren't watching the squad through the game. Eyes widen and chins drop at my appearance, but I ignore them. Everyone knows me as a stone-faced whore, so that's the mask I'll slip on and give them what they expect.

I stand on the edge of the crowd where I can see the guys emerge and hopefully catch the attention of the one I want. My stomach flutters with nerves as I wait. The excitement around me only increases as the minutes tick by. But nothing could have prepared me for the eruption of noise when the door opens for the first time.

A few of the guys emerge and the crowd goes crazy, engulfing them into the mass of bodies. The noise level only increases when the captain appears with his boys at his sides. The wide smile on Jake's face makes something twist in my stomach. But it's no longer jealousy as he searches for Amalie in the crowd. For many, many years, I thought Jake was it for me. I mean, the captain of the football team and the captain of the cheer squad are meant to be, right? No, apparently not. It didn't stop me from spending the best part of the last few years following him around like a lost puppy while trying to do anything to get his attention. It worked... once. I gave him my V-card one night when he'd had way too much to drink. I don't think he even realized he was my first... or it was even me he was fucking, to be honest.

A sigh passes my lips as I think about that night. It was only a few weeks before Amalie arrived and she swept him straight out from under my feet. Not that he ever showed me there was anything between us, other than that night.

I was gutted. There had only been two guys up until that point that I'd really wanted and although the first one thinks of me as a little sister, the second had used my body and still didn't want me.

Am I really that unlovable?

Zayn appears, quickly followed by the one I want.

My stomach somersaults as I take in his shaggy blond hair that's still wet from his shower and his clean Bear's jersey that clings to his sculpted chest.

My mind takes me back to the one time I got up close and personal to that chest. I vividly remember what my hands looked like as I pressed them against his pecs to get some leverage.

Heat fills my veins as I relive that fateful night.

He takes two steps from the building and my stomach drops thinking that he's going to walk straight out and not see me. Taking matters into my own hands, I reach out and grasp his wrist. He stills for a beat and I panic that he's about to rip himself away before even acknowledging me.

He keeps his eyes on the ground for the longest time. I just start to think that he's going to refuse to look at me when his head lifts.

I gasp when his green eyes connect with mine. But they're not like I remember. They're not soft and kind. They're hard and angry, rightly so. My heart aches as I look into them. Has the boy I've been craving gone?

My skin prickles with awareness as our eyes hold. But the longer it lasts the darker his get and the tingles of excitement I first felt give way to a different kind. Fear. Fear that he's going to break our connection and walk away from me, much like I did that night. I guess it's what I deserve. No. It is what I deserve.

He steps toward me, and my hope rises. He might be angry, but at least he's going to acknowledge me. When he looked away the first time our eyes connected when he was playing, it hurt. Really fucking bad. He's the one person I need on my side right now. I just need to figure out how I'm going to make that happen because right now, he looks like he's barely restraining himself from sending me back to where I just came from.

The second he's before me, he wraps his hand around my wrist and pulls me back into the shadows, away from prying eyes. Oh great, he's ashamed of talking to me. Good start.

I roll my eyes at myself and allow him to drag me to where he wants me.

"What the fuck are you doing here, Chelsea?"

"Waiting for you." My voice is so sickly sweet it hurts my own ears and makes me wince.

"Did you really think that was the best idea? No one wants you here."

My heart drops at the truth in his words. "Even you?"

He stares at me, his jaw popping as his teeth grind before he lets out a sigh. "Chels."

"No," I snap. "Don't *Chels* me. Tell me how it is. Tell me how you really feel."

"You shouldn't have turned up tonight. If we lost, it would have been your fault."

"But you didn't, did you, champ?" I step forward and run

my hands up his chest, desperate to know if that connection is still there between us.

Before I get a chance to feel it, my hands are ripped away.

"Not here. Not tonight."

His eyes hold mine, his warning loud and clear.

I open my mouth to say more, but he steps away before any words pass my lips.

His eyes drop down the length of my body, a little heat creeps into them and pushes the anger away.

He remembers as well as I do.

"Go and find a more willing member of the team. They all want to celebrate tonight, and I'm sure they'd be more than happy to get you on your knees."

My chin drops. I'm not shocked by the suggestion, it's the fact the words are coming from his mouth that surprises me.

He's always been the kind one, I always thought the pushover. Maybe I don't know all there is to know about the quietest member of the team.

I don't get to say anymore because when I come back to myself, he's gone. Swallowed by the crowd who are overjoyed to celebrate with their champions.

I stay where I am, watching the excitement that I should be in the center of with a heavy heart.

Before long, everyone starts to disperse. Tonight's celebrations are happening in the Dunn household. We haven't had a proper party there—that I know of—since Shane's eighteenth, but knowing his dad, I'm not surprised he wants to take charge of tonight.

Mom's been friends with Maddie, Shane's mom, since before I arrived in town. Everything that goes on under that roof is football related or somehow a reminder of Brett's success and the future he wants for all his boys. Mom always jokes about what it would have been like if they'd had three girls who weren't at all interested in the game. It doesn't really bear thinking about.

I wait until the area is clear before stepping out of the shadows. After how Shane just was with me, I don't really want the wrath of anyone else.

I had hoped that he would be nice, maybe have some weird understanding that I needed to do this, that I needed time away and that I had to be here for this.

I know it's crazy to ask that of him. He has no idea about anything, well other than the basics.

Mom's friendship with both Maddie and Kelly, Ethan's mom, means they know some things about my life, some of the darkness that my parents rescued me from.

Just because I felt like we had some kind of connection that night, that when he looks at me, he can see deeper than the others, it doesn't mean he knows any of the shit that follows me around and why I do the stuff I do.

He sees me the same as the others do. I'm disposable to him. Just a cheer slut to use and abuse when the time is right.

I thought he was different.

With a sigh, I emerge to find a few students and their families loitering by their cars, but no one gives me a second glance.

I look down at myself. I've never felt more out of place or uncomfortable, but equally, I've never been one to do things to give me an easy life.

I jump in my car and start the engine. The rumble races through me and I can't help feeling a little better. I haven't driven since I left this place, and suddenly having this freedom once again fills me with excitement.

I could drive and just keep going. I could leave Rosewood behind for good. Would anyone besides my parents actually miss me? I very much doubt it.

I could set up my own life and embark on a new future.

I rest my head back and blow out a long breath.

It doesn't really matter if I stay here or if I skip town. Life is going to be unrecognizable for me, it seems, and I can't see it getting any easier any time soon.

I should drive home, make myself a hot chocolate and dive into my bed in the hope that I never have to emerge ever again. But when I pull out of the stadium parking lot, I don't head for home. I turn the same way almost all the others have and in the direction of the Dunn household.

What's the point in hiding, I may as well rip the Band-Aid off in one night, right?

Seeing as I'm probably one of the last to arrive, I can't park anywhere near his house. The Dunn residence isn't a stranger to a party. Hell, it's where I learned that I could drink most guys under the table and that if I touch them the right way, then they'll be like putty in my hands.

Jesus, I sound just like the woman who gave birth to me.

A sobering chill runs down my spine at the thought. I guess it's true what they say, the apple never falls far from the tree.

I told myself I'd never be like her. Never reduce myself to the things she did. I was too young to know what it was she was really doing at the time, but I sensed it. And as I've gotten older, it's become clearer and clearer the reason why she used to take all the random guys back to her bedroom and be high as a fucking kite when they eventually left.

My stomach turns over as I think back to that trailer. I can still remember the smell as if it were yesterday.

I heave as my memories get too much. I've been with my parents for over ten years, yet that life is still as vivid as the day I moved here.

Bringing my car to a stop about a million miles from the Dunn house, I throw my door open and climb out. I tug at my uniform in an attempt to feel like I used to in it, but it's pointless. I fear that I no longer belong in it, and I have no idea what that means for me. Being the captain was who I was. Without it, I'm just some lost girl who seems to have no control over her life despite the fact she's the one who did all the things to make it explode in the first place.

Luca and Leon, Shane's brothers, have thrown some massive parties over the years. But then I guess they never won the state championship when they both played for the Bears because I've never seen anything of this scale before.

I wonder how much Mr. Dunn paid the neighbors to ignore this tonight?

Cars litter their usually quiet street, there are people everywhere, some moving to attend the party, others just watching the commotion and probably wondering what the hell is going on.

As I round the final corner, I have to weave in and out of the cars to even get close to the house.

"Jesus," I mutter when I find a press van and a load of reporters huddled in the front yard. But I'm not surprised to find Brett at the front and center of the attention. He lives for the fame.

As I get closer, I find the twins with wide proud smiles on their faces and their arms thrown around a very reluctant looking Shane.

This is his idea of hell, I don't need to see the pained expression on his face to know that. He's done everything he can to stay out of the spotlight over the years. This is his dad and brothers' thing, it's not his.

Brett chats away despite the fact the questions are most probably about tonight's game.

I stand to the side, hidden in the bushes as Brett continues to take the limelight until four other people join them. The press immediately turns away from Shane's fame-hungry father and to Jake and Mason, who both have their girls pinned tightly to their side.

That pang of jealousy I felt earlier hits me. I want someone to hold me that tightly. Just once. Is that too much to ask?

Jake and Mason answer questions, but they don't look entirely comfortable about it. They need Ethan. He'd lap up this kind of media attention.

It's weird not to see the three of them together.

Regret fills me for not responding to the messages he's sent me over the past few weeks. I know Kelly has left and it was selfish of me not to at least ask how he was handling everything. I need to remember that while my life is falling apart, others' are too.

At some point, Shane manages to slip away because when I drag myself from my thoughts, he's nowhere to be seen.

Taking that as my cue to also head inside, I step around the tree and walk around the back of the house.

There are people everywhere. Most of which I don't recognize as Rosewood students.

As I make my way to the kitchen, I get more than a few dirty looks. I keep my head high and smile in return.

Yes, I've made mistakes. A lot of them. But I refuse to cower down to these people who suddenly seem to think they're better than me.

I find myself a soda in the kitchen and sip it as I look around the room.

Everyone chats and laughs as if they don't have a care in the world.

"I hope you dropped a few of your own pills into that," Shelly barks, coming to stand in front of me.

She has Victoria and Krissy standing right behind her. All three have their hands on their hips and fierce looks on their faces.

"It's funny," Krissy pipes up, breaking the crackling tension between us all. "I thought we'd made it clear that you weren't welcome here."

I push from the counter and get in Shelly's space.

"Oh yeah. And you should probably remember who got you your place on the squad," I spit at Krissy. She was nothing before she tried out. I made her what she is today. I was the one who allowed her to attend these kinds of parties and hang out with the football team.

"Krissy deserves her spot on the squad. Much more than you do right now," Shelly barks, speaking for Krissy, who fumes behind her.

"Ladies, ladies, ladies. Put the claws away, eh?" Zayn says, sliding up beside me and wrapping his arm around my shoulder and making me cringe. I know it's my fault that the guys think they own my body, that they have the right to touch, but they really fucking don't. Not anymore. "I'm sure Chelsea has a reason to be here that doesn't involve drugging us all."

"Fuck you," I spit, pushing his arm from me and stepping away from them.

"Here you go, Chelsea. I made you a drink. It's a special cocktail, especially for you." A wicked smile pulls at Zayn's lips as he holds out a cup for me. "Go on, drink it. See how you like it."

We stand, locked in our stare. Him daring me to take it and me begging him not to make me.

"No," I bark, not taking my eyes from his.

"What's wrong, Chelsea? You too good to drink your own poison?" He lifts a brow.

"I'm not drinking that." My stomach turns over at the thought alone.

"Prove to us that you're sorry, that you belong here. Come on, the Chelsea I used to know never turned down a drink. We'll start to think they're something wrong with you."

My heart pounds, and my hands shake. I can't let these assholes see beneath my mask. I hate to do it, but I know there's no other way out of this.

I stare at Zayn a little longer, really study him. He's not a bad guy. He doesn't go out of his way to hurt people, girls especially. I really doubt he spiked that drink.

I guess I'm about to find out.

"Fine," I spit, taking the drink and downing it in one.

The girls' eyes go wide as Zayn continues staring at me.

Sweetness explodes on my tongue the second the liquid hits and I instantly know it's just fruit juice. It's still yet to be seen if there're any drugs in it though.

I feel weak for doing it. I shouldn't bend to them. I need to stay strong. Focus on what I want and why I'm here.

I look back up to Zayn and hold his dark stare. He's usually the joker, but right now his eyes hold a viciousness that I'm not sure I've ever seen. Would he take things this far? Have I just played right into his hands?

My stomach turns over and I worry I'm about to puke on my own feet.

Not wanting to show any kind of weakness. I take a step forward.

"What are you trying to prove, Hunter?" I sass, popping my hip out.

His top lips curls in a way I'm not used to when I'm this close to him before he dismisses me with a tilt of his chin.

Glancing to the side, I find Shelly and Krissy staring daggers at me.

Needing to get away from their burning, hate-filled stares, I turn on my heels and run.

I push people aside as their too-loud whispers, all directed at me, fill my ears.

"Why the hell is she here?"

"Doesn't she know we don't want her anymore?"

"Karma will kick her ass into next year."

"She looks like a whore."

"She's put on weight."

"Why did we ever think she was that pretty?"

All of them swirl around my head as I fight to find an escape.

I shouldn't have come here.

I should have driven home, or better, just kept going.

Finally, I make it out of the packed room and out into the hallway, reaching for the handle of the first door, I slip inside and breathe a sigh of relief.

4

SHANE

Everything about this party is exactly as I feared. It's meant to be about us celebrating a successful season and taking the championship, but predictably, Dad is making it about him.

"Shane's skills and success are down to me. I made sure he had a ball in his hands from the day he was born. I made him practice. I encouraged him to join the team. I, I, I, me, me, me."

I'm fucking sick of it.

Everything is about him. About his NFL career, about his success as a father, about his wealth.

Fury bubbles in my veins as I push through all the people, most of which I've never seen before in my life to find some space, some peace.

If I knew he was going to have the fucking press here waiting for us, then I never would have come back. But I needed to get away from her. From those large dark eyes that do things to my insides. The way they practically begged for me to give her a chance, to listen to her.

I might be the only one who will do that. She might have never wanted to admit it, but she's been in my life longer than anyone realizes thanks to our mothers. But she needs to realize that I'm not the pushover she thinks I am.

While Chelsea might have spent our entire school careers avoiding me, pretending I'm nothing to her, she's spent hours under this exact roof, mostly hanging out with my brothers, but also me too on occasion. I know the things she keeps hidden from the outside world. I've even had a glimpse of the real girl hiding beneath the hard outer shell on occasion. And it's those little glimpses that keep me going back for more because she calls to me in a way I can't ignore.

I fall down onto the chair behind my dad's desk and stare around the room.

His career is proudly displayed on every single wall as well as lining each shelf. There are jerseys, posters, trophies, everything to remind him of what a success he is every time he looks up. But that's not all. His golden boys' journey to the top is also proudly displayed. Photographs of Luca and Leon in their first jerseys, a ball between them which is bigger than the almost newborn babies. Images of them playing at little league, proudly holding their first trophies, and an array of other similar photos right through to them now playing for the Maddison Panthers.

What's glaringly obvious as I sit here, ignoring the party that's booming on the other side of the door, is any evidence that I even exist.

I let out a long sigh, rest my head back and close my eyes in an attempt to block it all out. It does fuck all though. My reality is still pounding around me. I should be enjoying myself, reveling in our team's success. But no, I'm hiding like a fucking pussy.

The sound of the door opening drags my head down from staring at the ceiling and when I look over, the person who's leaning back against it is the last I expected to see.

The anger that was already beginning to get the better of me reaches all new heights at the sight of her.

"What the fuck are you doing?" I bark, pushing the chair out with so much force that it clatters against the wall behind me.

Her wide, startled eyes find mine. If I weren't so lost in my frustration over tonight, then I might see her shock, but I don't, all I see is red.

Stalking toward her, my fists curl at my sides.

"I asked you a question."

She swallows, the skin of her long slender neck rippling.

"I needed a breather."

I don't stop until I'm right in front of her.

"You weren't welcome in the first place."

Her already dark chocolate eyes darken further with my words.

"I'm pretty sure this is an open house tonight."

"Yeah, to anyone but you," I snap.

"But—"

"There are no buts here, Chelsea. You fucked up. Big fucking time."

"Yeah, and I'm sorry, all right?"

A bitter laugh falls from my lips. "No. It's not fucking all right. First you drugged Amalie, and then not happy with causing all that drama, you had to go for Mason. What the fuck were you even thinking?"

Her eyes narrow. I know I'm getting to her and that the best thing for both of us would be for me to send her away, but now we've started, I can't stop, and it seems she's in the same mood too.

"Ah, I forgot about your obsession with the supermodel."

"I'm not obsessed with her. She's just a decent person, unlike someone else I know."

"Pfft." She rolls her eyes at me and I lose my shit.

Reaching out, I take her chin between my fingers and squeeze.

"You don't get to walk back in here after disappearing out of the blue and expect to fit back in," I seethe.

"No one cares I left." She tries to avert her gaze, but I hold her in place and meet her eyes once more.

"Is that what you really think?" I ask, my eyes drilling into hers.

"Well no one wanted me to come back so clearly no one missed me."

Something twists in my chest, but I refuse to tell her that I spent the past few weeks trying to find out where the hell she was. I was aware that Ethan knew, but he wasn't giving that information up for shit. Nor was my mother.

"Oh, I don't know. I'm sure a few of the guys missed you. There was one less slut to suck their cocks with you gone."

"Fuck you, Shane. You're just jealous."

"Really?" I laugh. "You think I'm jealous of those assholes?"

Tears begin to pool in her eyes, and it feeds something inside me. Something dark that I don't really want to acknowledge, but I'm powerless to keep going.

"That night only happened because I wanted to see what the big deal was about."

She gasps.

I lean in so my lips brush the shell of her ear. She shudders, but she's about to learn there's going to be nothing pleasurable about this. "All I hear is how good you suck, how tight your pussy is. Thought it would be a damn shame to be the only one on the team not to experience it."

"No," she cries.

"What? You think I actually wanted you that night?" A bitter laugh rumbles up my throat. "You offered it to me on a plate. Did you really think I'd refuse?"

"Shane," she warns. "Don't do this."

"Don't do what? Treat you like the cheap slut that you are? You're nothing, Chelsea. No one wants you here. Now fuck off."

A sob rumbles up her throat, but she somehow manages to keep the tears that fill her eyes from dropping.

She stares at me for a beat before pulling her face from my grip and wrenching the door open.

At the last minute, she turns back.

"You're lying, Shane. I know you're fucking lying." It's then her tears fall, but she runs before I get a chance to do anything.

"Fuck," I bellow into the room, but the sound gets swallowed by the loud music coming from the wide-open door.

A huge part of me screams to chase her. To pull her into my arms and tell her that she's right. That I was lying. But I can't. Not tonight. Maybe not ever.

Chelsea doesn't want me. She's made that abundantly clear on many occasions. Hell, most of the time she doesn't even want to be associated with me.

I know as well as she does that that night between us meant nothing. We'd both been drinking. Noah and Tasha had disappeared upstairs, and I was fucking livid that he was screwing around on Camila. Chelsea was just there. A distraction from going and rearranging one of my best friend's face for disrespecting one of my closest friends and the girl I thought he was in love with.

Needing to do something other than just hide in my dad's office. I storm through the open door and go in search of some alcohol. Anything to stop me from chasing after Chelsea and doing what I really want to do.

5

CHELSEA

I manage to keep it together until I'm safely inside my car. Everyone inside that house might not want me there, but I'll be fucked if I'm going to show any of them that they're getting to me.

I blow out a shaky breath and stare ahead through blurry eyes.

I didn't really know what to expect from Shane. He's always been the quiet one, the one who sits back and watches all the drama unfold around him. I thought he'd probably be angry, after all, he was the one who got the blame for drugging Amalie seeing as Jake found them together that night. It had worked out kinda perfect for me because everyone believed Jake and no one even bothered to look for another suspect.

I shouldn't have done it. I knew it at the time and I really know it now. But I was desperate. It's not an excuse, I'm aware of that. I spent a lot of time with counselors while I was away dealing with the guilt and I fully accept that I was wrong and that I have no excuses for my appalling behavior. I just have to apologize and hope that at least someone will forgive me, or I don't know what my future looks like here in Rosewood.

I've applied for colleges out of state. I never intended to hang around once I graduated. But everything's changed now.

My priorities have changed. The easiest thing would be to stay. I've got my new pool house and the support of my parents here. But if I bump into someone who hates me every time I turn a corner, then I'm not sure they're enough to really keep me here.

Once my tears clear enough for me to drive home safely, I make my way back.

It's not all that late, but still the house is in darkness when I pull up into the driveway. I make my way around the back and let myself into my new little home.

I breathe a sigh of relief the second I shut myself inside.

No one can hurt me here.

No one can look at me like they hate me.

And most importantly, while I'm alone, no one can learn my secret.

I don't get much sleep. I spend most of the night tossing and turning, trying to get used to my new bed. It's too soft, too comfortable, and nothing like what I've spent the last eight weeks sleeping on. That was like lying on a fucking rock compared to this.

The sun's only just risen when I give up and go in search of something to drink.

I make myself a cup of coffee and put a Pop-Tart into the toaster that my parents left for me. I do it all with a smile on my face because despite everything that's going on outside my little sanctuary, I'm overjoyed with this little bit of independence my parents have granted me.

I need this breathing space to come to terms with everything.

My life has been turned upside down, by my own doing of

course. But that's only the beginning of the changes that are on the horizon.

Dragging on a pair of yoga pants and an oversized hoodie, I pull my curtains open and head out for a morning walk along the beach. I've missed the sea while I've been away. I'd usually run, but I'm not sure I've got it in me this morning.

Finding my favorite playlist, I drop my cell into my pocket and pop my earbuds in to block out the world around me and I take off.

Being so early on a Saturday morning, I have little concern about running into anyone from school who might be tempted to drown me in the ocean.

I feel like I breathe for the first time in weeks when I step down onto the sand. I tug my sneakers off and pull my yoga pants up a little so they don't get wet, and then I walk down to where the waves are crashing onto the beach.

The warm water surrounds my feet and I sigh in relief.

I feel at home here and I can forget all the bullshit and just be me. I can pretend for just a little while that everything is okay. That I still have friends and a life here and that I'm not the biggest fuckup that Rosewood High has ever seen.

I don't keep track of the time or how far I've walked, I just keep going as the sun begins to rise higher and higher. It's late in the year but with the sun beating down, I soon end up shedding my hoodie and tying it around my waist as I continue walking.

I'm lost in my own head, staring at my feet as they splash through the shallow water so I don't see anyone approaching until it's too late.

"I'm going to start assuming that you're stalking me." His familiar voice sends a shudder down my already heated body, but that's nothing compared to when I look up and find him shirtless and in only a pair of low-slung shorts. His golden skin glistens in the sun and his hair is dripping with sweat. I'm fairly sure I've never seen him looking better.

"Oh yeah, I slept outside your house last night and followed you here. Guilty," I say sarcastically, holding my hands up in defeat.

He silently stares at me and I hate that I can't get a read on him.

He shocked me last night with those vicious words he whispered in my ear. It was so unlike him. But then again, I've never really made the effort to get to know him better.

He has every right to hate me. To say the things he did. They were true. I didn't start things with him that night because I wanted him. I was lonely. Bored. Jealous of Tasha finding that connection with someone that I was so desperate for. Even if it was with a nerd like Noah.

Their relationship just showed that we don't have to fall for a football player to find love. Maybe I'd had it wrong all this time.

I remember looking at him on the other end of the sofa after Tasha and Noah stumbled out of the room to find a little privacy, and I wondered if maybe I should try something a little different.

One thing's for sure, he blew me away that night.

It was nothing like the night I lost my V-card with Jake. We'd been drinking but we weren't wasted, and it didn't feel like the only thing he wanted was the release. There was more to his touch, more to the words he whispered to me. He made me think I'd been focusing all my efforts on the wrong guys this whole time.

But there's a good chance that just like everything else in my life, I'm wrong about that too.

"Are—" He stops himself and looks out to the water. His hand comes up and he wraps his fingers around the back of his neck and tugs.

"Are..." I encourage, not wanting this weird exchange to be over quite yet.

"Fucking hell," he mutters to himself. "Are you okay? You know, after yesterday." And there he is, the sweet guy I remember from that night.

"I'll survive. You know me, stone face, hardened heart." I roll my eyes. I'm not naïve to what the rest of the school thinks of me. They think I'm some heartless bitch who only cares about herself. The reality is far from that.

"Chels, you don't need to do that."

"Do what?" I shrug, looking down at my feet.

"Pretend that everything's fine when it's very much not."

"Yeah well. What's the alternative? Everyone hates me. No one wants me here. And I can't see it changing anytime soon."

"Can you blame anyone?"

"I never said they were wrong."

"Me either."

"Ouch."

"What do you want me to say, Chelsea? Everything about what you did was wrong."

"I know."

"And you let me take the fall for it. Because I wasn't already enough of an outcast with the team, you allowed them to think I was capable of that."

"I'm sorry," I whisper, but it's too quiet for him to hear it.

"What was that?" he asks, reaching out so I have no choice but to look at him. The second his fingers connect with my chin, tingles erupt.

I have no idea if he feels it too. I can only hope this isn't a one-sided thing. Even if he never forgives me, I'd like to think that maybe that kind of connection does really exist.

"I'm sorry, okay? I'm sorry I did it. I was in a bad place. I shouldn't have let you take the fall, that wasn't fair."

He steps closer and my heart rate picks up.

His eyes leave mine for the briefest second and when they come back, they're colder, angrier.

"Prove it."

"W-what?"

"Prove. It."

"How?"

"I don't know. Use your imagination. But I know for a fact you have some skills that can make guys do whatever it is you want. Maybe try that." There's no emotion in his voice. The change in him confuses the hell out of me.

"Y-you want me to get on my knees?" I stutter, not quite believing what he's suggesting. I'd expect it from some of the other members of the team, but not Shane.

He quirks an eyebrow impatiently.

"Here? Now?"

"Why not? It's what you deserve."

My chin drops as we engage in a silent battle of wills. Where's the sweet guy from a few moments ago?

It's another second when I hear it. The booming voice that can only be from another member of the team.

"Chelsea, what a fucking surprise to see you here." Zayn's arm wraps around my shoulder and he pulls me into his body.

Shane's eyes narrow at him, but he doesn't say anything.

"I'm surprised you wanted to show your face this morning after the way you left the party last night. Everyone really fucking hates you, girl."

It's only when I turn to look into his eyes that I remember the drink he forced me to have last night. I guess it's safe to assume that there was nothing in it.

"I know," I mutter. "Shane was just suggesting a way I could make it up to the team."

"Oh yeah, what's that then?"

Ripping my eyes from Shane's, I turn to Zayn. He's clearly out on his morning run too, but he's still wearing a shirt.

My eyes hold his for a second before I make a show of running them down his body.

"You know me, Zayn. I've got certain skills that can make up for things." I use similar words to what Shane just said to me to prove a point before licking my lips enticingly.

I take a step toward him and run my fingertips down his chest before slipping them under his shirt to find his abs. They tense as I flatten my palm against them ready to slide it under the waistband of his shorts.

His eyes widen, but I don't miss the heat that fills them. Zayn's never been one to say no to a good offer.

Just as I'm about to push my hand lower and into his boxers, a low growl comes from beside me. Fingers dig into my upper arm and I'm pulled away from Zayn and into a hard, heaving chest.

"I'll catch up with you," he says over my shoulder.

Zayn immediately nods and jogs off down the beach.

"Don't fucking touch him." His large hand lands on my stomach and my breath catches in my throat.

"You jealous, Shane?"

He growls again as something tickles around the shell of my ear. His nose? Lips? I'm not sure, but fuck if my knees don't want to buckle.

"Nah. I just don't want anyone else to get you on your knees before I'm finished with you."

He might be threatening me, but his words send a wave of heat between my legs.

"Is that right? If the first time was so good that you need a repeat, all you need to do is say the words."

"Nah. It's not that easy, Chelsea. This isn't about pleasure. It's about revenge."

"R-revenge?" I stutter, totally thrown for a loop.

"I'm glad you're confused because so am I. My head's a fucking mess and it's all because of you."

Something crackles between us as his hand snakes up my body. My nipples pebble as it brushes over my left breast, but he doesn't stop like I need him to, instead his hand wraps around my neck.

"Oh god," I moan. I don't mean for it to come out loud, but fuck, he's turning me on right now with his dominance. I had no idea that he had it in him, but I am all in with this side of Shane Dunn.

"You might want to lock your door because I'll strike when you least expect it. Things are on my terms now. Not yours."

I shudder in his hold, but instead of giving me more, he releases me with a shove. If I had my wits about me, then I'd be able to catch myself, but he's just rendered me useless and I tumble to the soft sand at his feet.

"You look right at home on your knees."

$$6$$

SHANE

I turn away from Chelsea before I do something else I'll regret. I'm not sure what it is about her, but she brings out a different side of me. One that I'm not sure I like. Although if the way her body shuddered against my hold told me anything, I'm pretty sure she liked it.

My lungs burn by the time I catch up with Zayn.

"Hey, man," I pant as he comes to a stop beside me.

"What the fuck was that about?"

"What, Chelsea? Fuck knows. Trying to apologize or some shit," I lie.

His brows draw together. "And what exactly did you have against her grabbing a handful of the goods?" He thrusts his hips forward in a way I never need to see any other guy do.

"We're on the beach. There are kids around."

"Riiight. Is there something you need to tell me?"

"Uh... nope, don't think so."

Since I started hanging out with the team more in my pathetic attempt to find out where she'd gone, Zayn and I struck up an unlikely friendship. We're polar opposites in every way, other than our love of the game, but we just kinda clicked in a way I never have with any of my teammates. I'm not complaining because it's not like I ever got Noah or Wyatt out to train with me. It's kinda nice having some company.

"Okay. Just watch your back, if you're playing games with Chelsea, you're more than likely going to lose."

"I can handle Chelsea."

"Bro, I'm pretty sure there's not a man on this earth who can handle Chelsea Fierce."

I laugh at his comment in a lame-ass attempt to cover up how it really makes me feel.

We workout together on the beach for a little over an hour before I head home to shower.

The house was a disaster when I left first thing this morning, but as I walked down the street, the cleaning company my dad hires were all arriving, so I have no doubt that it will be like a show home again once I get there.

"It was a great night last night, eh son?" Dad says when he strolls into the kitchen as I'm grabbing a bottle of water from the refrigerator.

"Yeah. Great."

Clearly it passed him by that after I disappeared from the press, I only emerged from hiding when I needed more alcohol, something that I seriously regretted when I first woke up this morning knowing that I was meeting Zayn.

He'd wanted to cancel seeing as it was the morning after our big night, but I refused to hear it. Just because the season is over, it doesn't mean I'm letting up. I might not want the football career my father has planned for me, but I still want to play. Plus, it's not like Coach is going to let up on us just because we're state champions. He'll want to send us all off to college in prime condition. My muscles ache just thinking about it.

Leaving him behind, I take my bottle up to my bedroom. I

don't have the patience for his self-centered bullshit this morning.

Closing the door behind me, I pull my discarded shirt from the waistband of my shorts and throw it toward the laundry basket. I take a step forward, my eyes land on the bed in the center of the room.

Suddenly it's that night again...

I was so fucking angry having just watched my best friend disappear off upstairs with a girl who wasn't his girlfriend. I'd been suspicious for a while as he just wasn't himself, but until that point, I'd had no evidence to accuse him of anything.

The second she turned up at my house with Chelsea in tow while Noah and I were shooting the shit over an old NFL game, I knew exactly what was going on.

I let them in because, well, I'm not a douchebag, and the second Tasha was in the room she climbed on Noah's lap and started kissing him. There was so much familiarity between the two of them that this wasn't some one-off, random hook-up. They'd been bumping uglies for a while.

My fists curled as he pulled her out of the room, telling me that they were going to make use of one of our many guestrooms. In one respect, I was grateful. It meant I no longer had to watch them, but on the other, I was devastated for Camila.

It wasn't the first time he'd been accused. Mason took him to the ground at Noah's own birthday party, but Camila waved it off as her ex-childhood best friend throwing his weight around. Turned out, Mason was right.

I had no idea that while I was still sitting there with my head spinning that Chelsea was anonymously messaging Camila to make sure she walked in on them.

Had I known that was the reason Camila randomly turned up not long later, the evening might have gone very differently.

Images of our time together play out in my mind like it only happened days ago, not weeks. I rub at my stubbled jaw, it's not even weeks, it's months since that night. I've watched Camila and Mason reunite, Ethan find Rae, and I'm still here harboring some weird feelings for a girl I should hate for all the shit she's caused. Yet I can't get her out of my fucking head.

I tell myself that it's just because I'm angry with her. She framed me as the one who drugged Amalie, she viciously went after Camila, one of my oldest friends. Yet all I can think about is that night.

Maybe it was just because it was a long time coming. Maybe I've just latched on to her even more than usual because she was my first, not that I have any intention of telling her that.

Chelsea's been in my life for years, she's followed Luca around like a lost puppy for most of that time waiting for him to throw her a bone, but while she was clearly after him, I was in the background wishing she'd give me a chance. I'd have given anything back then for her to look at me like she did him.

That night she did just that and I was powerless but to fall for her charms.

I shouldn't have done it, I knew that. Allowing myself to go there made me no better than the guys on the team that I spend my days moaning about and trying not to be like. It made me like my father. I shudder at the thought.

But the way she touched me, the way she kissed me. It meant something. It wasn't just a meaningless night, a way to pass the time. Of that I was sure, until she was gone anyway.

"Fucking hell." I slam my head back against the solid door, wishing that I could forget all about her and that night. She doesn't deserve my time or my attention. But she calls to me like no one else ever has. She always fucking has.

She's like a fucking drug that I know I shouldn't want, yet

I'm powerless to resist even knowing that it'll make me more desperate after another taste.

I push from the door and drop my shorts and boxers as I make my way to my bathroom to wash this morning's sweat and sand from my body.

My semi-hard cock taunts me. The memories of that night threatening to make it go full mast in its need for another round. My cock doesn't care that we should hate her. That she doesn't deserve another chance. It just wants her. The same as the organ beating in my chest, but I manage to ignore that a little easier.

I stand under the hot spray and allow it to soothe my tense muscles, but it does little to help. My head and heart seem to be in a constant battle for how I should handle Chelsea. I spent weeks trying to find where she was, wanting to know she was okay after everything that happened. But one look at her and the anger I should have felt when she disappeared hit me like a truck.

Attempting to push her out of my head, I get dressed and make my way back to the kitchen for some food.

Mom sits at the counter in her yoga outfit and sips on a cup of coffee.

"Morning."

"Morning, baby. How are you feeling this morning?"

"Great, why?"

"Last night was… intense," she says with a wince.

"You can say that again. Did you know he had the press coming?"

"You know your dad. He's in a lane of his own. He gets an idea in his head and he makes it happen." Mom sounds as exhausted as I feel with Dad's antics.

I grunt some unintelligible noise.

"He just wants the best for you."

"And what about what I want?"

Sadness washes over her. She's well aware that I don't want to be forced into the NFL, but she's about as successful at talking Dad out of it as I am.

"He thinks you've got what it takes."

"Maybe I have. That doesn't mean I need to want it though."

"I know. Would you like some breakfast?"

"Yes, please."

I sit as she gets up and pulls the refrigerator open. "Grilled cheese?"

"Sounds good."

"So I was at yoga with Honey this morning," she says, mentioning Chelsea's mom.

"Oh yeah," I mutter.

"Did you know that Chelsea is back? Honey said they've moved her into the pool house to give her some breathing space."

"Yeah, she was here last night," I say, ignoring her comment about her new living arrangements but tucking the information away for later.

"Was she? I didn't see her."

"She didn't stay long. She's not exactly everyone's favorite person right now."

"Understandable. Honey said she's in a better place and ready to get back to reality."

"I don't think it's going to be that easy."

Mom sighs. "I told her that I'd ask you to keep an eye out for her at school next week."

"Mom," I complain. "Chelsea won't want me being her bodyguard."

"I'm not asking you to attach yourself to her hip. Just keep an eye out."

"And what if I don't want to? What if I think she deserves all that's coming to her?"

"Shane, don't be like that."

"She drugged Amalie and Mason, Mom. She hurt Camila." I don't go in to any more about what happened with Camila, she really doesn't need to know the details of what Noah's been up to.

"She made a mistake or two. No one's perfect, son. Sometimes people just need a little forgiveness to be able to turn a corner and make a fresh start."

"And what if I can't forgive her?"

"Then I guess that's up to you. I just hoped you might be a little more mature about it."

"Not forgiving her after she hurt people I care about doesn't make me immature."

"Okay, maybe that was the wrong word. Just... just give her a break. She hasn't always had it easy, and I think she deserves a second chance."

Mom places my breakfast down in front of me before she turns and leaves the room.

"She's had about a million after all the drama she's caused over the years," I mutter to myself.

I drop my plate into the dishwasher before leaving the house in favor of spending the day at Wyatt's on his Xbox. It sounds much more appealing than spending the day at home with either Dad going on about what college team will give me the best shot at the NFL or Mom trying to convince me to give Chelsea the benefit of the doubt.

Thankfully, as usual, Wyatt keeps the conversation away from anything to do with football or last night. As much as I might want to continue celebrating our epic win, I'm also relieved to have a break from it all.

At some point in the early evening, Noah turns up to join us. Sadly, he has other opinions on dissecting last night.

"I can't believe Chelsea dared to show her face. Tash said

the squad was less than pleased to see her. She said Shelly was vicious."

I recall the tears that filled her eyes as I gave her a few of my own truths last night and guilt hits me. I knew she hadn't had the best return. The girls' frustration at her sudden reappearance was palpable, but I didn't really put much thought into how they might have spoken to her.

"What did she expect?" Wyatt asks, shocking the hell out of me. He usually steers clear of having any opinions where the cheer squad or the football team are concerned.

"To be welcomed back into their loving arms and be reinstated as captain, I think."

We hang out for a while longer, but now they've mentioned her name, I can't get her shocked face from this morning when I accidentally pushed her to the sand out of my head.

She looked like a scared little mouse that I was about to crush with my foot.

"I need to head out. Thanks for the pizza," I say to Wyatt, nodding at the boxes littering the coffee table of his den that we ordered earlier.

"No worries. See you tomorrow."

I grab my hoodie from the back of Wyatt's couch and make my way out of his house.

If I were to cut through the alley behind Wyatt's house, it only takes me ten minutes to walk home. But instead of turning right, I turn left up the street. I know why, even if I don't want to accept it. This way leads me right to the house I shouldn't be going anywhere near. Only, it's not the house that interests me. It's the pool house.

7

CHELSEA

I spend the afternoon and evening with my parents. My intention was to lock myself away and pretend anything that happened yesterday was just a dream... fucking nightmare more like.

They both try to dig into my time away, but other than the generic 'it was good and exactly what I needed' that they want to hear, I don't go into any more detail.

That place is depressing enough, the last thing I want to do is talk about it.

I'd like to think it's the closest I'm ever going to get to jail, but seeing as I've already done some seriously questionable things in the past few months, I'm not all that confident.

It's regimented with its routines. I understand why, the teenagers inside are fucking up at every possible turn and need some serious boundaries put in place, but fuck, it's hard work.

Wake up at seven-thirty, chores, school, therapy sessions, more chores, bed. Every fucking day.

The girl I was roomed with was the best part about that place. The stories she told me about her past made mine look like child's play, but she got me like no one I've ever met before. I'm not sure how I was lucky enough to be roomed with her, but I'm so fucking grateful. She made my few weeks bearable.

Those routines soon became second nature and unbelievably I miss them even after being home for barely twenty-four hours. Suddenly being free to fuck up my life all over again is a pressure I really don't need.

I have no idea how I'm supposed to go from that kind of life and back to school in only a few hours.

My head spins at the possibility of trying to reenter my life once again. If last night was anything to go by, then it's not going to be smooth sailing.

With my belly full of Mom's cooking, I lay out on my couch watching old episodes of the Kardashians, they make me feel a little better about my life as I take in all their drama.

At some point, I find my eyes shutting and despite the fact my bed is only feet away, I cave to my exhaustion and allow myself the sleep I need.

I have no idea how long I'm out for but when I wake, I can't shake the feeling that I'm being watched.

It's crazy. The only people who know that I'm in here are Mom and Dad and I'd like to think they're not here watching me sleep. I know they're protective, but shit, that would be just creepy.

Cracking my eye open, I expect to find the place empty and prepare for feeling ridiculous, but that's not what happens.

A scream falls from my lips when I find a figure sitting on my coffee table in the dark.

Sitting up so fast my head spins, my eyes focus and I'm able to make out my nocturnal visitor's features despite the dark hoodie he's hiding behind.

"What the hell are you doing? Trying to scare me to death?"

He shrugs. "We've got unfinished business."

Resting his elbows on his knees, he leans forward slightly. His emerald eyes catch the small amount of light that's streaming in from the moon outside and I gasp at the darkness within them.

I have no idea if he's angry or turned on right now. And it's just another of those times where I wish I'd paid more attention to him in the past. I should be able to read him better than this by now.

"H-have we?" I stutter, pushing the blanket from my legs and sitting forward.

If he thinks I'm going to back down, then he's got another thing coming. I'm not some weak girl that he can put in her place. I thought he'd know better than that.

Maybe he does.

Pushing from the couch, I turn my back on him and walk to my kitchen for a drink.

A low growl rumbles from behind me. It confuses me for a second, that is until the short hemline of my Bear's jersey catches my eye.

"You like my shirt, Shane?" I ask, knowing exactly what he's looking at right now. A smile twitches my lips that he cares enough that he's unable to keep his feelings about it locked down.

"Take it off," he demands.

Bending over slightly, I pull a bottle from the refrigerator and twist the top, making a show of drinking some down.

"Why? You want your number on my back?" I ask innocently as I place the bottle on the counter.

When I spin around, I find him standing halfway between where I am and the coffee table where I left him.

"You don't deserve my number. You don't even deserve to be wearing that shirt after the shit you pulled."

I shrug once again. I can't argue with his words. I know what I did and I won't hide from the mistakes I made.

"So because of my questionable judgment, you think I should forget the team I've supported for years like I don't care?"

His eyes burn down my body, but linger for a little longer than necessary on my bare legs. The hem of the jersey kisses the top of my thighs so there's not much of my skin that's not on show below my waist right now. I may have chosen a different shirt had I known I was going to have company.

Although, when his dark, hungry eyes come back to mine, I wonder if it's actually had a pretty desirable effect.

"What are you going to do, Shane? Rip it from my body?"

One side of his lip curls up in a sinister smirk as he takes a step toward me.

"I'm not going to make you do anything, Chelsea. We both know you get yourself in enough trouble without any encouragement."

"Things are different now," I argue, thinking of the hours of counseling sessions I've had over the past few weeks.

"Is that right? So you're not willing to do anything to reclaim your place at school?"

He tilts his head to the side, usually I'd describe it as cute but with the intense look on his face that I'm not sure I've ever seen before, it's far from cute. If anything, it's... hot.

Fuck.

Heat races through my body as memories of how his hands felt on my body slam into me.

"N-no," I stutter, trying to remember what it was he just said to me as he takes another step forward. His scent fills my nose and does nothing to tamp down my desire.

I've always wanted the bad boys, the assholes. It's a

weakness I've never been able to rid myself of. I always dismissed Shane because he was a good guy. But this Shane standing before me right now is anything but a good guy. He warned me on the beach earlier that he was after revenge. Have I stirred something inside him that I never should have been close enough to in the first place?

I should regret that night.

I was desperate. Lonely. Lost. But he gave me something that I'd never experienced before and fuck if I don't want to find out if it was a one-off thing or if it really exists.

"No?" he asks.

"No. If I get my place back, my squad back, it's because I deserve it, because I've earned it."

"Pfft. Little chance of that happening."

"So be it."

"You're lucky, you know."

"How's that?"

"Because you could be dealing with a lot worse than me right now."

A shudder runs down my spine as images from my past flash through my eyes. I've dealt with worse.

"You don't scare me, Shane."

"I wasn't expecting to. Now," he says, closing the final bit of space between us.

My breathing increases with his proximity and when his eyes drop to my heaving chest, I know he doesn't miss it.

"Take. It. Off."

"Fuck you." I laugh, although the serious look in his eyes makes me think this is anything but a joke.

"Been there, done that, Chelsea. Or did your time with me just blur into all the time you've spent with the rest of the team with your legs open?"

"No," I argue, my fingers gripping the hem of my jersey tightly.

His eyebrow quirks. "Tell me, what number was I? How many team members came before me?"

I shake my head, refusing to answer that question.

"Or was that night just about you getting a full house? Was I the last one? One more ride so you could score a home run."

"No," I cry. He's so far from the truth, but I don't want to confess all my secrets.

Turning away from his angry stare, I look toward the house, but all I see is our reflection in the glass doors.

"I'm waiting, Chelsea. I've been waiting a long time."

"You wanted a repeat, you should have just said."

"No, that's not what I was waiting for." Something flashes in his eyes and I wonder how true that statement really is. "I've been waiting to hear what you've got to say for yourself. To hear your excuses. To understand why you happily walked around while allowing people to think that I was capable of the things you did."

"I've said I'm so—"

"I don't want your fucking apologies. Your words mean nothing. As you're aware, actions speak much, much louder."

I swallow nervously, but still heat fills my veins.

His eyes roam my body once more. "Come on, Chels. It's not like I haven't seen it before. Hell, our entire class has seen your naked body more times than we can count. You never used to be shy about showing anyone who'd look what you're rocking."

Fed up with his taunting, and knowing that he's right, I pull my jersey over my head and throw it at him.

"Better? You got what you wanted now? Remove my armor and hope that it makes me weak? Well, let me tell you something, Shane." I push from the wall with my head held high. He's right after all, I've spent way too much time at parties naked and trying to tempt guys to like me. I shouldn't care that I'm standing here in just a small pair of panties. But unlike when I've had half the class looking at me, standing here before Shane right now, I feel bare and it's not just because of my lack of clothes.

My breasts press against his chest and he gasps. "You might think you're in charge here. You can spit your vile words, tell me what a whore I am, make assumptions about the things I've done, but we both know that right now, I'm the one who holds all the power."

I drop my hand to his crotch and just like I suspected, he's hard as fuck.

8
____

SHANE

"**F**uck," I groan as she wraps her fingers around my length.

It was probably no secret what her naked body was doing to me, I'm wearing sweats for fuck's sake. All she had to do was glance down to see the imprint of my cock against the fabric.

"Tables have turned now, huh, Shane?"

My brain misfires as she presses the length of her body against me, her hand trapped between us as she continues to hold me.

Suddenly my revenge mission seems so far from my mind with the scent of her floral perfume filling my nose and the heat of her skin against my body.

"I warned you, I'm not the kind of girl who's going to play your games, Dunn. I set the rules around here."

She strokes me over the fabric and my head spins.

"That night, you didn't stand a chance. I got exactly what I needed. You were like putty in my hands, very much like right now."

Finding some strength from somewhere, I lift my hand

and manage to wrap my fingers around her wrist, stopping her movement before I come in my pants like a fucking kid.

I tell myself it's not her, that it's just the touch I haven't had since she was in my room that night. The second she left me with nothing but memories, I craved more, but I knew I wasn't going to get it. She played me, I knew that. Just like she's trying to now. She didn't want me. She just wanted someone, a distraction while her friend was busy elsewhere.

"What are you doing, Chelsea?" My voice is rough and deep, and it gives away what I really want.

Fuck.

I shouldn't even be here right now, let alone even considering allowing her to do this.

I probably well deserve all she can give me after what she did. I told her I was coming after revenge, but I wasn't really expecting this. I didn't think she'd turn the tables like this.

How naïve I was.

I wanted to tell her how it felt being on the other end of her betrayal. To have the entire school look at me like I was the fucking Devil while she swanned around ruling the school like she always has.

"Trying to make you feel good. Isn't it obvious? I'm trying to make up for everything, just like you suggested on the beach this morning."

I squeeze my eyes shut in an attempt to keep my focus, but it's really fucking hard with her fingers gripping me so tightly.

"I wouldn't have—" My words are cut off by her bitter laugh.

"Oh really? So you would have said no if I had pushed my hand inside your shorts like I did Zayn's?"

The thought of her touching him has jealousy eating at me. It's ridiculous, she was only doing it to make a point but still, I hated the idea that he might have actually gone through with it.

"No."

"Why not? I deserve it. I deserve to be the whore on her knees in front of everyone who was on that beach."

My teeth grind as I try to keep the truth hidden. "Chelsea," I warn.

"Come on, Shane. You had so much to say earlier. Cat got your tongue all of a sudden?"

She releases me and I breathe a sigh of relief, but it only lasts the briefest of seconds because before I have a chance to get my head straight, she wrapped her fingers around the sides of my sweats and pulled harshly.

My length is in her hand in a second and she strokes slowly, her huge chocolate eyes staring up at me.

"Is this what you wanted when you came here tonight, Shane? Did you want a quick thrill so you could say you'd fucked me when I was down?"

I open my mouth to answer, but no intelligible words come out. My head screams at me to move, but I'm trapped between the counter and Chelsea's parted lips. My muscles are fucking frozen to the spot.

"How badly do you want my mouth, Shane? How desperate are you to feel my lips wrap around your cock? To have me suck you until you're dry?"

"Fuuuck."

"Well, it seems tonight really isn't your lucky night."

"Huh? What? Chels—"

She pushes away from me and stands, a triumphant smile on her face.

"Shane, put your fucking cock away and get out of my pool house. You're not welcome here."

My jaw drops.

"What?" She chuckles. "You thought you could walk in here, threaten me and that I'd drop to my knees and make up for my mistakes? Fuck off, Shane. I might have regrets, but they don't make me weak. Especially where you are concerned."

I swallow harshly as I pull my sweats back up. With her arms crossed over her breasts in a way that only makes them look more appealing, she takes a step toward me.

"If you want to play, Shane." Her eyes drop down the length of my body, tingles erupt in their wake. "Then let's play. But I can assure you that you'll lose."

Why do I get the idea that she's right? I came here tonight to have it out with her, yet I'm the one leaving after being chewed a new one.

"I'm not playing your games. I wanted you to understand what your mistakes did to me." My eyes trail down her body much like she just did to me. "But I see it was pointless. You don't care about anyone but yourself. Goodbye, Chelsea." I push from the counter and march through her pool house toward the door I entered through not so long ago.

"Hey, Shane?" her soft voice calls out to me. I shouldn't turn back. I should keep walking with my head held high and not give her the satisfaction. Of course, that's what I should do. Just like the night I became Chelsea's newest victim; I do the opposite of what would be sensible.

I look back over my shoulder to find her holding her arms out at her sides. Except for her tiny pair of panties, her body is bare for me.

"Get a good look. It's the last time you're going to see it."

I keep my eyes on hers. I've already fallen for too many of her games tonight.

"Get rid of Jake Thorn's jersey, Chelsea. His number doesn't belong to you," I demand before ripping the door open and stepping out into the night beyond.

"Fuck you, Shane," she shouts at me, and despite the fact I'm still hard as fuck from her touch and the sight of her body, a triumphant smile tugs at one side of my lips.

I might have played right into her hands back there, but there's one thing I'm certain of. If I made the right move tonight, I could have taken back power.

She wanted me as much as I wanted her. And it's only a matter of time until it's going to happen again.

My cock throbs and my mouth waters.

She might think she's fierce, but I'm going to prove that she has more weaknesses than just her need for power.

9

CHELSEA

A sob erupts the second he closes the door behind him. Tears burn my eyes and I'm unable to stop them from falling as I wrap my arms around my middle in an attempt to hold myself together.

This isn't what I wanted for us when I came back. I know it's what I deserve. Probably less than what I deserve. But the fact he's talking to me, turning up here even, shows me that there's a chance I can rediscover the sweet guy that I know is hiding inside from that night.

Thoughts of how he touched me, the things he whispered in my ear cause another sob to rumble up.

I need that Shane. I need the boy who's going to pull me into his arms and make me feel safe. Not the cruel replacement that turned up here tonight looking for revenge.

With my head spinning, I take a step toward my bedroom, bending down to pick up my discarded jersey as I go. It's the one I've always worn with Jake's number on the back. Why would I wear any other when he was the one I wanted? But Shane is right. It's wrong of me to wear it now. Even in private. Jake's not mine, he never was, and he never will be.

He rejected me, just like so many others in my life before him. I guess it's something I should be used to by now.

I drop it in the laundry basket as I pass with a sigh. It's time I moved on with my life and start focusing on the future instead of everything I've fucked up in my past.

Pulling open a drawer, I find a tank and pair of sleep shorts and curl up in the center of my bed in a ball as my tears soak my pillow.

I shouldn't have come back here. It's been barely twenty-four hours of my fresh start and I'm already fucking everything up.

The guy I want more than anything to pull me into his arms and tell me that everything is going to be okay has just slammed the door in my face and walked away without looking back. None of my squad wants me, and the rest of the school looked at me as if I was a piece of trash.

I deserve it, I know that, I do. But I couldn't help hoping it wouldn't be quite this bad.

It was delusional.

I'm delusional.

I blow out a shaky breath as I come up with a plan. Just finish school and then start over somewhere else, anywhere else. The thought of leaving my parents at a time when I'm going to need them the most terrifies me, but I know they'll be better off without me. It might have been their choice to allow me into their home all those years ago, and then to keep me when they thought they saw something redeemable inside me or some bullshit, but they don't need the drama I bring to their lives. I bet they had a great time the past few weeks without me being here. They could go to bed at night not wondering if they were going to get a drunken wake up call, or worse, blue and white flashing lights on the doorstep again as Dad's cop friend dragged my ass home.

Jesus. I was a mess.

. . .

When I wake the next morning, my eyes are sore from crying and my chest still aches as I remember watching Shane walk away. But knowing I need to do something, anything to try to feel normal once again, I find my cell and risk a message to someone who's always picked me up in the past.

Chelsea: Hey! Are you still in town?

Luca: Yeah, heading back to MKU later. Breakfast?

A smile twitches at my lips that he knows exactly what I need.

Chelsea: Would love to. Pick me up in an hour?

Luca: I'll be there x

I bite down on my lip as a little bit of the old me creeps in. Luca has always been my go-to Dunn brother. I can't lie, I gravitated to him at the beginning because he was so hot. He was the older brother that all the girls fancied but would never have a chance with. As much as I didn't want to accept it, I didn't have a chance either, but unlike my friends, I got to spend time with him and in my naïve little head, attempt to convince him I was the one for him. Reality was that I was a prepubescent girl who he saw as a sister of some sort.

He's always been so sweet and always ignored my advances despite my best attempts over the years. I never really gave up, but as my boobs grew and I found my place as a varsity cheerleader, I discovered I could get the attention of almost every other boy in our class, so I shifted my attention.

Luca's always been there though, acting like the brother I never had and helping to steer me in the right direction more often than not.

I have a quick shower, blow dry my hair, and apply my makeup just like I always do. I do it without thinking about my reality as I focus on such mundane tasks.

It's not until I pull my closet open and stare at all my clothes that I allow reality to seep in.

My cheer uniforms hang proudly at one end beside shelves of sports bras and yoga pants. It's only been a few weeks really, but even still, I feel different. I still want the same things, I want my squad, my future, I want to find love, but all of that suddenly seems a little less important these days.

Reaching in, I pull out my favorite pair of pants and pull the hot pink fabric up my legs before grabbing the matching sports bra and dragging an oversized tank over the top. I'll go for pancakes with Luca then head to the beach for a run after, burn off the excess sugar.

There was a gym at the center, but it was nowhere near as kitted out as I needed it to be in order to attempt to stay in shape. I might not be rejoining my squad anytime soon, but I'm not losing the years of hard work I've put in.

I give myself one final glance in the mirror before I head for the door. I look the same on the outside. My large eyes still hold the dark memories from my past that I'll forever hold inside, only now, there's an extra secret to keep to myself, for now at least.

I'm just closing the pool house door when the beep of his horn sounds out. Mom and Dad are sitting at the dining table when I pass through the kitchen.

"Morning, Chelsea. Did you sleep well?"

I think about my late-night visitor but quickly push him aside. "It was great," I lie easily.

"Have you got plans for today? I was thinking we could head to the mall and start our Christmas shopping." The hopeful look in her eyes damn near kills me. She's so desperate for us to be a normal family.

"Sure," I concede, unable to disappoint her once again. "I'm going for breakfast with Luca, then I'll come straight back."

"Okay. Have fun, sweetie."

After swiping a strawberry from her plate, I make my way to the front of the house when Luca beeps again.

Jogging down the steps from the house, I almost feel like my old self when I find him smiling at me through the driver's window of his truck.

"Looking good, beautiful." He makes a show of checking me out as I jog around the front and pull the door open. I'm sure a few years ago I'd have died a million deaths if he ever looked at me like that, but that's not how things are between us now. He's off killing it at MKU and I'm here pulling the pin out of the grenade on my life.

"Hey. Is that a bit of girl on your face?" I joke, reaching over to wipe an invisible mark off his cheek.

"Glad to see they didn't take away your smart ass."

"There's nothing to worry about where my ass is concerned, Dunn."

He chuckles at me before putting the car in reverse and backing out of my parents' driveway.

"And if you must know, there was no girl last night. I just hung out with Leon, Shane, and Dad watching old NFL games."

The mention of Shane is like a baseball bat to the gut.

"You okay?" he asks, glancing over when he pulls up at an intersection. "All the color's just drained from your face."

"Yeah, yeah. I'm good."

"You hanging, Chels? That why you needed this breakfast?"

"Something like that," I mutter.

"So what? You head to the beach with your squad and celebrate returning to your tribe?"

I look over expecting to find that he's joking, but I do a double take when I find him looking deadly serious.

"What?" he asks when the silence between us gets a little too much.

"I don't have a squad, Luc. The only celebrating my *tribe* will be doing is that they've gotten rid of me."

"What the fuck?" he barks.

"Oh come on, you've heard the rumors. You know why I left. Don't tell me you really expected me to be able to turn back up and reenter my old life like nothing happened." I take from the opening and closing of his mouth that he did. "We're not like guys, we don't have a fight and get over it. I'm done as far as the squad, hell the school, are concerned."

"You made a mistake, Chels. It'll blow over."

"I drugged the new girl, let your brother take the fall, and then went after one of our players. There's no coming back from that, Luc. I should just be glad I don't have a criminal record to go along with it."

He blows out a long breath as we make our way to the other side of town and our usual diner for the best pancakes in Rosewood.

"You fucked up. We all do it. They'll forgive you. They have to, that squad is nothing without you."

"They seem to be coping fine." I think of my butchered routines on Friday night. I mean, it wasn't the kind of performance that'll get them anywhere at regionals, but equally, it wasn't terrible.

"You've got this, Chels. I have faith in you."

"I'm glad someone does. Fancy coming to school with me tomorrow to hold my hand?" I ask with a laugh.

Luca pulls the car to a stop in the parking lot behind the diner and turns to me. His eyes are full of sympathy that I really don't want to see. Sitting back, I stare at the brick wall ahead instead of his familiar green eyes.

"Chelsea, you don't need anyone to hold your hand. You never have. Fierce isn't just your last name, girl. It runs through your fucking veins. You need to pick yourself up and walk back into that school like you fucking own it. But you really don't need me to tell you this, do you?"

For the first time since I can really remember, I think I do need to hear it.

Since I turned up in Rosewood after being dragged from my old life, I've made a point of showing everyone a certain side of me. And right now, I need to find that girl that Luca is talking about once again. It's no good being this broken girl who's been beaten down by her past and her mistakes. That won't get me anywhere.

I've got to hold my head high. Even if it is easier said than done.

"Come on, let's go eat our weight in pancakes."

I follow into the diner and we take a seat in our usual booth. The waitress comes over immediately, but she doesn't need to ask for our orders we're here so much.

I thought that when Luca left for college that it would be the end of our mornings, but apparently, he enjoyed them as much as me because at least once a month I'll wake on a weekend to find a message from him.

"The usual for both of you?"

"Please," Luca answers for us.

"A-actually, could I get an orange juice instead?"

"Of course, sweetie."

"Thank you."

"What, no black coffee this morning to go with your black heart?" he asks lightly, repeating the joke I've made on many occasions.

"Nah. So how's things been? I missed this."

Luca smiles before recollecting his tales from college while I've been away and successfully distracting me from my own life. It's the exact escape I need.

. . .

With stomachs full of pancakes and syrup, we make our way back toward our side of Rosewood and back to real life.

"You heading back to MKU this afternoon?"

"Yeah. Only a couple of weeks and I'll be back for the holidays," he says, clearly sensing where my thoughts are at. I need an ally in Rosewood right now, not all the way over in Maddison.

The thought of the holiday joy I'm going to have to spend the rest of the day faking with my mom doesn't fill me with happiness, but I guess it's better than the alternative being alone and miserable. I may as well have some company.

"Thank you for this morning. I really needed it," I say, leaning in to give him a hug.

"You've got this, Chels. You know where I am if you need me."

"I really appreciate that, Luc. But you've got a life to live, you don't need me cock blocking you."

He looks me up and down, his eyebrow quirking. "You think you could stop me getting some. Now that I'd like to see."

"On that note." I jump down from his truck and wave him off when he disappears from my view.

With a sigh, I make my way inside to find Mom and discover what plans she has for us for the rest of the day.

10

SHANE

The last thing I want to do when I get back from my excruciating time with Chelsea is to be forced to sit dissecting old NFL games like it would actually help me with my future progression. Luca and Leon don't give a shit, they'll happily watch games for hours with Dad and point out everyone's mistakes.

Thankfully, the obvious effect Chelsea had on my body has long vanished by the time I fall down on the couch, but that doesn't mean my muscles still aren't pulled tight or that my balls aren't blue as fuck.

That one night with Chelsea might be the only real experience I have, but fuck, I know enough to know exactly what I need right now.

I shift in my seat as images of that night threaten to reignite my earlier desire.

"You all good over there?" Leon asks, amusement curling at his lips. "You enjoying this a little too much, bro?" He nods to my crotch and to the TV.

My lack of female action is something that both my brothers like to rip me for. Just because I'm not like them with a different girl bouncing on my cock every night, it doesn't mean I'm not interested. Both of them have sat me down before now to tell me it's okay if I'm gay and that it shouldn't stop my football career, like it should even need fucking saying. It's twenty fucking twenty, it shouldn't matter who I chose to love. They just don't understand that I don't get all that excited about testing out every available pussy while I have the chance.

"Fuck you. I'm going to bed."

"Oooh someone's touchy."

I flip Leon off over my shoulder as I walk out. Luca looks over but he just rolls his eyes at the two of us.

I lie in bed staring at the ceiling running the events since she showed her face last night through my mind. Did I play it all wrong?

I think about her dark eyes begging for me to listen to her in the shadows after the game, I think about the tears that filled them while we were in Dad's office. Was I too harsh? Or, not enough?

I remember what she did, how she could so easily hurt people I—she—cares about.

One thing is for sure. I shouldn't have gone there tonight. I shouldn't have gone anywhere near their house. I shouldn't have stepped foot inside her pool house, and I certainly shouldn't have gotten her to take that fucking jersey off.

The sight of her standing before me, confident as anything is burned into my eyelids. She's so fucking perfect and I remember all too well how that body lined up with mine, how we moved together, how soft her skin was.

Groaning to myself, I shove my hand under the sheets and wrap my fingers around my length. It's got nothing on Chelsea's gentle touch but it's all I've got.

Resting back, I close my eyes and put myself back in that pool house. I forget everything, the vile words we hurled at each other, her reputation, the fact I should hate her, and I just focus on how good I know she can make me feel.

All too soon, my cock jerks in my hand and I stifle the groan that wants to erupt. Knowing my luck, Leon will walk past the door at the exact same time and think I'm jacking off to a football poster on my wall or some shit.

Unable to sleep and not wanting to lie in the dark with thoughts of a girl who shouldn't take up my headspace, I turn my Xbox on and spend almost all night playing online with Wyatt who is more than happy to give up a night's sleep to gaming.

I have no idea what time I eventually crash. All I do know is that when I wake the sun is high and my dad and brothers' voices boom from downstairs.

Groaning, I turn over and grab my cell from the nightstand.

Finding no messages, I open up Instagram and start scrolling, anything so that I don't have to crawl out of bed yet. I soon regret it though when I find a photo of none other than Chelsea with my fucking brother out to breakfast this morning.

Anger stirs in my belly as I grip my phone tighter. How dare he take her out like everything is normal.

Hearing footsteps pounding up the stairs, I throw the covers off and march for the door.

Ripping it open, I wait to see which one of them is about to appear around the corner.

Something explodes within me when it's the one I want.

"What the fuck do you think you're playing at?" I bark at Luca as he gets closer.

"What the fuck?" he asks in shock as I stand in the middle of the hallway, effectively stopping him from getting to his room. "Get the fuck out of the way, Shane."

"No. What the fuck were you doing with her this morning?"

"Oooh," he sings as realization dawns. "We went for breakfast. So what?"

"So what? Don't you know what she did?" I balk.

"Yeah. She fucked up. She's been gone weeks. She's paid for it. She doesn't need shit from me too."

I stare at him, my mouth hanging open. "You're fucking serious?"

"Yeah. She fucked up, Shane. We all do. Give her a fucking break."

I look him up and down, my lip curling in disgust. "You've fucked her, haven't you?"

"What? No. of course I haven't fucked her. She's like my little fucking sister. What the hell is wron—oh."

"What?" I spit.

"Jealousy doesn't look good on you, little brother."

My teeth grind. "I'm not jealous."

"No. That why you're stalking her Instagram? Finding out where she's been? That's why you kept ringing me while she was gone, wasn't it? I thought you were concerned about her, but no, you just wanted to fuck her."

"No. No. She's been around half the team, I'm not going there too." He lifts his brow and all it does is piss me off further.

"Get the fuck out of my way. I need to go back to college. And you, you need to sort your shit out."

"I don't fucking want her," I argue after he pushes me aside and storms past.

"I didn't say anything about wanting her. I said sort your shit out, but I'm glad you just admitted that she's the issue. She's lonely, Shane. Go see her. Be nice to her. You might even get what you want." I watch him stop when he gets to his door and turn back. "But don't fucking hurt her. She's been through enough."

"Don't hurt... fucking hell. What line has she spun you this morning?"

"The truth, Shane. She needs some friends right now, how about you try to be one."

"What the fuck ever." Marching into my room, I slam the door behind me, hoping that I can leave his words out in the hallway.

How can he say that? Be her fucking friend. I've never been her friend. She's followed Luca around for years like a fucking puppy, she never had any intention of ever being my friend.

I was just a means to an end. A toy for her to enjoy when she was bored. She said it herself last night.

I am nothing to her.

I shouldn't even fucking care.

I open up my cell again, ready to unfollow her. My finger hovers over the button as her large chocolate eyes stare up at me.

"Motherfucker," I bark, throwing my cell onto the bed and storming toward the shower.

I don't fucking need this bullshit.

After showering off the lingering scent of her perfume from last night that continued to taunt me even while I was sleeping, I head to the gym to work out some of my frustrations.

I could stay at home and use Dad's state of the art home gym but the second he discovers me in there he usually insists on 'helping' and his brand of helping usually means pushing me until I can no longer feel my legs. I might need the burn right now, but I also need to be able to walk into school tomorrow.

I shoot Zayn a message as I jump in the car, and he agrees to meet me there.

We hit the gym for a little over an hour before finding ourselves in the sauna.

"You coming to mine tonight? Mom's away?"

"Uh... I guess."

"The rest of the guys are coming, the girls too."

The fact that he means the squad, minus Chelsea, makes my chest clench in a way it shouldn't. I shouldn't feel bad for her missing out on this stuff after she was the one who fucked it all up, but I can't help it. It's her squad, her senior year. Shelly can make out that she's taken over all she likes, but we all know Chelsea made them what they are. Their coach sure didn't do it.

"Sure thing, man," I say, pushing thoughts of Chelsea to the back of my head. If she can go out for breakfast with my brother like everything is normal, then I can have a night with the team and her squad of bitches.

"Yo, catch," Rich shouts the second I walk into Zayn's den later that night as a bottle of beer comes flying for my head.

"Fucking hell. A little warning would have been nice."

"You don't get no warning in the NFL, my friend," Rich says, making me want to turn around and walk straight back out again. I've already had to endure one of Dad's pep talks before I managed to leave the house this evening, I really don't need it from them too.

Twisting the cap, I throw it at him and it bounces off his temple.

"Someone needs to get laid," he mutters. My entire body freezes and suddenly my head is back in Chelsea's pool house last night.

Shaking her from my head, I fall down onto one of Zayn's beanbags and tip the bottle to my lips.

"It's all right, bro. The girls will be here soon and they all wanna fuck a champ."

"Shut the fuck up, man," Zayn says, attempting to come to my rescue.

As far as they are concerned, I haven't gone past second base with any of the cheer bitches that throw themselves at us at every available opportunity.

I used to be happy to watch it all from the sidelines while hanging out with my other friends, but then she happened, and I found myself in the middle of this world.

I just wanted to find out where she was, I needed to know that she was okay, all the while wishing that I didn't care that much.

That's the thing with Chelsea Fierce, she fucks with my head until I don't know which way is up.

A ruckus is raised at the door behind me, and when I glance over, I find the rest of the team and the cheer squad piling into the room.

"To the state fucking champions," someone shouts before a round of hollers and cheers sound out.

Fucking hell, was that only Friday night? It already feels like a lifetime ago.

Everyone grabs a drink, someone turns the music up and the party really gets started.

I'm more than happy watching everyone enjoy themselves from my seat, but Victoria gets other ideas and pulls me up to join everyone else.

"There's nothing wrong with enjoying yourself, Dunn."

"I am," I argue, although I'm not sure my face matches my words.

"Dance with me," she demands, pressing her body up

against mine. She moves in time with the music and I forget everything and move with her.

The next thing I know, I'm rolling over on Zayn's sofa and falling flat on my face on his wooden floor. I have no idea how much I had to drink last night, but everything is pretty hazy.

Ow my fucking head.

I rest it on my forearm and I'm pretty sure I fall back to sleep.

"Rise and shine, ladies," someone announces way too loudly before the blinds are opened and the sun comes streaming in. "The bitches are waiting."

Glancing at the owner of the noise, I find Zayn standing with a shit-eating grin on his face as he looks between Rich and I who are both groaning in frustration. Why the fuck does he look so good this morning?

"Fuck. Off," Rich grunts, clearly sharing my thoughts.

"No can do, girls. School is calling."

Fucking hell, it's Monday.

"And you know that Rosewood High needs its champion Bears to show their faces this morning."

"This is all your fucking fault, Hunter," I mumble, pushing myself so I'm sitting against the edge of the couch.

"Me? I didn't pin you down and poor that vodka down your throat, Dunn."

"No, I'm pretty sure that was Victoria right before you did a body shot off her—"

"Enough," I bark. The events of last night are fuzzy at best, I really don't need a first thing refresher of the bad decisions I made.

11

CHELSEA

I'd hardly looked at my cell while I was away, and I certainly didn't open any social media apps. I could only imagine the exaggeration and lies that were flying around on there about what happened and where I'd gone to. The only messages I opened were from Ethan, but even then, I mostly didn't respond. It was nice to know that someone other than my parents did actually miss me.

After a fitful night's sleep full of nightmares about what the next day might hold, I sit up in bed and lift my cell from the nightstand.

Six a.m. The mornings I'm usually up this early, it's because I requested the squad start the day with a morning workout session. That's far from my reality today though. I'd love to don my sports bra and yoga pants and burn off some of my excess fat until my legs feel like jelly and all of us help each other limp back to the locker rooms to put ourselves back together.

I blow out a long sigh, wondering if I'll ever get a chance to return to that life. Cheerleading is everything to me. It was always my plan to secure a scholarship so my parents didn't need to bankroll my future, hell knows they've already done more for me than I deserve. But now, with no squad and my future up in the air, I have no idea what my plan is.

Unlocking my cell, I hesitantly open Instagram. I'm hit with more notifications than I can deal with, and not wanting to see what people are saying about me, I focus my attention on my feed. It's fine, just the usual high school images until one makes me stop. My stomach turns over at the sight of Victoria with her hands all over Shane.

My lips purse as I scroll through the many variations of the same photography. My hands shake. I want to scream at her to get her hands off him, he's mine. But I know he's not. All we had was one intense night. I can't stake any claim.

Unable to continue looking at the familiarity of their touch, I slam my cell facedown on the bed.

I've been gone weeks. I'd be stupid to assume that he's not moved on. That another member of the squad hasn't got her claws into him. He's always acted like he wasn't interested in what we had to offer, but then he wasn't exactly turning me away that night. Maybe I was just the one to give him the push and the confidence he needed to turn into one of them.

Tears burn my eyes, but I refused to cry over whatever this weird infatuation is I have with Shane Dunn. We had one night, one that I'm sure he probably regrets after everything that happened after it.

I need to forget about all of that. Forget about the past. I need to focus on the future and trying to find myself some kind of a life as I figure out what comes next. I once thought it was easy. Go to school, cheer, win regionals, get a scholarship and get the hell out of Rosewood. I still want to leave, to get away from those who'll continue to whisper things about me, but suddenly disappearing off on my own somewhere across the country is less appealing.

With a sigh, I climb out of bed and set about getting ready for my big return to Rosewood High.

Dread rolls around in my stomach as I think about what the day might hold. I guess, I've already had it out with the squad, they're going to be expecting me. Fuck, that could be worse.

I try to focus on other things but it's impossible. By the time I walk through the kitchen of the main house where Mom is having her morning coffee, I'm worried I might puke at any moment. The second I pull the door open, her beloved festive music sounds out and I stifle a groan.

"Aw, it's so good to have you back again. This place just isn't the same without you," she says, smiling softly at me.

"It must be like I'm not here being out in the pool house," I mutter, raiding their refrigerator instead of mine.

"Not at all. I feel your presence even if you are out there." A silence falls between us as I swipe an apple from the bowl in the center of the island. "Thank you for yesterday. I know it wasn't exactly your idea of fun, but..." She trails off, leaving me to think about our afternoon at the mall. Mom loves the holidays, almost to an obsessive level. Every room of the house gets decorated within an inch of its life, and Dad and I are forced to endure hours of Christmas music throughout the entire house. Usually she'd have done it all this weekend, and I can't help but feel relieved that I didn't come home to the chaos of Mom bossing Dad around in her quest to make everything perfect.

"It was great, Mom." It's a lie, and she knows it. She had this huge list of gifts to buy and I had no one. Well, that's not true, I had the two of them but I couldn't exactly buy them with Mom there.

The look of sympathy on her face when I told her I had no one to buy for was one I remember all too well from my former years when people discovered just what a disaster my life was. It's a look that had mostly vanished from my life once I was adopted.

The squad and I had always done secret Santa. I have no idea whether they're doing it again this year or not, but I do know that I'm not going to be invited to take part.

With a sigh, I say goodbye to Mom and regretfully leave the house.

My stomach is in knots. I should eat the apple that I picked up, I know that, but I feel like all I'll do is puke it back up if I even attempt to eat it.

As I sit in the parking lot behind the wheel of my car with my classmates loitering around and heading for the buildings to start their days, I can't force my muscles to move.

This place has been my playground for years. I ruled this school along with my squad and the team. I shouldn't now be afraid to step foot inside.

It's all my own fault. I know that. If I hadn't made such stupid, fucked-up decisions then none of this would have happened. I'd still have my position, my future, my friends.

A few students eventually notice me sitting here, and I'm forced to move before I change my mind and drive back home again to hide in my pool house. That's not the girl I am. I don't hide. I stand proud with my head held high and my shoulders back. It's time to rediscover the old Chelsea, the one I pushed aside in my time away. It's time to take back control of my life.

Throwing the door open, I climb out and pull my purse over my shoulder. I focus on the building ahead and ignore the burning stares of everyone around me.

The voices start out as whispers but as I get closer to the main building to find my locker the gossip surrounding me becomes loud enough that I've got no choice but to hear it.

"Did you hear the cheer squad refused to take her back?"

"Can you believe she had the audacity to turn up to the

game on Friday night. Like she supports them, pfft. She probably just wanted to drug them again."

"Does she really think she's welcome back here?"

"She needs to watch her back. I've heard the squad are gunning for her."

A shiver runs down my spine. No one in Rosewood, other than my parents, know the real me. So the threat of the squad coming after me doesn't really scare me, but out of everyone, they know me the best. They would know how to hurt me. Hell, they already have. They know the only thing I want is to cheer, and they've already taken that away from me. So what's left?

This should have been my year, but from the get-go it's been anything but. First Amalie stole Jake, not that he was ever really mine, then my ankle stopped me from cheering and now this.

Most will probably tell me it's karma and that I deserve it, they'd probably be right, but it doesn't stop it hurting like a bitch. I've spent all my life working toward this point, toward regionals and my future and to watch it just fall away hurts like hell.

The whispers and gossip only get worse and I make my way inside the building. My only saving grace is that I haven't seen any members of the squad. They'll be outside in our usual spot trying to bag a player. I roll my eyes at the kind of behavior I was front and center of not so long ago. It's amazing how quickly things can change.

Students' stares burn into my back as I make my way toward my locker. In the past I've always loved that it's close to the girls' locker rooms, it made my life easier but as I get closer to possibly bumping into the squad, I start to wish it was situated at the other side of the school.

I'm just sorting my books out when a shadow falls over

me. Swallowing down my nerves, I risk a look over my shoulder.

"Chelsea," Miss Kelly, our cheer coach, says on a sigh. "I think we need to go and have a chat, don't you?"

Dread churns in my stomach that she's going to attempt a therapy session with me. If she thinks that she's going to unearth any more than the counselors did at the center then she needs to think again. I'm not sure there's a counselor on earth who could sort out the mess that my head and life is right now.

Grabbing the couple of books I need, I slam my locker closed and follow Kelly toward her office within the girls' locker room.

I have serious mixed feelings where our cheer coach is concerned. She's got a great reputation from her own cheer career and the teams she's coached in the past. But I can't help feeling like she's lost her enthusiasm. That or it's been misplaced onto Mr. Knight, one of the other gym staff. He's married with a couple of kids but we're all convinced they're having an affair. She spends more of our training sessions either in the office with him or just markedly absent. It's how I've ended up being more than just the squad captain, a role that I'm more than happy to take on board. I've been choreographing routines for as long as I can remember. Even before I lived here, dancing was my escape. I'd take my radio out to the fields behind where we lived and lose hours making up routines, teaching myself moves. I used to watch the cheer team at my school, when I was there, in awe. I wanted to be them so badly, but most days it was all I could do to get to class let alone anything else that would take up my time. But I wanted it, so fucking badly.

When I moved here, the cheer squad was the first thing I looked into. I was desperate to at least make something of my new life, hell knows I needed something to keep me from drowning as my world once again was flipped upside down. I might have found myself with incredible new parents who had enough money to give me everything I could need, but that was far from going to fix my issues. I had more of those fuckers on the day I was born than Derek and Honey had probably had all their lives.

Pushing away thoughts of my past from my mind, I drop down on the chair in front of Kelly's desk.

"It's so nice to have you back, Chelsea. It hasn't been the same without you."

"Really? It seemed to me on Friday night that no one had noticed I wasn't there."

"You've always been my best flyer, Chels. Of course we missed you."

I quirk a brow at her. I don't even remember seeing her on Friday night. She clearly has no idea what when down.

"Whatever. I want my squad back."

"Um... I understand that, Chelsea. I know how much this squad means to you."

"Do you? How? You're never here. There wouldn't even be a squad if it weren't for me, let alone one that's going to regionals in a few months," I seethe.

"I'm sure you of all people can understand that life can be... complicated."

"Yeah, I sure as fuck know that. Look," I say, standing from the chair and pacing back and forth in front of her desk. "I know I fucked up. I'm willing to take responsibility for my actions and I'll apologize to anyone, however you'd like me to. But I need my squad."

Kelly stares at me, her eyes narrowing.

She can't possibly know that I'm hiding things, can she? She probably knows me as well as my parents after all these years working side by side, but she can't know.

"I know you do, Chelsea. But I don't think it's going to be that easy. You've been gone weeks and the girls have—"

"I don't give a fuck. They were a mess on Friday night. They've trashed my routines, they were out of time, uncoordinated."

"They've worked hard to compensate for you not being there."

"Well, I'm here now."

"Look, Chelsea—"

"No," I interrupt. "Don't *Look, Chelsea,* me. This is my squad, Kelly. My fucking squad." I hate that my voice cracks and my bottom lip starts to tremble.

"I'm sorry, Chelsea. I need to focus on you, and right now, you need to get back into class and make sure you're going to graduate."

"Jesus, I didn't go on an extended holiday. I went to school every day. I haven't fallen behind. I will graduate."

"Prove it. Meanwhile, I'll speak to the squad, to Shelly, and see how they feel."

"This is bullshit," I spit, knowing full well that Shelly won't take me back. She wants the fame and attention of being captain and to be able to control my life. *Just like you used to,* a little voice in my head says, but I push her down. There's no point in focusing on the past. I need to fight for my future.

"Go to class, get those grades up. We've still got a few months before regionals. We'll be ready no matter what."

"You can't go to regionals without me. I am this squad. They never would have had a shot without me."

"Chelsea, I hate to say it, but maybe you should have been focused on that during the past few months instead of..." She waves her hand around not wanting to finish the sentence.

"Yeah well, shit happens, Kelly. I thought you of all people would understand that. How is Mr. Knight's wife, by the way?"

Kelly turns beet red with anger. "Get to class, Chelsea, before you cause even more damage to your cheer career."

"Whatever." I pull the door open so hard it slams back against the wall.

Every set of eyes now filling the locker room now turn to me and who should be front and center but Shelly.

"Aw, you having a little tantrum because you didn't get your way. Such a shame, right, girls? The all-powerful Chelsea Fierce has fallen from her throne, losing her crown on the way down. Mind you don't hurt your ass when you hit the floor."

"Fuck you, Shelly. This is my squad and you know it. You don't have what it takes to make it anywhere near regionals. You're unorganized, lacking dedication, you spend more time on your back with your legs open than you do training." By the time I've finished, we're practically nose to nose.

"Pfft, that's rich. You're the one who's been with almost the entire football team."

"Is that right?" I seethe. I know how I've made it look over the years, but everyone's opinion of me is far from the truth.

"Who's left? Just Shane probably, and I know for a fact that he wouldn't touch you with a barge pole."

"Is that right? I'd put money on having a better chance than you."

An evil smile curls at her lips. "Of course, you just drug the ones who aren't willing."

My arm has moved before I even register, and my palm stings against her cheek.

"You bitch," she squeals as the squad surrounds her. "You're finished here, Chelsea. Get. Out."

"I'm fucking leaving. But I'll be waiting."

"Waiting for what?" Victoria asks.

"For you to all be begging me to come back. I know you all want to win, and you know as well as I do that you need me."

"No one needs you, Chelsea. You're nothing but a raging bitch."

"Just wait," I repeat as I back out of the locker room.

I keep my head high and my eyes locked on Shelly's but inside I'm crumbling faster than I can control.

The hallway is empty when I stumble out, thank fuck because I'm on the verge of breaking.

No one needs you, Chelsea.

Shelly's words run on repeat in my head and mix with those of my past that I've locked down in a little box.

My chest heaves as I fight not to lose control. I make it to the bathroom without anyone seeing me. I'm just about to push inside when a figure at the other end of the hallway catches my eye, but whoever it is disappears around the corner before I get a chance to see who it is.

Standing in front of the mirrors, I fight my need to cry. I refuse to allow them to break me, especially only minutes into my first day back.

I'm better than this. I'm stronger than this.

I refuse to be beaten down by Shelly and her band of bitches who should have my back, not hers.

After fixing my makeup, I walk out to the deserted hallway and make my way to the first class of the day.

It seems that if I had any ideas of slipping in unnoticed today then it's all been shot to shit when I knock on my physics class door and walk inside.

Every single set of eyes drill into me, including that of the teacher.

"Oh... um... welcome back," he stutters. "Please take your seat. We've only just got started."

I nod, trying to appear totally unfazed by everyone's attention. After all, attention is what I've craved all these years, it should come naturally. But as I make my way across the room toward an empty desk, all I want is for the ground to swallow me up.

I keep my eyes on the one person I know I'm safe beside. Ethan.

Our teacher continues with whatever he's talking about as I fall into my chair and blow out a breath.

I've lost the attention of some, I can feel it, but the majority are still staring at me like I'm some alien creature they've never seen before.

"It'll get better," Ethan says, turning his back on most of the class. "It's good to see you back, Chels."

"I wish I could say it was good to be back." I blow out a breath as I pull my book from my purse. "Thank you, Ethan. For the messages. For thinking of me."

A sad smile pulls at my lips as he reaches over and squeezes my hand.

"Life can be tough. Sometimes we all need a friend." A lump forms in my throat at his kindness. He could quite easily be the leader of the Chelsea hate campaign seeing as it was one of his best friends I stupidly went after, but thankfully, Ethan sees a little deeper than my bullshit decisions.

"I think you might be the only one I have left," I mutter, more to myself than him, but he still hears.

"Just give everyone time. They're pissed, rightly so. But this is your home, Chels. You'll find your footing again."

"But what if I don't?"

"Then you'll find new footing. Be a new you. Everything will be okay."

I nod, wishing that I could feel just an ounce of his positivity.

I look at him, his kind eyes sparkle in a way I've never seen before and he looks happier than I think I've ever experienced.

"We looked for you at the party on Friday night."

"I didn't stay long, it was... intense."

"One day at a time. Things will be fine, you'll see."

"Mr. Savage, Miss Fierce, I'm sure you've got loads to catch up on, but if you could please save it for lunch."

"Sorry," we both mutter, turning to focus on whatever it is we should be doing.

I sit back in my chair, aware that I've still got one too many sets of eyes on me and trying to block them out to focus. Kelly might have been right about one thing this morning. I really fucking need to graduate. And as the next few months go on, it's only going to get harder, that I'm sure of.

12

SHANE

As I watched her all but run toward the girls' bathroom, every muscle in my body ached for me to follow her. She was upset, that much was obvious. I'd watched the squad run back into the locker rooms not long after she was dragged in there by Miss Kelly. There was never going to be a good outcome for her.

I'm just about to take a step toward where she disappeared when Zayn appears around the corner.

Taking a step back, I walk his way.

"Hey, man. How's the hangover?"

"Fucking great," I complain. "No better way to start a Monday at school."

"So I hear that Chelsea has shown her face."

I focus on the hallway ahead, but he keeps his eyes firmly on the side of my face. I know he's suspicious from Saturday morning. He might not have said anything last night, but I saw the look on his face when I was dancing with Victoria.

"Well, I guess she couldn't hide forever."

"So you haven't seen her?"

"Uh no. I went home for a shower and now here I am."

"Right."

"Right what?" I bark, already fed up with this conversation and his suspicion. I don't need anyone digging into my history with Chelsea. The fewer people who know about that night and my fucked-up head, the better.

"Oh nothing. I'm just watching you, that's all." He gestures between his eyes and mine.

I raise a brow at him.

"Don't act all innocent. I saw that thing between the two of you on the beach. You're hiding shit."

"Whatever. We're late." I turn away from him and toward my first class of the day, the sound of his laughter filters down to me. I don't need him looking too closely, I really fucking don't.

Grateful that she's not in my class, I find my seat and slump down in the hope I can be ignored while I drown in my hangover and the memories of my bad decisions. Sadly, those bad decisions all include one person who stirs something inside me she shouldn't.

Whispers and gossip ripple around the room and I hear her name mentioned more than once proving that no matter how hard I try, I can't escape her. Maybe I should have followed her earlier and just got it over with.

She thinks she's won sending me away like that on Saturday night. I should leave it there, but there's this nagging voice within me that demands I don't let her have the last word.

By some miracle, I get through the entire morning without seeing her. I was expecting her in math, but rumor had it that she was with the guidance counselor. Fine by me seeing as Zayn was sitting beside me just waiting to discover something. He's like a fucking dog with a bone, and I fear he's not going to stop until I give him something.

"Can you believe she just walked in like nothing ever

happened?" Camila asks Amalie when I drop down beside them with my lunch.

"Jesus, not you too," I complain. "She's all anyone's talked about all morning."

"Well, it's quite big news. What's got your panties in a twist?" Camila asks, studying me.

"Nothing. I'm just sick of hearing it all. Of course she turned up, this is her school."

"We know that. She's just not said anything about anything. You'd think she could at least apologize."

"I'm sure she will. I can't imagine walking back in after everything was easy. Give her a break."

"Whoa," Camila says, holding her hands up in shock. "Are you actually defending her after what she did to you?"

"No, I'm just saying that it must be hard. I'm bored with hearing it, imagine how she feels."

"I don't really give a shit how she feels, Shane. She hurt three of the most important people in my life not so long ago. I couldn't have cared less if she never returned."

"Bit harsh?" Amalie asks, making Camila shrug.

"Don't say you agree with him."

"I've been the school outcast. It's not something I'd wish on anyone."

"Even your worst enemy?"

"She's not exactly my worst enemy. She's just... lost, I guess."

I nod because I have a feeling that Amalie has just hit the nail on the head perfectly.

"Well, I think you're both fucking crazy and should be heading up the *we hate Chelsea* movement that's sweeping through the school." Camila is soon distracted when Mason steps up behind her and drops a kiss to her temple. "Hey, baby. You'll back me up here..." she goes on to explain her point of view and when Mason sides with Amalie and I, Camila's face starts to turn pink with frustration.

"Just give her a break. She fucked up."

"Fucked up. She fucking drugged you."

"Yeah, I know. But no one died, we're all good. Stop getting involved and maybe just focus on your own life."

"Ugh, please. We don't need to see that much tongue," Amalie complains when Mason pulls Camila onto his lap and drops his lips to hers. Camila flips her off over Mason's shoulder.

"Because you're so much better with Jake?"

"Meh. Anyway, it doesn't look like you're one to talk. Care to explain this?" Amalie asks, pulling her cell out and opening Instagram on an image of Victoria climbing me like a tree.

"If I knew there was going to be photographic evidence, then I might have put up a bit more of a fight."

Amalie looks from her cell to me and back again, her face full of amusement. "You put up any kind of fight?"

I think back to my fuzzy memories of the night before. "I have no idea. There was too much vodka."

"Shane, Shane, Shane. I thought you were better than them."

I shrug. "Boys will be boys."

"Ain't that the truth. I just thought you had better taste than a cheer slut."

"Me too," I admit. "Sadly, there wasn't much choice."

An eruption of noise at the cafeteria entrance cuts off our conversation and when we look over we find none other than Amalie's boyfriend lapping up the congratulations from our win on Friday night. Ethan is beside him with the entire cheer squad behind them.

"Oh look, the entertainment has arrived," Amalie mutters.

I watch as Jake looks around, the second he finds her, his eyes light up and he marches over. The moment he's in touching distance, he pulls her from the bench and straight into his arms.

A smile forms on my lips as I watch them. I always thought Jake was an asshole, I mean, he is an asshole, but when he's with Amalie, he's a totally different guy. A guy that I'm starting to discover that I actually like. Although I'm never going to tell him that.

Excitement vibrates through the students as they recall Friday night. The noise level becomes deafening as we celebrate the win we've waited all our lives for.

Everyone is laughing and enjoying themselves when suddenly the room quietens down. People turn toward the entrance and when I follow, I find the reason for the break in excitement.

Chelsea is standing in the wide doorway. She looks beautiful, like she always does. Her long dark hair is pulled over one shoulder, her dark eyes are wide as she takes in the view before her and her full red lips are parted. But the confidence she usually wears is disappearing faster than I can compute as the cheer squad turns on her.

A few people call out that she's not welcome, that she should go back into hiding.

"Jesus, people are cruel," Mason mutters as he stands from the bench.

I do the same, my need to protect one of our own overriding my need to see her get some justice.

A second before she's surrounded by the cheer squad, our eyes lock. Fear fills hers and it hits me right in the chest.

I don't think I breathe as she's swallowed up by the girls who used to support her every move.

"Fucking hell," Mason barks before both him and Jake take off for the crowd.

They quickly force their way into the huddle, but my legs refuse to move.

That is until a scream sounds out, one I recognize all too well. Then my body moves without any instruction from my brain. My need to go to her, to help her, is too much to ignore.

By the time I break through the now much larger crowd, it seems the show is over because Shelly is standing front and center with a shit-eating grin on her face. Her loyal followers standing behind her and backing her all the way.

Glancing up to the hallway beyond, I find the girl they've just sent away running as fast as her legs will carry her.

I'm pushing through the rest of the crowd before I even know what I'm doing, and I run after her.

"Chelsea?" She doesn't stop, her movements don't falter as she flees from whatever just happened with Shelly. "Chelsea stop, please."

She flies into the girls' bathroom and slams the door behind her.

"Chelsea?" I ask, poking my head inside.

"Go away." Her voice is broken and rough and it pulls at me.

Ignoring her warning, I step farther into the room.

"Chels?"

"I said go away, Shane. I can't do this. I can't—"

Placing my hand on her shoulder, I spin her around and gasp.

There are bright red scratch marks across her cheeks, but surprisingly that's not the most shocking thing because what has my eyes widening is her tears.

"Fuck, Chels." Before I know what I'm doing, I have her in my arms.

Her small frame trembles as I hold her tight.

"No, no," she fights, trying to push me away from her. "Shane, no."

I hold tight, knowing that she needs this right now, but

when she reaches up and twists my nipple, I have no choice but to release her.

"Ow," I complain, rubbing at the sting.

"You should have let go," she snaps.

"You should have let me hold you."

"Why?" she asks, wiping at her wet cheeks. "So you could say that you helped me when I broke. So that you could go back to your little friends and tell them how weak I am? So you can tell them that they're winning, that they're ruining my life?" The fire that I'm so used to starts to burn in her eyes.

"No, I was coming to make sure you were okay."

"Jesus, you really are pathetic. You that desperate for another round?"

I close the space between us so she has no choice but to back up until she hits the wall.

Our bodies are only an inch apart and her heat burns into me.

"You may have left me on the edge the other night, but no, that wasn't my intention."

I stare down into her tear-filled chocolate eyes.

She swallows nervously before biting down on her bottom lip. My eyes flit between them and her quickly darkening eyes.

"Go on then. Take whatever you want. You might as well kick me when I'm down."

As much as I might want to take her in my arms and look after her, I won't. Not like this.

Lifting my hand, I gently touch my fingertip to the scratches down her cheek. She startles and gasps at my contact.

"They have no right laying a hand on you," I whisper, ignoring her previous comment.

She shrugs one shoulder. "I deserve it for all the people I've hurt."

"Many would probably agree."

"You don't?"

"I don't know what I think when it comes to you."

Her breathing catches at my honesty.

"One thing I do know though, I don't just take. I don't take things that aren't offered to me, and I certainly don't take from others when they're down."

I take a step back and suck in a lungful of air now that I'm not surrounded by her scent.

"You want something from me, this isn't how you get it."

She opens her mouth to respond, but I'm done. I came in here with good intentions and I'm not going to stand here while she unleashes more hate and frustration my way.

Turning my back on her, I'm almost out the door when her voice stops me.

"Shane?" Resting my hand on the doorframe, I stop and hang my head, waiting for whatever she has to say. "I'm... I'm sorry." If the room weren't so silent, I would think I misheard.

"I know," I say before disappearing from her sight and allowing the door to close behind me.

13

CHELSEA

A sob rumbles up the second the door slams behind him.

I shouldn't have said those things. I knew the moment I looked into his eyes that he didn't follow me for a fight, but I freaked out.

I didn't want him to see me broken, to see me cry, but he was standing before me while I crumbled.

Shelly shouldn't have this power over me, but she ambushed me, spurred on by the girls who used to stand behind my every move.

As she raised her hand to get her revenge for the slap I gave her earlier, all I could do was stand there and take it.

I expected the slap, I didn't anticipate her nails as they clawed at my cheek.

"Fuck," I bark, turning to look in the mirror to inspect the damage.

I run my finger over the deepest gouge and hiss when it stings.

Movement over my shoulder has my heart jumping into

my throat. My first thought is that he came back without me hearing but I soon realize it's not him.

"What?" I bark at the short, dark-haired girl who clearly was hiding in one of the cubicles this whole time.

"Nothing," she says, walking toward the sinks to wash her hands. "You're welcome, by the way."

I give her a double-take. "Um... for what, exactly?"

"For giving you some kind of privacy. I must say though, I was disappointed that he didn't kiss you. That would have been hot."

"Fucking hell, creepy much. You were watching?"

"No, just listening."

We stare at each other, other than our dark hair we're opposites in every way. I might not be currently wearing my preppy cheer uniform but that's the persona I try to give off whereas everything about this girl is dark. The exact kind I'd usually steer clear of. So why I feel drawn to her, I have no fucking clue.

"They've all got you very wrong, don't they?"

"They? Who? What?"

She finishes washing her hands before coming to stand in front of me.

"I've heard so much about you, it's good to finally meet the woman behind all the stories." I narrow my eyes at her. Who the fuck is this girl? "Rae," she says as if she can read my mind. "Ethan's girlfriend. He's told me all about you."

A laugh rumbles up my throat. "You're Ethan's girl? For real?"

She smiles, gesturing at herself. "I know. Shocking right? I don't even own a cheer uniform."

"Maybe not," I muse. "But I think I'm already understanding why he didn't stand a chance."

"Oh yeah?"

"Ethan always loved a challenge, and why do I think you're

the ultimate one?"

She pops her hip and rests her hand on it. "Because I am."

"I think I like you already."

"That's good because most people are just scared, or jealous."

"You bagged Ethan Savage. Girl, that group out there will be about as jealous as it comes."

"I fucking love it. Seeing the frustration in their eyes on a daily basis is what gets me up in the morning. Well, that and Ethan's co—"

"Okay," I say with a laugh, halting any more words. "Ethan and I might be close, but there's always been a line between us."

"More than you have with the rest of the team, I hear."

"Fucking hell. You don't hold back, do you?"

"What's the point? What you see is what you get. Like it or fucking lump it."

I shake my head at her in total amazement.

"You fancy getting out of here. I'm not really feeling it, plus I've got gym later and I really don't have the patience for that."

"You want to skip?"

"Yeah. You don't actually want to be here after that, do you?" she asks, nodding at my cheek.

"No, I really fucking don't."

"Perfect, come on then. Let's head to the beach, I'm sure your tan could use some work after weeks of being locked up."

I follow her out of the bathroom and for the first time today, I'm able to ignore the stares and harsh words that are muttered as we pass.

"You know, I wasn't in prison, right?"

"Some center full of fucked-up teenagers and counselors who want to know your deepest thoughts and feelings? Sounds like prison to me."

I can't really argue because she does kinda have a point.

"You've got a car, right? I rode with Ethan?"

"Um… yeah. Over there." I point to my white convertible BMW.

"Wow, of course."

"What?" I ask.

"Just wondering if you could be any more stereotypical. You must have looked like something out of the movies getting out of this in your cheer uniform."

"I guess you won't find out seeing as they've kicked me out."

"I'm sure you'll get over it."

We climb in and in seconds we're heading out of the parking lot and away from Rosewood High.

"So how much has Ethan told you exactly?"

"Adopted, cheer bitch… sorry, head cheer bitch, team bike, life of the party, drink spiker, did I mention bitch?" She ticks each item off on her fingers.

"Oh my god," I mutter.

"What? Did I miss something?"

"No, no, I think you nailed it."

"If it makes you feel any better, I'm about as screwed up. You're in good company."

I've never really had what I would class as a close girlfriend. I spent all my time with the squad, but I never really connected with any of them, not in a way I would hope. I guess I wasn't the only one who felt that way, seeing as they all turned their backs on me at the first possible opportunity.

I glance over at Rae, someone who I never would have considered spending time with and much like with Shane, I start to wonder if I had everything wrong.

I clung to the squad, thinking they were what would make me happy. I attached myself to the football team thinking that I was destined to be with the best of the bunch, but was I just trying too hard?

Cheer is always going to be my life. But maybe I can have that and not the toxic relationships that come with it.

It's a sobering thought.

"Everything okay?" she asks after a few seconds.

"Yeah. You're... I'm not even sure what you are. But I needed this, so... thank you, I guess."

"You're welcome. Shall we?" she asks, gesturing to the beach outside.

"Yes." I grab a hoodie from the back of my car before following her down toward the shore.

We walk along in silence until we find a spot between the dunes where we're hidden from the world and we sit our asses down.

I wrap my hoodie around my body while Rae happily stretches her fishnet-clad legs out in the sun.

"How aren't you cold?"

"How are you? This is like summer in some of the places I've lived."

"Where have you lived?"

"Most recently, Washington. Before that, everywhere."

"So what's your story then. And don't even try to tell me you don't have one."

"Oh, I have one. Much like I believe you do. I'll just skim the basics. Desperate mother, too many almost stepdads to count, some of which were more questionable than others. We moved. A lot. She ended up fucking Ethan's dad and here we are."

"Wow, okay then." She raises her brows at me, waiting for me to return the favor. "So... crack whore mother, some very dodgy men, in the system by seven, moved here by eight and been with my new parents ever since."

"Well, aren't we a pair." She laughs.

"It must be boring having the perfect life. Imagine not dealing with all that baggage on a daily basis."

"I literally have no idea what that must be like."

We lose the afternoon chatting about bullshit and steering away from our pasts. I know that I shared more than I have with almost anyone in Rosewood since the day I arrived, and I have a feeling that Rae might have done the same.

Hearing her talk about her past, albeit briefly, made me wonder if that was the connection between us, why I felt instantly at ease with her unlike most others. I think... I think she might get me in a way that no one else does. She's been through hell, she knows what it's like to try to rebuild a life after that kind of nightmare.

"We should probably get back. Ethan will wonder where I am if I'm not waiting for him after practice."

We stand and brush the sand from our bodies before heading back toward my car.

"I never thought I'd see the day that Ethan Savage settled for one woman, you know."

"From what I've heard, you're not the only one to think that."

"He was a whore. Sorry." I wince.

"No need. I'm fully aware of that side of Ethan. We all have pasts, Chelsea. We know that more than most. I refuse to judge someone based on what's happened before."

"And that is why we're going to get along. Everyone else can't see past my mistakes."

"I understand why, you hurt people they care about. But one day they'll fuck up and they'll need a friend. You just need to hope karma works her magic and they get back what they gave to you."

Her words are on repeat in my head as we climb back into the car, ready to return to school.

"So, tell me about Shane," Rae asks, sitting back and waiting for me to reverse the car out of the space. "Chelsea?" she prompts when I don't do anything.

"Shit, sorry." I don't say anything else until we're on the road. "Shane is... Shane," I say on a sigh.

"There's history there, though, right? The tension in that bathroom, shit you could have cut it with a knife."

"Yes, no. I don't know. There was something. I don't know," I repeat. "My head was so fucked up back then. Hell, it still is now, possibly worse actually. I've got no idea what's going on."

"It sounded to me like he cared."

"We're toxic. We'll never work."

I shrug it off and thankfully she leaves it there.

We're just about to get out once we're back in the school parking lot when I find my voice again.

"Rae, please don't... please don't say anything about Shane and me. I think it's for the best if it all just stays in the past."

"Whatever you want. I won't tell a soul, not that you really told me anything."

"Nothing to tell."

"Fair enough. I'll see you tomorrow then, yeah?"

"Sure. Thank you for today. I really needed it."

"Anytime. Us fucked-up folk need to be normal sometimes too."

I laugh as she climbs from the car.

She turns back when she's halfway across the parking lot.

"Chelsea?"

"Yeah."

"Don't let the past define you. Only you have the power to change your future."

I nod and watch as she disappears toward the boys' locker room to meet Ethan.

I should just drive home and spend the night hiding in my pool house, but some part of me that's a glutton for punishment has me pushing the car door open and walking toward the gym where the squad will be practicing.

I pull the door open and silently make my way down.

The sound of them counting as they work through the routine is painful to hear. I should be doing that. I should be leading them.

I stand slightly back of the open doors and keep hidden in the shadows as I watch them. Kelly is nowhere to be seen, as usual, and Shelly is at the front barking her orders. Although she misses all the important things that need to be picked up like Victoria not locking her knees out on the lift she's working on.

"All in. We're going to hit it from the top. Harley," she barks, referring to one of our JV cheerleaders. "You're going to be our flyer."

Fucking bitch. You can't replace me with a JV.

Harley swallows nervously and looks around at the girls. "B-but I thought Tasha was doing it."

"Yeah well, Tasha keeps fucking it up." Tasha huffs out her frustration, but this is one decision I can't help but agree with Shelly on. Tasha is no flyer.

"Just get in position. You're the best we've got and you know it."

A few of the varsity girls turn their noses up at the decision, but I get where Shelly is coming from.

I stand watching them with a lump in my throat and my fists clenched so tightly that my nails dig into my palms.

My need to go marching in there and set them straight is all-consuming, but nothing good will come of it.

Watching Harley do what I should be doing, and doing it well, is the final straw. With tears once again filling my eyes, I turn and run.

Unfortunately, I barely get around the corner before I collide with a very hard and warm wall.

"Fuck. I'm sorry."

"Chels?" Large hands wrap around my upper arms, but I

have no intention of breaking down in front of anyone else today.

"No. Just no." I spin out of Ethan's grip and run for my car so I can fall apart in private.

I run past a few other members of the team, some of whom offer to cheer me up. My stomach turns over at the thought. The second I'm in my car, I put it in drive and speed home to the safety of my pool house.

The second I'm inside, I strip out of my shirt and skinny jeans and pull on some yoga pants and a sports bra. I shove my earbuds in and hit play on my usual workout playlist and I take off.

I don't allow thoughts to enter my head about what today has been like. I just run. I focus on the pulling of my muscles, on the movement of my limbs, of the music in my ears. I keep it all bottled up until I hit the park that I usually run around before heading back.

Seeing as schools out, it's full of happy, laughing kids and it's the last thing I need to see after my short conversation about my past with Rae earlier.

I fall down onto a bench and watch as a couple of small children chase each other around as their mother watches with a smile on her face.

I never had this growing up. I never had this kind of freedom to just be a kid. To forget about the stresses of young life and to play like my life depended on it. Survival was my only focus as a young kid.

I wrap my arms around myself and fight to keep the tears that are threatening in my eyes.

Was I always destined to be a fuck-up? Is it laced through my genes from my birth mother, just like the poison of her drugs?

Not wanting to draw attention to myself, I drag my already sore body from the bench and force myself to run back home.

I've had nowhere near the exercise I need, and I'm already suffering the consequences.

I have a shower the second I get back and intend on heading up to the house to find out what Mom's cooked for dinner, only when I emerge from the shower voices filter down from the living area.

Dread fills my veins.

Who the hell would willingly turn up and wait for me?

I quickly pull on some clothes and reluctantly poke my head out of the bedroom.

"Here she is," Ethan announces, making Rae look in my direction.

"Hey," she says as if she belongs in my pool house.

"Hey... um... what are you...?"

"We figured that you'd kinda had a rough day, so we ordered pizza. Thought we'd come and entertain you."

"Aren't you lucky?" Rae adds with a wink.

"You're just here to hang out?"

Ethan's brows draw together in confusion. "Uh... yeah. Is that okay?"

A smile curls at my lips and just for a moment, all of the weight I've been carrying around lifts from my shoulders.

"Yeah, it's really great. Thank you."

"We brought beer too."

I stare at it before shaking my head. "Nah, not on a school night."

"What the hell did they do to you in that place?" Ethan jokes. I laugh along with him because I understand how different this is for me. But everything is different now. I'm different now.

After grabbing myself a soda, I fall onto the other couch just as the food arrives, and for the first time in what feels like forever, I have somewhat of a normal night hanging out with friends.

14

SHANE

"You not going to go chasing after her this time?" Zayn asks, his arms resting on my shoulder as Chelsea flies past us and out of the building.

I tense at the question, and I have no doubt that he feels it.

"Shelly dragged her nails across her face, someone needed to make sure she was okay?"

"Did they though? Chelsea is more than capable of looking after herself."

I agree, but that's not the point, she shouldn't have to.

"You coming to Aces?" Rich calls from in front of us.

"Sure thing," Zayn shouts. "You're coming, right?"

"Yep. Wouldn't want to be anywhere else." As I say it, the image of Chelsea's pool house pops into my head.

I know she skipped this afternoon. She was meant to be in both my classes. I'd be lying if I said I wasn't nervous as I waited for her to walk through the door, only she never did.

I was disappointed, I wanted to see if she was okay after what happened in the bathroom and her fight with Shelly, but mostly I was worried.

She must have been dreading coming back here. No

amount of time away was going to erase what happened before she left. No one has forgotten, even if some like Amalie and Mason are happy to let things lie and move on with their lives, the likes of Shelly certainly are not.

Cheer to Chelsea is like football to Jake and the other guys. It's their life. It's their purpose. It's why they get out of bed every morning. But have that taken away and what's left, other than the broken shell of a person who's full of regrets.

"Fucking hell," I mutter, scrubbing my hand over my rough jaw. I need to get her out of my fucking head.

"What's wrong?" Zayn asks, dropping down into my passenger seat.

"Nothing," I grunt.

After waiting a few seconds to see if any others are going to join us, I start to back out of the space.

"Nothing, yeah sure. That's why you're acting like a moody motherfucker. This morning I assumed it was the hangover, or the fact you allowed yourself to get up close and personal to a cheer slut, but it's only gotten worse. So what gives, Shane?"

"I don't wanna talk about it," I mutter under my breath.

"Well that really fucking sucks for you because I think you're gonna have to."

I blow out a breath. Even if I did want to talk about it, I have no idea where I'd start. Luckily—or unluckily, I'm not so sure—Zayn seems to know exactly where to kick off his questioning.

"Something happened with Chelsea, didn't it?"

My grip on the steering wheel tightens, turning my knuckles white. I haven't told anyone about that night. As far as I'm aware, only the two of us know about it.

"Yeah," I admit.

"So what's the big fucking deal? You're just another notch on her... wait..." He holds his hand up in the space between us. Thankfully, I need to focus on the road, so I don't have to see him connecting the dots. "You... you like her, don't you?"

"No. No. No, I fucking hate her for what she did," I argue, but even to my ears, it's weak at best.

"So what are we talking here. She just suck you off, or did you get further?"

"Does it matter?" I ask, not really wanting to get into the details. Mostly because I have no idea if he's already been there and has first-hand experience himself. The thought has heat racing through my veins that all the guys I spend time with have seen her like I have.

"Of course it matters. When and how many times?" I glance over to find a shit-eating grin on Zayn's face. "What?" he asks.

"You're acting like you didn't get laid last night."

"Who said I did?"

"Uh... the girl crying out your name in the next room most of the night."

"The girl?" he asks, amusement filling his voice. "That wasn't one, Dunn."

"Fucking hell," I mutter.

"Why have one when you can have two? Laurie and Ruby together. Whoa, man. I'm telling you that you haven't lived until you've had one suc—"

"Okay," I say, cutting off whatever he was about to describe. "Ruby is a junior, man. Not to mention your sister's friend. Don't you think you should lay off the young ones a little?"

"What? I didn't stand a chance."

"Whatever. You're a dog."

"At least I'm not hung up on one pussy."

"I'm not... fuck."

"Bro, the fact you're even trying to deny it is highly amusing. So what's the real issue here? You hate her, yet you want to fuck her again? I don't see the issue, there's nothing wrong with a good old hate fuck. They're the hottest kind if you ask me."

"Says the expert," I mutter, rolling my eyes.

"Two in one night, bro. Two in one night," he repeats as we climb from the car.

"Zayn," I say, my voice suddenly taking on a serious tone. "Please don't—"

"Your secret's safe, man. You don't even need to ask. But do us both a favor, yeah?"

"What?"

"Go and fucking bang her. Fuck this asshole mood out of your system."

I can't help but laugh as we make our way toward Aces. It's either that or I spin on my heel and go and find exactly what he just suggested. The temptation to do just that is almost too high to ignore.

The squad turned up not long after us and filled the final spaces in the team's usual booths. Just like since she disappeared, her absence is ever noticeable when we all hang out, and similarly, no one Except for me seems to care or even notice.

Although it shouldn't, my heart aches for her that she's been so easily forgotten by the people who were meant to be her friends.

Would Noah, Wyatt, Camila and now Zayn miss me as little if I were to suddenly up and leave? I'd like to think I'd had a little more impact on their lives and that they would notice my sudden disappearance. It makes me wonder what Chelsea's life is really like if those who are meant to be her friends just don't care.

Burgers and shakes are delivered to our table via Rae's friend Cody. I eat and try to join in with the others, but my head's not in it. I'm too busy wondering what she's doing and if she's sitting at home alone while all her so-called friends are out enjoying themselves as if she doesn't even exist.

When my cell rings, it's the perfect excuse to make my excuses and head home, although the second I pull it out and find my dad's name staring back at me, I start to wonder if I should be so relieved or not.

"I need to go," I say, turning to Zayn. "You okay getting back or do you want a ride?"

"I'm good. You go and get what you need." He winks at me.

"What? No. My dad," I say, waving my still ringing cell at him.

"Sure. Sure. I'm good. See you tomorrow."

I nod at him and the rest of the team who are huddled around our table before heading out.

Deciding against calling him back, I put my car in drive and set off on the short distance home.

I don't bother calling out for him, or even looking for him. I know exactly where he'll be. He only ever calls me for one thing and that means he'll be in his office talking 'business', aka my dreaded future.

"Ah there you are. I was calling you."

"I know and here I am," I mutter, falling down onto one of the giant leather couches in the center of the room.

"Right, well... I spent the afternoon on a call with the Steelers' coach. He is very interested. I've sent him some extra footage of you in action. He's going to look it over, but he thinks you might be a great fit for their team. Do you know how many players left his team last year and walked straight into the NFL?" Dad asks, his brows raised in excitement.

"I have no idea, but I'm sure you're about to tell me."

"What's wrong? This team is one of my top picks for you. It could take you all the way."

"All the way where? To your dream. I'm not interested,

Dad." Standing, I walk toward the door, already over his conversation.

"Shane, get back here."

"No, we're done."

With my teeth grinding in frustration, I fly through the door, slamming it behind me and marching straight for the front door.

Anger swirls in my belly as I storm for my car. I'm so fucking fed up with having this same conversation. Why can't he just hear me?

I don't want the fucking NFL. I'm not good enough and I don't have the desire. I love football, I do. But it's not my future. Although I've got no idea what is.

I am not my dad. I am not my brothers. The NFL is their dreams and I'll support them all the way, but it is not mine and I just wish he would listen to me.

I drive around town as the sun sets with nowhere to go. I could go to Wyatt's and lose myself in a game, or I'm sure Zayn would welcome me in, his mom is never there to care what he does. But neither of those places hold any kind of appeal right now. I don't want to hang out with friends. I just want to... forget. I want a few moments of quiet where everything in my head just stops.

I find myself pulling into Chelsea's driveway.

I shouldn't be here. I should just go home and lock myself in my room away from Dad and his unrealistic ideas, but I can't get her out of my fucking head.

She's the one who makes everything go away. And I need that. I need that more than anything right now.

The sun has almost totally set by the time I slip around the side of her house, her parents are in their living room watching the TV but thankfully don't notice me.

As I approach the pool house, movement inside has me jumping into the bushes slightly.

I stand in the shadows, watching as both Ethan and Rae emerge. Chelsea smiles at them. It's a real genuine smile that she doesn't give out very often, and my own lips twitch slightly at the sight. That is until they disappear off around the edge of the pool and toward the driveway, thankfully the opposite way that I came. The second they're out of sight, her face drops. Sadness washes through her as she closes the door behind them and walks back into her pool house. Her shoulders are down and her head lowered as she falls onto the couch.

Stepping from the shadows, I make my way over, keeping my eyes on her defeated form.

I come to a stop at the door and just watch her as she lifts her fingers to her cheek to wipe away a tear.

My fists clench with my need to storm inside and pull her to me. I might have wanted to see her suffer after what she did, but watching her fall apart is ripping me open.

As if she knows I'm here, her eyes lift.

Her lips part in shock and I can only imagine a squeal of shock leaves them as our eyes hold.

She stands, she makes no move to invite me in, but she doesn't send me away either.

When another tear drops, she doesn't wipe it away this time, and it's my undoing.

Pulling the door open, I march inside and take her in my arms.

"Shane, what the hell are you doing?" she asks, her eyes wide as I wrap one arm around her waist and pull her into my body. Lifting my other hand, I wipe away the wet trail her tear left behind with my thumb.

"What I should have done earlier."

Leaning forward, I press my lips to hers. I want to give her a chance to pull away, to tell me where to go, but the second we connect I lose all restraint.

Walking her backward, she bumps up against the counter.

Her hands slide down my back before slipping inside my jersey.

Dropping my hands to her thighs, I make quick work of lifting her onto the counter, her legs instantly part allowing me to stand between them.

"Shane," she moans when I begin kissing across her jaw and down her neck. "Off," she demands, pulling at the fabric around my body.

Releasing her for a beat, I drag it over my head and drop it to the floor beside us.

Her eyes land on my chest before she lifts them to meet mine. They're dark, hungry, and it only spurs me on. My need to lose myself in her is too much to deny her. Being here right now with her hands on me and her legs locked around my waist, nothing else exists. There's no bullshit outside of these four walls. We're just two people who need to escape everything that's going on in their lives that's totally out of their control.

"I shouldn't be doing this," I whisper, taking her cheeks in my hands. I don't know why I say it, some fucked-up need to make sure she knows there's nothing more here than what I'm about to give her.

"So are you planning on stopping?" She tilts her head to the side and bites down on her bottom lip.

"Fuck no."

I've got her in my arms in a heartbeat and carrying her toward the back of the pool house where I'm hoping her bedroom is.

As I walk, her lips trail across my neck, only increasing my need for her.

The second I find her bed, I lower her down onto it and crawl over her body.

"Shane, what are—"

"No," I say, placing my finger against her lips, cutting off any more words she might want to say to me. "No talking or I'll leave. No bullshit, I just... I just need..." She raises her brows, waiting for me to finish. I swallow down my pride because I need this too much right now to do anything but tell the truth. "You, okay? I just need you."

Her heels dig into my lower back and I fall on top of her, pressing her tiny frame into the mattress.

"Give me everything," she moans when I release her lips once again.

Gathering up the fabric of her tank, I push it up her stomach, my lips kissing across the smooth skin as I do.

Once I've got it over her breasts, she takes over and rips it from her body.

Her chest heaves as her breaths race past her parted lips.

She needs this as much as I do. I have no idea what I'd have done if she'd have turned me away like she did the other night. Hell, she might still do so.

That thought spurs me on.

The second she arches her back for me, I slip my hand behind her to unhook her bra.

She moans loudly as I pull the fabric from her body.

Her nipples are pert and ready for me.

Fuck, this girl has my head all kinds of fucked-up.

I hate her.

I want her.

I shouldn't have her.

I can't help myself.

"Shane," she moans. "Please."

I stare up at her as she looks down at me.

I should walk away and not look back. There's no way that this is anything short of a disaster waiting to happen. But I fear after just one taste all those weeks ago that I'm already in too deep.

Tension crackles between us as neither of us moves and only the sound of our heavy, labored breathing can be heard.

"Shane? I thought you came here with a plan in mind," she taunts. "Or aren't you man enou—fuck," she cries when I dive forward and suck one of her rosy nipples into my mouth.

Her fingers dive into my hair to hold me in place and she groans in pleasure under me. I switch to the other side as my fingers trail down her sides to pull at her pants.

My lips leave her as she lifts her hips, allowing me to drag the fabric down her legs. She kicks her pants from her feet so I don't have to pull away to rid her of the clothing.

Sitting up, I stare down at her laid bare before me.

She's so fucking beautiful. Her slim body is flawless perfection and clearly shows all the hours she puts into her sport.

I can't get e-fucking-nough.

Skimming my hands down her thighs, her hips writhe with her need for more.

"What do you need?"

"You," she moans. "Y-your mouth."

I swallow nervously. She has no idea—I don't think—that our time together before was a first for me. Unlike most of the rest of the team, I don't spend every night of the week with a different girl. I wasn't waiting for anyone in particular. I just knew that I didn't want it to be just anyone. I never in a million years would have thought Chelsea would have been the one to take my V-card, but now it's happened, I can't imagine it any other way.

"What's wrong? You going to leave me high and dry?"

I stare at her, my head spinning with my need.

"I deserve it. You should get up and walk out now and not look back. Everyone else would."

"Enough," I bark, ensuring her lips slam shut immediately. "I said no talking."

Lowering to my stomach, I wrap my hands around her thighs and focus on her core.

She's so ready for this, and the sight has desire racing through me. My cock is impossibly hard and desperate for her touch, but for some fucked-up reason, I want to give this to her first. I want to help her leave everything behind just like I'm craving for myself.

Closing the space between us, I flatten my tongue and press it against her. I'll be the first to admit that I don't really know what I'm doing, but as she moans, her fingers once again find their way into my hair and pull painfully hard. Not that I'm about to complain. With her taste on my tongue and her sweet scent surrounding me, I'm so fucking lost I barely know my own name. It's exactly what I needed. What I knew she could give me.

"Shane, fuck," she moans, her back arching in her need for more.

Releasing one of her hips, I find her entrance and slide one finger inside her.

"Yes, yes. Fuck yes," she chants, spurring me on. I lick faster before grazing her with my teeth and add another finger stretching her open. "Oh god. Oh god."

Her muscles clamp down on me and I keep my rhythm, desperate to feel her fall apart against me.

I remember all too well how tight she was when she came around me last time, the little noises she made as she came down from her high. It was fucking mind-blowing and I need to experience it again more than I need my next breath.

"Shane. Shane. Shannnnnne," she screams as her body quakes beneath me. Her thighs clamp around my ears as she falls.

Standing from the bed, I drop my hands to the waistband of my pants and pop the button. My eyes stay on Chelsea as she lies lax on the bed, trying to catch her breath.

"Shane, I—" Propping herself up on her elbows, her words are cut off as she watches me push both my pants and boxers down my thighs and take myself in hand. "Fuck."

"What?" I ask, kicking the fabric from my ankles and taking a step toward her. "You thought that was all I came for?"

She shakes her head, her eyes still locked on me. "N-no. I just thought..." She trails off as I place one knee on the edge of her bed and then the other.

"You just thought..." I prompt, reminding her that she was in the middle of saying something.

"I thought you were about to leave."

"Not yet. I need to take what I came for first."

Something flashes in her eyes, the fire I'm so used to as she rips me a new one, but the words don't follow. She knows full well that she'll only be denying herself if she turns on me right now.

However fucked-up this might be. However much we might hate each other. This right now is happening because we both need it too much. We need each other too much.

That thought is fucking terrifying.

I shouldn't need anyone, let alone Chelsea.

Forcing the thought from my head, I crawl between her legs and find her entrance.

"Condom?" I ask, realizing that I don't have one. *Fuck.*

"It's okay, it's safe."

"But..."

"I haven't been with anyone, Shane. Not since..."

My eyes fly up to meet hers. All I see is honesty staring back at me.

"Contrary to popular belief, I'm not actually a whore."

"No, that wasn't..." She quirks a brow. "I was just surprised."

"No talking, remember?" she sasses, wrapping her legs around my hips and dragging me closer.

"I didn't forget."

She squeals as I thrust my hips forward, filling her in one swift move.

Fuck. My eyes squeeze tight as I give myself a second. She's so hot, so tight, so fucking incredible.

Leaning over her, I wrap my hand around the back of her neck and tilt her up so I can capture her lips. I thrust again as my tongue delves into her mouth and my hand comes up to cup her breast, my fingers pinching her nipple.

"Oh god, Shane," she mumbles against my lips as I play her body.

I was nervous as fuck that first time. I had no idea what I was doing and she was, well... Chelsea, expert at all the things. But the second I got my hands on her, everything just fell into place. It was like my body just knew what to do and the nerves fell away as she moaned and writhed against my touch.

Our tongues duel as our bodies find a rhythm that has me racing toward my release long before I'm ready for this to be over.

Chelsea's nails scratch down my back as her slick walls ripple around me, telling me that she's about to fall over the edge with me.

"Chelsea," I groan. It's half in awe and half just to remind myself that it's her, that this is happening again.

Dropping my hand down her body, I find her clit and circle it.

She cries out, her nails digging into my skin, but the bite of pain only adds to the pleasure that's coursing through my veins.

"Fuck. Fuck," I groan against her lips, desperate for air but refusing to pull away from her.

"Shane," she cries. "Oh god, Shane."

Her entire body locks up as her pleasure slams into her. Her back arches and she throws her head back. I miss her lips immediately, but the second I open my eyes and get a look at her, it's soon forgotten.

With her eyes squeezed shut, her swollen lips are parted in pleasure as she rides out her climax. Her pussy clamps down on me impossibly tight and I can't help but fall over the edge with her.

Falling to the side of her, we both lie lax and trying to catch our breath.

The silence surrounding us becomes heavy, but it's not with the tension that was filling the room not so long ago, it's quickly becoming more and more awkward as neither of us says anything.

Chelsea is the first to break it, but I never could have guessed the words that fall from her lips.

"Well, that was unexpected but enjoyable." A laugh bubbles up my throat. "But you can leave now."

Sitting up, I stare down at her. Her hair is all over the place, her cheeks pink with exertion and her lips red from my kisses. She doesn't make any attempt to hide the fact she's naked and if her words weren't so final, I'd probably have a job keeping my eyes on her face, but as it is, I'm too shocked to really notice.

"I can leave now. Wow."

"What? Did you expect to spend the night cuddling? You got what you came for. You can go now."

She rolls on her side, turning her back toward me.

"What? I didn't... Chels?"

"Just go, Shane. We both know you don't want to actually spend time with me. You just wanted that revenge fuck you talked about Saturday night. Well, you got it so off you fuck."

"You don't actually believe that, do you?" I place my hand on her waist and her body locks up at my touch.

"Leave."

Knowing that I've got no chance of getting through to her. I reluctantly push from her bed and drag my clothes on.

She doesn't move an inch as I prepare to leave.

With a sigh, I walk to the door, bending down to pick up my jersey as I do. Unable to stop myself, I look over my shoulder. She's staring at the wall, but I know she's aware of my attention because her body tenses as my eyes run up the length of her.

"Here," I say, throwing my jersey at her. "This isn't over."

She opens her mouth to respond but doesn't say anything. Assuming she's done, I turn to leave. I'm halfway across her living area when her sob sounds out.

My fists clench, my nails digging into my palms, but I don't turn back. I might not know her all that well, but I do know that I wasn't meant to hear that.

The second I get in my car, I regret it.

15

CHELSEA

I shouldn't have let him go. I knew that the moment he stepped out of the room. I should have called him back, allowed him to spend some more time distracting me.

While he was here, I forgot about everything that happened today. For those few moments, I felt like me once again. Like I belonged somewhere, like someone wanted me.

I'm not stupid enough to believe it's the truth. He might have said it wasn't about revenge, but I'm sure he would have said anything in those few seconds before getting what he came for to make sure I agreed.

When I wake, my eyes are sore from crying once again and my muscles ache from our short time together, but that's not the most noticeable thing.

That's his scent.

It's everywhere and for the briefest of moments, I believe I dreamed that he left, I allow myself to believe he's still here with me.

But the second I open my eyes, it all comes crashing down. The bed beside me is empty, just like the rest of my pool house.

He left. He left after getting what he wanted. He's just like the rest of the guys on the team, only he's left more of a mark. He's the only one—other than Jake—that I've ever wanted more from, needed more from. Only he has no idea. Because just like the rest of the team, he just sees me as an easy piece of ass. I allowed him to have me and now he thinks it's his God-given right. He's probably enjoying that everyone else hates me. It means he's got no competition. I now really am a sure thing.

My chest aches as those short few moments from last night run through my mind. I don't want to think about it, but I can't stop. It's like my brain just wants to torture me.

I think about the gentleness of his touch, the way he played my body like he had a fucking map. The way he moved, the softness of his lips. None of those actions screamed revenge and hate fuck, but it couldn't have been anything else or he would still damn well be here.

Wouldn't he?

If he cared, he wouldn't just walk away. If it were anything more than a quick release, a way to prove to me that he has the power then he wouldn't have left.

You told him to, a little voice says, and I remember the exact words that fell from my lips as I dismissed him like he was nothing.

I cover my mouth with my hand, wanting to stop the sob from erupting.

What the hell was I thinking?

Sitting up, I discover the reason for his slightly overpowering and mind-spinning scent. I'm wearing his jersey.

I should have showered after he left, but I didn't have it in me. Instead, I pulled his shirt over my head and curled up in bed, willing my body to sleep to take me away from the memory of his touch. Only when it did claim me it was filled with vivid memories of him.

This is such a fucking mess.

Pushing from the bed, I set about getting myself ready for another shit show of a day at Rosewood High where I'm sure I'll be chewed out by Shelly and the squad and ignored by Shane like I'm nothing more than a piece of trash he threw away.

With a sigh, I pull his jersey over my head, but before dropping it to the laundry, I can't help but gather the fabric up to my nose and breathe him in.

I want to cling to the feelings that race around my body while I'm surrounded by him. The safety, the contentment, the belonging. But what's the point? They're all lies.

I'm sitting in English later that morning, my many regrets spinning around my head. I seem to be adding more to my already endless collection.

Will I ever make the right decision?

I was first in, much to our teacher's surprise. I'm not sure I've ever been early to class in my life, but right now it sure beats risking running into Shelly or anyone else in the school who wants me gone, which sadly is almost all of them.

She starts talking to me about what I've missed while I was gone after expressing her half-hearted delight at having me back. I half listen. I know I should be more interested in what she's telling me, but right now, as I wait for the rest of the class to appear and turn their hate stares on me, I really can't find it in me.

A few students start to file in, most of which I don't really know, although each and every one looks my way, even if for a very brief second.

I keep my head down, but it doesn't mean that I don't feel their stares or hear their constant whispers.

The class must be about half full when the atmosphere changes. I don't want to look, I already know the cause but I'm powerless but to lift my head.

The second I do, my eyes lock with his green ones. His face is blank and I have no idea what he's thinking or feeling. I hate it.

Does he regret last night? The lack of expression or care seems to hint at that.

My stomach knots. No matter how naïve, I was still hopeful things might be different this morning.

Dragging my eyes from Shane's, I focus on the guys standing behind him. Zayn's standing with his usual smirk playing on his lips as he looks between the two of us. Great, seems another person knows our secret. How long until the rest of the school finds out? Shane will be lynched for even talking to me, let alone touching me.

But it's not Zayn's amusement that really catches my attention because that's the furious eyes of their captain who's standing just behind Shane's shoulder.

I gasp at the darkness of the blue eyes I used to think I knew better than my own. His stare pins me to my chair and a shudder of fear runs down my spine.

Jake Thorn might be an asshole, but he'd never hurt me on purpose, of that I'm sure. But I hurt the one person who means more to him than anything else, and I know that I'm going to have to accept whatever consequences he has for me.

I know it won't make much difference, but my lips part anyway.

"I'm sorry," I mouth to him.

His lips purse in anger as his stare holds but it's only a few second later when our teacher barks at them for blocking the entrance and the three of them are forced to move.

He holds my stare until he's got no choice but to look toward his desk.

My stomach rolls and I worry that I'm going to end up running to the bathroom any minute. Thankfully, the rest of the class arrives, the teacher starts and I'm able to breathe through the nausea.

Regrets are horrible things. I hate that I hurt people that were my friends. I hate the way they look at me now with disappointment and anger laced through their features. But other than apologize, I have no idea how to fix everything I did. I know it was wrong. I know it was a massive mistake. I was just... I am... lost. I'm so desperate for those connections that I see everyone has around me. The friendships, the relationships. I've never had them. Never.

It should have been a natural thing with my mother, but she was too concerned about getting her next hit than she ever was about me. Honey and Derek are great, I love them in my own way, but they're not my real parents. I don't feel that natural bond with them. Our relationship has taken years to evolve to what it is now, and at times it wasn't easy, but together we found our way through. They have proved to me that people don't always let you down. They could have so easily given up on me over the years. Hell, I've given them enough reason to, but they've stood by me through every one of my mistakes and bad decisions.

I let out a sigh, wishing I had all the answers and that one day I won't feel like such an outcast. Everyone walks around the hallways here like they belong, like they've found their place, but even before all of this, I never felt at home. It's why I forced the relationships I did form. The girls in the squad needed to be friends with me if they wanted to keep their place, the football team accepted me because I had something to offer. Not one of them wanted me for me. I'm pretty sure no one has ever wanted me for me.

A smile curls at my lips as I think about the time I spent with Rae yesterday. Despite everything she'd heard about me in my absence, she genuinely seemed to want to spend time with me yesterday, genuinely seemed like she wanted to know the real me, not the bullshit Barbie doll persona I give everyone else. She saw the cracks, the dents and the broken parts of me that I keep locked inside, just like I did in her.

We'd be the most unlikely of friends, her with her goth look and me pining after my cheer uniform, but then I guess the connection that I've always craved runs deeper than our preferences and our style. Its strength comes from our fears, our nightmares, the things we keep hidden from the outside world.

As our teacher continues, I start to wonder how trustworthy she is. Could she be the one I confide in? Fuck knows I need to tell someone my secret.

The last thing I expected last night was Ethan and Rae to turn up to keep me company because they were concerned about me. Okay that's a lie, the last thing I expected was what happened after that, but I need to not think about him right now. It's bad enough that his stare is burning into the back of my head.

Ethan's words resonated with me. He's not usually one to be so wise, but I guess Rae must be having a good influence on him.

"You're Chelsea fucking Fierce. When have you ever sat back and allowed shit to happen around you? You want your old life back? Get out there and fucking take it."

He had a point. The only issue is that I'm not sure I'm that same person anymore.

My time away certainly gave me the opportunity to reflect. It gave me much more than that, and it changed my life in ways I'm not sure the counselors could even imagine.

I want my old life back. Well... I want my squad back.

Everything else. The fake friendships, the bending over backward to keep my position at the top of the school and the bullshit that came with that, not so much.

I just want my team. My future. The rest is so up in the air right now.

I'm still lost in my thoughts when the bell rings. I make quick work of packing everything up and trying to get out of the room as soon as possible. I might be keen to make amends for all my wrongdoings, but I don't want to have it out with Jake in the middle of a classroom with an audience.

"Get out of my way," a familiar voice barks from behind me as I take a step from behind my desk. My shoulder gets banged and when I look up, I find one of my previously loyal cheerleaders pushing me out of the way so she can get past.

I want to say something, but I bite my tongue. Making a scene isn't going to help anyone right now.

I eventually manage to make it out of the room before Shane and Jake even get up from their desks, clearly neither of them have any desire to talk to me. Right now, that is fine by me. I just want to get through the day without any more scratches or bruises.

My next class is just a repeat of the previous one. Constant stares and gossip. I'm actually starting to get used to it in a weird way. The old me would have loved all the attention, it's a shame that the new me mostly just wants to hide in the closet until they're all bored with me.

I'm surrounded by students and heading toward the cafeteria for lunch when the chatter around me suddenly drops out. The second I look up, I know why. Shelly and her bitches are walking this way, and every set of eyes is drilling into me.

Blowing out a frustrated breath, I take a step to go down the stairs to escape them. I'm hungry and I really don't have the patience for their bullshit right now.

"You're supposed to be staying out of my way," Shelly spits, coming to a stop in front of me and placing her hands on her hips.

The hallway around us falls almost deadly silent as they wait for a repeat of yesterday's fight. I had no intention of partaking in that one, I really don't want to be standing here now.

"I'm not in your way. I'm just going for lunch."

"You're not welcome."

"I'm not welcome in the cafeteria? Fuck off, Shelly, no one made you God."

She takes a step forward, a scowl on her face.

"Careful, those lines will set and you'll need to beg daddy for some more Botox." She gasps, as do the rest of the squad, although I have no idea why, it's no secret that Shelly's looks aren't all natural.

"You bitch," she squeals, raising her hand, much like she did yesterday, and I move to avoid her. I forget that I'm standing at the top of the stairwell. That is until I place my foot down and there is no floor for it to land on.

"Fuck," I squeal a beat before I begin to fall.

My arm releases the books I was holding to my chest like a shield from Shelly, but I don't manage to find anything to stop myself.

The last thing I hear is a collective gasp as my back hit the wall before I was tumbling down the stairs.

I vaguely remember hitting people's legs, but I'd pick up so much speed that none of the hands that reach for me successfully stop me.

16

CHELSEA

The pounding of my head is the first thing I feel when I come back to myself.

I wiggle my toes and then my fingers and breathe a sigh of relief. At least they still work.

"Chelsea?" a soft female voice says from beside me but I can't register who it belongs too.

A warm hand slips into mine and squeezes.

"Everything's okay. You're in the hospital."

"Should we get a doctor?"

I know that voice. The English accent is a dead giveaway.

"Amalie?" My voice is a rough whisper, but the shock is clear.

Dragging my eyes open, I have to blink a few times to make my vision clear, but when they do, there she is sitting at my bedside.

"What are you..."

"Doing here? I've been asking myself the same question to be honest."

"I'm..." I swallow and lick my lips. "I'm sorry."

She nods but I'm positive it's not to accept my apology more so just to prove she heard it.

"Here, have a drink." I turn to the sound of the other voice and find Rae.

A smile pulls at my lips despite the blinding pain in my head.

"T-thank you," I say once I've had a sip of the water. "W-what happened?"

"Shelly pushed you down the stairs."

I allow her words to run around my head for a second or two as I try to drag up my hazy memory of what happened today.

"N-no she did—fuck," I shout.

"What? What's wrong?" Rae is up off her chair, her eyes wide as she looks me over.

"Fuck, fuck, fuck," I chant, trying to push myself up to a sitting position. "What's wrong with me? What have the doctors said?" I ask in a rush.

"Nothing much, just that you had quite the hit to the head. Why, does something hurt?"

"No... um... I'm... fuck." I drop my head into my hands as both of them come in closer, intrigued by my freak out I'd imagine. "I'm pregnant," I mumble into my hands.

"What?" Amalie screeches in total disbelief.

"I need the doctor. I need to know. Fuck." I press my hand to my stomach, praying that Shelly hasn't just ruined the one good thing in my life. The one good thing to come out of all of this.

"Okay, yes. I'll go find her." Rae pulls the curtain back and runs from the room.

Amalie's attention stays on me. "You're not joking... are you?"

I shake my head. "No, I'm not. If I've lo—fuck. I can't.

Fuck." My voice cracks and my chin trembles at the thought of losing this as well as everything else in my life.

To my utter disbelief, Amalie wraps her arm around my shoulder and holds me to her.

"I'm sure it'll be fine."

I want to agree, but all I feel right now is dread. I haven't even had the chance to fully accept my reality and it might already be over. No. No, it can't be. I need this. I need everything to be okay.

By the time Rae reappears with a kind looking doctor trailing behind her, I've got tears running down my cheeks faster than I can control.

"Good afternoon, Chelsea. I'm Dr. Francis. Your friend here tells me that you think you might be pregnant."

"There's no might. I am."

"Okay, we've done blood work but it hasn't come back from the lab yet. How far along do you think you are?"

"About eleven weeks."

I might not be looking at either Rae or Amalie, but I don't miss their chins dropping in shock.

"Okay. Have you had an ultrasound?"

I shake my head. I visited a doctor at the center who had set the ball rolling but I don't have a date or anything although I know it must be soon.

"Okay." She reaches for my hand and squeezes in support. "Do you have any abdominal pain, any reason to believe something may not be right?"

I focus on my body for a moment, but other than my head and a few aches and pains, nothing seems wrong.

"N-no, I don't think so."

"Right, let me go and make a call or two and I'll see what I can do to get an ultrasound machine brought in."

With a soft smile and a glance at my shocked audience, she disappears back through the curtain.

"You're pregnant?"

Rae asks as if she needs to hear me say it again just to believe it.

"Yeah, but no one knows. I haven't even told my parents. You're the only ones."

"Jesus, Chelsea. You really know how to bring the drama don't you?"

"It wasn't meant to happen."

"For the love of God, please tell me that it's not Jake's." I'm not sure if she's asking that as a joke or not, but as I look at Amalie, I see a flicker of fear in her eyes.

"Of course it's not. That boy hasn't looked at me twice since you turned up."

"G-good. That's good." She lowers herself back to the chair, deep in thought.

"So whose is it?" Rae asks.

I shake my head. "Now's really not the time. Plus, I have a feeling he's not going to want anything to do with it."

"You haven't told him?"

"Not yet."

I was intending on telling my parents when I first got back from the center. But they were so happy to have me home and hopefully in a more positive place that I didn't have it in me to confess.

I know they're going to be disappointed in me. I see the way they look at me when I've been out partying. They're not stupid, they know the things we all get up to, and I've always promised Mom that I'd be sensible. I had a future, a cheer career to think of. Having this kind of accident certainly wasn't part of my plan.

"I-I know that I have no right to ask anything of you," I say directly to Amalie. "But I'd really appreciate it if you kept this to yourself."

She blows out a breath. Her eyes leaving mine for a beat.

"You're right. I don't owe you anything. I should go straight back to Rosewood and shout through the PA system." Every muscle in my body locks up at the thought. "But I won't. That's not the kind of person I am."

"Okay," the doctor sings, reappearing with a machine and another woman who I unfortunately recognize behind her. "Let's see what's going on then, shall we? This is—"

"We already know each other," the other lady says, and I just about manage to stifle a groan. "Nice to see you, Chelsea."

"You too," I say tightly, staring at the older version of the person who put me in this place. Shelly might not have actually pushed me, but she was the catalyst for this whole disaster.

Of all the people, the woman who turns up to do my first ultrasound has to be Shelly's mom. I have no fucking chance of keeping this secret now.

The doctor pulls the sheet from me and I discover that I'm still in my skirt and top that I put on this morning.

"If you could lift your top and lower your waistband a little. I'll get this all set up."

"Would you like some privacy?" Dr. Francis asks, nodding to Rae and Amalie.

"N-no. They can stay if they like."

Smiling, Rae moves closer to my side and takes my hand in hers. Amalie remains standing somewhat awkwardly at the end of the bed.

"I'm going to squeeze some gel on your tummy and we'll have a little look."

The gel is warmer than I'm expecting, and in only seconds a plastic wand thing is being pressed against my skin.

Shelly's mom tilts her head this way and that as she stares at the screen I can't see while tapping away at a few buttons.

My heart pounds in my chest and my hands begin to sweat, not knowing which way this is going to go.

"Right, Chelsea." She turns the screen to me and a fuzzy black and white image flickers on the screen. "Everything looks good. Can you see that there?" She points at a little blob in the middle of the screen. "That's your baby."

A sob erupts from my throat. "It's okay?"

"Yes, everything looks good. All the measurements line up with your eleven-week prediction. Congratulations, I guess."

"Oh my god." Tears pool in my eyes as I stare at my baby. My baby.

It's surreal.

I knew this day was coming. I knew I'd get to see it, but it's utterly mind-blowing.

"I can't believe you're growing a person," Rae mutters, equally as mesmerized by the screen.

"Trust me. I know."

"Would you like a printout?"

"Yes, please."

Sadly, Shelly's mom removes the wand from my stomach and the image of my baby disappears from the screen. I miss it almost immediately. It's the weirdest feeling that has me on the verge of a breakdown.

The doctor hands me some tissue to wipe my belly and before long I'm being handed a strip of paper with a range of images of my baby on it.

"Are we all okay here?" Shelly's mom asks before wheeling the machine out and leaving us to it. I don't see her go, I'm too fascinated by the images before me to even consider warning her about not saying anything.

"Your parents are in the waiting room. They're getting a little frantic," Dr. Francis says with a wince.

"We'll go and leave you to talk to your parents," Rae says.

"Uh... okay."

Fear fills my veins at the thought of admitting all of this to them. They're going to be so disappointed in me.

Just before Amalie and Rae pull the curtain back to leave, I call out.

"Amalie?"

She looks back over her shoulder at me, but she doesn't say anything.

"I really am sorry."

She nods, her eyes softening as she accepts it before they both continue through the curtain.

I'm alone, left alone with my own thoughts for all of three minutes. The entire time I have the ultrasound images grasped tightly in my hand.

Everything is okay. She didn't ruin the only bit of positive in my life.

"Chelsea, thank god you are okay. Principal Hartmann said you'd been pushed down the stairs, what on earth..." Mom comes rushing over and carefully pulls me in for a hug.

"I'm okay. And she didn't actually push me. I thought she was going to." I gesture to my face that she has yet to notice, seeing as I hid in the pool house from the second I got in from school last night.

"Jesus, Chelsea. Shelly did that?"

"I had it coming. I thought she was going to do it again, I stepped back and, well... here I am." I shrug, playing it down. Yes, my head throbs, but I'm okay. We're okay.

"You might want to sit down though. I've got something I need to tell you both."

Mom pulls back and looks at me suspiciously.

"I'm okay, I promise. It's just that..." I trail off until they're both in the chairs beside my bed. "I'm pregnant."

If I weren't so terrified by their reaction then the cartoon wide eyes and dropped chins might be amusing but as it is the sight only tightens the knot of dread sitting heavy in my stomach.

"Y-you're pregnant. Like... having a baby pregnant?" Mom asks in total disbelief.

"Yes. I'm so sorry. I should have told you sooner, but I was scared."

"You're having a baby now?"

"What? No, no. Not yet. Here." I reluctantly release my ultrasound pictures and allow her to look at them.

"Oh my god," she gasps, her own eyes getting a little wet.

"How far along?"

"Eleven weeks."

They're both silent as they stare at the images, and I sit nervously for the anger to come once the shock has worn off.

"How long have you known?"

"Quite a while."

"And you've kept it secret all this time? Even in the center?"

"Well, I saw a doctor, but yeah."

"Oh, Chelsea," Mom says, standing back up and pulling me into a hug. She sobs on my shoulder and although I hate that I've made her cry, I'm just glad neither of them are shouting at me. "You should have told us."

I look between the two of them, not missing that Dad is yet to say anything about this. "I was—I am—terrified."

"Oh, sweetie. You don't need to be scared of us. You know we'll support you no matter what." Mom runs her hand gently over my hair and a lump forms in my throat.

"I-I really want this baby, Mom. I want..." I blow out a breath, trying not to break down. "I want something of my own, you know. I didn't plan it. I was too focused on my future to even consider it. But now it's happened... I wouldn't have it any other way."

"I know, baby. I know." Mom holds me tighter as she cries.

She had a baby when she was not that much older than I am now. I remember the day she told me about it, the joy as she talked about discovering that she was pregnant was clear in her eyes all these years later. Despite her parents' opinion about things, she was excited about what her future held but sadly, it wasn't meant to be and the baby was born with a genetic disorder and died before he was six months old. She's never been able to conceive again.

I know that it's something that rips her apart to this day. She and Dad have always been desperate to have their own kids. But thankfully they decided to give back and started fostering kids about ten years before they were lucky enough to find me standing at their front door.

To this day, I've got no idea what it was about me that made them decide to go through all the legal stuff and adopt me unlike all the others they'd cared for, but I can't really argue because they've given me everything I was missing in my former years.

When Dad does speak his voice is so loud compared to the soft sound of Mom's sobs that it startles me.

"Who... um... who's the father."

"Derek," Mom chastises. "That's not the most important thing right now. When she's ready, I'm sure she'll tell us," Mom says, squeezing my hand and thankfully giving me a way out of this conversation. "Everything is okay with the baby though, yeah?"

"It seems that way."

She takes my hand and sits on the bed beside me.

"I know I probably should be mad, you are still in high school after all, but I think this could well be the best thing that's ever happened to you."

Dad looks at her like she's just grown an extra head, whereas all I do is smile because I can't help but agree.

"I know things are scary and unknown right now. But I do know that you are going to be a fantastic mother. I do wish you'd told us sooner, just so we could have supported you. But I need you to know how proud I am of you."

She smiles at me and I look from her kind eyes to my dad's. He doesn't seem quite so thrilled by this turn of events, but they both know me well enough to know that when I set my mind to something that nothing is going to stop me.

"What about college? Cheer? The scholarship you were so desperate for?" he asks, always the voice of reason.

"Oh Derek, give her a break."

"I'm just curious."

"I'll figure it all out. Everything happens for a reason, right, Dad?" I lift a brow and wait for him to agree.

"I guess," he mutters, but we all know he believes the words. He's said them himself enough times over the years.

17

SHANE

"What the fuck is going on?" I ask Zayn as we make our way toward the cafeteria for lunch. The kids around us are buzzing with something. Excited chatter and gossip get louder and louder.

"She pushed her right down. It was brutal."

"She fell top to bottom like a rag doll."

"No one knows if she's alive."

What the actual fuck?

I may be clueless, but it doesn't stop a trickle of dread from running down my spine. After yesterday's public fight, my imagination is running on overdrive right now.

"I have no clue but it sounds dramatic whatever it is," Zayn mutters.

We're almost at the cafeteria when the crowd in front of us parts and Principal Hartmann appears along with three other teachers all frog-marching Shelly, Krissy, and Aria, down the hallway.

Something uncomfortable sits heavy in my stomach as realization starts to hit. There really is only one person those students could have been talking about.

"Chelsea," I mutter to myself before running for the cafeteria to find some answers.

I have to fight my way through the crowds that seem to have appeared out of nowhere to watch Shelly, but in seconds I'm through and running toward someone who'll know.

"Cami, what's happened?"

"That," she says, glancing over her shoulder. "Fuck knows. Some cheer slut drama probably. I don't have time for that bullshit."

I purse my lips. I want to shout at her that that bullshit she's talking about could very well mean something to me, but I can't.

Instead I force out, "Yeah you're probably right."

"Shane." Spinning on my heel, I find Zayn talking to Ruby and Harley. Ruby blushes bright red just looking at him, whereas Harley looks bored by having to stand in her brother's vicinity. "Go on," Zayn encourages once I join them.

Harley rolls her eyes in frustration before turning to me. "Shelly pushed Chelsea down the stairs."

"What? Is she okay?" I ask in a rush, probably looking like I care too much, but I really don't give a shit right now.

"I have no idea. She's been taken to the hospital."

I'm out of the school building before I've even realized I've moved. My need to get to her is all-consuming, but the second I turn the engine on, I freeze.

There's a very good chance she won't want me there. She's shown me time and time again that she doesn't care, that she doesn't want me, and I keep running back like a sad little puppy.

My grip on the wheel tightens until my knuckles turn white. I need to go there. I need to know she's okay.

"Motherfucker," I bark, slamming my palm down on the wheel and resting my head back.

My head spins as it screams at me to get out of the car and continue with my day as if nothing's happened.

It's what she would want.

But what about what I want? What I need?

"Fuck it."

I put the car in drive and speed out of the school parking lot. Only, when I get to the turn for the hospital, I don't take it.

My head's too fucked-up after last night and everything else that's happened in the past few weeks.

I just need it all to stop.

I breathe a sigh of relief when I find our driveway empty. The last thing I need right now is another lecture from my dad.

Thankfully, I managed to sneak back into the house last night without him spotting me. I didn't need a rehash of our previous conversation. Nothing he can say to me can change my mind. I don't care about the fame, the success, the money. Professional football and the NFL will not make me happy. The pressure he puts on me for high school football is bad enough. I watch what he's like with my brothers. He's relentless in his need for them to be the best. It's exhausting.

I blow through the house, not stopping as I descend the stairs to the basement and Dad's home gym. I hate being in it but needs must and all that.

Pulling my hoodie and shirt off, I drop them to the bench before coming to a stop in front of what I really need.

The punching bag.

I run my fingers over the smooth black leather before pulling my other arm back and plowing my fists into it over and over.

I didn't bother wrapping them, so after only a couple of hits, they split open.

I punch over and over, taking everything out on the bag. I picture my dad and all his bullshit demands, Chelsea and the way she repeatedly keeps turning me away. I'd never hit a woman, but Shelly's face pops into my head as I throw another. How fucking dare she lay her hands on Chelsea. Who the fuck does she think she is? She's already taken away her captaincy and enjoys rubbing it in her face. Isn't that enough?

My hair sticks to my forehead, my chest heaves with exertion as I fight through the pain of my exhausted muscles to continue. But no matter how many times my fists connect with the leather, it's not enough.

The door opens behind me and breaks through my angry haze. I throw one more punch at the bag before turning to find the inevitable. My furious father because I'm not at school where I should be. But to my surprise, when I turn around, I find Luca staring back at me.

"What are you doing here?"

"I left a textbook in my room. More importantly, why are you here? Shouldn't you be in class?"

"Fuck off," I grunt, turning my back on him and giving the punching bag my attention once again.

"You need a partner to take that out on?"

By the time I look over my shoulder, he's dropped his bags and pulled his shirt over his head.

He stands a few feet in front of me and puts his fists up, ready to fight.

"I'm not fighting you," I mutter, taking a step back. We might have fought many times over the years but I'm not taking this out on him.

"Yeah you are," he taunts, coming closer and jabbing me in the shoulder. "So what's wrong? Dad riding your ass about the NFL again?"

"When isn't he?"

I move around him to get some space, but he's not having it and follows, continuing to taunt me.

"So if it's not Dad then it can only be one other thing."

"Oh yeah, what's the…?" I ask, better his arm away when he starts to hit me harder.

"A girl."

"Luca, will you just leave me the fuck alone?"

"No can do, brother. You need to get this out and I'm offering it to you. Plus, I could use a good workout and seeing as your fists are already busted up, I stand a pretty good chance of winning."

I don't point out that he always wins. He's bigger and stronger than me. Both of them are which is why they're better at the game.

Wiping my face with my discarded shirt, I turn back to him.

"It's her, isn't it?"

"Who?" I bark.

"Chelsea," he practically sings her name in delight and it reawakens my anger once again. "Don't think I don't see it, little brother. You've pined after her for years."

"What does it matter? She's only ever had eyes for greater things. You…" I roll my eyes. "Jake fucking Thorn." I regret my admission the second his lips twitch in achievement. "Oh, just fuck off back to college."

"So what? You think you're not good enough for her, is that it?" Luca's fist connects with my cheek but it's not a punch, more a tap to get me worked up and make me fight back. "It's what Dad says, right? You need to push hard, play harder, work harder if you're going to make it. He wants it for you, but he doesn't really think you can do it."

Fury races through my veins. I know he's just saying it to rile me up, but fuck if it's not working.

"And as for Chelsea, she wants a winner, Shane. Someone she can be proud of. Someone she can show off to make her feel better about herself. That's not you, is it?"

"Motherfucker." I fly at him, but not before I see the smirk on his face.

My fist connects with his jaw and his head snaps to the side before he comes back at me.

"That's better, little brother. Let it out. Show me how you really feel."

He pushes me back, but I don't let it put me off.

Fists fly, bodies connect and unlike when I hit the bag, I actually get some relief from the stress that's been pulling at my muscles.

"Fuck, fuck," I say, stumbling back from him after a few minutes. I'm dripping in sweat and my body is aching.

I'm fairly sure he didn't hit me with everything he's capable of, but still, it hurts.

I fall down onto the bench a second before a bottle of water is thrust in my face.

"Drink."

"Who are you, my fucking father?"

"No, thank fuck."

He drops down beside me, equally out of breath as he rests his elbows on his knees and sucks in a few deep breaths.

"You've got better, faster. I'll give you that."

"Fuck you."

He chuckles. "Nah, save it for Chels."

"That's not—"

"Cut the bullshit, Shane. You're fucking good enough for her and you know it. You want her? Take her. You want the NFL? Have at it, you're good enough. You want to be a fucking ballet dancer? Go for it. What I said earlier was bullshit and you know it. Don't listen to that asshole, nothing you ever do will be good enough for him, it's just something that you need to accept. But you don't need to be good enough for him. You just need to be good enough for you."

I sit back and let his words sink in.

"Chelsea's a good girl, Shane. But it's no secret that she's been screwed up by her past. She's… complex. And just like you, she doesn't feel like she's good enough. You manage to see beneath the mask she wears, you know the vulnerable girl that's beneath. The one that hardly anyone else sees. She's not as strong as she makes out but she won't accept it. She'll fight until the bitter end, until she gets what she wants. Rightly or wrongly.

"You want her. You're gonna have to fucking fight too, bro. Because she won't drop those walls easily."

"Fucking hell, Luc. How did Mr. Fuck 'em and Chuck 'em get so wise when it comes to women?"

"I'm not fucking wise. I just know her. And you're wrong. She never wanted me. She just wanted me to want her. She's lost, Shane. The question is, are you strong enough to help find her?"

I blow out a breath, not even knowing where to start with all of that information he's just unloaded on me.

"I need to get out of here. Dad'll bust my ass if he finds me here. You too. I suggest you get washed up and disappear. Maybe go and visit that girl that's got you all tied up in knots."

"The new cheer captain pushed her down the stairs today."

"She fucking what?" he booms, anger rolling through him in an instant. "Is she okay?"

I shrug. "I have no idea. She was taken to the hospital."

"And you're here fighting with me because…"

"Because I have no idea what to do. She keeps sending me away. She doesn't want me."

"And you're going to allow that? She needs you. Be there." He collects his stuff and looks over his shoulder at me before he disappears. "Call me if you need anything, yeah?"

"Thanks, man. Sorry about your eye," I say, nodding to where it's starting to swell.

"Nah, the girls will love it. They get all kinds of wet for a bad boy."

"Fucking hell. Go. Please, just go."

I'm still shaking my head when the door slams behind him. He might be a fucking idiot, but he's kinda got a point.

Collecting any of the evidence I was here, I take myself up to my room for a shower. I can hardly walk into the hospital with my knuckles in the state they're in now.

Turning the shower on, I avoid looking at myself in the mirror. Luca might not have gone full force on me, but that doesn't mean I can't feel myself bruising from his hits.

My hands sting like a bitch when the hot water hits them. Gritting my teeth, I stare down as the water washes the blood away.

Scrubbing them down my face, I make quick work of washing myself before getting ready to go and find out what happened to Chelsea.

The drive to the hospital is quick and as I park, I can't help regretting not just coming here first. Although I think I needed that time with Luca more than I'm willing to admit.

With a sigh, I push open the door and head toward the ER. I have no idea if that's where she'll be or if she's even still here, but it seems like the best place to start.

I've barely walked through the doors when I see two people I wasn't expecting heading my way.

"Hey, what are you doing here?" I ask Amalie and Rae when they come to a stop in front of me.

"We came with Chelsea. Did you hear what happened?"

"Yeah, Shelly pushed her down the stairs or something."

"She said that Shelly didn't actually push her, but whatever happened, Chelsea ended up at the bottom unconscious."

"I-is she okay?"

The two of them share a look and dread twists in my stomach.

"Yeah, just a bang to the head. She'll be back to her usual delightful self in a few days, I'm sure," Amalie says with a roll of her eyes.

"I'm surprised you helped," I say.

"What was I supposed to do? Feed her to the wolves so they could have another go? Shelly is taking it a bit far now, even if she didn't push her."

"We should go. Ethan and Jake are going to be waiting." Thoughts of school and missing practice with the guys should concern me, but now I know she's here, my need to see her has only increased. "Why are you here anyway? Shouldn't you be with the team?"

"Oh yeah, I... uh... I've got an appointment," I lie, badly.

"In the ER?"

"No, I'm cutting through."

They both eye me curiously, but when I take a step forward, they both stand aside and let me pass.

"I'll see you tomorrow," I say, waving them off and disappearing into the building, grateful that they can't see me walk straight up to the reception desk.

"Um... hi," I say when the woman eventually looks up from her computer. "I'm looking for Chelsea Fierce."

"And you are?"

"I'm... um... her boyfriend?" I cringe as I say the word, and I can't help that it comes out like a question.

"Her parents are with her. You're more than welcome to go through as long as it's only you. Or you can wait." She points with her pen to the chairs behind me and I look over my shoulder.

"I'll wait, thank you. Wouldn't want to overwhelm her if she's not feeling great." Plus, the last thing I need is a grilling from Honey and Derek.

I find a seat in the corner but where I can keep an eye on the exit.

Pulling my cell from my pocket I open my Snapchat notifications. My eyes almost pop out when I find images and videos of Chelsea as she tumbled down the stairs and was left helpless at the bottom.

What the fuck is wrong with people?

I end up waiting so long that I begin to wonder if I missed her parents leaving, but only a few minutes later I spot them emerging from the ER doors. Derek pulls his crying wife into his side as they move toward the entrance.

My heart is heavy as I stand and make my way through the doors.

I have no idea what I'm going to find on the other side, and my pulse begins to race as I get closer to where I know she is.

18

CHELSEA

When the painkillers I've been given start to kick in, my parents say their goodbyes so that I can rest. The doctor reappeared while Mom sat holding my hand and explained that although everything looked perfectly fine that they wanted to keep me overnight just to keep an eye on me.

I hated the idea of a night in the hospital, but I could hardly argue. I had just had a flight down a set of stairs.

My arms ache where I must have hit them, my hip smarts when I shift in the bed but it's my head that is still throbbing and if I look around the room too fast, it starts to spin. Maybe a night here where I know I'll be looked after should anything go wrong won't be so bad.

I place my hand to my belly, feeling like a huge weight has been lifted now that people know about my little secret.

I hadn't even registered that my period was late while I was in the center. It wasn't until I'd been there three weeks and realized that I hadn't had one for ages that I started to panic. Turns out I was right to because when I did the test, it almost immediately turned positive.

I panicked for about two minutes as I sat there on the closed toilet seat, but as I thought about it, I soon realized that it might not be such a bad thing. Yeah, I was young, I'd only celebrated my eighteenth birthday the week before, but I knew I could do it. I could be a mom. I might not be able to look after myself at the best of times but even in those few moments, I knew that I loved the small person growing inside me more than anything.

I'd lived through hell as a child. I could be a better mother than the one I was forced upon. I could give a child a better start in life than that bitch gave me. Hell, I've already done a better job seeing as no drugs or alcohol have passed my lips since I found out. I'm sure that's more than she could have said during any of her pregnancy with me.

I have no idea how much time has passed before I come back to again. The sound of people milling around outside the curtain fills my ears. It's so loud at times I wonder how I slept through it, or the pain that's still pounding away in my head.

Knowing that it was the pain that woke me, I reach out to find the buzzer for the doctor to see if I can get some more Tylenol. When I don't immediately find it resting on my pillow where I left it, I drag my eyes open to look for it.

"Fucking hell," I gasp, not expecting to find someone staring at me. "You're turning into a stalker," I snap, my heart racing in fright.

His eyes burn into mine. There's an intensity within them that makes me panic.

Fuck. Does he know?

My heart races so fast that my head begins to spin.

I quickly locate the call button and press my finger on it.

My stomach turns like I might be about to puke and my mouth waters.

"Are you okay? Can I get you anything?" He sits forward in the chair and reaches for my hand.

My entire body locks up. I can't do this. Not now and certainly not here.

"No, and you shouldn't be here."

"W-what?" he asks, his eyes widening in shock.

"Shane." I suck in a breath and focus on the curtain in front of me. If I so much as look at him, I'll break and I can't afford for that to happen. "What I need is for you to leave."

"That's bullshit and you know it," he says, getting closer but I hold my nerve despite the scent of him filling my nose and begging me to turn to his green eyes that I know are going to be dark like when he's hungry or well... hungry.

I blow out a shaky breath and pray that he doesn't notice.

"Thank you for coming to check on me. As you can see, I'm fine, but I need you to leave."

His entire body tenses before he moves even closer. The heat of his breath hits my cheek and my traitorous body shudders with his proximity.

"This is the last time you're going to get to send me away, Chelsea." His voice is low and angry, and it has a ball of emotion crawling up my throat. "You make me walk out now and I'm not coming back. Ever. I've tried to be nice, to reach out to you when others dismissed you, but you've turned me away every time. Well, this is it." He holds his arms out. "You tell me to go now and we're done."

Every single part of me wants to break down and tell him to stay, to be honest about everything and be brave. But I can't. I'm terrified that he won't want me. Won't want us. And I can't allow that to happen. I've been rejected over and over my whole life. That needs to stop now, so I'll send him away before he gets the chance.

I might have wanted to see him when I first came back but he's proved to me that anything between us wouldn't be a good idea. I've got to focus on me right now, not everyone else. I've got something more precious to look after.

My fists clench, my nails digging into my palms as I try to muster up the strength to say the word I need to.

"G-go."

An unamused laugh falls from him as he takes a huge step back from the bed.

"You know, I thought you were different from what they all said. I thought it was all an act. I thought that beneath it all you were different. That you didn't mean to hurt people, that all that shit was just you being hugely misguided, but it seems that I'm the idiot because they're all right, aren't they? You really are just a bitch who doesn't care about anyone but herself." At those words, my eyes search his out. I regret it instantly because the green is darker than I've ever seen and they're full of unshed tears.

Fuck.

"Whatever this was. It's done. Goodbye, Chelsea."

Without a second glance in my direction, he disappears through the curtain. I swallow the sob that erupts from my throat because I need to know he's gone before I fall apart.

Curling in on myself. I wrap my arms around my belly and cry. "I'm sorry, I'm so sorry," I whisper to my baby. "It's for the best, I promise."

It's not until the next afternoon that I'm finally discharged and able to leave the hospital. Everything is still fine and finally they've got the pain in my head to subside a little.

Mom insists on holding on to me all the way out to the car as if I'm going to drop to the floor any moment. She tried to get me to sit in a wheelchair. I wasn't having any of that. Everything is fine, I'm just a little sore with a bump to the head, there's no need for the mollycoddling.

"We've got your room all ready for you," she says once I'm settled in the back of the car and she's in the front beside Dad.

"I'm fine to go back to the pool house."

"Nonsense. We need to keep an eye on you for a few days at least."

I catch Dad's eyes in the mirror and they crinkle at the edges. I know it's his way of begging me just to comply to make both our lives easier.

I do, but mostly because I'm too exhausted to do anything but.

I spent what felt like all of last night crying after sending Shane away and with the constant noise of the ER outside the curtain, I got hardly any sleep. I would prefer to hide in my pool house, but to be honest, any comfortable bed in a quiet room would be hard to refuse right now.

The ride home is tense. I know it's because they're both worried about me and what my plans are now that college is clearly out of the question but they seem to both be avoiding bringing it up, which really is fine by me because I don't have any answers.

The second we get home, I'm escorted up to my old bedroom and told to get in bed. I do because I'm exhausted, but I really don't need Mom fussing around me like I'm about to break any moment.

"Mom, I'm really okay. You don't need to do any of this."

"I know. I just want to make sure you're comfortable."

"I just hit my head."

"Chelsea," she sighs. "Someone pushed you down the stairs."

"She didn't push me and the second I'm back at school I'll tell Hartmann that. I'm not exactly innocent here. I brought all this crap on myself. I've just got to see it through. Everyone will get bored with me eventually and move on to someone else."

"Do you really believe that?"

I shrug. If I don't believe it then what hope do I have?

"You're not stupid, Chelsea. All of this might blow over, but then what? You'll turn up at school one day no longer able to hide your secret and you'll be hot gossip again."

"What are you suggesting here, Mom?"

"I... I don't know. I just hate that you're going through all this."

"It's fine. It's karma."

She opens her mouth to argue once again. She might be fully aware of my misdemeanors, but that doesn't stop her from trying to defend me. It's admirable, but I'd rather she just call a spade a spade. I was wrong. I hurt people that I should have cared about, and I'm just learning my lesson. They're fighting back, and rightly so. It might be misplaced because the people who should hate me, Amalie, Mason, S-Shane—I can't even think his name without getting emotional—seem to be fine. It's those who are fighting for their honor, like Shelly, who seem to have the biggest issue.

"Any chance we could get takeout pizza for dinner?" I ask, attempting to change the subject.

"Of course. Anything you want." She sits on the edge of my bed. "How have you been, you know, with the pregnancy? Any morning sickness or cravings or anything? Is there anything you need? Prenatal vitamins?"

I smile at her enthusiasm. Why I was ever scared to tell her I don't know. I should have known she'd be nothing but supportive.

"I've felt a little nauseous but nothing much. I've been a bit off food to be honest, although I wake up in the night starving some days. I've got all the vitamins I need. Thank you." I take her hand and squeeze it in both of mine. "Thank you for being okay with this."

"Oh, Chelsea. Sometimes things in life are out of our control. We just have to trust that someone up there has our best interest at heart." She glances out the window. Over the years, Mom's battled with her faith. She really wants to believe there's something out there, but then she'll remember all the hard times and it'll make her question everything. She was brought up in a religious household and I know she feels guilty for questioning her parents' beliefs and the way she was brought up. I just hope she finds the answers she craves one day.

"It's crazy," I say, dropping my hand to my belly. "But it feels right. I know everything about it is far from perfect, but it just feels... right," I repeat, unable to explain it any better. Once the shock wore off, something within me settled. I've got something that's mine. Something that's going to rely on me and look at me like I'm the most important person in the world. Something to give me purpose, a reason for being. It already fills me with more joy than anything in my previous eighteen years.

"I understand. Being pregnant is a wonderful gift and a beautiful thing. I'm so glad you've shared it with me. Anything you need, all you need to do is ask. I'll leave you to get some sleep." She drops a kiss to my cheek and leaves the room, closing the door behind her.

Climbing out of bed, I find my purse that Dad dropped to the chair when we first got in here and I dig out my ultrasound pictures. I lay in bed just staring at them for the longest time before sleep eventually claims me.

Everything in my life might be all kinds of fucked-up right now but I've got my little one. Everything will be okay.

When I wake again, it's to a gentle knock on the door.

"Sweetie, are you awake? You've got a visitor." Mom pokes her head around the door as I pull myself up to sit against the headboard.

My first thought is that it's Shane and hope swells in my chest that he's ignored my words once again and is going to fight for me. But the second she stands aside and I spot a pair of fishnet-clad legs behind her, I know it was wishful thinking. After what I said, I have no reason to think he'll ever speak to me again. Although, I guess he's going to have to because at some point we're going to have to have a serious conversation.

"Hey, how are you feeling?" Rae asks, walking into the room with a box of donuts in hand.

"All the better for seeing those."

"I'm glad I could be of assistance."

"We were going to order pizza for dinner. Would you like to stay, Rae?" Mom asks.

Rae looks to me and I nod at both of them.

"That would be great, thank you, Mrs. Fi—"

"It's Honey," Mom says with a smile.

Rae walks into the room but waits until Mom has shut the door behind her before she drops down onto the end of my bed and places the box between us.

"So..." she starts. "You're pregnant."

"Can I at least get some sugar in me before you start on the hard stuff?"

She laughs, pulling the lid off and giving me first choice.

I fight a moan of delight when the sweetness explodes on my tongue. It's a million times better than the crap they gave me in the hospital.

"You can come again," I mumble around a mouthful.

"You might change your mind in a minute, I want all the details. Tell me everything. How did it happen?"

It doesn't escape me that we only met on Monday and yet this feels like the most natural conversation I've ever had with another girl despite the fact I really don't want to talk about this.

"Well, I spent the night with this guy. Now, I don't know what you do with Ethan but he stuck his pen—" One of the cushions that was on the bed gently hits me in the shoulder.

"That wasn't what I meant. I don't need all the ins and

outs." We're both silent for a beat before we simultaneously bursts out laughing.

Tears fill my eyes and joy fills my heart. I can't remember the last time I laughed like this, and it feels so incredibly good.

Once the giggles subside, a silence falls around us and Rae blows out a breath. "I might be way off the mark here but..." I look up at her, my breath catching as I wait for whatever it is that she thinks she's figured out. "It's Shane's, isn't it?"

I gasp in shock. I barely know this girl, we've spent no more than a few hours together, how has she figured this out?

"Um... how... um... what makes you say that?" I ask, trying and failing to sound like she hasn't just knocked my world off-balance.

"There was just something he said while you were away that stuck with me. Then I saw his reaction to you on Friday night. He was meant to be focused on the game, but at every opportunity, his eyes searched you out." My heart starts to race. Surely, she must have been imagining things. "Then we saw him at the hospital. He made up some bullshit excuse about having an appointment. I think Amalie might have fallen for it, but I saw right through his lie. He came to see you, didn't he?"

I swallow nervously as I try to come up with any words to answer her.

"Y-yes." I hold her eyes as she absorbs that one simple word. Mine fill with tears whereas hers brighten with accomplishment. "You don't need to look so pleased with yourself."

"When I was a kid, I used to imagine what it might be like to be a detective."

"Well, congrats, Sherlock. You seem to have this case all figured out," I mutter, reaching out for another donut just to give me something to do instead of stew on the admission I just made.

"Fucking hell, it's really Shane? I thought the idea was a little left field, but... fuck."

I shrug, what is there to say.

"He's..." She trails off, trying to find the right words. "He's different from the rest of the guys. He seems more... sensible, thoughtful, kind."

A lump forms in my throat and tears sting the back of my eyes, desperate to be released.

"H-he is. He's a really great guy, actually. Just... don't tell anyone I told you that." I laugh, but it's far from the joyous one that fell from my lips not so long ago.

"But you've still not told him?"

I shake my head. "I can't. What if he doesn't want us?"

19

SHANE

"Here, drink this," Zayn says, shoving a bottle into my hand.

"Doesn't Ethan have anything stronger?"

I'm in a bitch of a mood. Have been since she sent me away from the hospital like a fucking spare part on Tuesday evening.

By the time I go home, Dad had somehow discovered that I'd skipped school and ripped me a new one, claiming that I had no idea how good I had it and that I should appreciate everything he's given to me. As per usual, there was no mention of anyone other than him. I have no idea how Mom puts up with his bullshit. Anyone overhearing would think he was a fucking single dad who had to do everything alone. Truth of it is that he was absent for most of my childhood while he swanned around the country chasing fame and fortune. Mom was the one to bring me up, he just supplied the money in an attempt to make up for his absence.

Asshole.

"Vodka?" Zayn asks.

"Yes." Reaching out, I take it from his hand instead of the beer.

I'm not in the mood for a party but Zayn insisted that I show my face and at least attempt to enjoy myself while drowning my sorrows with the copious amounts of alcohol Mr. Savage always supplies for Ethan's parties.

"Cheer up," he says, falling down beside me. "So she blew you off? There's plenty of other pussy here tonight to distract you."

"Who said she blew me off?"

"Uh... have you seen your face?" I'm assuming he doesn't mean the bruises that Luca left behind.

"Fuck off," I grunt, twisting the lid of the bottle and lifting it to my lips.

The vodka burns as I swallow a shot, but I welcome it. It's better than the ache in my chest that's been consuming all my thoughts since I walked away from her.

Part of me thinks I should have fought, should have stood my ground and made her hear me out for once, but then another part of me thinks it's probably for the best. If she's not interested now, then why should I bother?

Zayn falls into conversation with Justin who's sitting beside him and they both ignore me as Ethan's house fills with more and more kids ready to see in the weekend in style.

The music is turned up in the other room and the rest of the team descends on the couches. As is usual these days, Jake, Mason, and Ethan are absent, probably too busy with their girls to bother with us. I get it. I'd rather hang with my girl—if I had one—than these assholes given the chance.

All of a sudden Zayn stops talking mid-sentence and stands, totally ignoring whatever he and Justin were discussing.

"Ruby, baby. You are looking fine tonight." His eyes drop

down her body and I roll mine at him before glancing over my shoulder.

She's wearing the smallest red dress that I think I've ever seen. No wonder Zayn's eyes look like they might pop out.

He stalks toward her but stops abruptly when two others walk into the room.

"Harley, what the fuck are you wearing?" he asks, turning to his sister who's dressed similarly to Ruby.

"So it's okay for you to eye fuck my friend but I can't possibly show any skin?"

"It's not the same, Ruby is…"

Ruby, Harley, and Poppy's eyes rise as they wait to find out how Zayn's going to dig himself out of this hole. He looks between the three of them.

"She's not my sister."

"Nor is Poppy, but I doubt you'd look at her like you just did Ruby."

"Ew no, why would I look at her like that?" He curls his lip up in disgust as he turns to Jake's cousin.

"You're a pig. Come on, let's go and get a drink."

"But—" Ruby complains as Harley slips her arm through hers and drags her away from her brother.

"No buts. You don't want to touch him with a barge pole. He's probably diseased by the number of skanks he's touched." Ruby blushes red. It seems she hasn't confessed about her time with Zayn last weekend.

The three of them disappear, but Ruby doesn't lose Zayn's attention until she's slipped around the corner.

"Fucking Harley," he mutters, dropping down onto the couch. "Things were easier when Mom refused to let her attend."

"She just needs someone to distract her," Justin suggests. "I can offer my services." He wiggles his eyebrows and Zayn's shoulders visibly tense.

"Don't even think about touching her, asshole. Anyone goes near my sister and I cut your balls off and feed them to you, got it?" he barks.

A couple of the team nod in agreement, but most just roll their eyes at him. I'm not sure why he's bothering, he knows full well that most of these assholes don't do as they're told. Ever. If one of them sets their sights on Harley, then they'll fucking have her, I've no doubt.

Conversation turns to college applications and I almost walk off when someone asks me if I've made a decision about which team I want to play for when our missing captain and team members join us with their girls.

"Ah, about time the captain showed his face," Zayn shouts, earning him the finger from Jake.

"What the fuck is she doing here?" Justin barks and when I look to the doorway, I find Chelsea standing with Rae.

Good question. What the fuck is she doing here?

She's not dressed like I'm used to. Instead of the barely-there outfits she used to select for this kind of party, she's wearing a decent length skirt and a shirt that covers almost everything she used to show off to get attention.

She looks good. Too fucking good and it has desire that I shouldn't feel filling my veins.

She hovers by the door as Rae tries to talk her into joining us.

"Come on, Chels. What's wrong? Forgotten how to make us compliant?" someone calls. My teeth grind as I think about them all having detailed knowledge of her body.

Her eyes lock with whoever said it for a beat. Before she rolls them and looks around the room. She visibly flinches the second she finds me. Her lips part and she takes a step back. Rae reaches for her but the second she looks at me, she seems to understand.

Great. If someone knows then no doubt everyone will

before long. I'll just be another idiot who's fallen for Chelsea's charm and beauty.

She whispers something to Rae before backing out of the room.

I swear I don't breathe until she's gone from my sight.

"Okay, you two need to sort whatever that was out," Zayn whispers to me once everyone is distracted.

"Nah. We're done."

"Really?" he asks, quirking an eyebrow.

"Yeah. She's expressed her true feelings. Time to move on." I sit forward, resting my elbows on my knees and glance around at the girls littering the room, most of whom are on the cheer squad and totally out of the question. I've been burned once by one of them, I'm going nowhere near another.

There is one who's noticeably absent though. Shelly hasn't been seen since being marched to the Principal's office on Tuesday. It turns out that she was already on Hartmann's shit list and he suspended her. With her gone and Chelsea at home recovering, it's been a quiet few days for Rosewood High which is unusual to say the least.

"Right, we need to set tonight's challenge," Zayn announces. Jake, Mason and Ethan all excuse themselves, not needing any kind of challenge to make sure they get laid tonight, leaving the rest of us waiting to hear what he's got to say. "Our little tagging game is fun and all, but how about we up the ante?"

"Go on," Justin says, leaning forward, intrigue filling his eyes. A few of the other guys follow the move. I, however, stay exactly where I am knowing that I won't be getting involved, just like every other time they've done this shit.

I have no intention of hooking up with a girl just for bragging rights. It's not really my style.

"Fuck the tags, let's make this a dare."

"Ohhhhh," someone says as more and more of the guys listen in to Zayn's plan.

"We name the girls, you must get some kind of evidence that you succeed or..."

"Or?" Rich asks.

"Or... winter formal is just around the corner." Zayn rubs at his chin in thought. "I'm sure none of you want the public humiliation that could come with failing."

Shaking my head, I entertain myself with my bottle of vodka while Zayn starts dishing out names.

"Shane," he barks, turning to me. His eyes twinkling with delight.

"Oh no, not a fucking chance, man."

"Oh, I don't know. I think you might like this particular challenge," he whispers so only I can hear. I quirk a brow at him, wondering if he's going where I think he is with this.

I take another shot of vodka. The strength of the alcohol no longer burning my throat, but it's having the exact effect I needed it to on the rest of my body.

"Go on then," I taunt, leaning forward much like the others did. I don't look to the guys, but I feel their eyes on me. They're used to me running away from these challenges, so I understand why they'd be surprised.

Zayn smiles, and excitement explodes in my belly. "Chelsea."

A couple of the guys gasp and a few laugh. "Oh fuck off, Shane isn't going to go for that," Rich barks.

"Well, there's no point in him being the only member of the team she's not been with." My lips purse in anger and I fight to stop my reaction from showing on my face.

"Fine," I say, much to their surprise. "What?" I ask when a few of them question me. "A dare is a dare, right?"

I take another shot and sit back, ideas forming in my head faster than they should as Zayn rattles off a few more names.

"Happy?" he says, turning to me once everyone has their target for the night.

"Yet to be determined," I say, pushing from the couch and walking away.

"Don't forget the evidence." I flip him off over my shoulder and head for the kitchen in search of Chelsea.

It takes me longer than I'd like to find her, but the second I step foot into Ethan's den, I know she's there. I feel her.

Looking to my right, I find her curled up into the opposite corner of the couch to where Rae and Ethan are. Jake and Amalie are on another, along with Mason and Camila, who are making out on a beanbag.

"Everyone out," I bark, successfully earning everyone's attention.

I lift the bottle again as all eyes turn on me.

Ethan barks out a laugh like it's the most ludicrous thing he's ever heard.

"What was that, Dunn?"

"I said," I repeat with a roll of my eyes. "Everyone. Out." Taking a step forward, I lock my eyes on Chelsea's. She swallows nervously as she sits motionless on the couch. "Except you. Chelsea and I need to have a little chat. Don't we, Chels."

"Oh my god," Amalie gasps from behind me. I know this is a little out of character for me. But the girl brings out the crazy in me, that plus the alcohol that's currently racing through my veins.

"I don't think so," Ethan says, standing in front of me and blocking my view of her.

We stand chest to chest, nose to nose. Ethan's not the kind of guy I'd go up against willingly. My brothers might have taught me to fight fairly well, but I have no reason to believe that he wouldn't squash me like a fly should he wish.

"I-it's okay, Ethan." Her soft voice fills the room before her slender hand wraps around his upper arm.

I want to rip it away. She shouldn't get to touch him with such familiarity. Red hot jealousy burns through me that every guy I know has had a taste of what I want.

Glancing to my left, I find Jake staring between the two of us. There's no love lost between him and Chelsea these days, but he was the one she pined after for all that time and he was the one who got her first. He always gets what he wants.

After a beat, Ethan stands down and allows Rae to pull him from the room, although it's not before she whispers a warning in my ear.

"Hurt her and I'll hurt you."

If it had come from any other five-foot nothing girl, I might not bat an eyelid, but Rae is kinda scary. I nod at her, although I don't take my eyes from Chelsea's.

They all leave the room, and soon the door is closed behind them, leaving the two of us alone with the tension crackling between us.

The silence is heavy as our connection holds. My heart races as I try to come up with the words I need to say to her, but being this close, and this drunk, all I can think about is kissing her.

"What?" she barks after a few long, quiet seconds. "What do you want?"

I take a step closer, running my eyes down her body. "I think you know what I want."

"And I think you know my opinion on that."

I lift the bottle to my lips before offering it to her. She pushes it away, refusing my gesture.

"How much have you had?"

"Enough," I say, placing in on the coffee table and taking another step toward her.

"So I see. I'm almost impressed that you had the balls to kick Ethan out of his own den."

"Almost impressed. Wow. I wonder what I'd have to do to really impress you," I tease, stalking toward her until she has to start backing up.

"To leave. I don't know how many times I need to—" Her words are cut off with a gasp as her back connects with the wall. "Shane?" Her voice is barely a whimper, I might be concerned if it weren't for the fact her eyes drop to my lips.

"Careful, Chelsea, that almost sounded needy," I warn.

The heat of her body burns against my skin, but I don't touch her. Not yet.

"No, I-I don't want you. You need to—"

"Is that right? So your heart isn't racing right now?" I ask, knowing full well that it's pounding just like my own. I can tell by the fast movement of her chest. Her breath catches at my words as I look down at her breasts. "And your nipples..." I reach out a finger and very gently tease around one. "They're not hard and desperate for my touch?"

"Fuck you, Shane," she spits, but she's only angry because she knows I'm right.

My eyes find hers once again. Excitement fills me at the fire I see shining in hers. It's been diminished more than not recently, and I hate it. There might be things that Chelsea has done that are less than desirable, but her passion, her desire. Fuck, it brings me to my fucking knees.

"That was kind of the idea, baby," I say, my cheek brushing against her so I can whisper it in her ear. She shudders and I can't help but smile.

She turns to me, and I pull back to meet her eyes, too intrigued to find out what she's about to say no to.

"Why me, Shane?"

A laugh falls from my lips. I wish I had the answer to that question. I could be going after any girl right now, but she's the only one I want, the only one I can think about even when I beg for my mind to stop.

"I have no idea."

"You've got a thing about being second best, don't you?"

"W-what?" I stutter.

"You're always the little brother, the one who's never quite good enough, always watching your big brother's get what they want while standing on the sidelines."

Anger swirls in my belly, filling my veins with red hot fury. This is the thing about Chelsea. She knows me better than anyone because she's been in my life just that long, not that she'd ever admit it. We're closer than anyone imagines. "That's not true," I argue, and she quirks a brow at me.

"No? And with me? You're once again picking up sloppy seconds, and Jake's no less. The guy you've had to follow for as long as you can remember."

"Enough," I bark, my fingers gripping her jaw, my eyes staring down into hers.

"Why? Can't handle the truth?" Our stare holds, anger, desire, passion crackling between us. "Cat got your tongue, Shane? I thought you were here to rip me a new one."

"No. You're wrong."

"Oh?"

"I came here to prove you wrong."

"About what?"

"About what you want."

"Wha—" I assume she's going to ask what I'm talking about, but she doesn't get the chance because I make the most of her parted lips and press mine to them.

She stills to start with and we stand with just our lips connected but then it's like someone flips her switch and her hands come up to tangle in my hair and I lean forward, pressing her body into the wall.

My tongue sweeps into her mouth and hers eagerly joins

in. My hands run up her sides and slip into the fabric of her t-shirt. I skim up her soft skin until I find the swell of her breasts. Her head falls back, banging against the wall as I squeeze, and I panic. A moment of reality through my drunken, angry haze.

"Y-your head. Are you okay?" The healing scratch marks the only visible reminder of what she's been through this week.

Her fingers tighten in my hair and she moves my head so I have no choice but to look at her.

"Don't do that."

"Don't do what?"

"Pretend that you care. That this is anything more than what it is."

I want to argue, to tell her that this is way more than she's willing to accept, but the words die on my tongue as I remember exactly why I searched her out in the first place.

The challenge. The dare.

Hurt her like she repeatedly does you and prove that she wants more than she'll admit.

With a nod to myself, I pull my cell from my pocket. She huffs in impatience, but I don't stop. I won't film it, I wouldn't do that to her. But there were no rules. Pulling up the microphone, I press play and place it on the dresser beside us.

"Okay, fine," I say, turning my attention back on her. Her eyes are dark with desire, her lips already swollen from my kiss. My cock strains against the fabric of my pants, desperate to be inside her once more. My hands drop to her thighs and after pushing her skirt up around her waist, I lift her.

"Oh god," she squeals as my fingers dig into the skin of her thighs.

"You don't want me to care? You want rough. I'll give you whatever you need, baby."

"Oh fuck, Shane," she squeals, as I lift her higher and press my lips to her neck.

Her thighs clamp around me as I run my tongue up her sweet skin. She shudders, her fingers once again diving for my hair.

I bite, suck and kiss hard enough that there's going to be no forgetting I was here the second it's over.

She might like to keep pretending that there's nothing here, that she doesn't want me, but we both know it's a lie.

When we're together like this. It's like nothing else exists. It's just us and it's fucking explosive.

Lifting the fabric of her shirt up her belly, she helps me out by pulling it off and dropping it to the floor as I drop my lips to the swell of her breast.

I smile in delight when I find the front fastener and make quick work of undoing it so her tits spill out.

"Shane, Shane, please," she chants above me as I kiss and lick everywhere but where she needs me.

"You don't want this remember?" I remind her.

"Fuck you, Shane," she groans, trying to direct me with my hair.

"All in good time. I want to hear you admit it first."

"Admit what?"

"That you want me. This. That you made a mistake every time you sent me away."

I lick up the underside of her breast and allow my nose to brush over her peak. She gasps as the sensation races through her. But the stubborn bitch still resists.

"No. I just want this."

"You just want me for sex?"

"Yes. Now please. Give me what I need."

"Why not one of the others? I'm sure they'd be up for it."

"No," she cries as my teeth sink into the softness of her breast.

I look up at her as I suck and lick at the bite. Her eyes are black, her cheeks red with desire.

"No, I don't want..."

"Go on. You don't want...?"

"I don't want any of them, okay?"

"So, say it. Say those three little words and I'll give you what you need."

My tongue brushes the very tip of her nipple and her eyes shutter with pleasure.

"Fuck," she barks. "I want you, okay. I fucking want you. Argh," she screams when my lips wrap around her tip and I suck her deep into my mouth.

Her heels dig into my ass, her nails scratch at my scalp as her back arches against the wall, giving all of herself to me.

Her chests heaves and my name leaves her lips with her cries of pleasure as I switch to the other side.

Just when I think it might be taking her too close to the edge, I drop her back to the ground.

"What the fuck are you doing?" she asks when I take a step back.

Rubbing at my jaw, I run my eyes down the length of her. Her neck, chest, and breasts are covered in my bite and suck marks, my cock weeps as I take in the sight. Her skirt is bunched around her waist, exposing her tiny black panties.

Shaking my head, I push my hair away from my face, pulling my shirt over my head and drop to my knees before her.

Sucking her bottom lip into her mouth, she watches me with heat filling her eyes.

Reaching forward, I wrap my fingers around the sides of her panties and pull until they come away from her body.

"Shane, fuck." Her eyes widen in shock as I ball up the lace and shove it deep in my pocket.

"For later, then you inevitably send me away." I'm only

half-joking. I have no intention of sleeping with them under my pillow or anything fucking crazy but I'm not against a little memento of tonight, alongside the recording of course.

Tapping against the inside of her thigh, she widens her stance for me, giving me just enough space to lean forward and find her clit with my tongue.

Her taste explodes in my mouth, making my head spin with my need to sink inside her. I could do that right now, hell knows she's ready, but I'm not okay with this being over too quickly. I already know that it'll never be long enough.

Her fingers return to my hair as I lift her leg over my shoulder to give me more access.

I'm a little more confident this time, helped by my recent experience but more so the vodka. Just like that first night, my inhibitions are a hell of a lot lower than usual.

Parting her lips, I suck on her clit as she chants above me. My fingers find her soaked entrance and I groan in delight as I slide them into her slick channel.

"Oh god," she moans as the vibrations of my low groan rumbles through her and she only gets wetter.

I lap at her and my fingers increase speed inside her. The one leg she's standing on begins to tremble as her pussy begins to clamp down on my digits.

As much as I want her to come like this, I won't allow it. There's no way I'm risking giving her what she needs only for her to walk out without looking back once again.

Just as I sense she's on the brink of falling over the edge, I pull back and wipe my mouth with the back of my hand.

"What the fuck are you doing?" she barks as she realizes that I've stopped and drags her head from where it was resting back against the wall.

"Changed my mind," I say with a shrug.

"You fucking what?"

Falling down onto the couch, I stretch my legs out in front

of me. The bulge of my hard cock obvious beneath the fabric of my pants.

"If it's good enough for you, then it's good enough for me, baby."

"I've never left you like that."

"As good as every time you send me away."

"No. No, that's nothing like—"

"Say it again," I demand.

"Say wha—oh." She places her hands on her hips. She's still totally on display for me to enjoy despite the patch of skin around her waist that's covered by her skirt.

"Say. It. Tell me you want me."

Her lips purse and her teeth grind.

"Tell me that you feel this. This thing between us when we're together."

"It's just sex, Shane."

"Is it? So it was like this with all of them, was it?"

Something passes across her face but she covers it before I get a chance to attempt to make it out.

She opens her mouth to respond but no words come out. I already knew I was right, but that's all the confirmation I need to know that this thing isn't one-sided. She feels it too.

"Strip."

20

CHELSEA

"**S**trip."

It's hardly the demand of the century, seeing as I'm basically standing here naked anyway.

I make quick work of undoing the button around my waist and shimmying the fabric down my legs.

Shane watches my every move, his eyes almost black with desire.

I stare at him resting back on the couch like he doesn't have a care in the world, but I know that's far from the truth. The darkening bruises around his eye and jaw, and his cut lip are just the beginning.

I really thought after I sent him away from the hospital that it would be the end of us. I know that Shane is nicer than most guys, that he's already given me one too many chances to admit that I want him but I really didn't think he'd come back for more once again.

He's drunk, a little voice in my head says, and as if he can read my mind, he leans forward for the bottle he abandoned not so long ago.

He swallows down a couple of mouthfuls like it's water,

only I know from the slight slur of his voice and the confidence in his touch that it's not.

I really fucking want some. But I can't. Not that he offers me any.

"So now what? I told you what you wanted to hear." Although, we both know I didn't. I might have said I wanted him in that moment but there is so much left unsaid between us. I should have told him the truth a few moments ago when he asked about this being like me with the others.

He has no idea that really, there aren't any others. Just like everyone else at Rosewood High, he has me marked as some kind of whore who puts out to everyone who shows any kind of interest, only it's not quite the truth.

"Show me. Show me what all the others rave about. I think I've forgotten the last time, maybe you're not that good after all."

He places the bottle on the floor after opening his fly temptingly.

I should walk away from what he's insinuating, but I know I've only got myself to blame. It may not be as bad as he thinks, but I can't lie, I've touched one too many of his teammates in the past. Those I haven't are happy enough to brag along with the others making out like they know. I should have set them straight the first time someone claimed to have had me on my knees, but I couldn't. Fucked-up, I know, but they were talking about me like I was something, like they cared and had a reason to keep me around. Like I said, fucked-up. But it is what it is.

I expect him to push his pants down, but he never does. He just keeps his eyes on me, daring me to give him what he needs.

"I should walk out right now," I say, although my body betrays me and takes me a step closer to him.

"Go on then. I'm getting used to seeing your back."

I hate this side of him. The angry at the world persona he's playing to try to hurt me like I have him. But as much as I might hate it and crave the sweet guy that I know he really is, I can't help but be turned on. Something inside me just can't resist that hint of a bad boy that I suspect only I've had the pleasure of witnessing.

I think back to him ripping my panties from my body not so long ago and a wave of desire washes through me. Who knew he had it in him?

"I never back away from a challenge, Shane. You want to play games, then you've chosen the wrong opponent if you want to win."

He swallows as he takes in my body as I close the space between us.

Once I'm right in front of him, I place my hands on the back of the couch on either side of his head.

He stares up at me, his eyes dark and his chest heaving.

"What are you waiting for? You owe me."

I can't really argue with that. I owe him a hell of a lot more than a blowjob though after all the bullshit I caused him.

"Oh yeah. What exactly do I owe you?"

"Everything. Now..." He shoves his thumbs into the waistband of his boxers and pushes.

"Stop," I demand, making his eyes widen in shock.

Backing away from him, I drop to my knees.

The sight of me before him has the vein in his neck pulsating.

"Allow me, I *owe you* after all."

His lips part to respond, but no words come out as I wrap my own fingers around the fabric and tug.

He lifts his hips to help and I pull his pants and boxers over his ass and down his thighs. His already hard cock rests against his stomach and I can't help but bite down on my bottom lip at the thought of taking him in my mouth again.

He wasn't wrong with what he said earlier, it's been so long I have almost forgotten.

Once he's free of his pants, I discard the fabric on the floor and push his legs wider so I can settle between them.

I drop my lips to the side of his knee and slowly kiss up his thigh. His fingers slide into my hair as his impatience starts to get the better of him, but I refuse to be rushed.

Leaning forward, he reaches for the bottle of vodka he left on the floor and lifts it to his lips.

"Want some?" he offers this time.

I shake my head.

"Your loss." He drains the bottle before throwing it to the other side of the couch and resting back.

He stares down at me, his impatience obvious in his eyes as I continue teasing him.

"Chels," he moans as I scratch my nails down his abs. "I need—"

"I know what you need, Shane."

His hands tighten in my hair, leaving me little choice but to look up at him. His eyes are still dark with desire but there's more there now. His usual softness has returned.

"No, I really don't think you do."

A lump forms in my throat and tears burn the backs of my eyes as our connection holds. Damn pregnancy hormones. I desperately want to believe that there could be something between us, but it would be dangerous to even allow a little bit of hope in. He doesn't want me. He can't, not after everything. There's a reason why no one knows about this situation we keep finding ourselves in. I'm his dirty little secret. One that he's happy to enjoy behind closed doors, but is probably ashamed to admit to the outside world. I'm not the kind of girl guys like Shane deserve. He should have a nice girl on his arm. Not one with a tarnished reputation who everyone hates.

Needing to break whatever weird connection has

developed, I do the only thing I know that will distract him. I lean forward and lick up the length of him. His cock pulsates beneath my gentle touch, his hips lift as he seeks more and his fingers tighten until his grip is almost too painful to bear.

"Fuck, Chelsea."

Spurred on by his words and reaction to my simple touch, I wrap my fingers around him and lick around the head of his cock.

He groans, the noise at the back of his throat reawakening my own lost pleasure from earlier.

Parting my lips, I suck him as deep as he'll go, loving the growl that rumbles up his throat.

Glancing up at him, I find his head resting back on the couch, his blond hair is a mess after having my hands in it not so long ago, his eyes are shut, his cheeks flushed and his lips parted.

I run my eyes down his body, taking in his chest and cut abs. Fuck, I want to run my tongue over every indentation. I want to be able to take my time, to enjoy this thing between us not just have stolen moments full of anger and hate as we battle against each other and what we really feel.

"Fuck, fuck," he chants when I lift my hand and cup his balls.

His length swells between my lips and I know he's almost at the end.

I suck him once more before releasing him with a pop and standing.

"What the fuck?" His head lifts, his eyes wide in shock.

He must realize my intention the second he sees the smirk on my lips.

Tit for tat, baby. You leave me hanging, then you can expect the exact same treatment in return.

"You set the rules, baby," I say in a sickly-sweet voice that I usually reserve for hooking up with the assholes he plays with. "Not my fault if you can't handle the consequences."

I step back, but he's quicker than I give him credit for. His fingers find mine and I'm pulled toward him with such force that I have no choice but to fall into his lap.

"Going somewhere?" he asks, his eyes glittering with amusement.

"Yeah, leaving."

"Not this time. I'm not finished with you. And for once... I'm calling the shots."

I stare at him, enjoying his more dominant side.

In seconds he's moved me so that I'm sitting astride his lap and his large hands wrap around my waist, holding me in place.

"Go on then, I think we've both waited long enough."

Reaching down, I grasp him. His eyelids lower at the sensation and I delight in the fact that even now, I hold all the power. It's how I need it to be. I need to be the one who can call the shots in an attempt to protect myself.

The moment I have us lined up, I sink down and watch as the muscles in Shane's neck strain with pleasure. His jaw pops as I drop lower and his fingertips dig into my skin.

"Fuck," he barks once I'm fully seated.

His eyes hold mine and I lift slowly and drop back down.

"Fucking hell, Chelsea," he groans, suddenly sounding much more sober.

"What?" I ask, confused by the change in him.

"It's not supposed to be like this." His voice is low and almost a whisper, and I lift once again.

"Like what?"

"This fucking good. This fucking addictive."

I fall silent, but I fear my feelings about what he just said are written all over my face. He's right. It shouldn't be like this.

It was supposed to be one night of distraction. It wasn't

supposed to turn into needing each other quite like this. It wasn't supposed to turn into this toxic thing that I can't help craving as much as I hate it.

Unable to look at the honesty in his eyes, I drop my head to the crook of his neck and push all thoughts aside as I ride him.

His hands help me move, but it's not long until his need for release has his hips pistoning up into me.

My fingers curl around the back of the couch and my nails dig in as I race toward my own orgasm.

"Fuck, Chelsea, fuck."

Sitting up straight, I throw my head back and cry his name as my body crashes over the edge.

Only seconds later, he pulls me down against his body, and with his face tucked in my neck, he stills as he growls out his release, his cock twitching deep inside me and igniting some of my own aftershocks.

His increased breaths tickle across my heated skin as he comes down from his high.

Knowing that I need to move, that our time together is over, I push away from him but his arms lock around me, holding me in place.

"Shane?" I question, needing him to release me before I start allowing myself to believe there could be more here.

"Just need a minute. That was..." He trails off.

"Yeah," I agree. What else is there to say? It was pretty incredible. Almost enough to make me believe that there could be something between us.

"Chelsea?" he asks, a weird emotion filling his voice that I can't place.

"Yeah?" I whisper, enjoying being in his arms a little too much.

His fingers thread into my hair and hold me in place as he moves his lips to my ear.

"That was a dare," he whispers.

For a second, the words don't register. But the moment they do, my entire body tenses in his hold.

Allowing me to move, his arms drop from around me and I sit up.

He's got a smug as fuck grin on his face as his eyes bounce between mine.

Something hot explodes inside me as I stare back. "You're a fucking asshole. You're no better than any of them, you know that?"

"Can't beat them, join them," he says with a shrug.

"Fucking prick." I climb off him, hating that him slipping from inside me feels so good it's almost a distraction from reality.

"You feel better now that you got one over on me? You win, Shane. You fucking win."

I tug my clothes on while he remains motionless on the couch. I don't look at him, I don't dare look to see that smirk again because I know how much it's going to piss me off.

I don't even have the energy to say anything as I blow through the door. I slam it as hard as I can behind me as I run from the house.

I didn't want to fucking be here in the first place, but knowing I was almost as good as new, Rae insisted I attempt to rejoin the world and Mom couldn't do much but agree. She couldn't keep me locked up in that bedroom forever.

I keep my head down as I push through the students all enjoying their Friday night. Seeing as I'm now the social pariah, hardly anyone even glances my way as I make my way to the front door.

Thankfully, Rae is nowhere to be seen or I know I'd never make it out. Thankfully, I do because by the time I dig inside my purse for my car keys, tears are streaming down my cheeks.

"You motherfucker," I scream, slamming my hands down on the steering wheel in an attempt to get some of my anger out.

I was the one warning him not to play games, that he'd be the one to lose. How fucking wrong was I?

He's supposed to be the nice one. The sweet one. Yet he just played me at my own game. Although I'm not sure it was ever my game to begin with.

It's not until I'm halfway home that I realize the car behind me has been trailing me since leaving Ethan's house.

My heart races knowing that he's followed me and is driving drunk. I have no idea if I'm angrier at the thought of having to see him once again or that he's put himself in danger. I'm tempted to say it's the latter, but I push it aside, not wanting to deal with how I really feel about him.

It's dark so I can't really make out the car other than its bright as fuck headlights, but it makes every single turn I do, even to the point of signaling a turn on the street I live on.

My fingers tighten on the wheel and my heart pounds in my chest. I'm tempted to lock myself in the car for fear of getting out and having to deal with him again. But after blowing out a breath, I find some balls, turn off the ignition and push the door open.

The car is still there, idling by the sidewalk, but now I'm able to see it, I realize it's a truck and not one I recognize.

I take a step toward it to see who the driver is, but before I get a chance to see inside, it speeds off.

Weird.

Telling myself it's just someone from school trying to freak me out, most likely Shelly. I shake my head and walk to the house. I'm desperate to go to my pool house but all my stuff is in my old bedroom. That's all going to be changing tomorrow. No matter what my parents think, I'm perfectly fine and I'm going back to my little haven to get away from the world.

Thankfully, the house is in silence, so after grabbing myself a bottle of water, I head up to my room.

I walk over to the window to close the curtains but a set of lights outside once again catches my eye. Fear trickles through me, but I push it aside. Plenty of people hate me now, it could easily be any number of them as they watched me flee from Ethan's.

21

SHANE

The second the words are out of my mouth, I regret them.

It's the reason I sit there and watch her dress without saying a word. She should walk out after learning what I'd done.

I'm no better than her. Playing games to win points.

I wanted to prove that she wanted me. I guess I achieved that. She told me as much. So why doesn't it give me any sense of achievement? *Because you hurt her, asshole,* a little voice says in my head.

"Fuck," I bark into the quiet room. The bass of the music pounding through the walls tells me that the party is still going strong outside. Thankfully, everyone knows the rule that if Ethan's den door is shut then no one enters.

Pushing myself from the couch, I sway a little as I get to my feet, proving just how much I've had to drink already. Sadly, it's not enough to help me forget that look in her eyes as realization hit her.

I'm such a fucking asshole. Yeah, she's pulled some dickhead moves in the past, but she didn't deserve that.

She's wrong. I'm not one of *them*. They walk around taking whatever they think they deserve, much like my dad. I am not like them.

I pull my clothes on with the intention of getting out of here. A huge part of me wants to find her and tell her that it was a mistake, tell her how I really feel but I know she wouldn't accept it, it would be pointless and probably lead to us doing something else we'll regret.

"Shane, my man. Where've you been, bro?"

"Busy," I grunt at Zayn as both him and Justin wrap their arms around my shoulders.

"Oh, getting busy with Chelsea?" His eyes light up as my entire body tenses. "You know we need evidence, right? Your word alone won't stand tonight."

"Not that it ever would. There's no way you'd get a shot with Chelsea," Justin slurs.

They navigate me toward the kitchen where some of the team are still loitering with drinks in their hand.

I grab a beer from the counter as we pass before falling down onto the same couch I was on before all this shit kicked off.

"So..." Justin prompts, causing everyone to turn to look at me. "Shane thinks he's completed his challenge."

"I didn't say that," I argue.

"You didn't need to, man. So come on, let's see the evidence. Give these assholes something to aim for."

Her panties burn in my pocket and the recording on my cell taunts me. But I don't move to grab either.

"I don't have any."

"No proof means it didn't happen, and if it didn't happen, then you lose."

Getting more and more frustrated with these douchebags, I push from the couch.

"I don't give a fuck. Do your worst," I say, lifting my hands from my sides. "Some things are more important than your fucking bullshit games. How about you stop playing for just a moment and find something more meaningful in your fucking lives."

I don't hang around to hear their response, I storm from the room and toward the front door.

Sadly, I don't make it that far before I'm collared.

"Shane, what happened to Chelsea? I can't find her."

Rae's concerned eyes stare up into mine. "I have no idea."

Her eyes narrow in frustration. "What did you do?"

I want to fire back at her that Chelsea deserves whatever comes her way, but I think we'd both know it would be a lie.

"Something I regret," I admit quietly.

"Jesus. You two are a fucking nightmare."

"And you need to keep your nose out. You have no idea what's happened between us, you've only heard her side of the story, I assume."

"I'm pretty sure I understand fairly well. I know she fucked up, but people make mistakes, Shane. Much like tonight." She lifts a knowing brow. "So how about you put all of that aside and do the right thing."

"I have no idea what that is," I admit.

"Well you'd better fucking figure it out before it's too late."

She spins on her heels and marches away from me, her cell in her hand, I assume calling Chelsea.

I double back on myself, grab a bottle of whatever I can find on the kitchen counter before finally leaving the house.

Ethan's place is almost on the beach so in only minutes, me and my new friend Jack find ourselves on the sand and watching the waves crash onto the beach.

The stars twinkle above in the inky black sky and I wonder what it would be like to lay here with Chelsea beside me. All the bullshit banished and to just be us.

Could there be an us, or are we toxic to even consider?

I don't drag my ass from the beach until the sun is beginning to rise. I don't want to go home, I know it'll only end up in an inevitable argument with my dad.

With a sigh, I walk that way. What I really want to do is go to Chelsea. But even in my drunken state, I know that's a really fucking bad idea.

The house is in darkness, and I breathe a sigh of relief. It wouldn't be unusual for Dad to be up working through the night. Hell knows he's caught the three of us sneaking in before now.

I make it to the stairs before I realize someone else is awake. Light comes from the basement and footsteps head my way.

"What fucking time do you call this?" Dad barks. He's wearing only a pair of shorts with a towel hanging around his neck.

"Too fucking early for you to be working out. Be fucking normal for once in your life and sleep."

His eyes widen in shock. "You've been drinking." It's a statement, not a question, so I don't bother answering it. "What the fuck is wrong with you? Skipping school, getting drunk, staying out all night. This isn't you, Shane, and this kind of behavior isn't going to help get you into—"

"Don't fucking say it," I bark, knowing exactly what's about to fall from his lips.

"No coach is going to want a fuckup, Shane."

"So, what about Luca and Leon? Did you give them this kind of shit every time they threw a party and got so drunk everyone trashed the house?" I already know the answer, he had the place cleaned up and ignored it ever happened. "What about when they used to sneak in late every weekend? Did you accuse them of fucking everything up? No, of course you fucking didn't because they can do no fucking wrong.

Your fucking golden boys who hang on your every word. It's fucking pathetic."

"That's enough," he barks. "I will not accept this kind of behavior from you."

"What, suddenly acting like this is unacceptable? Unbelievable. You're a fucking joke, you know that?"

"Shane, that's enough," Mom's soft voice calls from down the stairs.

Dad and I stand in our silent stare off for a few more seconds before I dismiss him with a lift of my chin and head up the stairs.

"What's happened?" Mom asks as I pass her at the top of the stairs. It's obvious that we've woken her.

"Nothing. Go back to bed."

"Shane, what—"

"I said it's nothing."

This time she lets me go and the second I'm in my room I fall face-first on the bed and pass out.

By the time I wake the next morning, the sun has long risen and it's so late that I've got a ton of missed calls from Zayn telling me that I missed our morning workout. It's probably for the best, he would have spent the entire time grilling me over what happened last night. He's the only one out of the guys who'll believe me without the evidence they apparently require.

I might have set up that recording last night, but I don't know why I bothered, I was never going to allow anyone to hear it. This thing between me and Chelsea is just that, between us. It's our fucked-up, messy, toxic little secret.

My head throbs as I drag my body to the bathroom to freshen up in the hope I'll feel a little more human once again.

I'm more than happy to spend the day hidden in my room,

stepping out means I'll probably have to see someone and deal with the regrets and memories from the night before.

I think about the argument with Dad, that's one thing I don't regret. It's about time someone stood up to him, I just never really thought it would be me. I recall my time with Chelsea and the ache that's been in my chest since she walked out only gets more persistent.

I shake my head. After our first time together, I told myself that I'd be able to just forget her, and I did to a point. I sat back and watched her be her usual self at school afterward when all I wanted was for her to look my way and give me even a hint that she remembered our time together, that it meant anything to her like it did me.

Then the truth came out, and I wanted to look at her once again for a very different reason. I wanted to tell her what I really thought of her. I wanted to accuse her of setting me up, of using me as a scapegoat and not giving two fucks.

But she disappeared, and everything changed once again. Yes, I still wanted to rip her a new one, but concern soon overtook. It was stupid, I knew that. I shouldn't have been concerned after everything but somehow she'd wiggled her way under my skin and no matter how hard I tried, I couldn't get her out.

My need for coffee and food eventually cause me to leave the safety of my bedroom. Thankfully, when I get down to the kitchen, it's only Mom who's sitting with a cup of coffee and her tablet.

"Afternoon," she says with a smile. "How are you feeling?"

"Better than I should," I mutter, thinking of the vodka and whiskey mix from last night.

"Your dad's out of town for a few days."

"Great," I grunt, pulling a bag of chips from the cupboard and throwing a couple into my mouth.

"I know he gives you a hard time, but it's only because he

cares."

"Oh yeah, that's why." I roll my eyes at her.

"Baby," she starts with a sigh, but I hold my hand up to stop her.

"Can we not? I'm too hungover to talk about him."

"Sure." She falls silent as she watches me crash around in the kitchen, making a sandwich and my much-needed coffee.

After a few minutes, I fall down beside her.

"What's wrong?" she asks.

"Other than what we're not talking about, I assume?"

"Yeah. What's eating you? I have no problem with you going out and partying with your friends but over the past few weeks, you haven't been yourself. I know he's giving you a hard time, but it's more than that, isn't it?"

I stare down at my sandwich as I consider how to answer her question. I'm suddenly feeling much less hungry.

"It's a girl," I mutter quietly. I don't really want to have this conversation with her but I know it's better to just come out with it or she'll be like a dog with a bone until I confess.

"Thought as much. Anyone I know."

"Yeah, but I'm not telling you who so don't bother asking."

She chuckles. "Okay then. So what's the issue?"

"It's just... it's fucked-up. I shouldn't like her. We shouldn't work. It's a disaster waiting to happen..."

"But you can't walk away," Mom finishes for me.

I can't help but laugh. "Oh, I've walked away plenty. Doesn't stop me going straight back though." I think of all the times she's sent me away, and I told myself that that was it. No more. But every time, I've gone right back for more. I'm like a fucking addict needing my next hit.

"Love's a funny thing."

"Calm down there, no one mentioned the L-word," I joke.

"No, but the heart wants what it wants regardless of what our heads think."

"Helpful, thanks."

"Is she worth it?"

I open my mouth to respond, but I soon realize that I have no answer. Most people would say absolutely not. Chelsea Fierce is a force to be reckoned with and whoever she touches ends up burned. I know, I've experienced it. But that doesn't stop me from wanting to jump back into the fire.

I think of the soft broken side of her that I've had glimpses of over the years. *That* Chelsea is worth it. The one who allows her walls to drop and shows who she really is beneath the mask and armor she wears on a daily basis.

"Yeah, I think she is," I answer.

"Then you've got to fight for what you want."

"What if it'll only end in disaster?"

"Sometimes it's a risk we've got to take. You want her, then there's always a chance it won't work and you'll end up getting hurt. It's part of the territory, unfortunately. You've just got to trust yourself, and if you think she's worth it then you owe it to yourself to try."

"Thanks, Mom."

"No problem," she says, getting up and rinsing her mug out. "Just promise me one thing."

"Sure."

"Be safe."

I nod, really not wanting to get into that kind of conversation with her. Plus, I can hardly tell her I have been. The last two times I've been with Chelsea, we haven't used protection. I trusted her when she said she was covered. I shake my head at myself.

I might still be none the wiser about what to do with her, but I do know one thing. We need to draw a line under whatever this thing is. Whether that's to put a stop to it or just to quit the bullshit games we're playing, I'm not sure. But I need to be the bigger man here. I need to go and apologize for last night and we need to sit down and talk, something that we haven't done... ever.

Butterflies flutter in my belly as I head out the front door. I'm more nervous walking over there to have a conversation than I have been for anything else we've done. It's fucking crazy.

I park beside her and her mom's car and kill the engine. My hand trembles as I reach out for the button, and I chastise myself for being such a pussy.

It's just Chelsea. A girl I've spent countless hours with over the years. Okay, so she spent most of them avoiding me until recently when all we've tried to do is hurt each other, but she's still the same girl.

She's not though. She's different and you know it.

Fuck. I scrub my hand down my face and climb from the car. There's no backing out now. There's a chance she's already seen that I'm here, so I need to man the fuck up and do what I came to do.

Walking around the house, the sound of soft relaxing music filters through the air, and when I get around to the back, I find both Chelsea and Honey bent in half on yoga mats beside the pool.

Chelsea's wearing a pink pair of pants and a small matching top, but I hardly notice with the way her ass is stuck up in the air as it is.

Now this wasn't what I was expecting.

Her mom softly says something and both of them move simultaneously into their next position.

I have no idea how long I stand there watching her, it's kind of hypnotic, but all too soon, a dark pair of eyes lock on mine. There's no shock on her face, making me wonder if she knew I was here all along.

Honey notices that Chelsea is distracted and follows her gaze.

"Oh, Shane. What a nice surprise. Fancy joining us?" she asks with a hopeful look on her face.

"Um..."

"I think we're done here anyway, right, Mom?" Chelsea says, helping me out.

Honey checks her watch. "Yes, you're right. I need to get moving. I've got a meeting in an hour. I probably won't be back until late and your dad is away on business overnight. Help yourself to whatever, order yourselves food if you want some," she offers, looking between the two of us like she's trying to figure this out. The two of us may have spent plenty of time together in the past but I'm not sure this has ever happened before.

"Thanks, Mom," Chelsea says. "Have a great day."

After looking between us for another second, Honey smiles and heads for the house.

"What are you doing here?" Chelsea barks, her demeanor changing the second her mom is out of earshot.

"We need to talk."

"Talk?" she asks, her eyes widening. "We don't talk, Shane. Plus, I've got nothing to say to you."

"That's a shame, because I've got plenty to say to you."

Her lips purse and she grinds her teeth in frustration as she stares at me.

"And it seems like you've got nothing better planned since you're about to be home alone, so shall we?" I gesture toward the sun loungers that sit around the pool.

She huffs when I walk over and drop down into one. I stretch my legs out and place my hands behind my head, making a show out of getting comfortable.

It might be late in the year but the sun warms my skin as I sit here.

"Jesus fucking Christ," she mutters, spinning on her heels and walking away from me.

I sit forward, ready to chase her but decide against it. She marches through the door to her pool house but in seconds she returns with a zip-up hoodie over her shoulders. Apparently, I'm the only one who thinks it feels like summer.

I run my eyes down her body as she makes her way back over to me.

"What?" she barks.

"N-nothing." I swallow how disappointed I am that she's covered herself up, I don't think she'd want to hear it right now anyway.

"I hope you've got the hangover from hell," she mutters, sitting beside me and folding her arms over her chest.

"Not as bad as I deserve."

She looks over at me but quickly averts her gaze when she finds me staring back at her.

"That's a shame."

"I'm sorry, Chels."

"Really? That's all you got?"

"Uh... yeah. I was pissed at you for continually sending me away. I wanted to hurt you back. It was stupid. But when Zayn dared me, I couldn't think of anything else but making you admit that this is... something."

"Fucking Zayn," Chelsea mutters to herself.

"He knows about... us—"

"There is no us, Shane."

"Yeah, no, yeah... I know. I meant, he knows we slept together, and he knew I was pissed. He thought he was doing us a favor."

"Great. So the whole team knows by now then," she huffs.

"He hasn't told anyone."

"Pfft. It doesn't matter. Everyone already thinks we probably have anyway."

"What's that supposed to mean?" I ask.

"Nothing." She sits back and stares ahead. "Anything

else?"

I'm silent for a moment as I consider what I want to say to her. When I don't respond she turns her eyes back on me. My mouth waters as I take in her flawless beauty. "I... uh... I like you." Unable to hold her eyes, I glance down at my feet.

She gasps as she moves to sit on the edge of the lounger like me, our knees are only a breath apart.

Reaching out, she gently touches her fingers to my chin and I have no choice but to look up at her. I didn't intend to say those words, the admission just kind of fell out, and now I'm feeling like an idiot.

Our eyes connect, her chocolate to my green, and something crackles between us.

She shakes her head, a small smile playing on her lips.

"What you did last night. I deserved it. I deserved it and so much more for everything I've done to you and the others."

"Maybe so, but I shouldn't have done it. I hate myself for setting out to hurt you. It's not who I am, Chels."

"I know, you're the sweet one." One side of her lip twitches.

"Oh yeah, real nice."

"If you weren't, you wouldn't be here right now."

Pushing to stand, I have no choice but to look up at her once she's at full height.

"Mom made smoothies. You want one?"

"Um... sure."

Before I have time to blink, she's making her way to the kitchen. I blow out a long breath, chastising myself for being such an idiot. I know I said I wanted to talk, but I didn't want to come across like a total pussy.

"Fuck," I bark into the quiet of the back yard, dropping my head into my hands.

"Everything okay?" Her soft voice flows through me and my spine stiffens. Fucking hell, there's no way I'm leaving here today without convincing her that I'm a total fucking idiot.

"Yeah, everything is fine." I turn to look at her, she's holding two fancy glasses with straws sticking out the top with the front of her hoodie wide open. Just that bit of skin makes my mouth water. I already know that she'll be sweeter than whatever is in those glasses.

"Uh... here." Heat hits her cheeks, and I relax for a moment. Is she as unsure about this as I am?

I watch her as she moves to her seat and lowers down. I have no idea if she's aware of my attention or not but at no point does she look my way. Instead she takes the straw between her lips and sucks.

My cock swells as I remember just how hot and smooth those lips feel wrapped around my cock. Fuck. I came here to apologize not to sit here with a raging hard-on.

"You weren't that drunk then?" Chelsea asks suddenly, startling me from my little trip down memory lane.

"Uh... w-what?"

"I can read you, Shane. I know exactly where your thoughts are at."

"Can you blame me, you give good—"

"I'm off now," Honey's voice cuts through what I was about to say and my face flushes with color while Chelsea barks out a laugh.

Honey appears in the kitchen doorway and looks between the two of us.

"Have a good day, you two." She smiles at Chelsea and then me before turning and disappearing.

Silence stretches out between the two of us until the sound of an engine revving hits our ears and a car backs out of the driveway.

"So... we've got the whole house to ourselves," Chelsea says, putting her now empty glass down on the side table and looking to me. "What shall we do?"

22

CHELSEA

My heart thunders in my chest as Shane's honest eyes stare back at me. I was not expecting him to apologize, let alone admit that he does feel something for me.

I should fall back to my usual protective measure and send him away for fear of him getting too close and finding out the truth but the thought of spending time with him like two normal people who aren't constantly fighting is too tempting.

I don't deserve his apology, especially when I'm the one lying to him right now. I should confess, tell him everything that I'm hiding. But the words get stuck on my tongue.

If I drop that bomb then everything is going to change again, and this right now, it feels... right. And I crave a normal day more than anything.

Should I forgive him so easily for that stunt he pulled yesterday? Maybe not. But after all the times I hurt him, I can't really say that he was wrong for doing it. I deserved it.

Pushing from my lounger, I stand beside Shane's. He's still holding his full smoothie in his hands and staring up at me with desire in his eyes.

I know he was watching as I drank my own drink and I know exactly what he was thinking. I don't need to see the shape of his cock beneath his pants to confirm it. And I also can't deny that it turned me on too.

I have no idea what it is about Shane. I've had guys in this position time and time again, but I've never wanted to climb them like I do him right now. Every single part of my body craves him, craves his touch, his kiss, his caress.

Fuck.

"I-I just came here to talk, Chels." He swallows, the tendons in his neck strain and his Adam's apple bobs.

"And we have. You told me you're sorry, I told you I deserved it and you admitted you like me. What else is there to discuss?" The question tastes bitter on my tongue. There is so much more we need to discuss but I can't do it right now. I need this. I need him.

"Um... e-everything. We've barely scratched the surface. Chels?" he asks as I straddle his lounger and lower myself to his lap.

His eyes darken as I settle myself and place my hands on his shoulders.

"We've got plenty of time. You heard Mom, she'll..." I place a kiss to his jaw. "Be." Kiss. "Gone." Kiss. "All." Kiss. "Day." My final kiss is to the corner of his mouth and seems to be the end of his restraint because his hand slides up my back and his fingers thread into my hair as his tongue sweeps into my mouth.

I whimper above him because being close, having his hands on me is just that good.

His kiss is addictive, all-consuming, and as I hand myself over to him completely, I don't ever want to stop.

My hands roam around his chest, desperate to find his bare skin. After a few seconds, I slip my hands under the hem of his shirt and brush my fingertips up his abs. His entire body flinches at my contact.

"Fuck, Chelsea. What are you doing to me?" he groans against my lips, sending red hot lust straight through my veins.

His hands grip on to my ass, pulling me down harder onto him. His length presses against me and the temptation to take what we both clearly need is almost unbearable.

Torturing both of us, I reluctantly stand and back away from him.

As my heart races, I run my eyes down the length of him. His hair is a disheveled mess, his eyes are unbelievably dark, his lips swollen and his chest heaves as he tries to catch his breath. He looks incredible and makes me wonder how I've managed to turn him away so many times.

"Ches?" he asks, panic starting to set in that I'm about to end this once again. Fortunately for him, he couldn't be more wrong. I couldn't send him away now even if I wanted to.

"I was wondering," I say, slipping the hoodie down my arms so it falls to the floor at my feet. He sits forward, eager to hear what I've got to say next.

I lift my hands to my bra and as smoothly as possible pull it over my head.

Shane's eyes drop and he swallows as he stares at my swollen breasts.

"If you wanted..." I shove my thumbs into the waistband of my yoga pants and panties and push them down my thighs. "A swim."

Before he has a chance to respond, I turn and dive into the warm water behind me.

I have no idea how he sheds his clothes so quickly but I'm still under the water when I sense him join me.

Just as I break the surface, his arms slip around my waist and he pulls me up against his hard, naked body.

Opening my eyes, I find his green ones staring back at me.

"Hey," I say, nerves assaulting me from somewhere.

A wide smile spreads across his face. "Hey."

I wrap my arms around his shoulders and my legs around his waist. His already hard cock teasing my entrance and reawakening the desire that was coursing through me not so long ago.

He walks me backward until my back hits the pool wall.

When he drops his head, I lower my eyelids, preparing to resume our earlier kiss but his lips don't find mine, instead they brush my ear.

"I thought we were done with the games." A shudder runs through me as his breath tickles my sensitive skin.

"Mind games, yeah," I breathe. "Sex games, I'm all in."

He growls in response and his mouth latches on to my neck. My head falls back, giving him all the access he needs. But he doesn't continue long enough before he speaks again.

"If we're doing this…" Just the thought of this being a thing has my stomach somersaulting. "I need you to promise me something."

"And what's that?" I ask, playing with the hair at the nape of his neck.

"I'm the only member of the team that gets to touch you, look at you, have you. You want me. You give them all up." It's hardly the demand of the century. I've used them over the years, just like they have me. Jake was the only one I ever thought I wanted more with. Not playing games with them isn't exactly a hardship, especially if I can have Shane.

Gripping on to his hair, I pull his head from the crook of my neck so I can look into his eyes. So he can see the honesty in my words.

"I don't want them. I've never wanted them."

His eyes bounce between mine as he thinks about my

words. "So, what do you want?" His voice cracks slightly as his nerves creep in.

"You."

"Fuck."

His lips find mine once again as he pins me back harder against the wall. His kiss is bruising, but I can't get enough. Our teeth clash as our tongues duel, desperately trying to get enough of each other but both knowing that we'll never achieve it.

He lifts me higher before lining his cock up with my entrance.

"Okay?" he mumbles against my lips before pushing inside.

"Yes, Shane. Always."

I love that he's sweet enough to ask. That he doesn't just take like so many of the others. But he needs to know that he already owns me. He can take exactly what he likes and I'll meet him move for move.

"Fuuuuck," he grates out as he stretches me open.

"Oh god."

The water laps around us as we move together. His hands grip on to my ass almost painfully as he thrusts up into me, taking what he needs and giving me exactly what I'm craving.

Seeking out my lips, his tongue plunges into my mouth, mimicking what's happening below the water as my body starts to race toward the end. I don't want this to be over. This connection, I want to feel it forever.

"You feel so good, baby."

"Yeah," I moan as he brushes his lips across my neck.

"So tight, so hot, so perfect."

One of his hands leaves my ass in favor of roaming over my body. He squeezes each breast, pinching each nipple and sending shockwaves of pleasure racing through me. Then he brushes his fingertips down my stomach to find my clit.

"Oh shit," I moan, my eyes closing as pleasure explodes within me.

"Look at me, Chelsea. Don't hide. Don't run."

I do as I'm told, and my eyes fly open. It's the first time I accept that he's as vulnerable as me right now. He's laid on the line how he feels, what he wants, and just like me, he's terrified that I'll reject him. Fuck, what I've been doing since I came back. Continually walking away, or sending him away like I don't care.

Admitting that I want him, that what we have here means something to me terrifies the shit out of me. What if I tell him the truth and he walks away from me? From us? The thought alone has a lump forming in my throat.

People always abandon me. Leave me. Why should I believe that he'd be any different? The only people who've stuck around are Honey and Derek and even all these years later, I have no idea why they chose me.

"Jesus, fuck, Chelsea." Shane's low, husky voice drags me from my inner turmoil and brings me back to the here and now. He stares at me, his eyes telling me more than his lips do and I can only hope that mine are doing the same. That he can read everything I'm too scared to put into words.

"Come, Chelsea." As he says it, he pinches my clit and thrusts up higher.

"Oh fuck," I cry not two seconds later, following his order.

I just register his smirk of achievement before I have no choice but to slam my eyes closed and ride out the waves of pleasure.

Shane thrusts three more times before his grip on my hips becomes almost painful as his entire body stills. A groan of pleasure rumbles up his throat as his cock twitches violently inside me.

His arms wrap around me and he holds me tight, our

chests crushed together as we fight to gain control of our racing hearts.

After long silent minutes with my ear pressed against his chest listening to his heart thunder, he releases me slightly.

Reluctantly, I pull my face away and glance up at him.

Reality comes crashing down that this is over now. Every other time we've been together, things have gone very wrong from this moment on.

Biting down on the inside of my cheek, I risk a glance up at him. His eyes are soft, full of something I'm not used to seeing on the guys I've spent time with in the past.

Reaching out, he brushes a wet lock of hair from my cheek and tucks it behind my ear.

"Stop waiting for something to go wrong," he murmurs.

"But... it always does."

"Not today. Today, we just enjoy." He leans forward and brushes his lips against mine. "No games, no bullshit. Just... us."

A smile curls at my lips. "Yeah?" I ask, hopeful that we could at least attempt to do this.

"Yeah. If you want me." That little bit of vulnerability I saw earlier creeps back into his eyes.

Cupping his cheek in my hand, I sigh when he leans into my touch.

"I do."

"Perfect," he says before dropping his hands to my waist and scaring the shit out of me when he lifts and launches me into the pool. I squeal before I go under but can't help laughing once I come back up.

It's been too long since I let go of everything and just had some fun.

With my past and bad decisions weighing me down, it's easy to forget that I am only eighteen and that I can have this.

We play around in the pool for the longest time. Our

hands barely leave each other's bodies as we enjoy ourselves and laugh like we've got no worries in the world. It's incredible and although we don't go any farther than a few naughty gropes and the odd kiss or two, I'm desperate for him to pull me to him once again so he can consume me. But he never does. I know it's not because he doesn't want to. He's been hard almost since he pulled out of me earlier, but he's made no move to take me again.

"We should probably get out," I say when our splashing comes to a stop. I hold my hands up above the water and inspect my wrinkled fingertips.

"Yeah, you're probably right. I'm hungry," he says, crowding me into the corner.

"O-okay, we can shower and order food."

"Food? Hmmm..." he mumbles into the crook of my neck. "I wasn't talking about food."

Heat floods my body as his front presses against me, his cock prodding me in the stomach.

"Then we definitely need to get out so you can get what you need."

His hands slide up the sides of my body before tucking under my arms and lifting me from the water as if I weigh no more than a feather.

Water runs down my bare body as his eyes follow its movement.

The cool air and his stare have my nipples pebbling.

"Oh yeah, I'm definitely starving."

Feeling brazen under his attention, I part my knees. His eyes immediately drop to my core and he licks his bottom lip. My muscles clench as I remember exactly how it feels with his tongue against me.

He leans forward. My fingers dive into his hair, halting his movement.

"Shane?"

"Lie back," he demands, pulling at my legs so my ass slides toward the edge of the pool.

I glance around at the houses surrounding us. None of them directly overlooks our back yard, but that doesn't mean they can't see what's going on right now.

"Chels?" He follows my line of sight. "You think they'll get off watching the show?"

My eyes widen at his words. I thought I knew the kind of guy that Shane was. It seems I was very wrong. He might not be a dog like the majority of his teammates, but fuck. His confidence is hot.

"Shane?" I repeat, my head spinning with lust, unable to think straight.

Do I want him to eat me right here for everyone to see how he owns me? Fuck yes.

Doing as I'm told, I rest back on my elbows. Placing my heels on the edge of the pool, I watch as his pupils dilate as he stares at me.

"I thought you said no games," I quip. "This definitely feels like you're playing me right now."

My words eventually cut through his daze and his eyes come back to mine.

"I don't mind these games so much."

Without wasting another second, he dives for me.

I fall back down, my back arching against the hard tiles beneath me, my shoulder blades smarting with pain as I writhe, but I couldn't give a fuck. Shane licks, sucks, and drives me fucking crazy with his fingers teasing my entrance.

Any thoughts of nosy neighbors evaporate from my mind as I focus on what he's doing to my body.

"Shane, Shane, Shane," I cry in pleasure as he pushes me over the edge. My fingers find his hair and I hold him in place until I've ridden out the final seconds of my orgasm. "Fucking hell," I pant when I eventually let up my hold and he moves away from me.

I'm still laying out on the tiles a sated mess when he jumps from the pool and stands over me. Water drips from his body, splashing over my now mostly dry one.

"Come on," he says, holding his hand out for me. "I think we've given your neighbors enough of a treat for the day. I'll save fucking you over the table for another time."

Despite the fact he's only just made me come, my thighs clench as the image of him thrusting into me from behind fills my mind.

Shaking the thoughts away before I tell him that it's exactly what happens next, I lift my hand up and allow him to pull me to my feet.

"Shower?" I ask, standing so close that my breasts brush against his chest.

"Sounds perfect. You do look really dirty."

I tilt my head to the side and look up at him through my lashes.

"What?" he asks.

"Where did the sweet, shy guy go?"

He chuckles. "You just weren't looking in the right places, baby."

"So it seems," I mutter as he pulls me along behind him toward my pool house.

"Just because I don't always act like them," he says, and I assume he means his teammates. "It doesn't mean that I don't want the same things."

"Me on my knees?"

The muscles in his shoulders tense as he continues dragging me through the living room and then the bedroom. He doesn't stop until we're in the walk-in shower, and then he spins me and backs me up against the wall. He takes my chin in his fingers and lowers his face so his nose is almost brushing mine. His eyes are hard, much like they were last night and nothing like the easy-going, fun-loving guy I've spent the last few hours with.

"Don't. Don't ever compare me to them like that. I don't want you for a cheap ride. And I'd really prefer not having the constant reminder that they did."

"Shane, that's not—"

"You're mine, but they all had you first. It makes me want to kill every last one of them."

I take his clenched fists in my hands and lift them to my lips.

I hold his eyes, hoping that he can read the truth in them. "Most of them are lying, Shane," I whisper.

His jaw pops and his eyes remain angry and hard.

"Shane," I repeat, knowing that he didn't hear a word I just said. I wrap my hand around his neck and brush my thumb along the line of his jaw. "I haven't touched most of them. They're bragging to make themselves look like a big man. I promise you, it's nowhere near as bad as it seems."

He blinks a few times, but he doesn't relax, and I worry for a second that my stupid comment has ruined this and that he's about to realize his mistake and walk away.

I might have forced him to do so in the past, but now I've somewhat allowed myself to believe that there could be something between us, it would kill me to watch him turn his back on me, on this.

"I hope to fuck that you are right." I don't get a chance to respond because as he says it, he reaches out and turns the shower on. We're both blasted with ice cold water for a few seconds before it begins to warm up.

I open my mouth to say more, although I'm not sure what exactly, but I don't get the chance because the second my lips part, his tongue sweeps inside.

23

SHANE

Just the thought of what she might have done with the guys I'm forced to spend time with has anger racing through my veins.

She can tell me that it's bullshit on their part all she likes. Hell, I believe her. I know what braggers and bullshitters they are, I experience it daily. But still, it doesn't do much to get the images I don't need out of my head.

I want her to be mine and mine alone. I hate that others have experienced this. Her.

"Stop overthinking," she warns, her soap covered hands rubbing across my abs and getting dangerously close to where I really need them. "Stop worrying about what's already been done. We can't change the past, Shane. I know that better than anyone."

She looks up at me, her dark eyes open and honest in a way I'm not sure I've seen before.

"Why did you do it, Chels? Why hurt everyone?"

"It was stupid," she says, bowing her head, too ashamed of her actions to hold my eyes.

"Explain it to me. Please. Help me understand."

She blows out a breath as she considers her words.

"You know my past, Shane. It was... bad. I was a nuisance, this unwanted, unloved small person who only got in the way. I had no use, well not until I grew up a little, not that that stopped some of the guys leering..." A shudder runs down her spine as she remembers.

Wrapping my arms around her, I gather her close in the hope it helps her to feel the opposite of those things she just described.

"I've just always wanted to be wanted," she says so quietly that I almost think I imagined it. "I know I had Honey and Derek, but they didn't choose me, not really. They had no choice but to take me in when I first turned up on their doorstep.

"I've watched everyone for years, finding their best friend. That person they can have a conversation with without even saying words. I've watched those around me fall in love. And I've always just felt alone.

"I was jealous. I won't lie, I thought Jake was it for me. Two broken souls who could fix each other or some bullshit. Then Amalie turned up and shattered anything I believed. He wanted her, *you* wanted her.

"Then Mason and Camila sorted their shit out, and one by one I was watching everyone find what I wanted so fucking badly.

"I lashed out. I was jealous and drowning in other's happiness. I've got no real excuse because it was a fucking stupid thing to do. It was misguided, immature, unnecessary, selfish, the list goes on.

"I'll never forgive myself for it. To this day I'm not sure what I was trying to achieve other than to stop everyone being so happy and moving on with their lives while I seemed to be forever stuck in misery. I was so fucking lonely, Shane. So fed up with everything. Of pretending, of trying to be the person everyone had to like. All of it was fucking bullshit."

We're both silent for a beat before she speaks again.

"I never set out to hurt you or to make it look like it was you. But once everyone assumed, I couldn't exactly scream it from the rooftops that it was me. Well, I guess I could have but..." she sighs. "I'm so sorry. So fucking sorry. Somehow, I intend on making it up to the others too. I don't know how; I just hope I'll figure something out."

"I'm pretty sure you just need to say the words, Chels."

Taking her cheek in my hand, I move her head so she has no choice but to look at me. Her eyes are full of tears, but I have no idea if any have fallen with the water pouring down over both of us.

"I'm sorry," she whispers, her voice cracking. "There are so many things I'd do differently if I could go back."

"You can't. You've got to accept it for what it was and move on. We all have."

She nods sadly.

Silence falls between us once again as her words from moments ago run around in my head.

"What about the squad?" I ask.

"What about them?" Her brow creases in confusion.

"I thought they were your friends."

"Like the team are your friends?"

"But—"

"My squad are my squad," she says, cutting me off. "I decided a long time ago that cheer was going to be my life. I love it. I live it. Becoming captain was never a question for me. It's in my blood.

"Those girls, they don't hang around with me because they like me, because we're friends, they do it because they have to.

I'm their leader, the reason they're on that squad, the reason they have the position in the school they do.

"They're not my friends," she repeats. "Just look how quickly they turned their backs on me when I fucked up. Real friends don't do that. They should be there no matter how bad you screw everything up, even if they're angry. L-like you," she whispers.

"The only people I've ever had any kind of real friendship with is Luca and Ethan. They both see beneath the act, they see me, not just the cheer bitch everyone else gets."

"So you and Ethan, you've never..."

Her lips curl in disgust before she chuckles. "Never. He's kinda like my brother. Luca too."

"And me?" I ask, running my thumb along her bottom lip and stepping closer.

"Are not like my brother," she says with a smirk.

"Thank fuck for that," I mutter with a laugh.

Tension crackles between us but no words are said as we continue to stare at each other.

Chelsea's lips part, but she doesn't say anything for the longest time.

"I-I think you might have been what I was searching for all along." Her eyes widen the second she realizes she said it aloud.

"Is that right?" I close in on her, pushing her up against the cold tiled wall.

"I'm not sure, you might need to show me again."

I have no idea what time it is when we emerge from her bathroom, but I do know that I'm hungry, and for actual food this time.

"Where are you going?" Chelsea asks in shock when I walk toward the door to her pool house naked.

"Well, I wasn't going to walk home like this if that's what you're worried about."

"Good. You're not the only one who gets to claim ownership, you know." Her eyes run down my body, staking her claim.

"All yours, baby."

I'm only gone seconds as I grab my abandoned clothes but when I get back, what I find is almost as good as her still being naked.

She's standing at her refrigerator wearing the jersey I left behind the night she sent me away.

"I sure hope there's nothing underneath that."

"You'll have to find out for yourself," she says, turning to me with two sodas in hand. "What do you want to eat?"

"Whatever. I'm easy."

"You sure are." She winks.

"Being corrupted by the chief cheer slut. I must say, it has its benefits." A brief flash of hurt flickers in her eyes and I feel awful for joking about it. I step up to her and take her hand in mine. "Hey, I didn't mean…"

"It's okay. Chinese?" she asks, grabbing her cell and opening it up to change the subject.

"Sure. Sounds perfect."

We spend a few minutes debating dishes before she places the order and we fall down onto her couch.

She turns the TV on and opens Netflix.

"Any preference?"

"Nope, whatever you want."

Her recommended programs open up and I can't help but laugh.

"What?"

"You're such a girl." I take in the cheer series that she's halfway through and all the chick flicks and romance that fills the screen.

"Yeah, and?"

"I was kinda expecting it to be full of phycological thrillers and murder documentaries."

"Fucking hell, Shane. I'm not a total psychopath. I do have a... softer side."

"I know, I know. I'm only joking. And I happen to like getting beneath your hard outer shell."

"Oh yeah?"

I wrap my arm around her shoulder once she's chosen some series to watch that I've never even heard of and tucks herself into my side.

It's really fucking comfortable.

"I believe you, you know," I say after a few quiet moments as the theme tune to the program plays out. "If you say it's not as it seems then, I believe you. Those guys can be real assholes."

"They can. Which leads me to my burning question," she says, looking up at me. "Why are you suddenly hanging out with them? You used to stay as far away from the team as possible but since I've come back, you seem to always be with them."

"Hmm... it wasn't by choice, I figured that I might be able to find the information I needed from one of them."

"Information? What could you possibly need from them?"

"I thought they might have known where you went."

Her chin drops. "Y-you were looking for me?"

"You just disappeared. I was still desperate for a repeat of that night and then everything blew up and you were gone. I didn't know what to think. I wanted to shout at you for what you did, I wanted to hurt you for allowing me to take the fall, but mostly, I just wanted you. I wanted to know you were okay, that you were safe.

"Mom refused to tell me where you'd gone despite the fact I knew she knew. I had no idea if you'd run or what."

"I was sent," she admits. "I'd already fucked up one too many times and when I got home that night and confessed to my parents they got straight on the phone and booked me a place at the center. They'd threatened time and time again but I didn't think they'd do it. It had been years since I'd been there, I was more than happy to never return. But looking back now, I think it was the best thing they could have done. I needed that time. I needed the space to figure out who I was and what I really wanted."

"What did you do there? What's it like?"

"It's basically a group home but they have teachers and counselors on site to work with all the kids. It's one of the better places to end up when you've got no home, that's for sure.

"I did schoolwork every morning, therapy sessions and exercise in the afternoons. It was regimented and structured, everything I needed to sort my head out."

"Did you speak to anyone from home?" I ask, thinking about how lonely that sounds.

"My parents called regularly, and Ethan messaged a couple of times. I needed the space."

I pull her tighter into my body. "I'm glad it helped. But I'm even more glad you're back."

"It gave me perspective. Helped me figure out what I want."

"And what do you want?"

She lets out a sigh and is silent for so long that I'm not sure if she's going to answer me. "I want to focus on my future. I want to forge meaningful relationships and if that means I distance myself from the squad and the team, then so be it. I'm done making myself miserable trying to be what others expect of me."

"But what about college? If you give up on the squad then..." I trail off, she doesn't need me to spell it out for her.

"What will be will be."

Her cell buzzes on the coffee table, telling us that dinner has arrived.

She jumps up and heads for the door.

"You can't go like that," I say, hopping up behind her.

"Then you can answer the door. Come on."

We make our way through her house. She stands to the side a little as I pull the door open to take our food.

I'm just about to close it behind the guy when her fingers wrap around the wood and she peers outside.

"What's wrong?" I ask, looking out in the same direction as her.

"Do you recognize that truck?" she asks, pointing to a black truck idling at the end of her driveway.

"No, why?"

She waves me off and closes the door when I try to see who's in the driver's seat.

"I'm sure it's nothing. I've just seen it a few times. Probably waiting for a neighbor or something."

Taking the food back out to her pool house, we put all the containers out on the coffee table and sit on the floor to eat.

We have the most incredibly relaxed night, eating, chatting and watching her girly TV. We both steer away from the hard conversations that we'd brushed on previously. Chelsea had a point when she talked about leaving the past where it was. It was time for fresh starts for both of us.

The sun has barely set when I look down to find Chelsea asleep. As smoothly as I can, I slip out from under her and sweep her into my arms. I carry her through to the bedroom and peel back the sheet before dropping her down and crawling in behind her.

She sighs and snuggles her ass back into my crotch as she gets settled.

I lay there for the longest time with her in my arms, thinking about all the things she told me today and trying to imagine what her previous life was really like. Eventually, I find myself drifting off with her and I swear to God, I have the best night's sleep of my life.

24

CHELSEA

The second I wake, a smile breaks across my lips.

Sighing in contentment, I tighten my hold around Shane's waist and snuggle closer.

"Morning," he whispers before pressing his lips against the top of my head.

Unable to resist looking at him, I tilt my head up. His hair is all over the place and he has a pillow crease in his cheek. I'm pretty sure he's never looked better.

"Hey."

"Why do you look so surprised to see me?" he asks, his eyes bouncing between mine.

"Thought you might have changed your mind and snuck out in the middle of the night," I admit.

"You're kidding, right? Why would I leave when I could be curled around you?"

"Many reasons," I say, looking away from his soft eyes.

"Chels," he warns.

"I'm sorry, this... this is just going to take a bit of getting used to. No one usually wants to hang around this long."

"That's because you haven't allowed them to get to know you."

I think about his words. They're true. For the last… well, forever, I've put on this act. Pretended to be exactly what I thought everyone wanted from me, and I've kept everyone at arm's length.

"What do you want to do today?" I ask, wanting to turn the conversation away from me.

"I could do with working out this morning."

"Why? Didn't you get enough exercise yesterday?" I ask with a wink.

His eyes darken before me and my core clenches with need.

Reaching forward, he tucks a lock of hair behind my ear.

"I could go for another day of that kind of exercise." A smirk curls at his lips. "After a real workout. Just because the season is over, it doesn't mean I can get out of shape."

Pushing the covers down to expose his abs, I trail my finger over them and smile when his body flinches beneath my touch.

"Looks pretty impressive to me."

"Oh yeah? I'm not sure how they look will help me with college football somehow."

"If the coach was a woman, it might."

"And you'd be okay with that, would you? Me showing off the goods to get my place."

"Hmm… on second thought."

"Exactly."

"Can I come work out with you?"

"You think you can keep up?" he asks, teasingly.

"Cheer is a sport, you know. I put a lot of hours in to stay in peak condition."

"As many hours as we do?"

Propping myself up on my elbow, I stare down at him.

"I guess we're about to find out."

I don't know why I'm baiting him. I'm sure he could outrun me any day of the week, but I'm not one to back down from a challenge.

"Seems like we are."

He slips from beneath me and sits on the edge of the bed.

"Hey," I complain, rolling over onto my stomach.

Standing, he turns and rips the covers away from me.

"You won't win by laz– fuck, I think I changed my mind."

I glance down at myself. His jersey is hitched up around my waist, exposing my bare ass.

"Oh yeah? Why's that?" I ask innocently, rolling over to my back and parting my knees just slightly.

Shane clears his throat as he stares down at me, his cock trying to break free from his boxer briefs.

"You wearing only my number. Fuck. Do you know how many times I've fantasized about this?"

"Nope. But I think you should tell me all about it." Lifting my hand, I trail my fingertip down my thigh. "Was I just like this?" He watches my movement, his lips parted and his chest already heaving.

"Fuck, Chels."

"Was I totally bare beneath?" I part my legs wider and hook my finger under the hem of the jersey so he can see beneath. My nipples pebble and heat floods my core, my own words and his stare enough to turn me on.

Slipping one hand up my stomach, I make a show of pinching my own nipples and moaning in pleasure. It's over the top but I can't deny that they're not a lot more sensitive since... no. I lock that down. Guilt hits me full force that I'm keeping this little–or huge–secret from him. He deserves to know, but spending this time together, getting to know each other, I don't want it to end and I know that's what'll happen when I admit the truth.

I just need this right now. I need him and I'm too selfish right now to give him up.

"Yeah." His voice is low and husky, it's exactly what I need to help push those thoughts away and focus on right now.

"And did I touch myself like this?" Running my hand back down my stomach, I shamelessly part myself and run my fingers over my clit.

I arch my back and moan, keeping my eyes on him, fascinated by the way the muscle in his neck pulsates.

"Mmm..."

"Did you get yourself off while thinking about this?"

"What the fuck do you think?" he barks before diving forward and ripping my hand away from myself and replacing it with this tongue.

"Oh fuck, Shane," I cry, my back arching for real this time as pleasure races through me.

Before we even leave the pool house to embark on our morning workout session, I already feel like I've run a few miles. My knees feel a little weak and my muscles pull from our earlier activity.

"We'll leave my car at home and run down the beach?" Shane asks as he backs out of my driveway. Mom's car is already gone but that's not a surprise. She and Maddie have probably met for a morning yoga session. I'm sure they're busy gossiping about the fact Shane turned up to see me yesterday afternoon by surprise.

"Yeah, sounds perfect," I say, looking around for that truck but thankfully it's nowhere to be seen.

"You okay?" he asks, obviously noticing that I'm not really with him.

"Yeah, yeah, I'm good."

"If you're worried that you're not going to be able to keep up then all you've got to do is say so, I can go easy on you."

"Shut up. I'll run circles around you, Dunn."

"That right?"

"Just wait and see."

His driveway is equally as empty as mine, confirming my suspicion that our moms are together.

"I'll get changed and then we can head out the back."

"Sure."

I follow him through his house but only once before have I followed him toward his bedroom. That night. The night when all this started and sealed our fate. My hand comes up to rest on my belly.

It was just meant to be a bit of fun. I was bored, lonely and pissed off that Tasha had left me alone to hook up. Tormenting Camila had been the wrong thing to do, so was sleeping with Shane some might say. But I can hardly regret it now. I'm pretty sure that decision might be the best of my life. No matter what happens when I tell him about what we created that night. I can't regret it. Excitement and anticipation swirl in my stomach as I think about what the coming months will hold.

"Didn't think I'd get invited back in here," I say as I take a seat on the end of his bed.

"I didn't think you'd ever be in here in the first place."

"I can understand that."

"You rocked my fucking world that night, you know that?" he asks as he pulls some clothes from a drawer and goes about changing.

"Oh yeah? You weren't too bad either."

"Whoa, thanks for the glowing report."

"I'm joking. You were amazing. I was shocked. I'd have put money on you being a virgin," I say with a laugh, but I soon stop when he stills and looks over his shoulder at me.

"I was," he admits, making my chin drop.

"Fuck off you were. You knew exactly what you were doing," I say like I was an expert that night. I'd only been with Jake before him, and that was forgettable at best. I had such high hopes for my first time and when I got the chance for it to be with Jake, I thought all my dreams were coming true. Well, a drunken, painful fumble wasn't exactly what my fantasies were made of.

I watch as he pulls a clean shirt over his head. "I'm not lying, Chels. You were my first."

"Well, shit." *And what a first that was.*

"Well, your male ego will be pleased to know that I had no idea."

"It wasn't exactly hard."

"I think you'll find it was," I say with a wink.

He chuckles. "What the fuck am I going to do with you?" He walks over to the bed and reaches for my hand.

I stand the second he tugs and our chests brush.

"So I stood up to the guys from your past then?" he whispers in my ear.

"Shane," I say on a sigh. "I told you, it wasn't like that. I'm not like that."

"You're not going to try to tell me that you were a virgin too, are you?"

"Um... no. But I have less experience than you think."

He pulls back and looks into my eyes. He studies me for a moment and I expect him to ask me to explain, but he doesn't. Instead he drops his lips to mine for a brief kiss before he pulls me from the room.

We make our way to the end of his yard and out to an alleyway that eventually leads us to the beach.

We warm up on the dry sand before taking off.

The sun beams down on us and sparkles on the calm sea

to our side. The beach is almost empty with it still being a little chilly despite the bright morning sun.

I breathe in lungfuls of fresh sea air and smile. I really fucking needed this.

When I first discovered I was pregnant, I did a lot of research on what I was and wasn't allowed to do. I was terrified that I'd lose the escape I got when I was working out and that I'd have to give up all my favorite foods. I had no real clue what growing a person entailed, but I was relieved to read that I could mostly continue as normal, for now at least.

My heart pounds as my muscles burn.

Shane runs right beside me, every few seconds he glances over to make sure I'm still keeping up.

He really does underestimate me. What does he think I did when I wasn't barking orders at the squad or partying?

I have no idea how long we run, but eventually Shane slows to a stop.

"That all you got, Dunn?" I ask as he bends at the waist and places his hands on his knees.

He looks up at me, a smile breaks across his face as he shakes his head.

"What?"

"You really are full of surprises, aren't you?"

"I told you. Cheer is hardcore, and I work out... hard."

"So I see."

Standing up straight, he steps toward me. His fingers wrap around my ponytail and tugs so I've got no choice but to look up at him.

He stares down at me, his green eyes sparkling with something I can't quite read.

"I really fucking like you," he admits.

He looks nervous when I don't immediately respond.

"That's good." He lifts an eyebrow. "Because I really fucking like you too."

He seals his lips over mine and kisses the life out of me in the middle of the beach.

"Get a fucking room," a familiar voice calls.

"Fucking hell," Shane mutters against my lips before pressing his forehead against mine. "Sorry."

"I can handle these guys," I say, turning to see who our visitors are. "Morning, Zayn, Ethan." I can't help but laugh at the shocked look on Ethan's face. Fair play to Rae because she clearly didn't share my secret with her boy like I expected her to.

"Should have fucking known you were otherwise engaged when you bailed yesterday morning," Zayn says with a laugh. "Thought you'd fucked it up on Friday night, man."

"It's going to take more than a stupid fucking dare to get to me, Zayn. You should know that by now."

Ethan remains mute as he looks between the two of us like he can't believe what he's seeing.

"I'm sorry but have I walked into the fucking twilight zone or something. You two?" he asks, pointing between us. "You and you?"

Shane laughs as he pulls me into his side and possessively wraps an arm around my waist. I fucking love it.

"Yeh," Shane agrees. "Us two."

"Fucking hell. I thought the most shocking thing to happen this year was me handing Rae my balls. Clearly, I was wrong. Shane Dunn and Chelsea Fierce. Fuck me," he mutters to himself, making us all laugh.

"I'm glad you weren't too hard on him. He was a miserable fuck without you," Zayn says, making me very happy.

"Oh, is that right?" I ask, looking up at Shane.

"And you need to shut the fuck up," he barks back, but the smile on his face counteracts his harsh words. He really couldn't give a fuck about Zayn's teasing.

"So when exactly did this happen?"

"Uh..." I start, not really sure how to answer that.

"She dug her claws in before she went away and left me wanting more."

"And here we all were thinking you hated her."

"Yeah, I kinda did, she can be pretty convincing though."

Reaching up, I twist his nipple, laughing when he squeals like a little bitch.

When I look back to the guys, Ethan is nodding like he's figuring something out. "I guess that makes sense."

"What does?"

"That motherfucker started being our friend after you left. Digging to get information on you. Guess I should have seen straight through it."

"You were otherwise distracted if I remember rightly," Shane points out.

"True that. You do know that the rest of the school is going to have a field day with this, right?"

A ball of dread forms in my stomach at just the thought. But it's not for me, it's for Shane. He's the one who's going to be on the end of the bullshit. Everyone hates me. They're not going to understand why he doesn't.

"It'll be fine," he says with a confidence that I really don't feel.

"Well, we've got your back."

"Thank you, Ethan. I really appreciate it."

"Tell me, did Rae know about this?"

"Um..."

"She's in so much trouble." A wicked smile curls at his lips as ideas form in his head.

"Well, this has been fun and all, but we need to get going," Shane says, releasing me and taking a step forward.

"Do we?" I ask. He looks back over his shoulder at me and winks. "Oh yeah, we do. See you both tomorrow?"

"Already looking forward to it," Zayn says with a smile.

"Zayn, we'd appreciate it if—"

"He won't say anything until you're ready, will you, Hunter?" Shane finishes for me.

"My lips are sealed."

We say our goodbyes before taking off down the beach back toward Shane's house.

We're both silent as we run, but I can't help but wonder if Shane's head is full of thoughts about how we'll handle this once tomorrow and school comes around.

There's no way we're going to keep it secret, we've already been discovered once, it's only a matter of time before it happens again. But I hate to think what kind of backlash he's going to get from this.

I must admit that by the time his house is visible in the distance that I'm more than ready to stop. My legs burn and my muscles ache, but I refuse to let him know that I'm starting to struggle.

"You ready to admit defeat yet?" he asks, getting ahead of me and turning to face me just to show off.

"Never."

He must be able to see that I'm lying but he doesn't say anything, instead he slows to a walk and comes back beside me. He reaches for my hand and tangles our fingers together as we make our way from the beach.

"I think I might have found my new favorite workout partner."

"Oh yeah?"

"You're much better to look at than Zayn."

"I'm glad you think so," I say with a laugh.

His house is still in silence as we make our way back up to his room.

"I need to shower then get food."

"How about you pack some stuff, we get food then shower at mine."

"You mean together?"

"I'm sure that can be arranged."

"Can we get burgers?"

"If you want," I say with a laugh.

"Okay, deal."

I fall back on his bed while he pulls out a bag and starts shoving stuff inside.

"Fancy packing enough stuff for the night?"

He stops and looks my way.

"I like you on my bed," he says, running his eyes down the length of me.

"I prefer you in mine. There's no one who can overhear while I corrupt you."

"I shouldn't have admitted that earlier, should I?"

I'm silent for a moment while I think. "Did I give you all your firsts?"

His cheeks heat, it's utterly adorable, although I don't tell him that.

"Yeah," he admits, not that he needed to, it was written all over his face.

"Mmm... I like that only I've touched you."

"I hate that others have touched you." He looks away and back to what he was packing.

"Hardly," I admit.

He stops immediately and finds my eyes. He wants to ask, he wants to know the truth, but he's scared of my answer.

"There was only Jake, and then you."

His mouth opens and then closes as he takes on board what I've just said.

"But..."

"It's all bullshit. Yeah, I've done more with them than I should," I say with a wince. "But they've not touched me."

"None of them?" he asks, his brows drawing together.

"Just one."

"Jake." He rolls his eyes.

Scrambling from the bed, I come to a stop in front of him and take both his hands in mine.

"Yeah, but let me tell you something." I reach up on my tiptoes and kiss his lips. "You're much better."

He can't fight the smile that pulls at the corners of his lips, and I'm so glad because it knocks me for a loop.

"Oh yeah?"

"Yeah. You might not want to tell him that though."

He barks a laugh and pulls me into his arms. "I know, that's all that matters."

"He was really drunk. It probably wasn't his finest performance."

Lifting his fingers, he presses two against my lips. "I'm glad to know I'm better, but I don't need the details."

"Okay," I say with a laugh, dropping his other hand so he can finish packing.

25

SHANE

I can't lie, knowing that Jake Thorn didn't rock her world makes me feel better about life than I have in a long time. It also helps that half, or more, of the guys I spend time with haven't had a taste of what's mine, like I once thought.

"Why are you smiling at me?" Chelsea asks from the other side of her coffee table.

We stopped off to get burgers after leaving my house and ate them in the front of my car. It's not exactly the kind of first date she deserves, but it was pretty perfect for us. One day soon I'll take her out and treat her right, but not when we're both covered in sweat and sand from our run.

"Just thinking about what you said earlier," I admit with a smirk.

"Wha– oh, I didn't tell you to stroke your ego," she mutters, rolling her eyes.

"Maybe not, but I like it."

"Fucking hell, I've created a monster." She throws her pen at me, but I easily catch it before it connects with my face.

We both continue with our homework, but I can't wipe the

smile off my face, or refrain from glancing up at her where she types away on her laptop every few seconds.

"You're never going to get that finished," she says, without looking up from the screen. "I can feel you watching me."

"Can't help it."

With a sigh, she closes the lid and looks at me. I swear just the sight of her takes my fucking breath away. She's so beautiful.

Color hits her cheeks and she smiles in a way that only a few see. It's unsure and shy and I freaking love it. I love that I can see under the mask, the act, the bullshit. Yeah, she's fucked up, but she knows that. She's opened up and I'm so fucking grateful she has because what I've found inside is exactly what I always hoped was in there. A really sweet, funny and warm-hearted girl.

"So what did you win the other night then?"

Her question confuses me. "Huh?"

"The dare you won when you fucked me, what did you win or get out of it?"

"Uh um... nothing."

"What kind of shit dare was it if there weren't any benefits or consequences?"

"There were consequences, something about the winter formal but I didn't get anything out of it."

"How come? You got me." Her brows draw together in confusion.

"There had to be evidence, or it didn't happen," I say with a wince. She's aware of how the guys act, I'm sure she's been in the middle of their games and tags before now but admitting that she was used in this doesn't make me very comfortable and only points out how wrong their stupid game is and why I've never gotten involved before.

"You didn't get any?"

I swallow nervously. I hate that I caved to their fucking demands that night. I blame the alcohol. "Yeah, I recorded it."

"So show them and get out of whatever bullshit they want you to do." She doesn't even look shocked, which amazes me.

"It wasn't a video, just a sound recording." She nods. "And no fucker is listening to that."

"But—" She starts to argue.

"You're mine, Chelsea. No one gets to hear you like that. I'll take whatever they throw at me, I don't care."

Pushing to her feet, she walks over to me and drops into my lap. She's once again wearing my jersey but thankfully she's wearing a pair of shorts underneath, making it almost possible to look at her without losing my goddamn mind.

She takes my cheeks in her hands and stares into my eyes.

"I don't deserve you."

She drops her lips to mine and I'm powerless but to kiss her back.

All too soon she's standing once again and walking to her kitchen.

"Drink?"

"Soda would be great," I mutter, rearranging myself in my pants.

Sadly, after handing me a can, she retakes her seat at her computer and opens it back up.

"Are you behind after being away?" I ask as she starts clicking around.

"Not really. All my teachers sent work, I spent most evenings doing it. Contrary to popular belief, I'm not actually an idiot," she says it lightheartedly, but I hear the underlying anger in that statement.

"Did I ever say I thought you were?"

"No, but I know what people think of me."

"Good thing I'm not *people* then, isn't it?"

"It really is."

We both get back to what we were doing, well, she does. I mostly stare down at the paper in front of me while my thoughts run at a million miles a minute.

"What changed?" I ask, my thoughts spilling from my lips without permission.

She finishes what she's doing before looking up at me.

"What changed with what?"

"After that first night, you left like I'd set your ass on fire and you ignored me from then on. I just assumed I was shit and that you were disappointed."

"I'm fairly sure I remember you making me cry out your name that night."

"Chelsea," I sigh. "You're the queen of playing the game. I had no idea back then if it was one or not. Seeing as you'd never looked twice at me before, I could only assume it was."

"Honestly," she whispers. "A lot changed." She looks down at her hands that are twisting in her lap. "I made some stupid decisions, and one of them was leaving that night. Going away made me realize a lot of things, and one of the biggest was that I wanted you. It's why I came to you first. Why I sought you out after the game. I needed to apologize. I... I needed you."

She looks up at me, her dark eyes full of honesty and regrets.

"Shane, I—"

Whatever she's about to say is cut off when the door behind me opens.

"Hey, I was just wondering... oh, hello, Shane. I wasn't expecting to see you again."

"We're just doing homework," Chelsea says in a rush.

When I glance over my shoulder to say hello, Honey is looking between us with a weird expression on her face.

"Mom, can we talk... outside."

"Sure, sweetie." Chelsea gets up and ushers her mom outside.

I watch the two of them interact but I'm unable to lip read any of what they're saying to each other, although when Honey points at me it makes it clear who they're talking about.

The conversation gets a little heated before Honey walks back to the house. Chelsea looks to the sky, sucking in a deep breath before reaching out for the handle and pulling it open.

"Everything okay?" I ask the second she's inside.

"Yeah, it's..." She takes one look at me and bursts into tears.

"Shit."

I'm up off the floor and have her in my arms in seconds.

"Shhh, it's okay," I whisper into her hair.

"I'm sorry, I'm just being stupid. She offered to make us dinner. I hope you're hungry."

We spend the rest of the afternoon working before heading into the main house to have dinner with Honey.

It's all very normal. Despite the look I keep getting from Chelsea's mom. I almost expect her to launch into the 'what are your intentions with my daughter' speech but it never comes.

Her eyes are soft as she looks between the two of us, but I can see questions swimming in them. Just like I'm sure everyone will tomorrow when we walk into school together.

The thought alone has my stomach in knots.

I've never exactly been in the spotlight like Chelsea. I might be on the team, but I've spent as much time hidden in the shadows as possible, much to my dad's annoyance. He wanted me to be just like him and my brothers and go after the top spot. Shame he couldn't see that his youngest son was too shy and happy being hidden.

But thanks to the girl beside me, I've spent a few weeks as the topic of everyone's gossip as they blamed me for drugging Amalie all those weeks ago.

Walking into that place with the real culprit on my arm is going to cause a stir, that's for sure.

Ideas for the things people might say, accuse me of, fill my mind but one glance at the girl beside me and I know it's worth it.

Our relationship might not be what anyone expected, it might have come from nothing but games and lies, but there's something so right about it. I don't expect anyone else to understand. They don't need to. All that matters is that we're on the same page, and as she meets my eyes, hers twinkle with delight and I know that we are.

We're us going forward and things can only get better... right?

26

CHELSEA

"Are you sure about this?" I ask Shane who's sitting in the driver's seat of his car beside me.

My stomach turns and I worry I might vomit in the footwell.

I blow out what I hope is a calming breath, but it does little to settle the nerves racing around me.

I'm not worried about me. They can throw whatever they like at me and I'll let it wash over me as if it doesn't sting. I'm worried about Shane. He doesn't deserve what they're inevitably going to say about him because of me.

"Yes, Chels. I'm sure. I refuse to hide this because of those assholes." Reaching over, he laces our fingers together and tugs me over to him.

His lips brush against mine, and I immediately relax.

"How about we just go back to the pool house for the day?" I ask against him.

Hanging out in there together yesterday was so incredible. I'm not sure I've ever felt so relaxed in my own home. Him being there with me was just so natural.

Everything was great until Mom turned up and

jumped to conclusions about Shane's sudden appearance. Okay so they're correct conclusions and she was not impressed when I admitted that I haven't told him the truth yet.

To be fair, I was trying to work up the courage when she interrupted us. I tell myself that if she didn't choose that exact moment to storm in then I would have confessed all. Although, a huge part of me knows that I'm only lying to myself.

I'm living in denial right now because I know once the truth is out that everything is going to change all over again.

This normal we've found is going to be shattered, and I'm terrified of losing him now that I've found him.

Someone knocking on the window scares the shit out of me and causes us to jump apart in fright.

When I turn to the window, I find a smiling Rae looking back at me with an amused looking Ethan behind her.

"Fucking hell, was that necessary?" I ask, pushing the door open.

"Good morning to you too."

I grunt at her as I climb from the car and grab my purse.

"Are you ready for this?" she asks as Shane walks around and takes my hand.

"No," I state.

"It'll be fine. I'm sure you've dealt with worse in the past," Rae says knowingly.

"Me? Yes, it's him I'm worried about."

"He's a big boy and can make his own decisions," Shane mutters.

"Is that right?" Rae looks up at him, wiggling her eyebrows in delight.

"Really?" Ethan barks. "Don't you think it's bad enough that you withheld information about those two from me, now you're checking him out?"

Rae winces. "I'm in trouble." She winks before Ethan lifts her over his shoulder and marches away from us.

"She's really good for him," I say to Shane as we watch her struggle and squeal against his hold.

"It's amazing what the right woman can do, don't you think?"

"You think I'm the right one?"

Tingles erupt within me as he drops his lips to whisper in my ear. "Yep, in all the wrong ways."

As we get closer to the school building, my skin starts to prickle. I don't need to look up to know that we're gathering attention.

"Huh, looks like the newest gossip just arrived," Shane mutters, clearly braver than me and looking around at our growing audience.

Sucking in some confidence, I lift my head.

Every set of eyes in the vicinity is trained on us.

"Fucking hell. This is going to be hell."

"Only if we let it. Come on."

Much to my horror, Shane guides me to where the team and the squad hang out. They're all too busy in their own conversations to notice us at first. But the second Rich looks up, he elbows Justin and in seconds all of them are glancing our way.

"Well, this isn't what I was expecting to see on a Monday morning," Rich announces, ensuring anyone who hadn't noticed turns our way.

Whispered comments filter around us. My heart hammers in my chest as I wait for the first attack to come.

Shane must get bored waiting for any kind of reaction, either that or he just really wants to nail the point home because he pulls on my arm until I have no choice but to step into his body. He threads his fingers into my hair and lowers his mouth.

Just before they brush against mine, he says, "Might as well give them something to stare at."

His lips press against mine and I forget that we're standing here in the middle of the school with almost everyone watching us. His tongue slips into my mouth and tangles with mine as he pulls me tighter against him.

"Well, fuck me. I didn't think Shane had that in him," Justin hollers when he eventually releases me.

Shane chuckles but doesn't look their way.

"Can I walk you to class?"

"I'd love you to."

Leaving our spectators and the comments they make loud enough for us to hear, we turn our backs and walk away.

While I'm with him, they can't hurt me.

"I wish I was in your classes this morning," Shane says, coming to a stop outside my first class of the day.

"I'll be fine." Reaching out, I cup his cheek in my palm, loving that he's worried about me.

"I'll see you at lunch though, yeah?"

"You can count on it."

I nod as he captures my lips in a sweet kiss before turning away and marching down the hallway.

My heart melts as I watch him move. I had no idea I could feel quite this strongly about another person, other than the one I'm currently growing. That thought has my guilt hitting me full force again.

I'll tell him soon, I say to myself as I make my way into the empty classroom with a goofy smile on my face.

As each class passes, I ignore the comments that I was expecting, the gossip that I hear happening around me. It means little to me, my reputation in Rosewood High was ruined all those weeks ago, I just don't want to bring Shane down with me.

For the first time since I came back, I find myself actually eating lunch in the cafeteria. But I'm not at the table I'm used to with the team and the squad, I'm at one I never thought I would be. I look up at Shane and then to his friends who surround us. Camila and Mason are opposite with Amalie beside her and Ethan and Rae next to me.

Camila doesn't hide the fact that's she's not happy about this, and I can't blame her. Knowing she's only looking out for Shane makes me like her that much more. Amalie, however, hasn't really batted an eyelid about my appearance.

She should be the one who's angry at me, much like Mason but it seems they've accepted it for what it was, a mistake, and moved on. I couldn't be more grateful, but that doesn't mean I won't speak to both of them when I get a chance to apologize.

They all chat around me as if my presence by Shane's side is normal. While the rest of the school looked shocked, if not slightly horrified by this turn of events, these guys just seem to roll with it. It makes me wonder if Rae had given them the heads up.

She told me that she and Amalie had seen Shane at the hospital last week and it was how she figured it out, maybe Amalie had similar thoughts.

While the football team mostly ignores us, I feel the cheer squad's attention throughout lunch.

I haven't spoken to any of them since my final run-in with Shelly and quite frankly, I don't have any intention of changing that.

I might not be happy about leaving my squad behind but if that's how it's going to be then so be it. I've got more important things to worry about right now.

I slip my hand into Shane's and squeeze.

Dropping his lips to my ear, his breath makes me shudder. "Are you okay? You wanna get out of here?"

"No, I'm fine. Your friends are nice."

"You've just got to give people a chance, Chels."

I want the ground to swallow me up as how I've acted in the past flashes through my mind. I've been such a bitch.

"I'm just going to the bathroom," I say as I stand, needing to get away and have a moment.

I head for the bathrooms that he chased me to last week, but when I glance back over my shoulder, I find he's not doing the same today, his eyes are firmly fixed on me though, concern laced through them.

I push inside and suck in a deep, calming breath, willing the tears filling my eyes to subside. I really don't need to break down and give anyone any more reason to gossip about me.

I get a few dirty looks from the girls inside, but thanks to my previous reputation, none of them actually say anything to my face. I guess it's one benefit of being known as the queen bitch.

"Hey, are you okay?" a familiar voice asks as I waste time washing my hands.

"Yeah, I just needed a breather."

"You haven't told him, have you?"

Turning, I find Rae's dark eyes and immediately look away.

"Not yet. I'm scared."

She walks over to the mirror and wipes at the dark makeup under her eyes.

"I understand that. But don't you think it's going to get worse the longer you keep it inside. Today must have been huge for him. What he's done for you takes some serious balls. You owe him the truth."

My stomach twists and I lift my hand to it in the hope it stops it. "I know. But what if he hates me?"

"He'll hate you more for lying to him."

"Touché."

"I can't imagine how scary it must be. But you need him. Both of you," she says, glancing down to my stomach.

I blow out a breath.

"I know. I know. Things have just been so... incredible. I don't want to ruin it."

"Who says it will ruin it? Yeah, it's gonna be a shock, but things might be okay."

I like her positive thinking, but I'm a little more realistic about the whole thing.

By the time it gets to the end of the day, I'm just about ready to go home and have a nap while Shane is at practice.

I'm standing at my locker, grabbing the books I need for tonight when a shadow falls over me.

A shiver runs down my spine as I slam my locker and turn on whoever it is that's brave enough to approach me. I might have been the hot topic around school today but at least everyone has kept their distance.

My eyes widen when I find Victoria, Tasha, and Aria standing before me.

"Shouldn't you be at practice?" I ask, pushing away from the lockers and moving for the exit.

"That's what we need to talk to you about."

I pause with my back to them. "Why?" I ask over my shoulder.

"Um... things aren't going so well."

I turn around and look at the three of them. They look nervous and it piques my interest.

"And that's my issue because...? I've been kicked out, remember?"

"Yeah but... we need you."

Something that I can only describe as hope blooms within me.

"You... need me? For what exactly."

"Ugh, cut the bullshit," Aria says, stepping forward. "Shelly was a shit captain. She can't organize shit. Kelly, well fuck knows where Kelly is, she's not turned up to practice since Wednesday and everything's falling apart."

I open my mouth to respond but no words come out.

"Please," Victoria adds. "Come back. We know things are... awkward, but Shelly was the one who didn't want you. We all know that we need you if we're going to stand a chance at regionals. Please, Chels."

"Wow, okay," I mutter in surprise.

"So what do you say?"

The thought of following them and doing what I love most fills me with joy, but then my reality slams into me. I can hardly climb onto a pyramid and be thrown around like I used to.

"I can't cheer," I admit. "After the accident last week, it's not a good idea for me to..." I trail off before I say too much and can be caught lying.

"But you can captain, you can lead us, right? One of the JV girls can take your place. Harley is really good."

"Um..." A smile twitches at my lips. "I'd love to." I try to contain my excitement, but it breaks across my face as they squeal in delight and run at me.

"Shelly is going to be really pissed when she gets back to school," I say as I walk in the opposite direction from where I expected to be going.

"Shelly can fuck off," Victoria mutters. "She doesn't have what it takes to be captain. Her head's gotten so big I'm surprised she can fit in the fucking gym."

I allow the three of them to go ahead of me as I pull my cell out to shoot Shane a message to tell him that I'm not heading straight home. He'd given me his keys so I could drive his car, telling me that he'd get a lift from one of the guys but it seems we're going to get to travel together after all.

The girls are all gathered in the center of the mats when I walk in.

"She said yes," Victoria squeals as they all turn my way.

Delight lights up their faces as I walk toward them and the final piece of my puzzle slots into place. This gym is my home. I belong here, and it's not until right now that I really accept just how much I'd missed it. I might not be able to cheer like before, but that's not an issue. I'm with my squad.

Dropping my purse and books to the side of the gym, I take my place at the front of the girls.

"You guys ready to fucking kill regionals?" I shout, a wide smile on my face as they all start jumping up and down and cheering.

27

SHANE

Chelsea: I'm in the gym with the squad. Meet me when you're done xx

I stare at my message with wide eyes and fear filling my veins. I know that Shelly is still suspended, but nothing good can come of her being with those girls. They pushed her down the fucking stairs for Christ's sake. She can tell me all she likes that Shelly didn't touch her but if it weren't for her, then Chelsea never would have ended up in the hospital like she did.

I dress as quickly as I can after showering off the session's mud and sweat. Our usual practice might be over along with the season but Coach isn't letting up with our conditioning. I'm glad, I need it. Although less so now I've got Chelsea to keep me active.

"You on a fucking promise or something?" Zayn asks as he watches me hop around trying to dress at the speed of light.

"Something like that."

"I hate to say this, but you two are seriously fucking cute together."

"Aw, Zayn. You jealous?"

"Of regular pussy? Hell yeah," he states as I roll my eyes.

"You might meet someone who'll put up with your brand of asshole one day."

"Someone? Nah, I want at least two regulars. One could never keep up with me."

"You're a fucking dog. This is why you have zero regular girls. They're worried they'll catch something."

"You're moody when you need to get laid."

"I don't need…" I trail off, and he laughs. "Whatever. I'm outta here. Not coming to Aces?"

"I'll see if Chelsea wants to."

As I leave, he makes whipping noises behind me. All I do is smile. I fucking love it.

Jogging toward the gym, I pray that I'm not about to walk into some kind of cheer torture scene. But to my surprise, what I find is very much the opposite. Thank fuck.

Music booms around the gym and Chelsea is front and center counting and barking orders at the girls who are somersaulting, cartwheeling, and flying through the air.

She's got the biggest smile on her face and I can't help but share her joy. I have no idea what's happened to get her here again, the one place she wanted to be more than anything but she looks right at home.

"Lock your arms, Aria. If Ruby drops, it's your fault," she barks as the JV wobbles on top of the pyramid looking terrified. "That's it. Better."

I stand and watch them all for long minutes before one of the girls spots me and causes Chelsea to also look my way.

"Hey," she says, bounding over to me and throwing her arms around my shoulders. Her eyes sparkle in delight.

"I wasn't expecting to find this," I say into the top of her hair.

"I know. Isn't it incredible? Let me just finish up with these guys and we can get out of here."

I release her from my hold and watch her lead her squad in a cool down before dismissing them to the locker rooms.

Pride oozes from my chest as I watch her taking back the role that was always meant to be hers.

"Okay, let's get the fuck out of here," she says, walking to me and swiping her purse from the floor.

"Don't you wanna..." I gesture to the locker rooms where the others disappeared.

"I'm sure they can shower without me." She laughs, reaching up and brushing a wet lock of my hair from my face. That's not exactly what I meant, but I'm not going to complain that she's not about to leave me waiting for her.

"The guys wanted to know if you wanted to go to Aces."

"They want me there?" she asks, and I hate that she even has to question it.

"Well, they invited me, I told them that we come as a package."

She smiles up at me. "You don't have to do that, you know. You shouldn't be punished for my mistakes."

"I'm not. I just don't want to go without you. You belong there more than I do."

She looks back to the now empty and quiet gym and lets out a sigh.

"What happened here exactly?"

"I'll tell you on the way. I could really use a burger and milkshake."

The team looks a little hesitant as we walk toward our usual table, that is everyone apart from Ethan who immediately makes sure there's enough space for us to join.

Chelsea gets a few looks that I'm not all that impressed by, but on the whole, the team are on their best behavior, which is unusual. They're too busy planning for winter formal and the party that follows.

It's not until we're joined by the squad and they engage with Chelsea like everything is normal that I start to relax.

Pulling her tighter into my side, I kiss the top of her head and she looks up at me and smiles. My chest aches and three little words that I know she's nowhere ready to hear almost fall from my lips.

My cell vibrating in my pocket thankfully stops any more crazy thoughts.

Mom: Dad's back and wants you here for dinner.

I groan and Chelsea doesn't miss it.

"Everything okay?" she asks, looking up at me with those huge eyes of hers.

I show her my cell.

"Want me to come too?"

My lips curl at her offer but the thought of having her there to hear Dad and I argue about my future isn't exactly my idea of fun.

"I really appreciate that, but I think it's probably best if I do it alone."

"Okay," she says snuggling into my side.

"Do you want a lift home or are you going to hang out with the squad?"

She looks up at them. "I think I'll stay for a bit. Call me later though, yeah?"

"Try and stop me."

Tilting her head back, I sweep my tongue into her mouth, not giving two fucks about our audience.

Hoots and hollers sound out around us but I barely hear any of them. As always, I'm too lost in her.

The last thing I want to do is leave her here, especially to go and spend time with my dad, but I don't really have much of a choice. If I don't go now, then it'll only make it worse.

With one final kiss, I leave her behind. She has a huge smile on her face, so I don't doubt that she's exactly where she wants to be. Ethan winks at me as I look back over my shoulder telling me that he'll keep an eye on her. I never thought I'd happily rely on him for anything, but it's weird how things change.

Dread fills me as I make the short drive home. The closer I get, the more I wish I took Chelsea up on her offer to come with me. She would have made this a little more bearable.

Both Mom and Dad are already in the dining room when I get there, waiting for me.

"What time do you call this?" Dad barks the second I step into the room.

"I got Mom's message twenty minutes ago. I came as fast as I could."

Dad tuts while Mom mutters that it's okay as she rushes from the room, I guess to get the dinner.

"You look like shit."

"Wow, thanks, Dad. It's nice to see you too."

"You need to take better care of yourself if you're—"

"Don't," I warn.

"Oh, you wouldn't believe who I ran into yesterday."

I roll my eyes but keep my attention on my empty plate.

"I did a speech at Penn. Do you know who their new coach is going to be next season?"

"I've got no idea, but I'm assuming you're about to tell me," I mutter.

Thankfully before he can launch into his story, Mom reappears with armfuls of food. Jumping up from the table, I help her lay it all out in the center.

"Kit Anderson," Dad continues as if Mom isn't currently acting like a servant and loading his plate with food. "Can you believe that?"

I shrug, helping myself to some chicken. I'm not hungry after the burger I had at Aces but I know better than to sit here and refuse food.

"He gave me some great insight into who's tipped for the top next year. I've reevaluated our options and I think..." He pauses as he reaches into his pocket and pulls out a list.

"Do we need to do this now?" Mom asks softly.

"It's important, Maddie. Shane's choice now will determine his future career. I have to make the right decision."

And that statement right there just about says it all.

"I know you just want the best for him, but don't you think it should be Shane's decision to make, not yours?"

Dad cuts her a seething look and she pales slightly. Dad's a force to be reckoned with, I think she learned years ago that trying to persuade him in a different direction is pointless.

"He doesn't have all the information. I do."

"He is also sitting right here," I mutter. "You can give me all the information you like, but I'm the one filling out the applications, and I'll apply wherever I see fit." Pushing my chair out behind me, I stand. "I'm sorry, Mom. I'm sure this is delicious, but I'm not sitting here and putting up with his bullshit."

"Shane, get back in here right this second," he barks from behind me as I race from the room and up the stairs.

I pace back and forth in my bedroom as the sound of my parents arguing downstairs filters up to me.

I can't fucking wait to get out of here and start my own life.

Sitting down at my desk, I pull open my bottom drawer and wrap my fingers around the college applications I've been working on. A couple are the same as the ones Dad wants me to apply to, but he's not the reason.

I flick through the brochures for the millionth time, hoping that something will jump out at me and tell me that it's the one. Nothing does.

Part of me wants to get as far away from here as possible, as far away from him as possible. But the other part wants to stay. I could apply to Maddison or Florida U and be close for Mom.

With a sigh, I rest back in my chair. I wonder where Chelsea is planning to go. We might have spent quite a bit of time together over the past few days, but talk about our futures hasn't really come up.

Even thinking about this is crazy. It's only been a few days and here I am allowing thoughts of her future to influence mine.

Unable to resist, I grab my cell from the side and shoot her a message.

It's fucking crazy, but I miss her.

If I thought I had some weird obsession before when she barely spoke to me or looked my way, then I know I do now. She's given me a taste, shown me what she hides beneath the mask she wears, and fuck, I never want to let her go.

28

CHELSEA

I hated seeing the dejected look on his face as he walked out of Aces, but I knew he was right. He needed to deal with his family alone. It's not my place to turn up and play peacekeeper between him and his dad.

My lips curl in disgust as I think about how his dad treats him and what he expects from him. Shane doesn't talk about it much, he doesn't need to. I've seen it with my own eyes over the years, heard his crazy unrealistic expectations. Shane's avoidance when it comes to talking about the future and what college he wants to go to is understandable.

His dad wants him to be the NFL's next big star, but anyone who knows Shane even a little bit can tell that's not who he is. Hell, I knew that even before anything happened between us.

Pushing thoughts of Shane from my mind for now, I focus on my squad as they sit and gossip around me.

The last thing I was expecting was to end the day back in my beloved role as captain, I thought that ship had long sailed but it turned out that I just had to be patient.

"Shelly is back tomorrow," Aria says. "She's not going to be happy about this."

A shiver of dread runs down my spine at the thought. I can't imagine she was too thrilled to be suspended when she didn't so much as touch me last week but it seemed that she was already on Hartmann's shit list and that it was the exact excuse he needed to give her some time out.

I can't really complain. It's been nice without her. I can't help but wonder though if my easy return to the squad is going to be very short-lived. She's going to come back gunning for me, that's for sure.

Our afternoon in Aces is just like old times, only now, I feel like I might actually belong. The squad wants me, whereas before I was sure they just put up with me because they had to, and I now know that I've got someone who's going to stand beside me no matter what tomorrow and Shelly bring.

Nerves flutter in my belly and remind me that those aren't the only differences. In a few weeks, I know I'm not going to be able to hide this secret anymore. I've been lucky this far with keeping it to myself but I know I'm on borrowed time, especially with Shane.

I need to tell him before someone else beats me to it.

"Hey, Chels. You want a lift home?" Ethan asks, dragging me from my thoughts.

Looking up, I find him standing with his arm around Rae. He's not looking at her yet he's got this smile playing on his lips that I don't think existed until she turned up in his life.

"Yeah, that would be great," I say.

After saying goodbye to the squad, I follow Ethan and Rae from the diner.

I'm too busy chatting to them to pay much attention to the parking lot and I jump into the back of Ethan's truck without much thought.

That is until we pull out and I spot that truck again, idling by the exit.

"Hey," I say, poking my head between the two front seats. "You have any idea who drives that truck?"

I know it's a long shot, but I figure it's worth asking because I don't have a fucking clue. I've racked my brain to come up with the answer but other than one possibility that I don't even want to consider, I've got no idea who it could be. They seem pretty interested in me, mind you.

Ethan looks in his mirror as we pull out in front of them and shakes his head.

"I have no idea. Why?"

"No reason," I lie, looking back over my shoulder to see if I can get a look at the driver. Sadly, the reflection of the windshield means I can't see shit other than the sun lowering in the sky.

Sitting back, I cross my arms and blow out a breath.

It's just a coincidence that I keep seeing it, I tell myself. But it doesn't settle the unease that's churning in my stomach.

I try not to look back, knowing that I'll drive myself crazy, but I do. The truck follows us all the way to the end of my street before it continues forward when Ethan signals to turn. He doesn't seem bothered after I pointed it out earlier. But why should he? He's not aware that it's been following me around like a fucking psycho stalker for the past few days.

I breathe a little easier knowing that he's gone as I wave goodbye to Ethan and Rae and slip into the house.

The sound of Christmas music fills my ears and unlike the past few years, instead of groaning, I actually smile.

"Hey, sweetie," Mom says when I poke my head into the living room. "I was hoping you'd be back soon. Want to help me?" she asks, gesturing to the bare tree.

She's been slowly decorating the house since I got back

from the center, but I'm surprised it's taken her this long to tackle the tree.

I was intending on having a shower and starting on my homework, but for once, hanging out with Mom and getting in the festive spirit seems more appealing.

"Sure," I say, dropping my purse to the couch and going to join her.

"Did you have a good day?" she asks as we wrap the fairy lights around the branches.

"Yes, actually." I go on to tell her about the squad.

"You know you probably shouldn't be cheering now, don't you?"

I stare at her for a beat, clearly my expression saying exactly what my words aren't.

"I'm sorry, I'm sorry. I can't help worrying."

"I know what I'm doing, Mom," I say, reaching into the box of decorations and pulling an ornament out.

"Is that why you haven't told Shane yet, because you know what you're doing?" She stops what she's doing and stares at me.

There was no hiding Shane's involvement in this whole thing when he turned up over the weekend and then never left.

"Things are complicated."

"You're telling me."

I let out a sigh and sit on the edge of the couch. "The time we spent together before I went away... it was... I thought it was a mistake. I was lonely, he was there. I don't need to spell that out for you," I say with a roll of my eyes.

"But then I found myself in that place again, and I started allowing myself to reflect and consider what I really wanted, and things started to change for me. The time I'd spent with him, albeit short, it was different. He was different.

"Then I found out about..." I gesture to myself. "And I

knew I needed to do something about it. I didn't for a second think he'd give me the time of day when I got back. I'd dragged him down along with the others I'd hurt. He had every right to throw my attempts at making up for it back in my face. Well, actually he did to start with but..." I trail off, not really needing to go into all of that.

"By some miracle, he forgave me and he showed me the real him and what life could be like if I just let someone in.

"He's..." I pause, thinking of our time together and trying to come up with a word to describe it. "He's been incredible. Everything I never knew I needed but always wanted. I don't know," I say with a shake of my head. "Everything just feels right."

Mom looks at me with soft, tear-filled eyes. "Chelsea," she says, dropping down beside me and taking my hands in hers. "Don't get me wrong, I'm thrilled you've found that in him. He's a really good kid and I don't think I could have chosen someone better for you if I tried. But," she says, and I groan. "You need to tell him. The longer this goes on and he doesn't know the truth, the more it's going to hurt him. If he's the kind of guy you think he is, then he's going to want to know."

"What if he's not that guy?" I ask, terrified of even saying the words aloud.

"If he's not, then you don't need him in your life. You are a strong, *fierce,* young woman, Chelsea. You don't need a man. You are more than capable of doing things yourself."

"I... I know that. Believe it or not, I'm not actually scared of doing this alone if I have to. I just... I don't want to. I know what it's like to come from a broken home, I don't want that." I pull my hand from hers and drop it to my belly.

"You need to trust that he'll do the right thing. And if that's not what you want, then you need to make the best of it. You're going to be an incredible mother, Chelsea. Just don't waste time and risk Shane not being the kind of dad he could be because he's too angry to see what's important."

"You're right." I nod. "I just don't know how I'm supposed to tell him."

"You'll figure it out. I have faith in you."

We spend the next hour finishing up the tree before Mom offers to make us both hot chocolates. I leave her to it so I can go shower and change.

The second I walk into the pool house, I can smell him. Disappointment floods me that he's not here and I pull my cell from my purse. I find a message from him from ten minutes ago.

Shane: I miss you. What are you doing?

Chelsea: Putting up decs with Mom. Did everything go okay?

It shows that he's read the message, but he doesn't respond. Dread sits heavy in my stomach that he's still in the middle of dealing with whatever his dad's got to be throwing at him.

With a sigh, I drop down on the edge of my bed and place my cell on my nightstand, hoping that I'll hear from him again soon.

Pulling the top drawer open, I lift up the notebooks and scraps of paper to find what I'd hidden beneath.

I pull my ultrasound pictures out and stare at my little person. Excitement races through me and I press my palm to my stomach, hoping that they know how much I love it already.

I run my finger over the tiny black and white image, wondering what the baby might look like. If it is going to have dark hair and eyes like me, or light like Shane. If it is going to be a little cheerleader or a football player.

I know I've got so many things to be worried or

apprehensive about but excitement is my overriding emotion whenever I think about what the future holds for me.

Placing my pictures on the nightstand, I push from the bed in favor of stripping off and getting in the shower.

I intend to pull on a pair of sweats and a hoodie and spend the evening chilling out with Mom and some Christmas movie she's sure to find on the TV.

I'm just rinsing the conditioner from my hair when I hear a crash.

My heart jumps into my throat as I think about the truck with the dark windows and beaming headlights.

"Fuck," I mutter, making quick work of finishing up and wrapping a towel around my body, feeling grateful that no one's walked in here with a knife or anything crazy.

With my heart almost pounding out of my chest, I poke my head from the bathroom. But there's no one there.

"Hello," I shout out as I tiptoe to the living area. But when I get there, I find it as empty as the bedroom.

I glance around, looking for something out of place that could have caused the crash, but I find nothing.

Assuming it was just Mom coming to get something, I walk back to the bedroom. Something on the floor by my bed catches my eye. The second I take a step toward it, I know exactly what it is. My ultrasound pictures.

I look around again, although I already know there's no one here but fear skates through me, nonetheless.

Who just walked in here and saw this?

Picking up my cell, I pray that there will be a reply from Shane letting me know that he's still at home.

Please, please, please, I beg silently as I tap the screen.

Nothing.

"Fuck."

Dropping the towel to the floor, I make quick work of

pulling on some clothes, although with how violently my hands are trembling, I'm not very successful.

The second I'm dressed, I grab my cell and car keys and run from the pool house.

"I'm sorry, Mom. I need to be somewhere," I call as I run through the main house.

"Is everything okay?" she calls back from her position in the kitchen.

"I hope so."

She shouts something back, but I'm already out the door, too far away to make out the words.

I don't bother looking around for my stalker, instead I wrench the door open and drop down into the driver's seat.

I fly out of the driveway and in seconds, I'm heading for the Dunn house.

If it was him, there's a very good chance that he didn't go straight home.

Fuck.

My hands tremble against the wheel and my stomach turns over as I think about him finding out like that.

He's going to fucking hate me.

My mouth waters like I'm about to throw up and for a moment I think I'm going to have to pull over so I can do just that. But after sucking in some deep breaths, it passes and I'm able to continue.

The second I turn on his street, I'm craning my neck to see if his car is parked in the driveway.

Please be here. Please be here.

"Oh my god," I cry when I get closer and see the back end of his car parked in the driveway.

Pulling my car to a stop on the street, I rest my head back and close my eyes for a second.

Maybe there was no one there. Maybe it was just my

imagination and I didn't put the pictures on the nightstand like I thought.

I almost turn around and head home, feeling stupid for overreacting. But what if I'm wrong? What if my first instinct was right and he's in there now hating me because he knows my—our—secret.

"Shit, shit, shit."

Letting out my breath in a long exhale, I push the door open and step out.

Walking up to the front door, I knock and wait. But nothing happens despite the fact I can hear voices—raised voices—inside. Hearing an argument in full force doesn't help settle my nerves at all.

Gripping the door handle, I push down to see if it'll allow me inside. Surprisingly, it does.

I silently slip into the house and peer around the kitchen door where the shouting is coming from.

Inside, I find Maddie and Brett barking at each other, arms flailing around in frustration. Moving before I'm caught, I turn for the stairs and quietly run up.

I pass the closed bedroom doors until I get to the one I want.

Okay, here goes nothing.

I push it open and step inside, but the room is empty.

My heart rate increases once more as I hesitantly take a step inside and look around.

I relax the second the sound of running water hits my ears and I turn toward Shane's bathroom.

Steam billows out from the adjoining room and a smile pulls at my lips, knowing that I'm going to find him naked behind that door. Things are definitely turning out better than I was expecting.

Placing my cell and keys on the dresser, I make my way over.

The heat hits me the second I step into the room. It's clear he's been in here for some time. Everything is steamed up and I can barely see him behind the glass door.

He's standing with his face tipped up to the water, totally still.

I make the most of my few minutes to rake my eyes down his sculpted body. He's not as bulky as some of the other guys on the team, but he's no less cut.

My mouth waters as I think about stripping naked and joining him. About running my hands over his smooth, taut skin.

I trail my eyes back up, enjoying my view. As if he knows I'm here, when I get to his chin, his head drops and our eyes connect.

As his eyes widen in shock, something crackles between us.

His lips part in surprise before a smile tugs at one corner.

Reaching out, he cuts off the water and steps out from behind the screen.

His eyes drop from mine to take in my body and my temperature soars.

"Fuck," is all he says before he closes the space between us and finds my lips.

His hands grip my ass as he lifts me and places me on the counter. My knees part and he steps between them, soaking me with his wet body.

His kiss is bruising as he slides his fingers into my still wet hair so he can tilt my face to just the right angle. His tongue sweeps into my mouth, tangling with my own as he claims me.

My hands run down his back, my nails scratching lightly until I find his ass and squeeze. It presses us closer together, his hard cock teasing at my core.

Heat floods me at the thought of him taking me here like this.

"Shane," I moan when he rips his lips from mine in favor of kissing down my neck.

His teeth graze as he kisses and sucks the sensitive skin into his mouth.

His hand finds its way under my shirt and he groans when he finds me bare beneath. His hot touch is a hint of a reminder of the panic I felt as I dressed and left the pool house.

But all that floats away when he pinches my nipple so hard I swear it has me on the edge of release.

"Shane, I need you."

"Fuck, Chels."

Gripping the hem of my shirt, he rips it over my head, throwing it haphazardly behind him somewhere. He continues kissing down to the swell of my breasts as he pushes my already high skirt up my thighs so it's around my waist.

He makes quick work of ripping the sides of my panties so they fall from my body before pulling me to the edge of the counter.

He's in a frenzy of need, but right before he pushes inside me, he rests his forehead against mine and looks into my eyes.

My breath catches at the emotions staring back at me. I can't decipher most of them, but one thing I do know. He needs this right now.

"Fuck me," I demand and he surges forward.

A garbled cry falls from my lips as he fills me in one swift move.

Thankfully, he stills for a beat to allow me to adjust before he pulls out, shifts me forward a little more and thrusts back in.

"Oh god."

I lean back on my palms and watch where we connect.

So. Fucking. Hot.

"Chelsea," he groans, forcing me to look up at him.

His lids are heavy, he's desperate to close them, to allow the pleasure to take him away from whatever it is that's causing the frown lines to crease his forehead.

"I'm here. Take what you need."

His fingers dig into my hips with a painful grip as he pulls out.

"How did you know?" His voice is so low that I almost don't make out the words.

"Know what?"

"That I needed you. Fuuuuck."

He hits me so deep that I lose all train of thought as he slams into me over and over, building me up for one incredible fall.

"Shane. Fuck. Fuck." My head falls back as he keeps going.

The only thing that can be heard is that of our heavy breathing and our skin connecting. The scent of his shower gel gives way to the smell of sex as the heat of the room has our skin slick with sweat.

"Lips. Chelsea. Need your lips."

Dragging my head up, I find him staring at me. His eyes almost black with his need. Sitting up, I wrap my hand around the back of his neck and crash my lips to his.

The new angle is mind-blowing and in only seconds I am racing toward my release.

Our kiss is messy as we try to get as much of each other as we can but soon our need for air as we both fall over the edge halts our movements.

"Oh fuuuuuck," he grates out as his cock twitches violently inside me.

Dropping my head to his shoulder, I fight to catch my breath, but he doesn't let up.

With his fingers once again in my hair, he pulls my head back and finds my lips.

He kisses me like it might be the last chance he gets. It's

wet, dirty, and full of emotion. It's like he's trying to tell me just how he feels, how desperate he is without saying the actual words. I accept all of it because the feeling is most definitely mutual. I may have told Mom earlier that I know what I'm doing. But the truth of it is that I have no fucking idea. I'm on the cusp of something so life-changing that I can't really even begin to comprehend what my future looks like. But being with Shane like this. All of it floats away and I know he needs this just as much as I do right now.

Lifting me into his arms, I wrap my legs around his waist, and he carries me into his bedroom before lowering me to the bed.

He stands back up and stares down at me. His chest heaves as droplets continue to fall from his hair and run down his defined muscles. His cock is hard once again and twitches under my stare.

"How'd you know?" he asks, repeating his question from earlier. "How'd you know I needed you?"

I bite down on my bottom lip, unsure of how to answer that question.

"D-did you come to the pool house tonight?" His brows pull together at my sudden change of topic.

"What? No, I was here. Wishing I was with you."

I can't fight the smile that spreads across my lips.

"Is everything okay?" he asks, clearly sensing that something is off with me.

"Y-yeah." I should come clean. I should tell him everything now.

I open my mouth to say something, anything, but at the same time, he falls on top of me and takes advantage of my parted lips.

"I wanted to come to you. But you were hanging with your mom. Fuck, Chels."

"What happened with your dad?"

"Normal bullshit. I'm not good enough. Will never make it. Need to decide which team I want to play for. He just won't fucking listen."

"Shane," I say, placing my palm on his rough cheek.

"You are good enough. You are more than good enough. You're incredible."

A smile twitches at his lips.

He shakes his head like he can't believe what I'm saying.

"Fucking hell, I can't get enough of you."

He quickly tugs my skirt down my legs and drops it to the floor so we're both bare before he rolls me on top of him.

"Your turn," he says with a wink, taking his length in hand and holding it so all I have to do is sink down.

"Jeez, I'm not your sex slave."

"The position is available should you want y..." His words trail off as I lower down onto him. "Fuck. Will I ever get used to this feeling?"

"I hope not."

I drop down until I've taken every inch of him.

He stares up at me with such adoration, such, dare I say it... love, that it brings tears to my eyes.

"Chels," he says, reaching for my hands and pulling me forward.

His eyes search mine. I have no doubt he can see my threatening tears but like always when I'm around him, I don't want to hide how I feel. My mask is well and truly shed when it's just the two of us. He sees me. The real me. And yet he's still here.

"I know," I whisper. "I know."

"You fucking slay me, you know that."

"The feeling is mutual."

Dropping my lips to his, I cut off whatever his response was going to be. I fear he's on the edge of admitting something he's going to regret when I'm finally brave enough to tell him the truth.

I'll do it after this, I tell myself, once again putting it off.

I move against him, keeping the pace slow this time. Trying to show him exactly how I feel about him with my body instead of my words. I need him to know how real this is, how much it means to me. Words are nothing. They get thrown around all the time. Lies are too easy. But this. This feeling of us together. There is no lie there. It's impossible.

Our tongues slide against one another's as I continue to grind against him. His hands find my hips, attempting to get me to go faster but I resist. I'm in charge this time and I set the pace.

Dragging my lips from his, I kiss across his jaw, sucking his earlobe into my mouth before dropping down his neck.

"So good," I groan in his ear. "Your cock feels so good inside me."

A low growl comes from the back of his throat.

"Do you feel it?" His fingers grip the nape of my neck.

"Every fucking time I look at you. Touch you. Think of you."

"Fuck, Shane," I pant, his words pushing me closer to release.

"You're it for me, Chels. This is it for me. Whatever happens from here on out, college, our futures. It's us, baby. Promise me."

His words make my heart swell to the point I worry it might burst. "It's us. Always."

The first clench of my release hits me and I just start to fall when there's a commotion at the door.

"Shane, I need—fuck." Brett's eyes go impossibly wide as they land on us before he lifts his hands to his hair and spins around. "What the fuck, boy? This is our house. Our fucking house. Get her fucking out of here," he bellows so loud I can't help but wince as I jump from Shane.

"Get the fuck out, Dad."

"What the hell—oh," Maddie says, racing in to see what's going on.

Her eyes land on me and although I register the shock that was in Brett's she looks nowhere near as murderous at finding me here.

"Get the fuck out," Brett barks at me, risking turning around. Thankfully, I'm now wrapped in one of Shane's sheets. He however is still standing naked with just a pillow covering his junk.

"Dad, stop. Don't fucking talk to her like that."

"You are a fucking joke. A fucking joke." He marches toward Shane with his finger pointing at him.

Shame races through Shane's features.

"No," I cry, attempting to run over, but Maddie catches my arm and stops me from getting between the two of them.

"Just go, Chels." Shane's voice is empty, cold, and it makes a sob erupt from my throat.

"No, I'm not leaving you with him like this."

"It's fine. I'll see you tomorrow."

"No. Shane."

It takes a few seconds, but eventually he rips his eyes from his father's and turns them on me.

"Please," he whispers, his eyes pleading with me not to make this harder than it already is.

The tears that were filling my eyes spill over.

"O-okay."

"Here." He throws a shirt at me that's on the chair beside him and after a second, I follow Maddie out of the room.

She shuts the door behind us.

"What are you doing? You need to stop them, stop him," I plead.

"I will. Don't worry about him. I'll tell him to call you."

Not worrying that she's standing before me, I drop the sheet and pull Shane's shirt over my head. His scent relaxes me instantly, well that is until there's a loud crash from his bedroom.

"Go," she says. "Everything will be okay."

I want to scream at her. How is it going to be okay? She saw the look in Brett's eyes just like I did. I want to run in there and drag Shane out with me. But I can't. I'm powerless to do anything but what I'm told.

With a nod, I turn and head for the stairs.

"Chelsea." My name is no more than a whisper.

Turning, I look over my shoulder at her sad expression.

"I'm glad it's you," is all she says before slipping back into the room seconds before shouts erupt and something else smashes.

I race down the stairs, tears streaming down my face as I flee their house. I don't want to leave without him, I want to stand beside him and fight his battles with him, but I know I can't. This is a family thing and I need to back away and let him deal with it in his own way.

I don't realize that I left my shoes on his bathroom floor until I step foot on his driveway and the stones dig into my skin.

"Motherfucker," I spit as I run toward my car.

I fire up the engine and speed away from his house. If I sit out here, I know the temptation to go back inside will be too strong to ignore.

I'm almost back at my house before I notice the lights behind me.

Fire burns in my belly as my grip tightens on the wheel. Now really isn't the time for this asshole.

Unlike earlier, when I turn onto my street, he follows.

Slamming my foot on the break, I bring my car to an

abrupt stop before jumping out and running toward the truck following me.

To my surprise, it slows to a stop in front of my house despite the fact I'm getting closer.

The passenger window lowers as I approach.

"What the fuck is your problem? Why the fuck do you keep following me, asshole?" I scream. I lost control of my emotions about the time I was sent away from Shane's room.

The car is in darkness as I approach but my eyes soon adjust.

"What is it you want from m..." My final word trails off as I look into a familiar set of eyes. "No," I cry, fear like I haven't felt for years filling my veins. "No. No." I stumble back, tripping over my own feet as I run for the house.

This time I don't feel the stones cutting through my skin as I fly around the back of the house and race toward the safety of my pool house.

I fumble with the lock and after what feels like the longest time, I fall through the door. My breaths come in harsh pants as I try to drag in the air I need.

Slamming the door behind me, I run for the bedroom and then through to the bathroom, the door closing behind me with a loud crash.

Those blue eyes are a permanent image in my head.

"No. No. No," I chant as I turn the shower on and drop to the floor beneath the spray.

The water soaks Shane's shirt but I barely notice. I just need the quiet that comes with the water.

It's the only place I used to feel safe. Safe from them.

A shudder runs down my spine.

I thought I'd left them all behind. I thought the men of my past were only in my occasional nightmare now. I had no idea one would be stalking me.

I have no idea who those eyes belong to. I never took the

time to learn any of their names. They were just one scumbag after the other who turned up for my whore of a mother. Some barely looked my way, some looked too hard. Some... my blood runs cold and I fight to keep the memories down.

Nothing good can come from recalling that time of my life. A time when no one cared what happened to me. When they forced themselves on me, thinking they could take things that weren't theirs to take.

Fuck. I want Shane.

Pulling my knees up to my chest, I wrap my arms around them and drop my head to my arms as I try to push away the images that have haunted me for years. It's only been in the past few months that I've mostly rid them from my life.

29

SHANE

"Are you trying to intentionally fuck everything up?" Dad barks, but I'm already tired of his bullshit.

As Mom slips back into the room, hopefully to help calm him the fuck down, I find a pair of boxers and pull them up my legs.

My muscles are pulled tight with anger, and unmoving when all I want to be doing is punching him, is physically painful.

The look on Chelsea's face as I sent her away haunts me. I didn't want to hurt her. I just needed her away from this, from him.

Dragging on a pair of sweats, I pull a clean shirt from my drawer and grab a bag.

"Are you even listening to me?"

I don't give him so much as an acknowledgment, and it only adds fuel to his already raging fire.

"Brett, that's enough," Mom tries soothing as I begin shoving clothes into the bag, preparing to leave.

Sadly, her words have little effect on him.

"So is that it then? You're going to throw away a chance at everything for a pair of tits and a nice ass?"

I turn on him, fire burning through my body to retaliate. It would be so easy to lash out. But that would make me as bad as him. And I'm nothing like him.

"That would involve me having something to throw away. I don't want it. Any of it. How many times do I need to say it before it registers in your dense head? I'm not throwing away anything for her. She *is* my future."

His chin drops. "That's bullshit. You're eighteen, you don't know what you want."

"And you do? How could you possibly know what I want?"

"Because I know best," he roars.

I don't think he expects me to laugh, but that's exactly what I do. His fists curl at his sides as his frustration gets too much to take.

"Go on, old man, hit me. See if it helps knock some sense into me," I taunt, taking a step toward him so I'm right in his face.

"Shane, stop," Mom begs. She knows as well as I do that Dad has a temper that can snap at any moment.

"Why? I think it's time we saw him for who he really is. Come on, show me how much of a disappointment I am."

His teeth grind as I prepare for the pain I know is coming.

Only it never does.

After long seconds, he takes a step back.

"Fucking pussy," I mutter, turning around and swiping the bag I'd haphazardly packed.

"Where the fuck are you going?" he barks at me.

"Someplace where someone wants me. The real me. Not the one they're forcing me to be."

With that, I storm past Mom, who sobs as I leave and race through the house.

The moment I'm in my car, I allow myself to breathe and take a moment to think about what just happened.

"Motherfucker," I scream, slamming my hands down on the steering wheel.

A huge part of me wishes he would have hit me, just so I could retaliate. Hell knows I've wanted to a million times over the years.

Once my hands have stopped trembling enough to start the car, I back out of the drive with my chest heaving and one thought in my mind.

I need her. I need Chelsea.

I tell myself it's to make sure she's okay. But I know that selfishly, it's more for me than her.

She gives me a calm that I don't feel all that often, especially not at home. I need it. I need some kind of sign that this bullshit is going to come to an end. I need to have some hope that I'm going to be able to make my own choice and not be my dad's puppet to do with as he wishes for the rest of my life.

The journey to her house only takes minutes and before I know it, I am pushing my car door open and jogging around the side of the house with my bag in hand.

I have no idea if she wants me here, but there's no fucking way I'm staying in that house and allowing him to rip me in two. I've put up with it for long enough.

I'm eighteen. I can do what I fucking want.

The pool house is in darkness and I worry that maybe she's not here. But where would she have gone? She left wearing nothing but my shirt.

When I get to the door, I find it ajar and it has my already racing heart picking up speed once again.

"Chelsea?" I call, pushing it open and stepping inside.

I make my way to the bedroom, dropping my bag to the bed as I pass.

A sliver of light from the bathroom and the sound of water running indicates where she is and a little excitement starts to push away the anger that's still running rampant.

Wrapping my fingers around the door handle, I push, expecting it to open and be met by hopefully a naked and wet Chelsea. Only, when I push, the door doesn't move.

I try again, thinking it's stuck and a swear to God a scream of fear comes from the bathroom.

"Chelsea?" I ask, concern snaking through my veins. "It's just me. Are you okay?"

Movement sounds come from inside before the lock clicks and she cracks the door open.

She's soaking wet, her hair stuck to her face, her makeup running down her cheeks but I can see from the redness of her eyes that it's not from the shower.

I drop lower and see that she's still in my shirt and that it's soaked through.

Pushing through the door, I take her in my arms.

She's ice cold and shivers against my hold.

"What the hell, Chels?"

Holding her tight, I walk us to the shower. As expected, when I put my hand under the water it's freezing cold. What the hell happened? This can't be because of my dad, surely.

Turning the shower off, I lead her from the room, grabbing a towel on my way out.

She clings to me as if I might disappear any moment. Her slim body trembling against mine, her wet through shirt, soaking my own.

"I'm just going to set you on the bed."

Thankfully, she releases me and drops down when I encourage her to do so.

I make quick work of peeling the wet fabric from her body and dropping it to the floor. I dry her off, squeezing the water from her hair before finding my discarded jersey tangled in the sheets and pulling it over her head.

"Get in," I say, nodding to the bed and she scrambles to do so, quickly covering herself.

I shed my clothes and climb in with her, pulling her cold body to mine and wrapping myself around her like a blanket.

She trembles in my hold, as she fights the tears I know are threatening.

"It's okay," I say, holding her to me as tight as I can.

She shakes her head, her breathing ragged as she tries to get control of herself.

She's silent for the longest time and although it kills me not to ask, not to know what's wrong with her, I know she needs this.

Hell, I need this.

Dropping my nose to her hair, I breathe her in. Reminding myself of why I came here. Why being here with her means so much to me.

I think back to the connection between us before we were interrupted and tonight went to hell. My heart swells as I remember the look in her eyes as she stared down at me. I remember the heat that raced through my veins as she told me she felt it too. I mean, I knew, I feel it in her touch, see it in her eyes but to hear her admit that I'm not the only crazy one here felt fucking amazing.

I'm so lost in my thoughts that when she finally breaks her silence, it takes me a second to register her words.

"That truck... the one that's been following me..."

Every muscle in my body tenses as I wait to hear what's coming next. Did he stop her? Has he hurt her?

"He's a man from my past." Her words are so quiet, muffled against my chest, that I hardly hear her. "One of my birth mother's... v-visitors."

My body jolts at her words. I remember all too well the

things she told me about her past. She didn't go into detail, understandably, and I was happy to allow her the time she needed to tell me, if she even wanted to.

"I-I..." She blows out a breath. "I don't remember which one he is exactly. They all kind of blurred into one. But I remember his eyes. They're so bright, I always used to think they were fake." She pulls back from me a little and looks up to me.

Her large, dark eyes are red-rimmed from crying and the sight is like a baseball bat to my chest.

"Did he..." I trail off, not able to say the words to form the question I need to ask.

"I-I don't know. Like I said, they all blur into one. Some of them were more interested than others. Some of them were even nice to me, but I was so young and stupid. I can't distinguish which was which from my memories. The good fades away and only the darkness stays with me."

"Fucking hell, Chels." I pull her back into my arms and hold her tight.

"How did he find me?" she whispers.

"I don't know, baby. But nothing's going to happen to you. I promise you."

She blows out a shaky breath before looking up at me again.

"How'd it go with your dad?"

"That doesn't matter right now."

"It does. This isn't just about me and my past, Shane. I want to be here for you too."

"I know and you are This," I say, squeezing her tight. "Is all I need right now."

"All you need?" She raises a brow and her usual sparkle begins to come back.

"You're in my arms. What more could I need?"

She smiles, but it doesn't meet her eyes like it usually

would. I hate that something from so long ago, a lifetime ago, can cause her this much pain. I'd do anything to take it away but as I lie here holding her to me as tight as I can, I know there's nothing more that I can do.

Silence falls around us and eventually, her breathing evens out and I know she's fallen asleep.

I smile to myself, knowing that she feels safe enough to do so, and I know in that moment that I made the right decision tonight. Coming here and leaving that cunt behind was the right thing to do. I'm not sure I've ever said truer words in my life than when I told him that Chelsea was my future, and tomorrow I intend to tell her.

It's time we stopped thinking about the past, about the nightmares and the mistakes and start looking forward to our future together because that's exactly how it should be.

"No. Don't touch me. No."

Chelsea's fear-filled cries startle me awake seconds before her elbow connects with my eye socket.

Ignoring the pain, I push myself up on my elbow and stare down at her. There's a deep crease between her brows as she thrashes about, fighting her nighttime demons.

"Chelsea, it's okay," I say, taking her face in my hands. "It's just me. You're safe."

Her eyes fly open, finding mine immediately. It takes a second, but the fear filling them starts to subside.

"Shane," she says on a sigh before her eyes close once again and she falls back to sleep.

This is repeated over and over as the minutes tick by.

It feels like every time I begin to drift off to sleep, she's crying out in terror.

By the fourth or fifth time, I decide it's time to wake her to drag her from her nightmares.

"Chelsea, Chelsea." I repeat until her eyes flicker open once more. "Hey," I say softly, leaning down to brush my lips against hers.

"Shane?" she asks, sounding confused.

"Shhh... it was a nightmare. Everything is okay. I'm right here," I soothe, my lips brushing against hers.

Slipping my hand under the hem of my jersey that she's still wearing, she noticeably relaxes against me.

"Make it go away. Shane. Please." Her plea guts me, fucking slays me.

"Anything." Sweeping my tongue into her mouth, I move my hand up her ribs until I find her breast. Her nipple is already pebbled for me and I pinch it, making her gasp into our kiss.

I tease her with my hands and lips until she's moaning, writhing and begging for more.

When I can restrain myself no longer, I settle myself between her thighs and slide myself into her.

We both moan as I move so slowly and gently inside her.

"Better?" I groan against the soft skin of her neck.

"Yes. More, Shane, give me more."

Lifting her hands, I take both her wrists in one of mine and stare down at her.

A tear trickles from one of her eyes and it wrecks me. Reaching out, I wipe it with my thumb.

"Shane, I..." She hesitates and I shake my head slightly. She doesn't need to talk right now. "I think I've fallen in love with you."

My breathing catches and I swear that my heart stops in my chest. The world around us ceases to exist as I stare down into her dark, haunted eyes.

"Chelsea, I—"

"No," she says after slipping one hand from my grasp and

placing her fingers against my lips. "Don't. Not just because I did."

My eyes plead with her, but I know she's right. She's not ready to hear the words, especially straight off the back of her admitting it.

"Fucking hell, Chelsea."

Dropping my lips to hers I kiss her as deep as I can, trying to put everything I feel into my actions.

No sooner have we found our releases than we fall back asleep in each other's arms. Thankfully, the next time I wake, the sun is shining through from the living room and Chelsea's stare is burning into me.

Cracking an eye open, I look to the other side of the bed.

"Morning," I croak when I find her staring back at me like I was expecting.

"I thought it was all a dream," she says softly.

I shake my head. "Sadly not."

She blows out a long breath. "What are you going to do about your dad?"

"No idea. Quite honestly, I don't care."

"But college."

I shrug. "I'd rather not go than have my life dictated by him."

"What about you?" I ask, thinking about my crazy thoughts for the future yesterday.

"I don't know. I've applied a ton of places, have a shot at a scholarship at a couple. But..." she sighs, looking nervous all of a sudden. "After school, can we... talk?"

My eyes bounce between hers, trying to read what she's not telling me.

"Chels?" I pull her toward me, hoping that she'll say something to squash the lump of dread that's just formed in my belly.

"It's okay, I'm not ending this or anything. I just think we need to talk about the future."

"You mean where we go to college."

"Yeah," she says, looking away from my eyes. "Stuff like that."

Her words don't make me feel better and I almost suggest that we blow off school and just do the talking now. But knowing that's not going to help at all with my dad, I drag my exhausted body up until I'm sitting back against her headboard and pull her onto my lap.

"Whatever you need, baby."

30

CHELSEA

The lingering fear from my recurring nightmare clings to me as Shane and I get ready for school. The nerves fluttering in my belly about the conversation we need to have later help to distract me but the revulsion I remember all too well from their touch refuses to leave me.

"Everything's going to be okay," Shane says as we walk hand in and around my house to find his car.

Every muscle in my body is pulled tight as I wait to see if *his* truck is going to be there.

Some movement at the window in the living room tells me that Mom is aware that Shane's here once again and he's the reason I ran like I did last night.

Thankfully, when we get to the front of the house, there's no sign of him.

I breathe a sigh of relief and drop down into Shane's passenger seat.

He's right. Everything is going to be okay.

By the time we're pulling into the school parking lot, I almost believe myself. Shane will accept what I have to tell him and we can continue on as we have been with our shared little secret for now and the guy will just disappear as fast as he appeared now that he's seen me.

It's wishful thinking, I know, but it's all I've got right now.

"Looks like we're still hot gossip, baby," Shane mutters as we walk toward the main building to go to our lockers.

My skin prickles as all eyes burn into us. It's much the same as yesterday morning but if anything, everyone is even more intrigued.

I really thought something else would have happened by now to take the heat off us. Someone does something stupid every hour here at Rosewood High. None of are hot gossip for all that long.

Students whisper things to each other as we pass but I don't make out what they're saying.

"What the hell is going on?" I mutter. Sensing that I don't need an answer, Shane continues walking silently beside me.

We step in through the open doors and I get my first look at what has everyone talking and my world falls out from beneath me.

Pinned to every locker and every available surface are posters with an image I'd recognize from a mile away.

The words start to blur before me as reality hits.

Who's baby Fierce's daddy?

The world spins around me and as Shane drops my hand, I feel like I'm going to be swallowed whole.

No. No. No. This is not happening.

It's like I'm in a dream and watching this whole thing play out as all eyes burn into me and kids laugh and gossip.

"Tell me this is a joke." Shane's voice breaks through the haze, it's rough and deep and I know that if I were to turn around and look at him the expression on his face would devastate me.

This wasn't how it was meant to happen.

"Um..." I stare at the image of our baby that surrounds me.

My little secret out in the world for everyone else to look at.

That should be mine—ours—not all of theirs.

My breaths start to increase as I try to make sense of all of this and what I'm meant to say to him with everyone watching us.

"Chelsea," he warns, his voice telling me that he's on the verge of losing his shit, but as I open my mouth to respond nothing comes out, instead my knees buckle and I begin to drop.

"I've got you," a familiar friendly voice says in my ear as large hands grasp my upper arms. "Let's go. Dunn, you too." I'm pushed forward before we halt for a second. "Get fucking rid of all this." People start moving behind me as paper starts ripping and getting wadded up.

"Wait," I cry, stepping forward to pull one of the posters from the wall. I stare down at my baby.

I'm so sorry, I screwed this up.

I squeeze my eyes shut, praying that I can keep the tears at bay, for now at least.

Ethan directs me toward and empty classroom but just before we walk through the door, someone steps from the crowd with a triumphant smile on her fake face.

"You," I bark, staring into the evil eyes of a girl I once trusted.

Shelly smiles back at me sweetly as if she has no idea what I could be accusing her of.

"You need to watch your fucking back."

Her smile doesn't falter, and it only serves to irritate me further.

All she does is laugh before she slips back into the crowd and disappears.

Anger races through me and I fight to pull away from

Ethan's grip to run after her, but he refuses to release me and instead directs me to the classroom.

I have no idea if it's just the two of us or if Shane followed orders, but as I stand there staring at the ultrasound picture, I'm too scared to turn around and find out.

The door opens and then closes behind me and the tension grows.

Losing the fight with my tears, they spill over as I continue staring at the ultrasound. I've done all kinds of unmentionable things over the years, but this makes me feel totally violated. This is my baby. Mine. No one should have the power to spread him or her all over the school. This image is mine to look at, mine to choose who I show.

A sob erupts and I lift my hand to cover my mouth in the hope it keeps more down.

This is what she wanted. Me broken. I refuse to allow her to see it happen.

"Chelsea?" His voice is weak, rough, and full of emotion.

"Oh god," I whisper, looking up at the ceiling in the hope of finding the right words.

"Is it true? Are you... is that... fuck."

Turning to look at him, I gasp at the tortured look on his face. His eyes are wide, staring right at me as he tugs at his hair.

Our eyes lock and his shoulders tense even more. He doesn't need my words. He knows me enough by now to read it in my eyes.

"I'm so sorry."

His hands drop as his body turns rigid. His lips press into a thin line and his eyes harden. If the situation wasn't what it was, I'd say it was hot, but that's the last thing on my mind right now.

He takes a step forward and I have to fight not to retreat. I know he won't hurt me but my need to escape just in case almost gets the better of me.

"Whose is it?"

My chin drops. Of all the things I was expecting him to say, that wasn't it.

"W-what?"

"I said... Whose. Is. It?" His eyes drop from mine, pure disgust dripping from them as he stares down at my stomach.

"It's yours, Shane."

A bitter laugh falls from his lips. "You really expect me to believe that?"

"Uh... ye—"

"You're nothing but a fucking whore, Chelsea. That could be any one of the teams', and you know it. Hell, you've probably been through the fucking chess club and the band for all I know."

"What? No," I cry. "It's yours. It can only be yours."

"Bullshit. Everyone knows what you get up to. All the guys on the team brag about what you let them do. You're a fucking liar."

His cold words rip me in two. He has every right to be angry, I know that. But the person standing before me isn't my Shane. He's cold, cruel, evil.

I did this. I turned my soft, sweet guy into this monster. All because I was too weak, too afraid to tell him the truth.

"W-what I said was true. There's only been you and Jake."

"So it's his then."

"No, that was too long ago. It was that night, Shane. That first night."

"We used protection," he spits, as if that makes it a sure thing. I'm growing the evidence right now to prove otherwise.

"It happens," I say with a shrug.

"You're fucking unbelievable, you know that? I can't believe I've fallen for your lies and bullshit. I can't believe..."

He trails off, his hands returning to his hair as he spins away from me.

When his eyes come back to mine, the sparkling green I'm used to is gone, they're dark and empty.

"You promised me the games were over. But you've been playing me this whole time."

He reaches out and swipes the contents of the teacher's desk to the floor before storming toward the door.

"Shane," I cry. "Please. I need you."

He looks over his shoulder and for the briefest second, I think I've got him. Then his eyes drop from mine once more before he says. "You should have thought about that before lying to me all this time." And then he's gone.

I stumble back, lose my footing and crash to the ground in a heap.

When I open my eyes, I find two concerned sets staring back at me.

"I'm so sorry," I whimper.

"Let's get you out of here."

Ethan and Rae each take one of my arms and together they lift me from the floor.

There are still hordes of students filling the hallway, all waiting to witness the fallout from this no doubt.

"All right douchebags, the show is over," Ethan bellows the second he emerges and the majority of the students scatter.

Looking around, I notice that almost all the posters have disappeared and the second we step outside of the building, I discover why. Jake, Amalie, Mason and Camila stand at the benches with their hands full of them.

The four of them rush over when they spot us.

I wince, waiting for the backlash from them but all they do is give me small sympathetic smiles.

To be fair, nothing they could say right now could make me hate myself more than I already do.

"We thought that maybe you'd want to dispose of these," Amalie says softly, handing over her stack of posters.

"T-thank you." I look from her to Camila. "Will you find him, please. Make sure he's okay. It wasn't meant to happen like this."

They both nod.

"Come on, we're taking you home."

Ethan and Rae gently push me in the direction of the parking lot but before we're out of earshot of the others, I stop and turn around.

As expected, I find their eyes on me.

"I..." I hesitate, not really wanting this to be the way I say the words but feeling compelled to express just how much he means to me. "I really love him. Please, please tell him that."

I sob as I turn around and accept the embrace that Ethan gives me as we walk. Rae slips her hand into mine.

Their support right now means everything to me. But they're not who I want.

A parking space two spots down from Ethan's taunts me.

He's already left.

The emptiness that I was already feeling as he blew through that door threatens to engulf me.

I press my hand to my chest as the ache radiates from it.

"I... I need to find him. I need to explain."

Ethan and Rae exchange a look.

"We're taking you home, Chels. I think you need to give him some space."

"But I need to explain."

"We know you do, but right now, you need to let him cool down and you need to take a breath."

I nod, knowing they're right but hating it at the same time.

The drive back home passes me by in a blur.

All I can see is Shane's devastated, furious face.

I need to fix this. Only, I have no idea how.

31

SHANE

I don't see the students who are eagerly waiting for something to happen as I storm from that classroom.

Things are shouted. Accusations are made but I don't hear a single one.

Blood rushes past my ears so fast that just a buzzing fills them.

Out of the corner of my eye, I spot Jake, Amalie, Mason, and Cami furiously ripping the posters from the lockers and walls.

Amalie spots me over her shoulder and runs to me.

"Shane, are you okay?" Looking from her concerned eyes to the posters in her hand, I reach out and snatch one. The rest flutter to the ground but I don't stop to help her pick them up. All I can think about is getting out of here. Getting away from the gossip, the prying eyes, the knowing looks.

I didn't give a fuck when I walked in with her on my arm yesterday. It was what I wanted. They could tell me whatever they wanted, give me all their bullshit opinions. As far as I was concerned, she was everything I wanted.

But now... I've just had exactly what they all expected rubbed in my face.

How can this even be true? How could she have kept something so huge from me?

Pulling my keys from my pocket, I jump in my car and start the engine the second I'm inside. I need to get away from here right now.

I can't deal with all of them, and I certainly can't deal with her right now.

My head spins as I drive and I have no clue if I run any lights or almost kill anyone at the intersections I pass through. I have no fucking idea how but somehow I manage to get myself to the beachside parking lot by Aces in one piece.

The piece of paper on my lap flutters and catches my eye. Any chance I had of this being a really bad joke stares back at me.

Grabbing it once again, I shoulder the door and climb out.

I'm on the sand in seconds and I take off running until I find a secluded dune in the distance.

It's only then that I stop, fall to the sand and hold the poster up in front of me.

The wording at the top taunts me and I make quick work of ripping it off and stuffing it into the soft sand beside me.

I don't need a reminder of the doubt over this. I don't need a reminder of the person almost everyone else thinks Chelsea is.

Or is she?

"Fuuuuuck," I scream into the surrounding silence.

I'm so fucking confused.

Is this a game? Has she been playing me this entire time? My heart constricts as I even think about that possibility. Everything felt so real, so raw. When she told me last night that she loved me... fuck.

My fingers tighten on the paper and it crinkles in my hold.

With my heart pounding and my head warring, I look down at the image on the paper.

My breath catches as I focus on the small black and white person in the middle.

"Fucking hell."

A ball so fucking huge clogs my throat and my eyes burn.

Is this mine? Did we fucking do this?

My hands tremble as my eyes remain locked on the small person before me.

Everything is so clear, I can make out all the important parts.

Then I spot the date printed in the corner.

Last Tuesday.

I think back to my visit to the hospital to make sure she was okay.

Did she know then?

Has she known all along?

Is that why she sent me away?

My teeth grind as all these questions fill my head.

Only one person can answer all of them. But right now, the last thing I want to do is look at her.

I'm fucking terrified. Although I'm not sure of what.

Her telling me that this is real. That it's mine and that our lives are about to change forever. Or that it's not, and it's someone else's.

That thought is like a knife straight through my heart.

I want to believe her. That she's only been with me, that it can only be mine. But for years the evidence has pointed toward her being much less innocent. Should I believe her, or the gossip from the locker room?

Falling back on the sand, I use the paper to block the sun as I continue to stare at it.

If this is mine, if this is really happening, what does that mean for my future? A future that was already up in the air and surrounded by arguments and disagreements. What's going to happen now?

I lie there for hours running everything over in my head again and again desperately trying to come up with answers that continue to elude me. Only one person holds the answers, and I have yet to decide if I can trust anything that comes out of her mouth.

Eventually, clouds gather overhead and everything darkens, much like my mood.

Knowing I need to move before I get soaked, I carefully fold the paper and slide it into my pocket before climbing to my feet.

Every step is hard work as I make my way back down the beach.

My stomach grumbles as the smell from Aces hits it telling me that it's now long past lunch.

What happened to Chelsea? Is she still at school lapping up the attention from all of this? Something tells me that she's not.

A huge part of me wants to go and find her, to see if she's okay, to hear her out. But then I remember everything, and I change my mind. She might just fill me with more lies. How am I supposed to know?

"Shouldn't you be at school?" Bill chastises when I walk inside the diner and take a seat at one of the stools at the bar.

"Yep." I don't even bother trying to hide the truth.

"Everything okay?"

"Oh yeah. Perfect. That's why I'm here in the middle of the day," I mutter.

His eyes widen at my attitude. He's used to getting shit off the rest of the guys, but not from me.

"You want to talk about it?"

"Not really. Just a girl."

"Isn't it always?" He chuckles. "What did you do?" I look

up at him and he must read the truth in my eyes. "Oh, what did she do?"

"Made me trust her."

"Ouch." He must know who we're talking about. He was here last night while she sat beside me with my arm wrapped around her. "Maybe things aren't as they seem."

"Yeah, maybe. Any chance of takeout?" I ask, already fed up with talking about this.

"Sure thing, you want your usual?"

"Please."

Thankfully, Bill takes off to place my order before a group of what looks like college kids pour through the doors and take him away from me.

The second my food is ready, I'm out of there.

I eat it in the car while the rain pours down around me.

I watch as the small rivers of water pour down the windshield and I can't help but compare their descent into nothingness to my life.

I'm drowning right now. It was bad enough with just the bullshit with my dad, but now this.

Fuck. I don't know which way is up.

I should probably drive home but the thought of bumping into that asshole puts me off immediately. I told him that I was done last night, that I chose Chelsea. Now look at me.

Starting the car, I head for a house that I hope I'll be welcome in and will give me the escape that I need.

The driveway is empty but I abandon my car nonetheless and walk around the back.

As always, I find a key hidden under a plant pot in the back yard and I use it to let myself in.

Knowing where the alcohol is stashed in this place, I swipe a bottle of Jack and make my way toward the den.

The guys are at practice, so I've probably got a little while longer with my own fucked-up thoughts before I get hit with a barrage of questions. I can only hope that when he gets home that he's alone. I can't be dealing with a team gathering this afternoon, that's for sure.

By the time I have company, half the bottle is gone and I'm half passed out on the couch with music pounding around me.

"Jesus fucking Christ, Shane," Zayn says, walking in, turning the music down and ripping the bottle from my hands.

"What?" I slur. "I couldn't stay there."

"I wasn't suggesting you could. I was also wasn't thinking that breaking into my house was the best idea either. If Mom came home first—"

"Did she?"

"Well, no, but—"

"But nothing. Give me that back."

"What the fuck are you doing?"

"Getting wasted and forgetting my problems. What does it look like I'm fucking doing, asshole?"

Zayn drops down on the coffee table in front of me, the bottle hanging temptingly from his hands.

"And what good is it going to do?"

I blow out a breath. "It's making me feel better."

"Do you think you should be sorting this shit out?"

"Talk to her? No thanks." An unamused laugh falls from my lips. "She's a lying fucking cunt."

Zayn's brow rises. "You really believe that?"

"I don't fucking know what to believe." Pushing from his couch, I stumble over to the floor to ceiling windows that showcase his back yard. "I've spent years listening to you guys talk about being with her. Then she tells me that she's not really been with any of you and that it's all lies and bullshit." I fall silent for a moment. "Have you fucked her?"

"No," he states, although I can make out a little guilt in his eyes.

"She's sucked you off though I'm assuming."

He hesitates for a second, and that slight pause is all the answer I need. "Motherfucker," I shout, slamming my palms down on the glass before me.

"It was ages ago, Shane. And it meant nothing. We were both drunk, one thing led to another."

"Did you touch her?"

"W-what?"

"Did. You. Touch. Her?"

"Uh... no. I k-kissed her," he admits with a wince. "But that was it. I fucking swear to you."

Although I'm fucking mortified, he's just admitted to having his cock and tongue in her mouth, I must say I'm relieved it didn't go any farther.

"Shane," he sighs. "As far as I know, none of the guys have actually slept with her."

"Bullshit, it's all they brag about."

"Yeah, exactly. Brag about. Justin's the fucking loudest but I know for a fact that's bullshit."

I spin to look at him so fast that the room moves around me. "Fuck," I bark, grabbing my head in the hope it stops the spinning.

"Why does it even matter? Even if she has slept with the entire team, which she hasn't," he quickly adds. "All that's in the past. I've seen the way she looks at you, man. She's never looked at any other fucker like that. Well... other than Jake, but that's old news. He's so fucking smitten with Amalie that he's never going to see his balls again."

Falling back down on the couch, I rest my elbows on my knees and hang my head.

"She's fucking pregnant, Zayn," I admit out loud for the first time. "She's growing a baby. A fucking baby."

"So I heard."

"This is so fucked up."

I look up at him. His usual easy-going smirk is long gone as he stares back at me looking deadly serious. It's an unnerving look on him.

"So what are you going to do about it?"

Reaching for the remote, I turn the volume back up and reach for the bottle he's placed beside him. He doesn't even try to stop me this time.

I lift the bottle to my lips and fall back on the couch.

"I'm going to get fucked up."

"Fair enough. I just so happen to have the exact thing you need."

Standing, Zayn reaches into his pocket and pulls out a blunt quickly followed by a lighter.

Lifting it to his lips, he lights up and takes a pull.

I know the rules of this house, and I know he's breaking the biggest one by doing this but I'm so relieved to have his support right now and so desperate for the escape that I don't say a word.

He passes it over and I waste no time in taking a hit.

I've only done it a few times. It's not something I want to make a habit of, but desperate times call for desperate measures.

"All right, calm down. You're meant to be sharing," he says, snatching it back before falling down beside me.

I pass him the bottle and he takes a shot after having another pull on the blunt.

"To worrying about our issues tomorrow."

"What the fuck are you worrying about?"

"Whose pussy I'm claiming Friday night."

"Oh to be you," I mutter, trying to push images of Friday night's winter formal out of my head.

School dances are not my thing, but I was intending to ask Chelsea. I guess that's off now.

One song rolls into the next as we sit here passing the alcohol and weed back and forth. That is until a shrill voice cuts through the bass.

"Mom is going to fucking kill you, asshole."

Looking to the door I find Harley, Zayn's little sister standing with her hand on her hips and drilling Zayn with a death glare.

"Oh look, the goody-two-shoes and her friends have arrived."

Looking behind Harley, I find Ruby and Poppy, Jake's cousin, loitering behind her.

"No weed in the house, how many times?" She marches in and makes a show of attempting to take it from him but he's not interested, he's got his sights on someone else.

He dodges Harley and she crashes to the couch beside me, growling in frustration as he stalks toward the door.

"Hey, baby," he coos at Ruby who shamelessly arches her back to push her tits in his direction. He wraps his hand around her bare waist and pins her to the wall, lowering his head but not enough to kiss her. She stares up at him as if he just hung the moon. It's sickening.

Poppy watches with her top lip curled in disgust.

"Careful, Ruby. That mongrel has probably got fleas, or worse."

Zayn glances up at her and blows a kiss in her direction. She shudders before turning her back on the two of them.

"Get your fucking hands off her," Harley snaps, physically pulling her friend from Zayn's clutches. "Cut that shit out or I'll tell Mom."

"Ohhh I'm so scared," Zayn taunts.

Harley rolls her eyes. "We're going to do homework in the back yard."

Harley and Poppy march off but Ruby hangs back for a few minutes.

"You're more than welcome to join our party, baby."

"Ruby," Harley calls.

She bites down on her bottom lip and lets her eyes roam down Zayn's body. "Maybe next time, big boy."

Zayn groans as if in physical pain as she disappears from view.

"Damn, that girl is a motherfucking tease," he complains as he falls back to the couch and reaches for the bottle.

"I thought you..." I trail off, vague recollections of that night last weekend filling my mind.

"A guy never kisses and tells, bro. But Ruby and I, we've got unfinished business."

The three of them walk in front of the glass wall, Ruby's hips swinging seductively purely for Zayn's benefit. When she looks over her shoulder, she smiles and winks, but when I look back to Zayn, I swear his eyes are elsewhere for a second.

"Poppy was right, you're a fucking dog," I mutter, reclaiming the bottle and draining what's left.

32

CHELSEA

"Thank you," I whisper as Ethan pulls up in my driveway beside Mom's car.

I barely looked up the entire journey here, not even the fear of being followed by my past was strong enough to drag my eyes up.

"Do you want us to come in or..." Rae asks.

"No, it's okay. You head back to school. I don't need to drag anyone else into this disaster."

"If you need us," she says, turning to look at me. "We're only a phone call away."

"Thank you. I really appreciate it."

Part of me wants to walk around the side of the house and go and hide in my little sanctuary, but it's the other part of me that wins out, the part that desperately needs a hug from Mom.

Slamming the front door behind me, I race toward where I expect her to be.

I'm right, because as I turn the corner into the kitchen, she stands from her stool.

"Chelsea?"

A sob rips from my throat as I run to her.

She gathers me up in her arms exactly as I need and she holds me so tight. Almost as tightly as Shane did last night when he found me mid-freak-out over the ghost from my past. That thought has my cries getting louder and my tears flowing faster.

"What on Earth has happened?" she asks once I've calmed down a little. "Is everything okay with the—"

"H-he found out, Mom. Shelly told the entire school and totally ambushed him. God, it's such a mess. You should have seen his fa–fuck," I say when I pull back and find Maddie sitting on the stool opposite where Mom was when I rushed in.

"Um..." Mom says, looking between the two of us.

My heart swells with the knowledge that she's kept my secret from her best friend, her friend who just so happens to be this baby's other grandmother.

"What's happened with Shane?" Maddie asks in a rush, standing with us and correctly guessing who we're talking about.

"You might want to sit down," Mom suggests, reaching out and taking my hand for support.

I really want her to say the words, but I know that this needs to come from me. Someone needs to hear it the way it should be said.

"I'm..." My voice trembles, giving away my fragile state. Maddie's eyes bore into mine, fear and apprehension lacing through. "I'm p-pregnant."

"What?" she asks on a gasp.

"I'm sorry, I'm so sorry." My tears reappear and I furiously wipe at my cheeks getting fed up with my overflowing emotions.

"I'm assuming you're telling me this because it's Shane's."

"Oh my god, this is such a mess."

"Sit down, I'll get you a drink," Mom says, pushing me toward an empty stool.

Maddie's eyes don't leave me as I move and after sucking a deep breath, I turn to her.

"Yes, it's Shane's. He didn't know. It happened before I went away, I found out while I was there. Then I came back and we reconnected in a way I never could have imagined. I should have told him right away, but I was so scared I'd lose him. I've wanted to tell him so many times but things between us have been so incredible that I just couldn't ruin that."

"What did Shelly do?" she asks hesitantly.

"I-I think she snuck into the pool house last night and took a photograph of my ultrasound picture. She stuck these all around the school."

Not wanting to hold anything back, I pull the poster from my purse and slide it over so they can both look at it.

"What a bitch," Maddie mutters.

"It can only be Shane's; I swear to you. What she's implying. It's not true."

They both nod at me.

"Where is he?"

I blow out a breath, pulling the poster back and staring at my baby once again.

"I don't know. He ran. His car was gone from the lot by the time I got there."

Maddie hops down from the stool to collect her purse and pulls her cell out. "I'm just going to..." She trails off. We don't need an explanation as she taps the screen and then puts it to her ear.

"I'm so sorry, sweetie. I know this isn't how you wanted it to go." She holds me to her again and thankfully refrains from saying any kind of I told you so.

I should have told him that first night when I found him in Brett's office at the after-party. I should have been brave and just laid out all my truths right there. But instead I got swept away by him and actually started to believe that we could have something.

"Nothing," Maddie says, dropping her cell and shaking her head sadly. "I should probably go in case he goes home. Things are already tense enough with him and Brett, this is the last thing either of them need."

"I think that's probably for the best," Mom agrees.

They both share a look, having a silent conversation that only lifelong friends can before Maddie turns to leave.

"Maddie," I call before she disappears. "I'm sorry. This really was an accident."

"Chelsea," she sighs. "Some things in life are never planned, but that doesn't always mean they're going to be a disaster. You'll get through this, we all will. Just have faith." With one final smile, she walks away.

Faith.

I wonder if that's what has kept her with Brett all this time.

"Do you mind if I just go to the pool house so I can be alone for a bit?"

"Of course, sweetie. You do whatever you need. I'll be here if you need me."

"Thank you, Mom. Thank you for everything."

"You're welcome."

Her eyes don't leave me until I slip inside the pool house and turn to the bedroom.

I don't even bother kicking my shoes off, I just curl up in the center of my bed and allow more tears to come.

The next thing I know, Mom is gently shaking my shoulder to wake me.

When I drag my sore eyes open, I find she's brought a tray of dinner out for me.

"You need to eat, sweetie." And just to prove that she's right, my stomach rumbles right on cue.

"Thank you." I pull myself so I'm sitting against the headboard and she places the tray on my lap.

I stare down at my favorite, Mom's homemade mac and cheese, and my stomach growls once again.

"Do you mind?" she asks, pointing to the other side of the bed.

"Of course not." As she gets settled, I reach for the fork. "Did Maddie find him?"

"She messaged about an hour ago and still hadn't then."

"Jesus. This is all my fault."

Mom doesn't say anything. She doesn't need to. We both know my statement is true.

All of it is my fault.

If I were on birth control, this would never have happened. If I were brave enough to confess all then this wouldn't have happened.

I'm a fucking mess, and all I've done is prove to him once again how untrustworthy I am.

He'd be stupid to ever look twice at me, at either of us again after this.

I blow out a frustrated breath.

"He'll be fine. Shane's got a sensible head on his shoulders. He's probably just taking a bit of time to get his head around everything. Don't forget, you've had weeks to get used to this huge change in your life, he's just had it dropped on him. That must be some kind of shock."

I nod because there's not really anything else to do.

What I really want to do is get out and start searching for him. But what good would that do? He clearly doesn't want to see me or talk about it because he would be here if he did.

"Are you going to school tomorrow?" Mom asks, dragging me from my plans of driving to the houses of everyone I know in the hope of finding him.

"I have no idea right now."

"I trust you to do the right thing for you. If you need a few days, then take them. Just please try not to fall behind. I know things are up in the air right now, but not graduating won't help."

"Don't worry, I have every intention of graduating and still going to college, even if it's a couple of years late."

"One step at a time."

Once I've finished eating, Mom kisses my cheek and takes the tray, leaving me to my own misery. After using the bathroom, I shed my clothes and pull Shane's jersey over my head before climbing back into bed and almost immediately falling back to sleep again.

I'm awake before my alarm the next morning but as it starts blaring, I make no move to get out of bed. The thought of walking into school where everyone knows my secret fills me with dread.

I probably should go just in case Shane does, but something tells me that he's going to avoid that place just like I am.

Rubbing at my sore eyes, I smooth my bed hair down with my fingers.

I need to see someone, I need to talk to someone. Someone who understands me.

When I woke in the middle of the night to pee, I found the strength to pull my cell from my purse.

I had so many messages, none of which I opened other than the couple from Rae checking in on me. No one else cared when I wasn't in the middle of the next big drama to hit Rosewood High so they can fuck off.

As expected, I had nothing from Shane. I almost shut it down without reaching out but in the end, I decided that I at least needed to try.

I found his name and typed out a million different messages to send him but, in the end, I deleted them all and went with something simple.

Chelsea: I'm sorry. Please let me explain x

I wanted to tell him again that I loved him, try to explain how much both he and this baby mean to me, but there's no way I could express it in a message, so I'll have to wait until I see him again.

When I light it up, I find a lot more messages but the only one I care about sits unread just like it did after I sent it last night.

With a sigh, I find the next best person.

Chelsea: Do you have classes all day? I need you.

The little blue ticks appear almost immediately, and the typing bubble pops up.

Luca: Breakfast? I'll be there in a couple of hours.

Chelsea: Thank you x

He sends me back a hugging gif. I have no idea if he knows, if he's spoken to either Shane or his mom, but whether it's my simple message or the big news, he knows I need him and he's dropping everything for me.

I want to feel guilty. It's the last week of the semester. He really should be in class but instead he's coming to rescue me from myself. I guess he's used to it at this point.

With two hours to waste, I have a shower and do my hair and makeup. On the outside, it makes me look almost normal but inside I'm still a broken mess and I fear I will be until I get the chance to be in his arms again.

Standing in front of the mirror in just my underwear, I stare down at my belly. I swear it's bigger today.

I run my hands over the smooth skin and try to imagine what it might look like in a few months' time when there is no more hiding it.

I turn to the side and I can't help but smile at the slight bulge that never used to be there.

When I first found out, I thought I'd hate my body changing. I've spent years working on it, to be strong enough to do everything cheer required of me, but standing here right now, I don't care all that much. All I want is for the little person I'm growing to be happy and healthy. There are plenty of women out there who have a baby and get back to their sport, that's my aim. My cheer dream is far from dead, just postponed a little while I do something more important.

Glancing at the time, I jump into action knowing that he's going to be here soon. I pull on a pair of yoga pants and an oversized hoodie before slipping my feet into my sneakers.

A knock on my pool house door has my heart jumping into my throat. I assumed he'd wait in the driveway. Thoughts of it being Shane standing there has my pulse racing as I practically run for the door.

My face drops the second I find Luca.

"Hey," I say, my usual cheer long gone.

"Seeing as you were expecting me, you don't look all that pleased about me being here."

"I-it's not that. I'm really glad to see you, I just thought..."

"It might have been Shane," he finishes for me.

"You know?"

He shakes his head. "I know something is going on. Mom rang to see if I'd seen or heard from him, but I have no idea what's actually going on. I'm hoping you're going to tell me though."

Grabbing my purse, I look up at his kind face and into those eyes that are so like the ones I so desperately need.

"Shall we? I'll explain on the way."

I wave at Mom who's watching us from the kitchen door. Luca nods at her so I can only assume they've already spoken.

"Your carriage awaits," he says, opening the passenger door for me.

"Thank you."

After jogging around to the driver's side, he makes quick work of turning the engine over and backing out.

"Go on then. Hit me with the drama."

"I'm pregnant."

"Fuuuuck, girl."

"It's Shane's."

"Jesus, no wonder he's gone MIA. I think I'd leave the country if the girl I was banging came out with that."

"Nice, Luc. Real nice." Crossing my arms over my chest, I stare out the window. I was kinda hoping he'd be a little more supportive.

"Shit, I'm sorry. I didn't mean... I mean, it's just my worst nightmare. But... fuck. I'm sorry. Ignore me. So, how'd it happen?" I turn to look at him. "No, shit. I didn't mean how, I meant... how far along are you?"

I laugh at him and it feels so good after the hours of stress I've had.

"Twelve weeks."

"Whoa, so really pregnant."

"I'm not sure anyone at nine months would agree with that, but yeah, it's not new."

"So you've known a while."

"Yeah. I should have told him by now but... it was just so huge, I didn't even know where to start."

"I get that, but yeah, you should have told him. So I'm assuming from his disappearing act that he's found out."

"One of the squad pinned my ultrasound picture all over school."

"What?" he spits. "Why would she do that?"

"She hates me," I mutter, rolling my eyes. "He freaked out, rightly so, and left school."

"Shit. No wonder Mom's losing her mind."

"Uh huh."

"Jesus, Dad's going to have a field day with this."

I tell Luca about their dad finding us together the other night and losing the plot, the grimace on his face as I explain has dread sitting heavy in my stomach for what's going to happen when he discovers this.

Luca takes us to our usual diner and we slide into our booth before we order the same food, the only difference is my hot chocolate.

"That's why you didn't have coffee last time," Luca says, figuring me out.

"Guilty," I say with a laugh.

"Don't take this the wrong way, I'm just asking because I care but..." I hold my breath as I wait for what's to come. "Are you keeping it?"

"Yes," I say without any hesitation. "I knew the second I found out that there wasn't any other option."

"Okay." He smiles softly at me. "I think you're going to be a great mom."

"I sure hope so."

Silence settles between us but it's not uncomfortable.

"Do you think he'll come around? Do you think he'll want this with me?" I ask, hoping like hell I get the answer I want.

"Honestly, I have no idea what he's going to do or want with this."

My heart sinks, it was the response I was expecting but equally the one I didn't want.

The bell above the door to the diner chimes making Luca look up but I don't bother, the chances of it being the guy I want is slim to none and I guarantee that if it were Shane, Luca would have said something instantly.

"Can you message him, see if he's okay?"

"I'll try but I sent one last night after Mom phoned and it's gone unread."

Our breakfast is brought over and I mostly poke it around my plate.

"You really should be eating that, you know."

"I know. I'm just worried."

"It will be okay. Just give him some time. He'll be back."

I sigh, hoping that he's right. But while his cell sits on the table, silent, I can't help thinking the worst. That things are done between us.

33

SHANE

Zayn's attempts to get me to school this morning we're pointless, there was no way I was showing my face. Not until I knew the truth, and that meant talking to Chelsea, and I can't see that happening anytime soon.

The alcohol did its job last night and by the time we'd drained that first bottle everything started to get a little hazy. It was exactly what I needed.

That being said though, when I woke this morning it was with a raging hangover and a massive reality check.

Other than a trip to the bathroom, I remain on Zayn's den couch. He and Harley disappeared to school over an hour ago and his mom's away on business, so I've got the peaceful house to myself to wallow in my misery.

Well, that is until the doorbell starts ringing.

"Ugh, go away," I call out, not that they'd be able to hear me from the back of the house.

It rings a few times before stopping and I breathe a sigh of relief that whoever it is has left. That's soon ruined though when it starts up again.

"For fuck's sake."

Assuming it's a delivery or something important, I pull on my pants and head for the front of the house.

I don't bother looking out, I just grasp the handle and twist.

"What?" I bark much to the surprise of the visitor. "Mom?"

"Hey," she says, almost shyly, rocking back on her heels holding a tray of takeout coffee.

"How'd you find—" It's a stupid question, everyone in this town talks, especially the moms, and I overheard Zayn telling his last night that I was here so I should have expected this really. I feel like an idiot for not even considering it would be her.

"Can I..." She gestures into the house. It feels weird inviting her into someone else's house but I stand aside regardless and allow her in.

She follows me through to the kitchen where I take a seat at the island, I can't take her back to the den, it probably still smells vaguely of last night's weed. I'm surprised she can't smell it on me to be honest since I haven't bothered showering or anything yet.

She sits opposite me, her eyes never leaving my face. Concern is written all over hers. I don't need to hear a word to know that she knows.

"How are you doing?" she asks softly.

"I have no idea," I reply honestly, dropping my attention to the counter in front of me.

"Here, I brought your favorite."

I take the cup when she hands it over but don't say anything. I have no idea where to even start.

"I saw her yesterday." That gets my attention. My heart slams against my ribcage as I wait for her to say more.

I might have lost myself in my own despair yesterday but at no point did I forget her and how she might be dealing with all this. It pissed me off that after everything, all the games and lies that I could still be concerned about her but I think it's time I accepted that it's just how this thing between us works. She's worked her way so deep inside me that I fear I'm never going to be rid of her.

"How is she?" I hate myself for asking but I know that if I don't, it'll only eat at me.

"Mortified. Embarrassed. Angry. Hating herself."

"Good."

"Shane," Mom warns.

"What? Do you have any idea what that was like yesterday? I thought we were…" I blow out a breath. "I thought it was serious. That she felt like I did." I feel like a pussy admitting this but I need to tell someone.

"Things aren't always quite so black and white, baby."

"You're defending her?"

"No. I'm just saying that she probably had her reasons. People make mistakes all the time, Shane. You just have to—"

"Like Dad?" I ask, spinning this back on her.

"Um… yeah, him especially. All I'm saying is that hiding in here isn't going to help with anything. You're both hurting and the only way to get all the facts is to talk." I run my hand down my face and rub at my jaw. I really don't need this little pep talk on top of the hangover pounding at my temples.

"How are you feeling, about… about the baby?"

My chest compresses as she says that one word.

Baby.

It's the realization I don't need that this is all very real and not the nightmare I hope I'd conjured up in my sleep when I first woke.

I shake my head, struggling to comprehend what all this really means for me. For us.

"She's really pregnant?" I ask, ever hopeful that yesterday was a really bad joke.

Mom reaches into her purse and pulls out the poster that

started this whole thing. I stare down at the image which is almost as familiar as the back of my hand after all the time I spent staring at it yesterday.

My breath catches as I stare down at it once again. My copy is folded in my pocket for when I feel the need to remind myself that this is all real.

"She is. Twelve weeks."

"Fucking hell."

"And it's... m-mine?"

"She assured me that there was no other option."

I blow out a shaky breath.

Flying off the handle and accusing her of lying was so easy. But even as I shouted those things at her, I remembered how sincere she was when she told me the truth about the other guys, about how she'd only been with Jake.

My hands tremble as I finally allow the truth to settle within me. I'm going to be a fucking dad. A fucking eighteen-year-old dad.

This was certainly not part of the plan.

Dad is going to lose his shit.

"Does he know?"

Mom shakes her head. "I haven't told anyone. But this is going to be hot gossip, it'll get back to him sooner than you think."

I see the same fear and trepidation flicker through her eyes as I feel.

"Shane, no matter what..." She reaches over, takes my hand and squeezes. "I'm here to support you. I'll do as much or as little as you need."

Tears burn my eyes as I stare at her.

"I'm not sure I'm ready for this," I admit, emotion clogging my throat.

"Oh baby." She gets up from her stool and comes to stand in front of me, wrapping her arms around me. "I'll let you in on a secret. No one is ever ready for a baby. Even those couples who appear to have it all together. They're just as scared. It's a huge unknown and even after having one, or two, the next is always different. It's the most challenging, but equally the most incredible, most rewarding thing you'll do in your life."

"But school, college..."

"We'll figure it out," she says, pulling back and cupping my cheek in her palm.

"I can't believe you're not angry," I mutter, pulling my cup closer before lifting it to my lips.

"What's the point? The deed has been done, quite literally." I groan as my face heats. I really don't need Mom thinking about what I've been up to with Chelsea, although she is sporting the evidence of our interactions, or will be very soon. "Plus, I think your dad might handle that all by himself."

Dread sits heavy in my stomach.

"I'll talk to him, okay. Soften the blow, if I can. But he's not going to be happy."

"Mom," I sigh. "I really hate him. I don't want anything he wants for me and I'm exhausted listening to it all."

"I know, baby."

"How do you put up with it?"

She shrugs, a sad look passing over her face.

"Are you happy?"

"This isn't meant to be about me."

"If you're not happy, you need to do something about it." She swallows nervously and I wonder just how close to home I've just hit. "Don't worry about us, we're all old enough to deal with whatever you need to do."

She looks up at me, tears filling her eyes. "When did you get so wise?"

"About the time I learned I was going to be a father maybe. Fuck," I bark. "How is this happening?"

She squeezes my hand again. "Come home, please. Your

dad's out of town until Saturday, maybe even Sunday. It'll be safe. You can at least be in our own space while you try to get your head around all of this."

The thought of spending another night of Zayn's couch doesn't fill me with joy.

"Okay. But if he goes off the second he's back. I'm gone again. I don't need his bullshit right now." Or ever, but I don't add that bit.

"That's fair. Go and get your stuff."

I don't have any stuff but I go back to the den just to make sure I haven't left anything before following her out of the house and driving back home.

"Are you hungry?" she asks when we step through the front door.

"Yeah."

"Pancakes?"

"That would be awesome. I need to take a shower really quick though."

"Please do, you smell like stale whiskey."

"Thanks," I say with a laugh.

I have a quick shower before heading back down to the kitchen, the smell of the sweet pancakes and salty bacon assaults my nose and makes my stomach growl. When did I last eat?

"So what are you going to do now? You can't hide forever."

I shrug.

"Shane, it's only Wednesday. You really—"

I fix her with a look that has her words faltering. If I ever deserved a few days off, then now is the time.

"Okay, fine. But can you do something for me?"

"What is it?"

"Can you talk to her?"

"I'll consider it, if you promise to do something for me."

"Go on."

"Think about your future too."

She sighs. "Deal. I guess it's time for both of us to grow up a little."

"Everything will work out," I say, my voice full of confidence that I don't really feel.

She smiles weakly at me before plating up our breakfast and we fall into a comfortable silence, both too lost in thoughts about our futures and what they might hold.

Eventually, I leave her and escape to the peace of my room. I know she's right. I need to see Chelsea. We certainly can't leave things like we did in that classroom. We're connected now whether we like it or not.

Mom gives me the space I need for a few hours before she pokes her head around the door, asking if it's okay for her to enter. I nod at her and when she pushes the door open, I find she's carrying a fresh mug of coffee and has a bag of chips in her hand.

"Thought you might need something."

"Thank you," I say, sitting myself up from where I was lying on my bed staring up at the ceiling.

"I was just thinking, isn't it winter formal on Friday?"

"Yeah and..."

"No reason," she says with an innocent shrug before backing out of the room.

34

CHELSEA

I don't pay any attention to the other diners around us until I stand and turn to leave. It's then that I lock eyes with a very familiar pair that I never want to see again.

My blood runs cold, just like it did when I looked into his car and found those icy blues staring back at me.

He pushes to stand as I start to run.

"Wait, please," he calls, but there's no way I'm sticking around to hear anything that asshole has to say, no matter how politely he asks me.

I don't realize that Luca isn't behind me until I'm outside of the diner and I risk a look back.

The only person who's there is him. He's standing in the doorway with his brows pulled together.

"W-what do you want from me?" I stutter, trying like hell not to show him that I'm scared and failing miserably.

"Please, Rose. I just want to talk to you."

"I'm not Rose. You've got the wrong person," I say, turning my back on him, hoping that Luca will appear at any moment and take me away before this gets out of hand.

"It's you, I know it is."

"Is everything okay?" Luca asks, finally emerging from behind the man. "Is this asshole giving you grief?"

"N-no, it's fine. Can we just go, please?"

"Of course." Luca looks between me and the guy, confusion written all over his face.

The second his car beeps to signal that it's unlocked, I jump in and lock it once again behind me.

My chest heaves as my breaths rush past my lips in my panic.

"What the fuck was that? Who was he? Fuck, are you okay?" he asks when he notices that I'm on the verge of a panic attack.

I nod, focusing on my breathing until things start to return to normal. His concerned eyes never leave me though.

"Do I need to go and beat the shit out of him for something?"

I can't help the laugh that falls from my lips. It's probably the least of what that guy deserves.

He's still looking at us from his place in the doorway of the diner, I don't need to look up to know he's there. I can feel his stare prickling my skin.

"It's fine. It's nothing."

"I beg to fucking differ. You're anything but fine."

"It's just a ghost from my past. One I hope to never see again."

"Your past? You mean before Rosewood?"

"Yeah. Can you just take me home, please?"

"Of course."

He starts the engine, and with the guy's eyes watching our every move, he pulls out of his space and onto the road.

I hold his eyes, I don't want to, but I'd be lying if I said his insistence to see me, to talk to me, didn't intrigue me.

Now my fear has subsided knowing that I'm safe in the car beside Luca, I see something else in his eyes. But before I get a chance to figure out what it is, we've turned the corner and he's no longer in sight.

"Are you sure you're okay?"

"Yeah." My hands tremble in my lap and my heart is still galloping in my chest but I'm fine.

What I need is to be in the pool house with the outside world safely locked on the other side of the door.

We drive back to my house in silence. I can sense the million and one questions Luca has for me, but thankfully, he manages to keep them inside.

"What are you doing for the rest of the day?" he asks me when he's brought the car to a stop on the driveway.

"Homework. What about you?"

"I should probably attempt to attend at least one of my classes today."

"Luca," I say on a sigh. "I said to come if you didn't have class."

Reaching over, he takes my hand in his. "You needed me, Chels. Shane needs me. There's nowhere else I'd rather be."

Emotion burns at the back of my eyes and I fight to blink the tears away.

"Oh no no. No crying, you know I can't deal with that."

I laugh at him as I tug his arm so I can give him an awkward car hug.

"I'll see you soon, yeah?" I nod as I push the door open. "And if you need me, just call me. Any time."

"Thank you, Luc. I really appreciate it."

"You take good care of my niece or nephew." He nods to my belly and butterflies take flight.

"I will. Thank you." He salutes me before backing out of the driveway.

Panic hits me as he drives off and I realize I should have told him not to tell Shane that he's seen me. I don't want him going to find him and attempt to fight my battles for me. Not that I think for a second that he would listen to me. With a smile, I hurry to the front door and let myself in.

I end up spending the afternoon with Mom wrapping presents. It's not exactly what I would have chosen to spend the rest of my day doing but I can't deny that the mundane task does relax me somewhat.

"Are you planning on going back to school this week?" she asks as she adds another present to the perfectly wrapped pile beside her.

"I have no idea what I'm doing. I used to thrive on the attention but now, I just want to hide."

"Understandable. I was just thinking that if you're off tomorrow, we could go to the mall. You're going to need new clothes soon and it might be nice to get you out of the house."

I sit and think about her offer for a few seconds. "That sounds really good, I'd like that."

"It's a date then. Just make sure you touch base with your teachers and get the work you're missing, young lady."

"I will, I promise."

It's late by the time I get to do what I craved so badly earlier and lock myself in my pool house. Mom and I made homemade pizzas for when Dad got home from work and we sat and ate like a real family. It was nice. Exactly what I needed.

After promising to meet Mom in the morning for our day out, I head to my sanctuary and let out a sigh.

The stress from the last two days pulls my muscles tight, all I want to do is curl up in a ball once more and fall asleep.

I'd left my cell in my purse on silent and told myself time and time again throughout the day not to check it but once I'm alone, my restraint snaps and I pull it out and wake it up.

I keep my eyes shut for a beat, praying that he'll have reached out, but there's nothing. Well, not from him. There's plenty from others.

I reply to Luca to thank him again for dropping everything for me this morning, and I also send an apology back to Rae for ignoring her all day when she's just worried about me. She replies immediately saying that she understands and that she's sorry for not coming to see me today, but they had forced family stuff after school. I get it, it's fine. I don't expect everyone to stop their lives because mine is falling apart.

I ignore everyone else, they're just gossip hunting.

After pulling on Shane's jersey once more, I climb into bed wishing that he'd turn up and pull me into his arms.

It never happens, and when I wake the next morning, I'm still alone.

Shopping with Mom is better than I expected it to be. I pick up some maternity clothes that I'm going to need before she drags me into a baby shop to start looking at things.

I'll admit that I don't know the first thing about looking after a baby, but I figure I've still got a bit of time to work it out and I hear people say all the time that it's something that usually comes fairly naturally once the time comes, so I'm hoping that is the case.

She's not happy about it, but I stop her from buying anything. Other than maternity clothes, I refuse to buy anything until after my next ultrasound. I think I'd like to find out the gender, and I really have no idea what Shane thinks about it, so until we've made that decision, hopefully together,

I'll refrain from any of the cute stuff that Mom waved under my nose in her attempt to sway me.

I need to think of him. I've already been through so much of this pregnancy without him being a part of it. I want to at least give him the chance to be there for everything that's still to come, should he want to of course.

I'm still putting everything into my closet when there's a knock at my pool house door later that afternoon.

With my heart in my throat, I once again run through to the living area in the hope it's him, but just like yesterday morning, my hopes are dashed when I find Rae staring back at me.

"Hey," I say, opening the door for her.

I never used to lock it, but since seeing *him* I've started being a little more cautious. He clearly wants something from me and a late-night visit like he used to give my birth mother is certainly not on the cards.

I shudder at the thought.

"Are you okay? All the color just drained from your face."

"Yeah, yeah, I'm good. Especially now that I've seen this," I say, my eyes widening at the sight of the box of donuts she has in her hand.

"You seemed to like them last time."

"They're donuts, who doesn't like them?" I take the box, place them on the coffee table and immediately pull the lid off to make my selection.

"Was he in school today?" I mumble around a mouthful of sugary goodness in the hope she can't make out the words. But when her lips curl up into a smile, I know she didn't miss it.

"Nope."

"And was everyone still talking about what a whore I am."

"Pretty much."

"Wow, don't sugarcoat it, will you?"

"I can if you want, I just thought you'd prefer to hear the truth."

I groan. "I would, I just equally don't want to deal with it all."

"There's nothing to deal with where they're concerned. They're a bunch of gossips. Who cares what they think?"

"I know. I do know that. It's just hard sometimes."

"I heard someone taking bets on if it was Shane's or not," she admits quietly.

"They fucking what?"

"Kids are assholes. Just let them get on with it. So I'm assuming you haven't heard from him then?"

I shake my head. "I've sent messages, but they've not even been read. I've seen his mom and brother though."

"What did they have to say?"

"To be patient."

"Helpful."

"Patience isn't really my specialty."

"They're right though. That must have been one hell of a shock to find out like that." Guilt twists my stomach that I allowed it to happen. "He'll come around. He's a good guy and he'll want to do right by you."

"He has every reason not to."

"Chels, that boy loves you. He'll be back."

"You think?"

"I know."

I narrow my eyes at her. "What aren't you telling me?"

"Nothing," she says, raising her hands in surrender. "I know nothing."

She leaves me after getting a message from Ethan to say he's finished with the team.

I flick through the TV channels but not finding anything that captures my attention, I pull out a book I picked up this afternoon with Mom about what to expect from childbirth and having a newborn and take it to bed with me along with a hot chocolate. It's not the kind of book I thought I'd be reading for a few years yet, but here we go.

When I wake the next morning, it's with the book poking me in the arm and still open on a page I vaguely remember reading.

I'd turned my alarm off last night knowing that there was no way I was going to school again today, so when I look to my cell, I'm surprised to see how late it is.

I'll go back next semester. It'll have given them plenty of time to get over the drama, and hopefully someone else will have done something that takes the heat off me.

I still haven't received a reply from Shane, but I send him another one anyway. I need him to know how much I miss him.

I get up, shower, do my hair, generally waste time because it's not like I've got a lot to do today. I should get out and go for a run but the thought of seeing someone when I'm alone doesn't sit right with me.

Eventually, I grab my laptop and get immersed in some work.

Mom pops in and out with food and drinks throughout the day to check on me, but other than that, I stay locked in my own little world, keeping everything and everyone else at bay.

That is until sometime after six o'clock.

Mom told me that dinner would be at seven so once I finished the assignment I'd been working on, I head to the bathroom to freshen up and get ready to meet them.

I'm just about to slip my shoes on when there's a knock at the door.

Knowing that I've only been disappointed when my

imagination has run away with me over the past couple of days, I don't even bother hoping that it's him because I know it's not.

I'm staring down at my cell, praying for a response as I walk into the living area so I don't look up to the door until I'm right in front of it.

And when I do, I can't help but gasp in shock.

35

CHELSEA

Standing on the other side of the glass door is Shane.

He looks exactly as I remember, his shaggy blond hair styled in its usual messy style, his emerald eyes staring at me as if he sees all the way into my soul and his full lips that make my stomach clench with desire. But that's where the similarities end because he's wearing a crisp white shirt and a pair of slim black dress pants, and in his hands is a giant box.

My hand trembles as I fumble with the lock to allow him inside.

"Hey," I say in a rush the second there's a gap in the door. "You look... amazing."

"Thanks. Can I come in?"

"Oh shit, yeah," I say jumping out of the way and holding the door open for him.

I stand, awkwardly rocking on the spot as I fiddle with my fingers, not knowing what to do.

Fuck, I've missed him.

I watch silently as he places the box on the coffee table and turns to me.

His eyes run down the length of my body, I have no idea why, I'm just wearing a massive hoodie and a pair of yoga pants, it's not sexy in the slightest.

"Shane." Just being able to say his name gives me tingles. "Fuck. I'm so fucking sorry. I had no idea... I should have told you... shit... I don't even..."

"Stop," he demands, reaching forward and taking my hand in his, tugging me into his body.

His heat burns, but in such a good way. My knees threaten to give way as his scent fills my nose.

"Oh god," I whimper as he stares down at me. "I've missed you so much."

"Chels, will you go to winter formal with me?"

My chin drops as his words register. "Y-you want to go to the dance?" One side of my lip twitches with the beginning of a smile.

"If you still want me."

A laugh bubbles up my throat, but not because there's anything funny about this situation but because it's so unbelievable.

"You're serious?"

"Deadly."

"Um..." I look around, my head spinning with this unexpected little visit. "I don't have anything to wear." I think about the dresses I've worn to previous dances and even though I'm not showing, I know they're not suitable.

"I've got you covered." He stands aside and allows me to see the box that I'd forgotten he carried in.

"What have you done?"

Without saying a word, he walks over to the box and pulls the top off. Inside is an abundance of tissue paper.

"Go on then. Let's see how well I know you."

I step up to the box and peer inside, but the contents are totally hidden.

"You chose it all by yourself?"

"Sure did. Go on the suspense is killing me."

Pulling back the tissue, I find fire engine red fabric staring back at me.

Tingles erupt in my stomach as I reach in and pull the dress free.

"Oh my god, Shane. It's stunning."

It's full-length with a deep V and a high split up one leg. It has a lot more fabric than the dresses I'm used to wearing, but it's so freaking sexy.

"Yeah?" I look to his hesitant eyes.

I relax for the first time in days, and a sob erupts from my throat out of nowhere. The relief of seeing him after not knowing what he was thinking, what he was doing, or even where he was the last few days is suddenly just too much to take.

"Shit," he mutters, gathering me up in his arms and pulling me tightly into his chest.

I breathe him in and it only makes me cry harder. Having him here, being able to wrap my arms around him. It's everything.

"Shush, it's okay."

"I'm so sorry. I'm so so sorry."

"Hey," he says, tucking his thumb under my chin and lifting my face up so I can look at him. "We'll do that later. Right now, I want to take my girl to formal. So dry those eyes, put on that sexy dress and let's enjoy our night together."

I swallow down my emotions and nod at him, a wide smile on my face.

"Sounds incredible."

He releases me, picks up the dress I'd dropped back into the box and with his hand in mine, pulls me toward my bedroom.

He settles himself in the middle of my bed. He looks

fucking breathtaking and all I want to do is crawl into it with him.

"You've got thirty minutes. You also need to pack an overnight bag."

"Shane Dunn, have you been holding out on me?"

"What?" he asks innocently. "You think you're the only one who can have secrets?"

"I guess not," I say lightly, ignoring the ball of dread that threatens to fill my stomach at the mention of my secret.

He said he wants to talk later. We can do that.

"Come on, time's ticking."

"Okay, okay."

With his eyes burning into me, I pull the zipper down on the hoodie I'm wearing, revealing the bra I've got on underneath. After peeling my pants down my legs, I turn to him and he groans.

"I should probably go and wait out there, shouldn't I?"

With his gaze locked on my covered breasts, I reach behind me and drop the fabric.

"This was a really bad idea."

"Too late now. If only you came sooner and gave me more than thirty minutes to get ready. Just imagine how we could have used the time."

I push my panties from my hips and smile when his teeth sink into his bottom lip.

"Now I know, I can see it."

My brows furrow for a moment before I realize that he's looking at my belly.

I turn to the side, looking at myself in the mirror, and run my hand over my stomach.

"You think?"

"Yeah."

Anticipation crackles between us. The possessive look in his eyes has heat flooding my core.

Pulling my eyes away from his in the mirror, I force myself to focus on what I should be doing.

Pulling a drawer open, I find a suitable pair of panties for that dress and pull them on before sitting at my dressing table and making quick work of my hair and makeup.

"You could do that with more clothes on you know," Shane grumbles behind me.

"And what would be the fun in that?"

"If you're trying to make a point by showing me what I've been missing, trust me when I say it's really not necessary."

"Been a *hard* few days, has it?"

"Like you wouldn't believe."

I know I shouldn't be winding him up right now but I can't help it. I'm so happy that he's here and happy to joke with me once again that it's too much to ignore.

I know we've got a lot of heavy stuff to talk about but he's come offering a little fun first and I'll grab on to that with two hands.

The fact he's here at all means everything to me, let alone the rest of it.

"How about you help me cover it up?"

I step up to the bed and hold my dress out for him.

He makes quick work of sliding to the edge of the mattress and holding it out so I can step into it.

I turn so my breasts aren't right in his face, feeling like that might be a tease too much.

He pulls the fabric up my legs before I feel the soft brush of his lips on the small of my back.

"Shane?" I moan as they begin trailing up my spine as the fabric encases my body.

Slipping my arms into the holes, he pulls them up until the straps are resting over my shoulders.

I shudder as the tip of his nose runs along the line of my shoulder until his lips brush against the column of my neck.

"Oh god." My nipples pebble against the fabric they're now hidden behind, and all I can think about is taking it back off again.

Pressing the length of his body against my back, the obvious bulge of his cock presses against my ass and his hand slides around to my stomach, resting gently on the very slight bump he pointed out earlier.

"You're mine, Chelsea. Are you ready to go and show the world?"

"Yes," I whimper, too overcome with happiness at having his hand possessively on my stomach.

Lacing his fingers with mine, he spins me away from him so I can face him.

"Whoa." His eyes rush around my body, not knowing where to look first. "I knew it would be perfect but... fuck."

As I find some suitable shoes in my closet, he takes hold of the small bag I'd packed as I was getting ready and we leave the pool house.

Clearly, he wasn't the only one in on this little surprise because I find Mom, Dad, and Maddie standing in our backyard ready to take pictures.

"Jeez, it's not prom night or anything," I say with a laugh when both Mom and Maddie get a little choked up at the sight of us.

The thought of prom suddenly terrifies me. How big will I be by then? Will I still even be pregnant, or will I have had the baby?

A shudder of fear races down my spine. Shane squeezes my hand and I wonder if he's having similar thoughts.

Our lives are about to change so rapidly, and although I'm excited and sure that it's what I want, it's still scary. Everything we'd planned for the rest of our lives has potentially been turned upside down.

We smile for a couple of photographs before our teary-eyed moms wave us off, wishing us a fun night. I'm assuming they're aware that Shane's just told me to pack a bag and that we're spending the night together. Although, I guess they've not got much to worry about now, the worst has already happened.

The second we're settled in his car, Shane reaches over and takes my hand.

"Are you ready for this?"

I think of almost our entire class in the gym enjoying themselves. The last thing they are probably expecting is for the two of us to turn up hand in hand.

I think back to when we walked into school together on Monday and he openly kissed me in front of everyone. Hell, how was that only four days ago? It feels like a lifetime.

Might as well give them something to stare at. His words hit me and I can't help but smile.

"Yes. I think I am."

He glances over at me with a smile playing on his lips.

"You always wanted the attention, looks like you're doing a good job of getting it, hey?"

"Yeah, once I decided that I no longer wanted it. Go figure."

"They'll soon get over it."

"What? When I've got a belly the size of a basketball? Yeah, that should really take the heat off me."

"A basketball, bit small don't you think. More like one of those exercise ball things."

I gasp in mock horror and swat his shoulder.

"Carry on and you won't be capable of making any more."

"You want more?"

"Who knows. It's not like I planned this one."

"Good to know," he mutters.

"Shane," I say, reaching over to rest my hand on his thigh. "I didn't... I wouldn't..."

"I know, Chels. That wasn't why I said it."

"I fucked this all up so bad."

"Not now. Let's just enjoy the evening."

I love his idea. It's so sweet and thoughtful after the way we left things the other day. Although I can't help but feel the huge elephant in the corner of the room—or car.

As much as I want to lose myself in him, in the connection between us and how electric it is when we touch, I know we're only masking our issues. Just like I've done since I came back.

It's time I ripped that Band-Aid off and expressed all my truths, my fears, and what I want for the future.

36

SHANE

I thought I was crazy doing this. I didn't think anyone would understand but the second I told Mom my plans, she was fully on board. Her eyes went all soft and I thought she was going to burst into tears on me.

She immediately sent me back up to my room to get dressed so we could go out shopping. She didn't take me to the Rosewood Mall but her favorite one a few towns over. She might have been there to help me, but I knew the dress the second I saw it. I didn't bother looking at any others. After taking a chance on the size, I walked out of that store with the first genuine smile playing on my face that I'd had in days. Something just isn't right without her. I'm not right without her.

That being said, walking up to her pool house with the hope she'd agree to this plan was one of the most nerve-wracking things I've ever done in my life.

She could easily have said no. I told myself time and time again that she probably would just so I could be prepared. But I knew the moment I looked in her eyes that she needed me there just as much as I needed to be.

The relief that flooded me was all-consuming. I desperately wanted to pull her to me and make her mine once again, but I knew I had to wait.

There're a lot of things that need to be said between us. And yeah, maybe we should have the conversations before spending the evening together at the formal, but fuck it. I just want a normal night with my girl. Is that too much to ask? I want to push everything aside, just for a few hours so we can enjoy each other's company before we allow reality back in again and accept that everything is about to change for us.

The parking lot at school is mostly full when we turn up. I know we're late, it's how I planned it.

I've always been the one to hide in the shadows, to shrug off the attention being part of the team brought me, but not tonight. Tonight I was going to hold my head high and show the world what I wanted.

After telling her to stay put, I jog around the front of the car and open her door for her.

Reaching in, I tighten my fingers around hers and pull her from the car. I don't step back so when she stands to full height her breasts brush against my chest and with her heels on her lips are in the perfect position.

It would be so easy. Every muscle in my body screams for me to close that little bit of space.

Her dark eyes stare up into mine, begging me to make the move because she knows she can't.

I've got to be the one to make the move tonight. I'm calling the shots.

"Ready to show that dress off?"

I feel the shudder that runs through her body at my question.

"You're not scared, are you?"

"I..." She hesitates, and I hate the apprehensive look in her eyes.

Leaning in, my lips brush against her ear, this time her shudder is for a whole nother reason as my breath races past her skin. "You're Chelsea fucking Fierce, baby. Walk in there with your shoulders back and show them that you will never hide from them."

She gasps at my words but after a beat, she nods.

"Only if you're by my side."

"I wouldn't want to be anywhere else."

"Okay. Come on then, let's do this."

She slips her hand into mine and after slamming the door behind her, we set off toward the gym where Rosewood High hosts all their events.

The music booms out long before we get there. A few students loiter around outside, probably trying to locate the alcohol that stashed throughout the week in the hope of sneaking some in.

A few of them look our way, but no one says anything.

As we approach the door, Chelsea's hand begins to squeeze mine harder.

I can't help but smile to myself. Only a few months ago, I wondered if she really was an ice queen. Nothing ever affected her. Everything anyone said or did just washed over her like water off a duck's back. But I see it now. I see her vulnerable side, her fears, her nerves, and I fucking love it because I know full well that I am the only one who can.

She sucks in a deep breath before we both push the double doors open and walk inside.

We go straight through to where all the action is. As if they're expecting us, the music bottoms out for a beat as we step inside and almost everyone in the room turns our way.

"Fuck," she squeaks beside me. But only a second later, she sets her shoulders and follows my lead toward the center of the room.

All eyes follow us as I pull Chelsea in front of me. As if on cue, the song changes and I pull her into my body.

"Might as well give them something to stare at," I say as she stares at me in total awe.

A shy smile appears on her lips as she shakes her head.

"You're amazing. You know that?"

I shrug. "You bring it out in me."

Unable to resist her any longer, I lower my head. It starts as a soft brush of lips knowing that our entire class, hell, the entire school, is watching. But I'm unable to leave it at that when she presses the length of her body tighter against mine.

With my hands on the bare skin of her back, I part my lips and lick into her mouth. She eagerly accepts my kiss as if it's just the two of us inside her pool house.

I can only assume that everyone gets bored with us because when we eventually part, a little breathless and dizzy a few songs later, most kids have gone back to their own conversations and dancing.

Chelsea laughs, and it makes my heart clench. "I can't believe you just did that."

"It was time for some new gossip around this place, don't you think?"

"It still focuses on us, though."

"Maybe, but at least it's different."

"Well, well, well," a familiar deep voice says making its way over. "Didn't think you had that in you, Dunn."

Looking up, I find Ethan's amused face with Rae tucked into his side.

"You don't need to worry about Shane. He's got plenty in him."

"Huh, I thought that was you," Ethan deadpans, looking at Chelsea and making Rae snort with laughter.

"I wasn't expecting to see you here tonight. I didn't really have you down as a school dance kinda girl," Chelsea says to Rae.

"Now whatever gave you that impression?"

I take in her dark makeup, black skater dress, fishnets, and combat boots.

"I have no idea," she says, having similar thoughts.

"It was Sindy and Barbie," she says with a roll of her eyes.

"Who?" My brows pinch at not having a clue who she's talking about.

"Them." She nods her chin over my shoulder and when I glance over, I find Amalie and Camila walking our way with my reluctant looking teammates trailing behind.

"So this is a torture-your-boyfriend kinda night, is it?"

"You'd think so looking at their faces, right?"

"Dunn, Chelsea," Jake says when he gets to us.

"Hey. Um..." Chelsea says, tensing beside me. "Can we talk for a minute?"

Jake looks between the two of us. It's as if he's asking my permission, a part of me wants to laugh. How the hell did we get to this?

"I've just got a few things I need to say to him," Chelsea whispers in my ear.

"I trust you," I whisper back. "But please, make sure you tell him that I'm the best you've ever had."

"Shane," she squeals, slapping my chest playfully.

She drops a quick kiss to my cheek before leading Jake over to a quieter corner.

"What's that all about?" Amalie asks me, watching my girl lead her guy away.

"I have no idea, but I doubt she's about to jump him."

We both watch as Chelsea says whatever it is she needs to say to him. Jake shakes his head, a soft smile playing on his lips.

She's apologizing, that much is obvious, and I couldn't be more fucking proud of her right now.

"So you two—or three—really going for it then?" Amalie asks, turning away to give him some privacy.

"Yeah, I think we are."

"I would say that I think you need your head checked, but I'm not blind. You two are pretty perfect for each other. Even if I never in a million years would have put you together when I first arrived."

"Can't help who you fall for."

"You don't need to tell me that. I could have gone for the nice guy, but instead I ended up with—" She squeals as Jake wraps his hands around her waist and pulls her back into him. "That," she says with a laugh.

"Why do I get the feeling you're talking about me?"

"Because we are," Amalie says. "I was just saying what an asshole you are."

"Yeah, well, it's a good thing you fucking love it."

Averting my gaze as he pushes his tongue into her mouth, I look to Chelsea when she slips her arm around my waist and tucks herself into my side.

"Everything okay?"

"Yeah. I just needed to say my piece after…"

"I get it," I say, dropping my lips to her temple.

"I need to talk to Mase too, but he's otherwise occupied right now."

I look over to find him grinding away with Camila to the beat of the music.

"Shall we join them?"

"I'd prefer to do it in private with less clothes on," Chelsea murmurs, making my cock twitch with excitement.

"We've got plenty of time for that."

Despite everything and the unknowns hanging between us, we have the most incredible, normal, night.

We dance, drink, chat, and laugh with friends. At some point, Zayn and a few others from the team joined us but after Zayn's tagging announcement for the night, they mostly spent their time trying to win their chosen girls while the eight of us watched with delight as most of them got turned down time and time again.

Zayn eventually got bored trying to capture the nerd he'd been challenged to and ended up dancing with a thrilled looking Ruby while his sister and Poppy glanced at their antics with disgust on their faces.

"Shall we get out of here," Chelsea eventually whispers in my ear when everyone around us is lost in their own conversations.

"Hmmm... that sounds like a perfect idea. Ready to see what else I've got planned?"

"So ready."

We say our goodbyes to those around us before leaving the dance behind.

It's not until we're both back in my car that I think I take a breath.

"That was kinda crazy," Chelsea says, her thoughts mirroring my own.

"Yeah, it was. It needed to happen though."

"Why do you say that?"

"Everyone knows now."

"Knows what?" she asks, nerves laced through her voice.

"That you're it for me." Reaching over, I take her hand and lift her knuckles to my lips. "Right, let's go."

With her hand resting on my thigh, I back out of the space and toward our weekend destination. I was going to book us a hotel, but Mom called in a few favors and she managed to find the perfect place for us to have the privacy we need to sort everything out once and for all.

"I'm hungry," Chelsea complains when I've been driving for about an hour.

"What do you want?"

"Er... burger and milkshake."

I chuckle at her. "Next diner we pass, we'll stop."

"Aren't we nearly there? We've been driving for ages."

"Hardly."

"Maybe I'm just impatient."

I glance over at her; her usually dark eyes are almost black. She sucks her bottom lip into her mouth, knowing that I'm watching, and it makes my cock swell. Dropping my eyes to her chest, I find her swollen breasts that are temptingly exposed by the dress.

"Eyes on the road, Shane," she says with a laugh, pointing forward.

I do as I'm told, but only because I don't want to kill us all before I tell her what I've been planning for days.

"There," Chelsea shouts, pointing to an illuminated building up ahead, proving just how hungry she really is.

I signal to pull off the road and slow to a stop in the diner parking lot.

Chelsea is pushing the door open and climbing out before I've even had a chance to turn the engine off.

"I think we're a little overdressed," she murmurs to me as we walk inside the tired diner. I glance around at the two other customers in old ripped jeans and oil-stained shirts and I can't help but agree.

Their eyes, along with the sole waitress' follow us over to a booth in the window. I expect Chelsea to reach for the menu the second we're seated, but she doesn't. Instead, she just waits until the waitress comes over.

"Hey there, what can I get you both?"

"A cheeseburger, please. The biggest you've got. And a strawberry milkshake," Chelsea says without taking a breath.

"Okay, and you, dear?"

"I'll take the same. Thank you."

She scurries off as I silently laugh at Chelsea.

"What?"

"It's a good thing she didn't hang around, you might have eaten her."

"It's not funny. Every now and then I just get so ravenous, it's like I haven't eaten anything ever and I suddenly need to consume everything in sight."

"Tell me about it. Tell me everything," I demand.

She opens her mouth and then closes it again. "I don't know where to start," she admits.

"When did you find out?"

Picking up one of the salt packets from the holder, she fiddles with it as she thinks back. "About three weeks after I left.

"I didn't want to be there to start with and my entire focus was getting back. But after a while, I settled in and realized that actually, my parents were right to send me.

"I woke up one morning and the realization that I'd not had my period in a really long time just slammed into me out of nowhere.

"I'm not the kind of girl who tracked that sort of thing, but I didn't need to try to work it out. I knew. I can't explain how I felt different, I just did. It was weird.

"I got myself a test, and there it was. That positive result stared back at me."

"Did you tell anyone?"

"Other than the doctor." She shakes her head. "Nope."

"Jesus, Chels."

She shrugs like it's not a big deal. "I knew in that moment that I'd keep it. I don't even really remember panicking that much. It just felt right. It still does. Yeah, I was nervous as hell about having to tell people, you. But I knew I wanted it." Her hand drops beneath the table, her palm pressing against her belly.

It's a sight I didn't expect to see, not for many years yet anyway but excitement begins to bubble up within me.

We might be young. People might think we're crazy, but I already know that I want this with her.

Is it going to be easy? No. I'm not under any illusion that it's going to be easy in any sense of the word, but that's not enough to scare me off. Nothing worthwhile is easy. And if I had to embark on this challenge with anyone, then I can't imagine it being with anyone but Chelsea.

"I should have told you. I wanted to tell you, but then that first night you were so..."

"Horrible?"

"Yeah, something like that. I deserved it though. What I did, it was... unforgivable. You had every right to treat me like that, worse if I'm honest.

"But then as things changed between us, it got harder. You were quickly becoming everything I'd ever wanted, and I knew that admitting the truth would potentially ruin everything we were building.

"I was scared. No, terrified, that you would hate me, that you would leave me, and then I'd be back to square one once again with no one."

Reaching across the table, I take her hand in mine. "You should have told me. Hearing it from you would have been a hell of a lot better than what happened."

She swallows nervously. "I know. I was going to tell you that night, remember I said we needed to talk? I knew I had to do it. I just never got the chance."

"Who was it?"

"Shelly."

"What? Why would she do that? Wasn't kicking you out of the squad and pushing you down the stairs enough?"

She shrugs. "They let me back in without her permission. We all knew she'd be pissed."

"How'd she find out?"

"The woman who did my ultrasound in the hospital was her mom. I can only assume it came from her."

"Fucking hell." I think back to her being in the hospital and a thought hits me. "That's why you kicked me out of the hospital. You thought I was going to find out."

Guilt washes over her features. "Things were... complicated between us back then."

"Only because you made them that way. If you didn't keep sending me—"

"I was scared, Shane," she interrupts. "I was confused. I spent the whole time I was away thinking about you, about that night, about all the reasons you had to hate me but praying that by some miracle that you didn't. Then I came back, and it seemed you did hate me. But then there were these little moments when you didn't and..." she sighs. "I didn't know which way was up. Everything was different. My life had totally changed in ways that no one knew about and although I had much more clarity about what I wanted since going away, I was drowning."

"I never hated you, Chels. I tried to, trust me, I did. I was so angry that you let me take the fall for all of that. That you allowed what happened between us, instigated it even, when you knew the truth. But still, I couldn't hate you."

I look down at the table for a beat.

"I've wanted you for too long." She gasps and I look up at her from under my lashes. "I watched you for years look at anyone but me. But suddenly you saw me, wanted me. I don't even..." I shake my head unsure of how to vocalize what I'm trying to say to her but the waitress chooses that exact moment to bring our plates over.

"Thank you," we both say as she hovers around asking if we need anything else.

Once she's gone, I look at Chelsea, who has already started on her fries, and I smile.

"What?" she asks, shyly.

"You're so much more than I ever imagined."

"I will be after I've eaten all this. It's the size of my head," she says, nodding to the burger.

"That's not what I meant and you know it. For someone who always wanted to be front and center, you're not very good with compliments."

"I didn't get them very often," she admits.

"Well, you'd better get used to it."

Chelsea demolishes her dinner, I have no idea where she puts it, especially as I struggle to clear my own plate, but she claims to feel better for it as she sits back and places her hand on her belly.

"Should we go? We don't have far to go."

We both slide out from the booth and I'm almost at the door when I realize she's not behind me.

"Chel—" My word is cut off when I find her staring at the desserts on show.

"Want a donut?" she asks like we haven't just eaten our body weight in food.

"No, I really don't," I say with a laugh.

"I'll get you one just in case you change your mind."

I'm still chuckling at her as she takes the box the waitress passes over and we make our way back to the car.

Only twenty minutes later, we're pulling up into a parking lot for an apartment building that overlooks the bay. The moon glitters in the dark sea. I can only imagine how stunning it might be in daylight.

"We're staying here?"

"We are. Come on." I jump out excitedly and grab both our

bags from the trunk before joining her at her side of the car as she stares out at the sea beyond.

Silently we make our way inside the building.

"Wow, this is fancy," she says, taking in the lavish surroundings.

The entrance is impressive with its huge artwork and solid oak desk for security to sit behind.

After giving the guy my name like Mom instructed. He gives me a card before gesturing toward the elevators and we make our way over.

I tap the card to the panel and the second the doors close behind us we begin to move.

Chelsea is silent but her excitement is palpable as the elevator keeps rising.

When we step out, our feet sink into the plushest carpet that I've ever stood on.

There is only one set of doors in this huge entrance hall.

"I guess this is us then."

Tapping the card to the box beside the wall, the doors click and I push them open.

"Oh wow," Chelsea gasps, coming to stand beside me as we take in the view of the entire bay through the wall of floor to ceiling windows. "That's incredible."

Dropping our bags, I pull her forward toward the doors.

The moon shines bright and the stars twinkle in the black sky above.

Pulling her in front of me, I wrap my arms around her middle and rest my chin on her shoulder.

Everything might be up in the air right now, but with her in my arms, everything also feels right.

37

CHELSEA

My heart races as I stand in Shane's arms, looking out over the tranquil night view before us.

I thought I'd be in my pool house alone tonight while everyone enjoyed winter formal. I never could have imagined any of this.

Him, the dress, this incredible penthouse apartment. All of it has been way beyond anything I could have ever wished for.

Spinning in his arms, I look up at him.

He stares back at me, his green eyes dark and full of emotion.

"Chelsea, I—"

Cupping his cheek in my hand, I shake my head. "I'm really sorry, Shane. But what I said the other night is true. I love you, and I want this with you, if you'll have me... have us."

Dropping his forehead to mine, he continues to stare into my eyes.

"I wouldn't have it any other way."

One minute I'm on my feet staring at him and the next my legs are around his waist and my back is pressed against the window behind me.

"Shit, that's cold," I gasp as the cold glass bites into my exposed skin.

He takes advantage of my parted lips and plunges his tongue past them and deep into my mouth.

I sag in his hold as I give myself over to him but his hold on me doesn't falter.

He kisses me as if he's making up for the past few days. As his tongue caresses mine, tears burn my eyes. I can feel everything he's trying to tell me, and it's totally overwhelming.

I don't deserve this guy. I'm fully aware of that, and I intend on trying to prove to him every day that I'm worthy of him.

The fire that's been burning in my belly all night begins to roar to the point that just being pinned here kissing him isn't enough.

"Shane," I mumble against his lips.

"I know, baby."

He pulls his lips from mine but only gets as far as my jaw as he lowers my feet to the floor once more.

The length of his body presses me against the glass, and I feel every inch of him. He needs this just as badly as I do.

"Bedroom, now," I moan as his hand comes up to squeeze my breast.

Without missing a beat, he takes my hand and tugs me from the glass.

I'm assuming that he's not been here before, but that doesn't stop him navigating us straight to the ginormous master bedroom, again with a view out over the bay.

"This is beautiful," I say, taking in all the cream and gold hues around the room.

"You're beautiful."

When I turn, I find Shane's eyes on me. Something tells me he's barely even noticed the room.

A smile tugs at my lips as heat hits my cheeks.

"This dress is hot as fuck," he says, taking a step toward

me. He lifts his finger and runs it along the deep V, teasing me as it tickles over the swollen swell of my breasts. "But I think it might look even better on the floor."

"I guess you'd better find out."

Tucking his fingers under the shoulder straps, he pushes them until the entire top of the dress falls from my body.

He bites down on his bottom lip as he stares down at my breasts, my nipples hard and begging for attention.

Reaching forward, I take the top button on his shirt between my fingers and make quick work of popping them all open until I'm able to push the fabric from his shoulders.

It falls to the floor before he steps up to me once again. The hot skin of his chest almost burning against my sensitive breasts. His fingers thread into my hair as he crashes our lips together once again.

My nails scratch down his back before finding their way to his abs and dropping lower.

He's rock hard beneath his pants. I rub him and he groans into my mouth.

"Fuck, Chels." His lips trail down my neck as I open his fly and push my hand inside both his pants and boxers.

He growls, sinking his teeth into my soft skin as I wrap my fingers around his length.

Kissing down his chest, I run my tongue along the indentations of his abs, before pushing both his pants and boxers down his thighs. His cock springs free, teasingly close as I sit on the edge of the bed.

Reaching out, I wrap my fingers around him once more and look up at him through my lashes.

His lids are heavy, half covering his dark emerald eyes, his lips parted as his increased breaths race past.

I stroke him slowly and his jaw tics as his teeth grind.

"Good?" I ask. I don't need to, his body is giving me all the answers, but I need to hear his voice.

"So good." It's rough, sexy, needy. I fucking love it.

Leaning forward, I lick the precum that had leaked from the tip. His entire body flinches at my soft contact, his fingers lacing through my hair as if he's going to take control, but he never does.

Parting my lips once again, I take him in my mouth.

"Jesus, fuck."

I watch as his head falls back, sucking him deeper until he hits the back of my throat.

I know he hates that I've got a bit of a reputation for this, but I'm hoping that I can make him forget all about it now he's the only one reaping the rewards.

Pulling back, I lick around the head before sucking him back down again.

His head drops and our eyes connect as I continue working him.

Before long, he gets even harder in my mouth and I work him faster knowing that he's getting closer to his release.

"Chels," he warns, his fingers tightening in my hair as if he's about to pull me back. But I have other ideas because I don't let up for a second.

Lifting my hand, I cup his balls and squeeze gently.

He groans a beat before he twitches in my mouth and his salty cum hit's my tongue.

I suck him until he's finished, then sit back and wipe my mouth with the back of my hand, a smug smile on my face.

Resting back on my elbows, I watch him. His chest heaves with his exertion, his hair falls over his face and a sated smile plays on his lips.

After a second, he kicks his shoes off before allowing the fabric around his hips to drop to the floor.

Scooting back on the bed when he steps toward me, he climbs onto the bed, straddling my legs.

His hands land on my waist and slide up until he's

palming both of my breasts. My back arches, offering him up more of me. He pinches my nipples before dropping to find my lips.

The second we connect once again, I lose myself to him. I forget everything that got us to this point in our lives, and I just take everything he's offering.

His lips trail down my neck, leaving goose bumps in their wake before he licks along the line of my collarbone and descends to my nipples.

"Shane," I moan, both of my hands diving into his hair to hold him in place.

He sucks and licks, sending fire straight down between my thighs.

"Oh god, Shane, please."

His fingers wrap around the waist of my dress that's still in place before he begins to pull. I lift my hips to help him out and in no time at all, it drops to the floor, leaving me in only my red lace panties.

He stares at them for a beat, before his dark eyes flick up to mine, a smirk playing on his lips before he reaches out and rips them from my body.

I gasp, desire for him pulling all my muscles tight.

Pushing my knees apart, he settles himself between them and rubs his cock through my wetness.

"I can't wait any longer to be inside of you," he admits.

"So don't." And he doesn't. Before I've even finished talking, he surges forward, filling me to the hilt in one smooth move.

"Fuck. I'm fucking addicted to this feeling."

"That good, huh?" I ask with a smirk.

"Yeah, but I don't just mean your body. I mean this," he says, gesturing between the two of us. "It's not just sex, is it? This... this is bigger than that."

A lump forms in my throat, because I know exactly what

he means. Neither of us has much experience with this, but even with my lack thereof, I know that this is bigger than anything in my past.

I nod. "I know. I feel it."

"Fuck, Chelsea." He stops moving and just stares at me, his hand sliding up my body until he grips on to the back of my neck. "I love you so much."

I gasp at hearing the words and tears fill my eyes. My chest swells to the point I swear that my heart's going to stop right there.

"Shit, I didn't mean to make you cry," he says, reaching up to wipe my tears as they slip from my eyes.

"It- it's okay. They're happy tears. I love you too."

"Jesus. I don't think I'll ever get used to hearing you say that."

"I hope you never do."

Unable to stay still any longer, he slowly pulls out of me before sliding back in.

"Shane," I moan, my back arching as he hits every single nerve inside me, pushing me toward another high that I know I'll never get used to.

Sitting back, he wraps my legs around his hips and picks up speed. In only a few seconds sweat is glistening on my skin as he thrusts into me hard, building me higher and higher.

"Come, Chels. I need to feel you."

He drops his thumb to my clit, and I detonate around him. My eyes slam closed as my back arches and I cry out his name.

Seconds later, his own growl fills the room before he jerks inside me and gives me everything he has.

We both still, the only sounds that can be heard is that of our heavy breathing.

Still inside me, he stares down at me. Something crackles between us despite what only just happened. Aftershocks from my recent orgasm fire off, revving me up for another.

Hesitantly, he moves his hand forward from where they were resting on my knees. I'm confused by the move for a moment, he's just had his hands everywhere, why is he suddenly unsure. But then his large palm lands on my belly.

I probably look more pregnant than I did before, thanks to the giant burger from not so long ago.

He continues to stare, his thumb rubbing back and forth over the taut skin.

"Our baby is growing in there." The awe in his voice has emotions hitting me full force once again.

"I know," I whisper. It blows my mind every time I think about it too.

"When's your due date?"

"July seventh."

He shakes his head as he tries to process it all.

Placing my hand on his distracts him a little and his eyes find mine.

"Lie with me?"

I move my leg to the side, and he pulls out of me and falls down on the bed, facing me.

His eyes search my face as if he can't believe I'm really here.

"Are you sure you want this?"

His brows draw together.

"It's going to change everything. Your entire life. I would understand if you didn't—"

"Stop. Stop talking right now," he says, placing two fingers against my lips. "We did this together. So we will continue to do this together."

"But your future, college, your career."

"And yours too. This isn't just about me having to make changes."

"I know but I chose this. I didn't have to..." I trail off, not able to even say the words. "You didn't choose this, you were ambushed with it."

"It doesn't matter. No matter how I found out, my feelings about it would have been the same."

A smile tugs at my lips.

"Clearly someone up there thinks this is meant to be so I think it's only fair we give it a good shot."

"I figure that I can screw it up as much as I am so..." I trail off, it's meant to be a joke but I can tell by the look of Shane's face that he's not amused one bit by it.

"You're not screwed up, Chels. You're just dealing with the fallout from all of that."

His words remind me of yesterday morning.

"What? What is it?"

"I went to breakfast with Luca yesterday morning."

He tenses at my word. "I know, he called me. Ripped me a new one for not being there for you."

"He didn't." *Of course he did.* "I told him not to. I needed someone to talk to, not someone to get to you from the inside."

"He cares about you, baby. He was only trying to help."

"I know. Anyway, we get to the same diner we always do and *he* was there."

"He? Who's... oh. Shit. What happened?"

"He told me that he just wanted to talk but I ran. But I saw something different in him, I can't figure it out but something is telling me that he might not be the man I remember him as. My memories from that time are so fucked up. I don't know what's nightmares and what's real anymore."

"Maybe you should talk to him," he says with a wince, making my heart rate pick up.

I know he's right. It's the only way to find out the truth, to discover why he's sought me out all of a sudden.

"Is there anything else you need to tell me? Any other secrets you been too scared to admit?"

I think for a minute, sucking my bottom lip into my mouth.

"I hate peanut butter," I say seriously.

"I already know that."

"Really? I try not to tell people because they think there must be something wrong with me."

"Chels, you've spent countless hours in my house. I've spent longer than I want to admit watching you. I know these stupid little things, I've seen them."

I open my mouth to respond, but I find I have no words.

"Um... how about... I want you to fuck me again."

He chuckles. "I don't think that's a secret, baby."

Rolling onto his back, he pulls me with him so I have no choice but to straddle his waist. His hands once again come to my belly before sliding down to my hips, ready to help me move.

"Go on then, rock my world."

"I'm pretty sure I've already done that." I smirk.

"I can fucking guarantee it, baby. But it's time to do it again."

38

SHANE

When I wake, the other side of the bed is empty and cold. I sit up in a panic that she might have left in the middle of the night. I feel stupid for it the second I see her curled up in the love seat in front of the windows staring out at the sea crashing onto the beach wearing my shirt from last night.

She looks so peaceful with her head tilted to the side, lost in thought and her hand resting on her belly. I bet she doesn't even realize she's doing it, but it fills me with joy. It's clear how fiercely she loves that baby already and I can't wait to see her with him or her in her arms.

Something possessive washes through me and my teeth grind. Thoughts of the man who's been trailing her have my fists curling in the sheets. Now more than ever I need to make sure she's safe, and I don't know how to do that with some random guy clearly stalking her.

Blowing out a calming breath, I climb from the bed and make my way over to her.

"Hey, baby," I say, dropping a kiss to the top of her head.

She startles as I touch her, showing just how lost in her own head she really was.

"Morning. Sorry, did I wake you?"

"Sitting here silently?" I ask with a laugh. "No, I just missed you."

She turns to look at me, running her eyes down my naked body.

"Hmm... I missed you too, but I was hungry."

I glance at the coffee table and gasp. "You ate my donut?"

"Well, you didn't really want it in the first place, so..." She shrugs.

"You know the kitchen is full of food for us, right?"

"Yeah, but I wasn't sure if I was allowed to eat it or not. I just took a bottle of water."

"It's all ours. Would you like a real breakfast?"

Her eyes drop to my semi. "That all depends on what you're offering."

"I was going to offer to make you pancakes, but now that you put it like that."

It must be over an hour later when we eventually make it to the kitchen. Both freshly showered, Chelsea still wears my shirt, her long bare legs sticking temptingly out the bottom and one too few buttons done up, giving me the perfect tease as to what's underneath.

She perches herself on a kitchen stool while I get everything out to make our breakfast.

"I didn't have you down as a chef."

"I'm not sure I'd describe myself quite like that, but I can knock out a few things. Pancakes being one."

"I guess it's a good thing that one of us can cook seeing as we're starting a family and will need to fend for ourselves."

My stomach twists, but I'm not sure if it's with fear for what's to come or excitement.

"You want us to live together and do this right?" I ask.

"Why do you look so surprised? I don't want you at your parents while I'm at mine. I don't want you to be a part-time dad like we're not a couple just because we're young."

"Okay, but how the hell are we going to afford all this. We're still in school. I know my dad's loaded, but I highly doubt he's going to put up any cash when he finds out about this."

"Good, your dad's a cunt." I spin to Chelsea just in time to see her lips slam shut and her eyes widen in horror. "Fuck, that wasn't meant to be out loud. I'm sorry."

"Don't be. He is a cunt. I fucking hate him."

"He's gonna lose it when he hears about this, isn't he?"

"I can't imagine him doing anything else. I only have to breathe the wrong way and he goes off. I don't know what I did to make him hate me so much."

I turn back to the pan I'd put on the stove so she doesn't have a front-row seat to the emotion that I'm sure if filling my face as I think of my dysfunctional family. Mom and my brothers are incredible, I couldn't ask for better, but he just poisons everything.

"Hey," she says, slipping her delicate hands around my waist, her breasts pressing against my back. Her touch makes me shudder and I relax into her.

"You haven't done anything wrong." Her lips brush against my shoulder blade as she says the words and my skin erupts in goose bumps. "He's the one with the issue. And if he doesn't support us, then he'll be the one missing out. He won't get to see his grandbaby grow up. That will be on him, not you."

"I think my mom wants to leave him."

"And you're surprised?"

"No, not at all. I don't know how she's put up with him for so long. I just worry about what she'll do."

"She'll be fine."

I turn in her arms and take her face in my hands. "I know

she will. Thankfully, they're not my biggest concern right now."

"Oh?" she asks as I brush the tip of my nose against her.

"Nope, that would be you two. My parents are capable of sorting their own lives out. We need to figure out how to start ours."

"We'll figure it out."

"I'm going to get a job," I announce. It's been something I've been thinking about since finding out about the baby, and I know that I need to step up to the plate. We can't expect handouts from our parents to help fund this. We're old enough for this to happen, so we need to be grown up enough to accept responsibility.

"Me too," Chelsea agrees.

"You don't need to. You just need to focus on this little one," I say, dropping my hand to her belly.

"We're a team now. I want to do my part too. Plus, there will be times once the baby is here that I won't be able to do much, and I want us to be prepared."

After dropping a chaste kiss to her lips, I push her back in the direction of the stool she was previously on so I can continue with breakfast.

"What are you going to do about college?" I ask as I pour some batter in to the now scorching hot pan.

"I'm thinking I might take a year off. Get used to being a mom and then see if I could maybe start part-time after that. What about you?"

"I don't know. We might need for me to just get a job."

"No, Shane. I refused to allow you to do that."

"I'll do whatever I need to to make sure you and our baby are looked after."

"You have no idea how much that means to me, but still, I refuse to let you sacrifice your future."

"I don't even know what I want from my future, besides you."

"Forget about your dad and everything he wants for you, what can you see yourself doing?"

"I want to be involved with football, but I don't want to play professional. I want to be in the background. Trainer maybe, something like that."

"You've got a little time, applications aren't due for a few weeks yet. Think about what *you* want, and I'll support you all the way."

I look over my shoulder at her and smile. "I love you."

"I love you too, but please, don't burn my pancakes."

By the time Sunday morning rolls around, I'm nowhere near ready to leave our little penthouse of heaven but I know that real life is waiting. Christmas might only be a few days away but with the number of things we need to deal with, my father being the most pressing, it feels like a million years away.

"I don't want to go," Chelsea whines as I hold both our bags in one hand and hold my other out to pull her from the love seat where she's enjoying the last few seconds of the view.

"I know, but it's the holidays."

A smile twitches at her lips. "We're spending it together, right?"

"Too fucking right. I can't imagine I'll be welcome at the Dunn family Christmas dinner. You think your parents will be okay with me gate-crashing?"

"He might surprise you, Shane."

"Yeah, and he might not," I say sadly.

I know he's home, I've had messages from Mom. What I don't know yet is if he knows, although unless he's come home and locked himself in the house, I can't imagine he doesn't. This gossip isn't contained to Rosewood High, it's all over the town now that the kids have had plenty of time to go home and tell their parents.

The infamous Brett Dunn's son has got his teenage girlfriend pregnant, I bet they're all fucking loving it.

With a sad sigh and one last look at our weekend escape, Chelsea and I make our way down to my car.

The drive home is much more somber than the one here, the tension in the car is palpable and I hate that we have no idea what we're about to arrive back to.

My intention is to take Chelsea home, make sure she's happy before going and facing the music. I know she's going to want to come with me, but much like the last time, I need to do this alone. She's got enough to worry about right now, she doesn't need my broken relationship with my dad weighing down on her more than it probably already is.

All those plans are shattered though when I pull into Chelsea's driveway to find a truck parked in it that has her tensing in fear.

"W-why is that h-here?" she asks, her wide eyes locked on the black truck that I recognize immediately.

"Should I drive away?" I offer, not being able to get a read on what she wants me to do.

"N-no. I think it's time to get to the bottom of this. Find out what the asshole wants. If he's brazen enough to turn up at my house like this, then I need to find out what his issue is."

"Okay, let's go."

I'm at her door before she's even got one foot out.

"I'll be right beside you, baby."

She nods but no words pass her lips as hand in hand we make our way to the front door.

"Chelsea, is that you?" her mom calls from the living room and Chelsea's grip becomes almost painful.

"It'll be okay. I'm here, your parents are here. They're not stupid enough to put you at risk."

"I know, I know," she says, blowing out a slow breath.

The second we turn the corner, my eyes lock on the man that I haven't seen before, I've only ever seen his shadow behind the windshield of his truck.

He stands the second he sees Chelsea and I get a second to study him. I've never seen him before, of that I'm positive, but I can't help thinking there's something familiar about him.

Chelsea gasps despite knowing that he was here, and stumbles back a little.

Reaching out, I wrap my arm around her waist and pull her into my side.

"It's okay. I've got you," I whisper down to her as her eyes remain locked on the man.

"Chelsea, this is Greg—"

She tenses in my arms before cutting her mom off.

"What the hell are you doing in my house? Isn't it enough that you've been stalking me everywhere I've been for the past week, now you've got to force your way into my home, my family?"

He swallows nervously, his lips parting to say something but no words come out. I have no idea who he is or what he wants but it's blatantly obvious that he's out of his depth right now.

"I'm sorry. I didn't mean to scare you. I just... I didn't know how to go about it."

"Go about what?" Chelsea spits. "Thought I was grown up now so it would be okay to take whatever you wanted?" She stands forward, finding her courage from somewhere, and holds her arms out at her side. "You're sick. All of you. The best thing that ever could have happened to me was being taken away from that place. From scumbags like you."

"What? No, no... I wasn't... I didn't..."

He looks to Honey and Derek for support.

"Chelsea, sweetie. Greg isn't one of them. He's your father."

"What?" Chelsea barks, her body rigid as she stares at the three of them, disbelief written all over her face.

I stare at the man she's been so scared of the past few days and it suddenly dawns on me why he looked familiar, although his eyes are blue and Chelsea's dark, they're almost identical.

Holy shit.

Chelsea shakes her head.

"No. I remember you. You used to take her to her bedroom like all the others. You're just one of them who used to fund her drug habit."

"No, I was trying to help."

"Help? If what you're saying is true. You left me there. You left me with all those disgusting men who used to…" She trails off as the blood drains from Greg's face. "Helping me would have been taking me away, feeding me, clothing me, caring for me. But you did none of that."

"I did what I could at the time."

"Well clearly it wasn't good enough. Do you have any idea what it was like for me? That place was hell on earth. And you left me there."

Guilt covers his face. He reaches up and rubs at his jaw as he tries to find the words to reply.

"I brought you food, clothes every time I came. I gave her money but no doubt she blew it all on drugs. I did what I could."

"Bullshit," Chelsea spits.

"If I could have taken you away, given you a better life, I would have. But I couldn't."

"Why? What so important you couldn't help a vulnerable child?"

"If I could go back, I would have done things so differently," he admits.

"But you can't, so tell me, why? Why couldn't you be the man that I needed?"

"Your mother was my student. Admitting you were mine, it would have exposed our affair and I couldn't risk my career. It was the only thing I had."

Shaking her head, Chelsea rubs her hands over her face.

"Your job? Your fucking job. You left me there, knowing exactly what she was doing, what the men were capable of because of your fucking job," she screams, her body visibly trembling with her anger. "Those men they..." She shudders as the memories hit her. "You need to leave. You need to leave and never come back. I'm not interested in anyone who could do that to me or any other child. Not doing anything makes you as bad as them. No, do you know what, it makes you worse. You actively left me there. Left me there to be neglected and abused. You're a fucking monster, just like them."

"No, Rose, please."

Rose?

"That's not who I am. That girl, that one you abandoned, is long gone. I'm no longer that weak and vulnerable child that you forgot about. My name is Chelsea, Chelsea Fierce and I will not forget about all of that, everything you have done or failed to do, just because you've now decided to try to make amends for all your wrongdoings.

"I don't need a father. I've got the most incredible parents now who have given me everything you failed to. You're too late. I don't need you."

The tension in the room is heavy as they continue to stare at each other. The weight of Chelsea's words pressing down on all of us.

"You're right. About all of that, you're right. I just needed to..." he sighs. "I needed to see you. To know that despite all my mistakes that you survived."

"Yeah, I survived. I'm fucked-up beyond belief, but I survived."

Both her mom and dad gasp at her words, both of them obviously wanting to argue but wisely they keep their mouths shut.

"Please, R—Chelsea. I need—" She cuts him a scathing look and he backs down. "Okay, I'm going to go. I'm going to leave this here, just in case you ever want to reach out, even if it's to yell at me. I'd really like to get to know you, if you'd ever consider giving me the time of day." He drops a business card on the table. The room is so silent the sound of it hitting the glass is like a gunshot through the house.

He turns to Honey and Derek. "Thank you for allowing me to do this, welcoming me into your home. I know it's more than I deserve."

With one last look at his daughter, he walks from the room and soon after the house.

The second the front door slams. Chelsea breaks.

The three of us rush to her, thankfully I get to her before her parents and gather her up in my arms as she cries.

I move us to the couch and sit down with her on my lap.

Glancing at her parents, I find a similar look of guilt on their faces that was on Greg's not so long ago.

They think they did the wrong thing. And although I understand, I can't help but think that it needed to happen.

He's been weighing on Chelsea's mind since she first saw his truck, she needed to know the truth, no matter how painful it might be.

Long agonizing minutes pass as we all wait for Chelsea to calm herself down.

As I rub my hand up and down her back, her mom goes to make us all some coffee.

Eventually, she pulls her head from the crook of my neck and wipes the tears from her cheeks.

"I'm sorry," she says weakly.

"Oh, sweetie. You've got nothing to be sorry about," Honey soothes.

"I should have told you about him following me."

"He told us before you came back."

"Is he really my father?"

They both nod. "Yeah. It seems that he's been looking for you for a while. I know it's easy to say, but I really do think he wants to try to make amends."

Chelsea blows out a shaky breath.

"You have no idea what it was like," she says quietly. "The things I've told you all, they're just the tip of the iceberg."

"We know, sweetie. And we won't tell you what to do here. If you decide to never see him again, then we'll respect your decision, he will too. He just had to try."

She nods, holding me a little tighter as she falls silent once again.

"I hate that he can take me right back there as if it was yesterday."

No one speaks. Not a single one of us can take any of that away, make it any better. Although I really fucking wish I could.

After long excruciating minutes, Honey attempts to lighten the mood with a subject change.

"Did you two have a nice weekend?"

"Yeah, it was amazing," Chelsea says.

"I'm glad you've sorted things out."

"We have. This is it now, right?" she asks, her big eyes looking up at me.

"It is."

"Well, welcome to the family then, I guess," Derek says, lifting his mug in our direction.

"We'll leave you to it."

Derek and Honey take their coffee and close the door behind them.

Chelsea snuggles back into me and breathes me in. The move, the knowledge that she feels safe in my arms like this makes my chest ache.

"I love you, Chelsea," I whisper into the top of her head.

"I love you too."

39

———

CHELSEA

I can only assume that somehow Shane managed to carry me out to the pool house because when I wake a while later, that's exactly where I am.

Thankfully, the second I crack my eyes open, I find him sitting beside me playing on his phone.

Reaching out, I place my hand on his thigh and squeeze.

"Hey, how are you feeling?"

"I'm fine," I say, although the memories of what happened when we got back here aren't far away, nor are the images of my past that I try to keep locked in a little box in my head.

"You don't need to put on a brave face for me, baby."

"I know. I just... I don't know what else to do right now. Talking about all that, it just makes it all come back... even after all this time, it's so raw."

He slides down until he's lying on his side facing me.

"You know you can tell me anything and I won't think any different of you, right?"

I nod, the size of the lump in my throat making it impossible to say any words.

He reaches out, wrapping his hand around the back of my

neck and squeezing possessively. I love it so much, a smile starts to twitch at my lips.

"So, you were called Rose?" Hearing the name makes my spine stiffen. I always hated it. I don't think I've ever been as happy as the day my parents told me that I could change it.

To me, Rose signaled someone who was weak, defenseless, and that wasn't who I was by the time Honey and Derek took me in. I was stronger, braver, I could look after myself to some extent. I was fierce. Or at least I wanted to be. Finding out that was their last name was the first time I realized that I was where I belonged.

It didn't take me all that long to settle on a new name. The second Chelsea hit me, I knew it was right. Chelsea Fierce was the perfect name for the new me. The girl who took no shit, gave zero fucks and got everything she wanted.

It was great until I realized those things didn't really make me happy. I isolated myself from everyone, put walls up even with those who were meant to be my friends. I see that now, and I vow to never allow myself to fall back into that old life. I've got Shane now, and hopefully a real friend in Rae. Things are definitely looking up.

"Yep. That's what the woman who pushed me out decided I should be called. She probably couldn't spell anything longer." It's meant to be a joke, but the expression on Shane's face tells me he finds the whole thing anything but funny.

"It's pretty, but I can't imagine calling that. You're definitely a Chelsea."

"I agree. Although I didn't lose it completely. I'm now Chelsea Rose. I figured that my past was always going to be a part of me, so I may as well embrace it to some extent."

"Although it's horrible, hearing just some of the things you experienced makes me feel murderous, it did make you who you are. And I, for one, think you're pretty incredible."

"Yeah?"

"Yeah."

We stare at each other for the longest time. No words are said, they're not needed. That connection I craved is right there, and it's everything I need.

"Are you hungry?"

"Is that a serious question?" I ask with a laugh.

"Your mom came down to ask if we wanted to join them for dinner. You were asleep, so I declined. Thought we could order pizza or something. What?" he asks when I fall silent.

"I kind of fancy going out. We've been inside the whole weekend."

"Okay. What do you want to do?"

Thirty minutes later, we're both changed and heading out of the pool house.

We embark on the long walk from my parents' house to the seafront. The sun is setting, casting a stunning orange hue all over the bay as the moon makes an appearance for the night.

We stop at a diner and order takeout slices of pizza. We steered clear of Aces end of the beach, knowing the chances of bumping into someone from school would be high. I don't want to avoid them really, but equally, I want to keep Shane to myself while I can. I'm not ready for our weekend to be over.

"How are you feeling?" Shane asks once we've both finished eating.

We're sitting on the sea wall, our legs dangling over with the sand below, watching the waves crash in.

"Honestly, I have no idea. I always assumed that my dad was just some random guy who donated his sperm. I didn't think I had a father, as such, let alone one who was present in my early years."

"Did you mean what you said about not wanting anything to do with him?"

Did I? I think back to what I said to him and I wince. My

words might have been true, he shouldn't have left me there, but now some time has passed, and I feel less ambushed by the whole thing, I know that the situation probably wasn't that simple. Things rarely are.

My biological father taking me in his arms and carrying me away from hell was a fantasy I had many times as a child. I imagined him being some wealthy businessman who desperately wanted me but for some reason couldn't get to me. It was one of the stories I formulated in my head to escape my reality. Sadly, that one, nor any of the others ever materialized and when I was taken away, it was by the state and I was dumped in some kids home, not a wealthy man's penthouse.

I sigh. "I don't know."

Reaching over, he takes my hand and lifts my knuckles to his lips.

"Well, whatever you decide. I'm here for you."

A sob erupts from my throat without warning.

"Chels?"

"I'm okay. You just really don't know how much that means to me."

I wipe away the tear that drops before he notices and breathe in a deep breath.

I don't deserve this. I don't deserve him. But fuck, I'm going to do everything I can from now on to keep him.

"I can come with you, it might soften the blow," I offer as Shane puts his sneakers on the next morning, ready to go home and face the music with his father.

"No, it's okay. Just be here waiting for when I get back. There's a good chance I'll need you." His eyes darken as he says the words and my insides clench with desire.

As much as I hate it when he argues with his dad, I can't

deny that it fires him up in the perfect way and I do love helping to take his mind off it after.

"How do you want me?" I say in what I hope is a seductive voice.

"Hmm... in my jersey with nothing beneath."

"Done. Message me when you're leaving."

Standing, he stalks toward me. "I've changed my mind. I think I'll stay and take that right now."

"As much as I want to agree. You need to do this. The last thing you want is it hanging over your head during the holidays."

"I know," he mutters, brushing his lips against mine.

As much as I hate to do it, I push my palms against his chest to put a stop to his attempt to put it off.

"Go, Shane. I'll be here when you get back."

"Ugh, fine."

Falling down onto the couch, I watch as he pushes the door open but instead of walking straight through it and disappearing around the house, he still for a beat.

"What?" I ask when the color drains from his face.

"Can you hear shouting?"

Sitting up, I listen.

"Fuck," Shane barks before running to the house. I jump from the couch, hot on his heels as he runs through the open kitchen doors and into the hallway.

The shouting ceases as he comes to an abrupt halt when his eyes land on the people before us.

"Brett, no," Maddie cries, pulling at his arm as he storms toward Shane.

"I told you that you were going to fuck everything up," he bellows at Shane.

I want to do something, say something, but I'm frozen on the spot as I stare at the fury rolling off him in waves.

"How do you expect to be successful now? No one will

want you with a kid attached to you. You're a fucking disgrace, boy. Fucking disgrace."

"I don't give a fuck, Dad. I don't want the NFL. I don't want your dream."

"No? Am I not good enough for you? Is all the legwork I've done to get you a chance at the best college teams in the country not up to your standard?"

"I don't want it. I never have, but you refuse to listen to me."

"No? So tell me now, what do you want?"

There's a beat of utter silence, the calm before the storm because all of us know that this is going to get worse before it gets better.

"I want Chelsea. I want Chelsea and our baby."

Brett lets out a laugh, but it's nowhere near amused. It's menacing, and it makes a shiver run down my spine.

"You're fucking delusional. You think you're able to look after a baby? And with her?" Disapproval drips from his features as he turns to look at me. "She's nothing but a cheap slut."

"Brett," Dad barks, his fists curled in anger. He steps forward, but Mom places her hand on his arm and stops him.

Shane's chest swells with anger as he steps up to his dad, his fists clenched, ready to fight.

"Leave it, please," I beg, reaching out to touch his arm but he doesn't acknowledge my touch, he's too lost to his anger.

"Take that back."

His dad laughs again. "You're a fucking idiot, boy. You're throwing everything away. You choose her and you're giving up everything I can offer you. Everything."

"How many times? I don't fucking want it."

Brett's eyes turn black, cold, as his lips press into a thin line and the vein in his neck pulsates menacingly.

"You ungrateful little..."

"Nooo," I cry as Brett's arm suddenly flies toward Shane.

"Brett, no," Maddie screams racing forward.

Dad jumps into action, but we're all too late.

Brett's fist connects with Shane's cheek. The crack is so loud it makes my stomach turn over.

Shane stumbles back, his shoulder connecting with the wall before he falls back.

"Shane," I shout. There's a commotion behind me as I drop to my knees beside him. "Shane? Shane?"

"Fucking animal," Maddie spits before joining me at his other side.

"Baby, wake up. Shane. Fuck." Her eyes are wide and full of fear as she stares at him.

Jumping to her feet, she marches over to Brett who's now being restrained by my dad as he attempts to push him to the front door. His lip split open and blood trickling down his chin from where my dad must have retaliated on Shane's behalf.

"If you've fucking hurt him, I'll kill you." She pokes him in the chest as spittle flies from her mouth. "I'll fucking kill you."

"I'd like to see you try."

"Who are you? What happened to the man I married, huh? When did he turn into such a vile asshole?"

Brett doesn't say anything, he just stares at his wife as if she's lost her goddamn mind. Anger and frustration burn in my stomach for her.

"We're done. Expect to hear from my lawyer. I can't spend another day pretending I love you." She turns away, her back to him, unable to even look at his face. "Get him the hell out of here before I call the police."

After putting up a bit of a fight, Dad eventually gets Brett out of the front door and slams it behind him.

Fucking hell.

Remembering that Shane's laid out next to me, I rip my

eyes from Maddie and down to him. The most incredible sight greets me. His beautiful green eyes.

"Shane, oh my god," I wail, dropping down to him and wrapping my arms around his shoulders.

"I'm fine. I'm okay," he says into my hair as his arms come around me as if I'm the one who needs it right now.

Who am I kidding? I fucking do. That was terrifying.

After a few seconds, I release him, and he pushes himself so he's sitting against the wall.

"Well, that went well," he jokes, looking up at the concerned, traumatized faces staring down at him.

Maddie bursts into tears before Mom ushers her toward the kitchen. Dad walks toward us and holds his hand out to Shane to pull him up, who in turn does the same to me seeing as I'm still on the floor.

"I'll go get you some ice," I say, looking at Shane's swelling face.

"I need a drink," Dad announces, shaking his hand out and marching in the same direction Mom and Maddie just left.

We follow to find Mom pouring Maddie a glass of whiskey before Dad takes it from her and tips the bottle to his lips.

"Can I?" Shane asks once Dad's lowered the bottle, and he reluctantly passes it over, clearly deciding that it's okay to break his no alcohol for minors rule after what just went down.

Shane swallows a shot before passing the bottle back.

Ten minutes later, we all find ourselves sitting around the dining table. Shane with an ice pack pressed to his face and the adults all nursing their drinks. No one seems to have noticed that it's only just past midday. Although, to be fair, if I weren't pregnant, I think I'd want a drink right now.

"I'll make up the guest room for you tonight," Mom offers

to Maddie. You're more than welcome to stay as long as you like.

"T-thank you. I should go to the house to get some stuff before he burns it all."

"I don't think he'd—" Maddie's look cuts Mom's words off.

"What about..." Maddie flicks a look to Shane and me and I swallow nervously.

Mom chuckles, the sound of it feels so good after the stress and tension of the past hour. "I think he's already moved in, don't you?"

They all turn to us.

"You've both proved to us that you're adults now who can make your own decisions. So what do you two want to do?"

"Honey was right," Shane says before I get a chance. "I'm pretty sure I've already moved in." A wide smile spreads across my face. "Of course, that's if it's okay with you both." He looks to Mom and Dad, who both smile at him.

"You're going to be parents in a few months. I'm not sure we're in any position to stop you."

"I'm going to get a job, part-time obviously, so we've got our own money. I'm not sure what I'm going to do about college yet, but I will be going—"

"We both will. We're going to make this work. All we ask is for your support. If we can stay in the pool house for now, that would be great, but we'll get our own place as soon as we can. We want to do this the right way, for us, and for this little one."

Both Mom and Maddie's eyes fill with tears once again.

"We'll be here for all of you, no matter what," Mom says.

"You're both going to be incredible parents," Maddie adds.

"Only time will tell," I say with a laugh.

40

CHELSEA

"We're going to be late," Shane says, dropping down on the edge of the bed, looking hot in his button-down and dress pants. His hair is styled and just waiting for his hands to run through it to mess it up, or I might in a minute because I've got a thing about his messy, just-fucked hair. That just shows the one-eighty my life has taken because his long shaggy locks used to be one of the things I used to mock him for. It might be shorter now than it used to be, but it's no less of a mess. Now I just spend my time running my fingers through it and using it to hold him against me instead of telling him to cut it off.

"I'm nearly ready," I say, but I'm too focused on his reflection in my mirror to finish off my makeup. "Are you sure they want me to go?"

"Of course. Amalie and Jake invited both of us. They know we come as a package deal now."

"Oh god, we're one of them now, aren't we?"

"What do you mean?"

"You know how annoyingly sweet Amalie, Jake, Camila, and Mason are? That's us now too."

"I should hope so," he says with a shit-eating grin on his face. "I was always jealous of them."

"Ah, I forgot that you wanted Amalie first."

"I thought I did, I was just trying to distract myself from wanting what I couldn't have."

"Who was that?" I ask innocently, batting my eyelashes at him.

"Oh, just this insanely hot cheerleader. She wasn't interested though."

I make quick work of applying my lipstick, the kind that doesn't immediately rub off at the first touch of a kiss, good thing really seeing as I intend on doing just that the second I get to him.

Pushing from the stool, I stalk over to him. He watches me, fire burning in his eyes as I get closer.

"That dress," he says, biting down on his bottom lip. I'm wearing a skintight, burgundy body con dress that shows off every one of my curves, including my very small baby bump. Anyone who didn't know I was pregnant wouldn't see it, but I can and I'm so ready to embrace it.

I stop in front of him and reach for his shirt. I wrap my fingers in the soft cotton and pull him from the bed until he's standing before me.

"I'm glad you like it, one of your gifts is hiding beneath it. If you're lucky, you can unwrap it later."

He groans as if he's in physical pain.

"Maybe we should cancel on the party."

"Nope, you said we were invited." Reaching up on my tiptoes, I brush my lips against his as I slide my hand down my body to find his already hard cock. "Down boy, you've got a few hours yet."

"You're killing me. Get your shoes on and let's go before I really do change my mind."

Regretfully, I take a step back from him and turn to get my shoes.

"Come on then, let's go," I announce once I'm ready.

I glance around the room, which is now filled with his possessions as well as my own. I loved this place before, but since he officially moved in and made the space ours, I love it that much more.

The day after the showdown with Brett, my dad escorted both Shane and Maddie to their house. It turned out not to be necessary as he wasn't there, we've since discovered that he's in New York, but there was plenty of evidence that he had been there because the place was smashed to pieces. They didn't stay long enough to do anything about it though. They just grabbed what they wanted and left without looking back.

Maddie hasn't decided what she's going to do next, whether she'll eventually move back in, or not. She's said that she'll get through the holidays and then try to make some decisions for her future.

Thankfully, our house is big enough so now not only is Shane in here with me, his mom is in a guest room and we've got Luca and Leon too so that we can all celebrate the holidays as one big family. It might not be perfect for some of them, but to me, it's everything and for the first time in possibly forever, I'm actually excited.

I've got Shane's gifts all wrapped and ready for tomorrow, and I can't wait to see if he likes them. Plus, there's the little sexy set I've got on under this dress as an extra treat of course.

The drive to Amalie and Jake's new house takes a little over thirty minutes. Seeing as they're both planning on going to Maddison once Amalie graduates next year, they wanted to be on the right side of town.

I shake my head at how crazy this all is. They've bought a house, we're having a baby. Shit, someone will get engaged next. It's insane seeing as we're all eighteen or thereabout, but like I've said many times before, it just feels right. I guess what they say is true, when you know, you know.

"This place is cute, although not your average house for two eighteen-year-olds to own," I say as we pull up on the street the GPS brought us to.

It's a stylish gray and white modern duplex with huge windows and a cute front yard.

My mind runs away with me as I picture Shane and me in a place like this with a toddler running around. Butterflies erupt at the thought.

"It's impressive, that's for sure."

"I bet Jake doesn't know what to do with himself after that shitty trailer."

Shane turns to me, his brows drawn together. "Jake lived in a trailer? I thought he lived with his aunt and uncle."

"Yeah until they banished him to the back of their property in a damn old trailer that you wouldn't wish on your worst enemy."

"How didn't I know this?"

"It's a closely guarded secret. He used to want you all to think he had it all, but the reality was that being captain was about all he had. Until Amalie, of course."

"Wow, I never would have guessed."

"Exactly as he intended."

Movement inside catches my eye and I watch for a second as Mason and Jake talk and laugh with each other.

Happiness tugs at my stomach that they've found their forever with their girls.

"Are you planning on getting out?" Shane asks, opening my door for me. I hadn't even realized he'd left the car.

"Yeah, sorry."

I can't help the nerves that assault me as we stand at their front door. The majority of the people inside have every right to hate me, yet here I am invited to their housewarming cum Christmas Eve party like I'm one of them.

"Alright," Jake says eloquently when he pulls the door open. He looks as gorgeous as ever, but unlike all the years in the past, it does nothing for me.

"Nice place," I say, stepping inside when he moves aside and Shane gestures for me to do so.

"It's going to take some getting used to, that's for sure."

"Hey," Amalie says, rushing down the hall to greet us, looking totally harassed.

"Hi. Is everything okay?"

"Yeah, just trying to get the food ready. Excuse me." She races back off in the same direction she came.

"Ignore her, she just wanted everything to be perfect. I keep telling her to chill out but she won't have it."

I stifle a laugh. I bet him telling her that is really not helping.

"I'll go and see if she wants some help."

"Rather you than me."

Leaving Shane with Jake, I go in the direction Amalie disappeared, assuming it's to the kitchen.

When I get there, I find her flitting around counters full of food and drink.

"Can I help with anything?" She startles and turns to me with wide eyes. "Sorry, I didn't mean to scare you."

"Sorry, it's me. I'm just... gah. I know I'm putting too much pressure on myself. It's just..." She looks away from me. "I'm sorry, you don't care about all this."

"Of course I do. What's wrong?"

"It's just my first Christmas without them," she says, tears filling her eyes before she averts them.

Of course, I should have thought of that before now. The first Christmas without your parents must be so tough.

Reaching out, I take her hand in mine. "It's okay to be sad. No one expects you to be okay during this time."

"I know, I just need to keep busy so I don't spend the entire time thinking about what I would be doing with them if they were still h-here." Her chin trembles, her voice cracking at the end of her words.

I have no idea if she wants one from me, but without putting much thought into it, I pull her into my arms for a hug.

It's only brief, but when she pulls back, she's got a small smile on her lips.

"Thank you. I needed that."

"Put me to work, what can I do to help?"

"Can you make me a drink, a strong one?"

"Sure. Any preference?"

"Surprise me."

Walking over to the counter with the bottles, I find everything from beers to spirits and mixers. Pulling my phone from my purse, I look up cocktail recipes and mix one up for her.

"What is it?" she asks when I pass it over.

"A Screaming Orgasm. I thought it might help right now."

She stares at me for a beat before she burst out laughing.

"Shit, I needed that," she says, taking a sip as we're joined by two others.

"We've been sent for more beer," Mason says, pulling the refrigerator open like it's his house.

"Ugh, why couldn't he do it himself?" Amalie grumbles before putting her glass down and stalking from the room. I wince, feeling a little sorry for Jake. Amalie's in a bad place right now, and he's about to be the one to feel the force of it. I'm sure he's more than capable though.

"Oh, looks like he's in the doghouse."

"Leave her alone," Camila says, stepping up to Mason.

"What? I'm just saying."

"Could I have a word with you two?" I ask, stepping forward.

Both of their heads spin my way and they stare at me as if they didn't know I was in the room.

"Of course," Mason says softly while his girl places her hands on her hips and raises her brows.

I'm not surprised, I knew which of the two of them was likely to make me work for it. Rightly so I guess after I sent her after her cheating boyfriend. Although it might have been a bitch move, at least she found of the truth before it went on any longer.

"I just wanted to say that I'm sorry, I really am. How I behaved before was unforgivable—"

"Yet here you are asking for it," Camila snaps.

"No, no, I'm not. I'd understand if you never did. I just want you to know how much I regret all of it. My head was a mess, and I was making stupid decisions."

"Like sleeping with Shane?"

I can't help but laugh. "No, that was probably the only sensible thing I did back then."

Camila opens her mouth to say more, but she must change her mind because she soon closes it again.

Mason, however, just gives me a soft smile. "You're all good, girl." Stepping up to me, he gives me a brief hug. Camila gives him death stares the entire time, making me wonder why he thought it was a good idea.

"Stand down, Cami bear. It's over." He chuckles.

Camila steps forward, but it's nothing like the friendly way her boyfriend did. She frowns and points at me. "If you hurt him. If a few weeks down the line this all turns out to be one of your sick games, I swear I'll... I'll fucking kill you."

"Okay, baby. That's enough." Mason wraps his hand

around Camila's upper arms and pulls her back into his chest and wraps his arms around her.

"What Camila is trying to say is that we're glad you're back and we hope things work out for you from here on out."

"No, I wasn't—" Camila protests until Mason spins her and cuts off her words with his lips.

While they're distracted, I take a handful of the beers they came in for and go to join the others.

Amalie is still busying herself arranging the food she's prepared on the dining table while Jake looks at her with concern in his eyes.

"Here she is," Ethan announces, distracting me from the obvious tension in the room as I place the bottles down. "How's Rosewood's next star doing," he drawls, clearly already one too many beers down as he places his hand on my belly.

I notice Shane tense as he watches Ethan touch me, but a quick shake of my head and he soon relaxes. Ethan is anything but a threat.

"Keep your hands to yourself, Savage," Rae barks, swatting his forearm to make him release me. "I'm sorry, please ignore him."

"It's okay, I'm used to him by now."

"Yeah, Chelsea has been my wing-woman for years, she knows the drill."

"Oh yeah?" Rae stands to her full height, all of about five foot two, and stares at him. "On the prowl tonight, are you?"

"Uh huh, got my sights on this feisty little thing."

"Jesus," I mutter, slipping around them and joining Shane on the couch.

"Everything okay?" he asks as I pass him one of the beers I kept hold of.

"Yeah, just a normal day in Rosewood," I say with a chuckle.

"What's up with Amalie?"

"It's her first Christmas since her parents died. She's struggling."

"Ah of course."

"Brit, come and sit down. None of these fuckers care how you've arranged the sausage rolls, baby."

Amalie shoots Jake a scathing look from where she's still moving things around, but she must see something in him because after a second she backs away and out of the room.

Jake sits forward as if he's about to follow her, but it's not necessary because in only seconds she returns with the drink I made her.

"What have you got there?" Jake asks, making Amalie smirk as she sits beside him.

"It's a Screaming Orgasm. Chelsea made it for me." She grins.

"Careful if she made it," Camila pipes up, earning herself the attention of the entire room. Alcohol sure does give her a loose tongue.

"That's enough," Mason says as the awkward tension begins to lift.

"No, it's okay. I deserve it," I admit as Shane's grip on me tightens.

Amalie shrugs. "I trust her," she says, lifting the glass to her lips and taking a huge mouthful.

Something inside me swells. The regret for what I did is still there, I think it always will be, but the happiness I now feel starts to push it down somewhat.

The drinks flow, well for everyone bar me, and thankfully everyone begins to relax into the evening. Everyone gets drunker and drunker and for once, I get to watch as they begin stumbling their way to the toilet and clumsily missing their mouths as they try to have another drink. I never realized quite how stupid we all look as the alcohol takes over.

I enjoy myself more than I should just watching them all,

and unlike I was expecting, I don't really miss not being a part of it. There's something very sobering about being the sensible one.

"I really fucking love you," Shane slurs as he pulls me onto his lap and pushes my skirt up my thighs so I can straddle him.

"What are you doing?" My argument is weak at best, I might not be under the influence right now, but any touch from him has a similar effect. He makes me lose my mind with need.

"Kiss me," he demands.

I stare into his desire filled eyes and I'm powerless, unable to deny him anything he asks. Leaning forward, I press my lips to his. His tongue immediately darts out and pushes past my lips.

I have no idea what the others are doing around us, not that I care. My entire focus is on Shane as I shamelessly grind my hips down on his growing cock.

"Get a room." Ethan's booming voice eventually cuts through my lust and I pull back, my chest heaving and my body strung tight to continue.

"Don't even think about taking his advice and having sex in our new house," Jake barks, earning himself a look from Amalie. I'm not sure if she's just annoyed in general with everything to do with this time of year because of the memories it's bringing up for her or if she's just pissed off at him, but there's a definite tension between the two of them. And the words that fall from Shane's drunken lips next sure don't help.

"Oh yeah, you worried someone will do a better job of it? You do know I'm the best she's ever had, right?" His final words are muffled as I place my palm over his mouth.

"Shane!" I whisper-squeal, mortified that he's just said that out loud for everyone to hear.

Ethan, Mason, and Rae burst out laughing, but Amalie and Jake are much less amused.

I turn to look at the couple as Amalie's face turns beet red before she pushes from the couch and storms from the room.

"Bro, I think you'd better go and prove your worth. Give her a real one of those screaming orgasms," Ethan says, a smirk firmly in place as he talks.

"I'm so sorry," I say to Jake as he looks at the door, torn over what to do.

With a sigh, he stands from the couch and follows, but he stops at the door and looks back at me.

"I was really, really drunk. I'm surprised I stayed awake long enough to finish that night."

Shame burns at my insides and colors my cheeks. Great, the night I'd dreamed of for years really was one big drunken mistake to him.

"Well, I know for a fact that one of us didn't finish," I mutter, my need to have the last word getting the better of me.

"Oh burn, bro. Burn," Ethan barks while the others snigger around us.

"Fucking hell," Jake mutters before ducking out of the room to go and find his girl.

"We should probably leave now."

"Why? Things just got interesting," Ethan says, his voice still full of amusement. "I want to hear more about sex god Jake Thorn not completing his duties."

Shane's hands grip my ass reminding me that I'm still straddling him like a hussy.

"Yeah, it's definitely time for us to go."

Climbing from his lap, I make quick work of pulling my dress down. It's not like they haven't seen my ass before, but I'm a different person now and the only one I want looking at me is currently half asleep on the couch.

"Shane," I shout, startling him awake. "Let's go."

He mumbles something incoherent as he rearranges himself in his pants. As glad as I am that he can keep it up while plastered, now really isn't the time to show it off.

Reaching for his hand, I pull him from the couch.

He stumbles a little before steadying himself and wrapping his arm around my shoulder.

"I love you Chelsea Fierce," he slurs.

"I love you too. Now let's go before I can't move you."

"Do you want help?" Both Ethan and Mason stand, but I shake my head.

"I've got him. You carry on enjoying yourselves."

"Because listening to those two make up will be so much fun," Rae complains with a roll of her eyes.

"Have a great Christmas," I say, ignoring her comment. "We'll see you New Year's Eve at Zayn's?"

"Sure thing. Have a good one."

With a few more goodbyes, I eventually manage to get Shane out of the house and into the car.

"If you pass out before we get home, you're going to have to sleep in the car," I warn him. I'm lying, of course. I wouldn't be able to sleep knowing he was out there alone, but I hope my words are enough to keep him with me.

Shane keeps me amused all the way home, muttering mostly incoherent things but every now and then he'll drop in how much he loves me, or how badly he wants to fuck me and explain in vivid detail the things he wants to do to me. I can't deny that by the time I pull up on my parents' driveway that I'm a ball of need.

Sadly, by that time, he's also fallen asleep and is snoring lightly beside me.

"Shane. Shane," I say, shaking his shoulder to wake him. "Come on, or I'll have to go and get your brothers to get you out."

Still he snores.

"For fuck's sake, Shane."

Trying a different tact to get him alert, I pop his seatbelt and skim my hand up his thigh, rubbing his cock through his pants. In only seconds, it starts to harden under my touch.

"Wake up, baby. You've got promises to fulfill," I purr in his ear.

He groans, thrusting his hips up to get more.

"Chelsea." His voice is slurred, rough and deep.

"Wake up and get to the pool house and you can have whatever you want."

Suddenly, his eyes fly open.

"Fuck," he barks, his chest heaving and his eyes almost black with desire.

"Hey."

"Hey." A smile curls at his lips as he stares at me and lust curls at my insides.

"Shall we go inside?"

"Yes."

He somewhat clumsily manages to get himself out of the car before I wrap my arm around his waist in an attempt to steady him.

We sway our way around the back of the house. He trips and stumbles but thankfully stays on his feet. It makes me think of all the times my parents have collected me in a similar state and had to deal with getting me to bed. This is making me realize that I should probably get them a better Christmas present.

Finally, we get to the pool house. Shane leans against the wall, his eyelids getting heavy once again.

The second we're inside, he heads for the bedroom before falling face-first onto the bed and almost immediately starts snoring.

I can't help but laugh at him, and I drop to my knees and slip his shoes off. Not exactly what I thought I'd be doing on my knees tonight, but hey. He deserves this. After everything both his father and I have put him through the past few weeks, he needed to lose himself for a night.

I manage to roll him over and get his pants off, but after undoing the buttons on his shirt, I give up trying to get it off him. He's totally out of it and no help at all.

Kicking my shoes off, I peel my dress from my body and look at the black lace underwear I'd bought especially for tonight. Not wanting to waste it, I find my cell in my purse and open the camera. I snap a couple of pictures before sending them to Shane with a sarcastic comment about what he's missed out on. I'm sure he'll enjoy those when he looks at his cell tomorrow.

After finding his jersey, I pull it over my head and make use of the bathroom before crawling into bed beside him.

He might be out of it, but the second I press my back against him, his arm wraps around my waist and I'm pulled back so that were connected in every way possible.

"I love you, Chels."

"I love you too, Shane. Merry Christmas."

41

SHANE

I have no idea what time it is when I wake, but the sun is streaming through from the living area and my head pounds.

It takes me a second to remember the night before.

Fucking Ethan insisting we all do shots.

I want to curl back into Chelsea and sleep away the rest of the day, but my need for the bathroom and painkillers are too pressing.

Sitting from the bed, I find I'm just wearing my boxers and open shirt from the night before. I glance over at Chelsea and smile. She tried to look after me last night.

My pressing need for the bathroom keeps me from watching her peacefully sleeping any longer and I stand from the bed, shedding my shirt as I go.

I do my thing before brushing my teeth in the hope it'll make me feel a little more human before going in search of some Advil.

I down a bottle of water with the tablets before heading back to sleep, but when I walk into the bedroom, a very different idea pops into my head.

Chelsea's shifted since I left and she's now lying on her stomach, the sheets pushed aside with my jersey up around her waist. Her round ass is on full display with the scrap of lace she's wearing.

My cock swells as my mouth waters.

Time for her first present of the day, I think,

Starting at her ankle, I kiss up her leg until I get to the swell of her ass. Palming one side, I bite down on the other.

"What the—oh," she cries, quickly relaxing beneath me. "As you were."

She rests her head on her arm and looks down at me as I continue.

Slipping my finger beneath the lace, she parts her legs a little to give me better access and I slide it through her wetness.

"Hmm... were you dreaming about this?"

"Always," she says on a gasp as I slide one finger inside her. Her muscles clamp down, hungrily trying to suck me deeper. "You promised me all these dirty things last night and then you went and passed out."

"I'd better make it up to you then."

She moans when I pull my finger from her and instead wrap my hands around her hips. I lift her until she's on all fours and wrap my fingers around the sides of her panties.

I pull them down until they fall to her knees but I make no move to remove them further, I'm too desperate for her.

Leaning forward, I lick up her seam.

She cries out and I spear my tongue inside her.

"Oh god," she whimpers as I focus my attention on her clit. She pushes back into me, needing more. Sliding two fingers deep inside her, I suck, lick and bite until she's crying out my name, her legs trembling as she reaches her climax.

"Fuck, Shane." Her arms give out and she falls down onto the pillow, her ass still temptingly up in the air.

Crawling forward, I push the waist of my boxer briefs down just enough to release my cock. I run the head through her wetness before slowly pushing inside her.

She groans as I stretch her open until she's full of me.

Gliding my hand down her spine, I slide my fingers into her hair and tug gently. Her back arches, allowing me to slide a little deeper.

"So good," I groan, slowly pulling out before sliding straight back in.

"More, Shane. More."

Picking up the tempo, I give her exactly what she craves until the only sounds that fill the pool house are those of our heavy breathing and our skin connecting as we both chase our orgasms.

The second her pussy clenches with the beginnings of her release, I fall headfirst into my own.

"Fucking hell, that was some wake up," Chelsea says between heaving breaths as I fall down beside her, trying to catch my own breath.

"Merry Christmas, baby."

A wide smile spreads across her face as it occurs to her what day it is.

"Merry Christmas."

Turning over, she pulls open the drawer of her nightstand before placing two beautifully wrapped presents in front of me.

"I was wearing your first present, but you seem to have removed the bottom half."

She lifts my jersey up to show me the matching bra to the set she was wearing.

"You'll just have to wear it for me another time."

"I'm sure that can be arranged. Go on," she prompts, nudging the gifts closer.

Taking hold of the biggest one first, I make quick work of ripping the paper away to find a nondescript black box. Narrowing my eyes at her, I lift the top off to find a stunning silver watch staring back at me.

"Chels," I say, knowing that it's more than she can probably afford right now.

"Look at the back."

Pulling the timepiece from its cushion, I flip it over.

Shane. My one and only x

Emotion clogs my throat as I stare down at her words.

"Thank you so much," I manage to say around the lump after a few seconds.

"You're welcome."

Removing my old one, I drop it on the nightstand and place the new one on my wrist.

"It's perfect."

"And this one."

Wondering what else she's done for me, I rip it open but soon realize that this one is even more sentimental because it's a photo frame with 'I love my daddy' engraved in the dark wood, and in the center, our ultrasound picture.

Reaching out, I run my fingertip over our baby.

"It still blows my mind," I whisper.

"Me too. I'm not sure I'll believe it until he or she is in my arms."

I nod, totally understanding where she's coming from.

Resting it on my pillow, I climb from the bed so I can get her gift.

"This is for you," I say, crawling back on the bed to sit beside her.

She smiles at me before taking the small gift. My stomach is in knots, it's nothing huge, but I really want her to like it. It took me long enough to find it.

I bite down on the inside of my cheek as she rips into the paper and flips open the lid of the jewelry box.

"Oh, it's beautiful,' she gushes as she stares down at the necklace and I breathe out a huge sigh of relief.

"Yeah?"

"Yeah."

"Can I?" I hold my hand out and she places the box in it.

I have the necklace out in seconds and I hold up the three interlocked bands and turn them over.

"Look closer." I hold it out for her and she gasps the moment she sees our names engraved in it. "And we can add the third once we decide on a name."

"Oh my god," she sobs, her hand comes up to cover her mouth as tears fill her eyes.

She quickly pushes from the headboard and holds her hair out of the way so that I can place it around her neck. Turning back around to me, she holds the pendant between her fingers.

"Thank you so much. I love it."

"I love you," I say, leaning forward and capturing her lips.

"I'm not sure you've ever gotten ready so fast," I say when Chelsea stands from her dressing table in record time.

"I'm excited," she says with a beaming smile. "I think this is the first Christmas in, well ever, that I've looked forward to."

Like me, she's wearing a novelty Christmas sweater that our mothers insisted on. hers has "baking my little pudding" stitched across the front whereas mine is a standard Santa design.

"You look cute."

"I feel like I should shove a pillow up my sweater so it makes sense. My minute bump doesn't really do it any justice."

"You'll regret even saying that in a few months." I laugh,

pulling her into my arms and tucking a lock of her hair behind her ear. "Are you ready for the craziness?"

"More than ready. This is the first of loads of amazing Christmases. Just think, this time next year, we'll be surrounded by toys and hopefully an excited baby."

"I'm not sure he or she will be all that excited at six months old."

"Well, we can be excited enough for the baby too."

"That sounds like a plan, baby. Shall we?"

"Yes," she squeals with delight before we grab the couple of bags of presents we have for our families and make our way to the main house.

Honey and Mom are busy in the kitchen making waffles, there's already a stack high enough to feed the five thousand.

Derek, Luca, and Leon sit at the table eagerly waiting for their food delivery.

"At fucking last," Luca barks when he spots us. "We're not allowed to eat until you two show your faces. Mom wanted to come and get you, we thought it probably wasn't a good idea."

Chelsea's hand squeezes mine and when I glance over her cheeks are a little red.

"We were exchanging gifts before heading up."

"Sure you were," Luca says with a wink. "Gifts. Seems to be that you gave her your gift a few months ago."

"That's enough you two. I want to have some appetite left for the waffles," Derek complains.

We take our seats and not two seconds later, Honey and Mom bring over breakfast.

Luca and Leon dive in as if they've not eaten in a month while the rest of us watch them in fascination.

"What?" Leon mumbles around a mouthful. "I'm hungry."

Laughing at them, I grab a waffle for Chelsea before placing another on my plate.

"How was the party last night?" Mom asks, reminding me

about the hangover that's still thudding away nicely at my temples.

"I'm not sure Shane remembers much of it." Chelsea chuckles.

"Overdo it all, did you, son?" Derek asks.

"Something like that."

Thankfully the conversation takes a different turn and I'm able to put aside the fact I don't remember how I got back into the pool house last night, let alone how the evening at Amalie and Jake's might have ended.

I shrug to myself as I look around the table at those I love. Things might be crazy right now. Chelsea and I might not have a clue what the next few months and years might hold for us, but at this moment surrounded by all these incredible people that I know will support us no matter what, I couldn't be happier.

We have the best Christmas I think I've ever had. We laugh, joke, eat incredible food, thanks to our mothers, and we enjoy each other's company. It's the exact kind of Christmas I've already dreamed of and I can only hope that those in our future are as heartwarming.

The sun's long set when I find myself alone with Chelsea in her parents' kitchen as she gets herself a snack. How she's still hungry after everything we've consumed today, I have no idea.

"Hey," I say, wrapping my arms around her middle and holding her tight.

"Hey."

"Have you had a good day?" I ask.

"Yeah. The best. Thank you."

"What are you thanking me for?"

She spins in my arms and stares up into my eyes.

"For everything. For just being you and making all my dreams come true."

I open my mouth to respond, but I have no words. Instead, I put everything I feel for her into my kiss.

"I love you, Chelsea Fierce," I whisper against her lips, my palm pressing tenderly against her swollen stomach.

"I love you too."

42

CHELSEA

"**I**'m not sure how I feel about saying goodbye to this year," I admit as we walk through Zayn's front door.

All our parents—minus Brett, who's still in New York—are at Rosewood's annual New Year's Eve celebration that Camila's mom organizes every year and tonight is Zayn's turn to host our party.

A huge part of me is ready to see the back of a lot of things that have happened this year, but another part of me wants to cherish them. Yeah, I fucked up. Yeah, I did things I'll regret for the rest of my life, but equally, I got the two best things in my life.

I glance at Shane as he leads us toward the back of the house and Zayn's den. I can't help but smile as I think of all the things he's taught me. How he's shown me that it is possible to have exactly what I always wanted. Someone in my corner. Someone who would fight for me no matter what and love me so hard that it's almost unfathomable.

"I know you're staring."

"As you should. You look hot tonight."

"I'm nothing compared to you. At least every guy at

Rosewood and beyond knows you're taken now," he says, and when I follow his gaze, I find almost everyone looking our way.

It seems that despite everyone being at home for the holidays, they've not forgotten the hottest gossip to hit Rosewood High in a while.

"Ignore them. They're just jealous that I got you and they didn't."

"I'm not sure anyone had any interest in me before you, baby."

I shrug, none of it matters. That's all in the past. We've got so much to focus on for our future, and that's where I intend on putting all my energy.

A cheer erupts as we enter Zayn's den, and when I look up, I find almost all of the team and the majority of the squad.

I haven't seen any of them since running from school the day Shelly exposed my secret.

Victoria, Tash, Aria, and a couple of the JV girls immediately see us and come over to congratulate me before taking great pleasure in explaining that Shelly is off the squad for good after that last stunt. Hartmann is on her case big time, one more wrong move and she's out of Rosewood for good.

Part of me is glad, she's clearly a conniving bitch with a seriously dodgy moral compass, but another part of me knows that it could so easily have been me. If my parents hadn't intervened when they did and force a reality check on me, who knows how far things might have gone.

I'd like to think that after finding out about being pregnant that it would have reined me in, but honestly, I have no idea what might have happened if I didn't spend those weeks at the center.

When I glance over to find Shane, he's been swallowed up by the team in a series of guy hugs and slaps on the back.

My heart swells that we're now able to celebrate our news with our teams.

"You're still going to lead us next year, right?" Aria asks once the excitement has died down.

"If you'll still have me."

"Hell yes. You're our way to regional success, girl."

A wide smile spreads across my face that my squad have that kind of faith in me.

After a few minutes, Shane finds me once again and hands me a drink while he takes a pull from his bottle of beer.

He's sworn to take it easier tonight after his Christmas Eve excess. He was mortified when I told him what happened that evening, although secretly I think he loves that he's not only got one up on Jake but that Jake knows about it as well.

Looking around the room, I find the six of them sitting on one of Zayn's couches. I breathe a sigh of relief when I see a genuine smile light up Amalie's face once again. Hopefully, now Christmas is done, she's been able to turn a corner and look forward to the year ahead.

We've all got so much to look forward to. Graduation, college, moving out, babies—well, that's just Shane and me as far as we know.

"Right, boys! Gather around," Zayn bellows around the room, totally unaware of what shenanigans are going on elsewhere in his house. It seems he thinks the only party is in this room while the rest of our class party outside the door. "It's time to set out the last challenge of the year."

Shane groans beside me as the excitement level skyrockets around the team. He leads me over to the couches to join the others who are no longer interested in the Bears games.

"You guys are all pigs, you know that, right?" Amalie asks, watching the action along with the rest of us as Zayn starts dishing out names.

"What?" Mason says as if he's going to argue. "If you're

going to accuse anyone, it should be the guy whose lap you're currently sitting on. He started this whole thing."

"Why am I not surprised?" she says with a roll of her eyes.

"You set me up with some stinkers one too many times, I know that for a fact," I say with a laugh. Shane doesn't react to my comment like he once used to. It seems that he's come to terms with my past and believes me when I say that it's really not as shady as everyone makes out. "Some of the pickup lines those guys use are appalling. It's no wonder they're over there still single."

"Look at the expression on Justin's face," Ethan says, pointing. "I wonder who he's just been given." He laughs.

We watch their delight and horror as all the names continue to be dished out until all eyes turn on the ringleader. At the same time, the door opens and Harley, Ruby, and Poppy walk through the door. Since Harley and Ruby became JV members of the squad, they've been spending more and more time with the team and it seems tonight that Poppy is being dragged along, despite the fact she clearly looks like she wants to be anywhere else on earth right now.

Rich and Justin watch the three of them enter before they share a look.

"Oh fuck," Shane says, clearly thinking the same as me. "This is not going to go well."

Looking to Amalie and Jake, I find that they got bored with the action and are busy entertaining themselves. That can only be a good thing because I don't think he's going to like what's about to happen.

Wide smiles spread across Justin and Rich's faces before they both point at Poppy.

Zayn follows their fingers before all the color drains from his face. He shakes his head, but I know as well as he does that his refusal is futile. The rules of the game state that you don't get a second pick.

Zayn barks something at the two of them, the only words I make out are a series of swears before he storms from the room, much to the amusement of everyone who was watching the exchange.

"Well, tonight might have just gotten more interesting," Ethan states, having just watched the same thing we did. He glances to Jake, who's still oblivious to what's just happened. He's going to lose his shit when he discovers his team is using the only family member he actually likes as a pawn in their games.

All the guys disperse, probably heading off to find their conquests for the night. We might not have been involved in all that, but we all know that they have until the sun comes up to score their girl.

Jake eventually allows Amalie up for air, but no one fills him in on what he missed. Instead, we break off into a series of different conversations about the upcoming year as they all drink and I sip on my fruit juice.

Before I know it, the final countdown is on and we're speeding toward putting this dramatic year behind us.

"Come on, let's get out of here," Shane whispers in my ear before pushing from the couch and pulling me with him.

I follow him, my hand firmly grasped in his, as he makes his way outside to Zayn's back yard.

There's a big crowd out here knowing that we'll soon be able to enjoy the fireworks that are going to light up the sky.

Ignoring everyone around us, Shane pulls me into his body, his hands resting on my hips as he stares down into my eyes.

"I can't wait to find out what the future holds for us," he whispers, his voice rough with emotion. I know he's worried about his Mom, she's adamant that the moment the holidays are over that she's filing for divorce from Brett and moving on with her life. Without his dad breathing down his neck, he's had the space to be able to really think about what he wants. He's got applications written up in the pool house ready to send off to start college in September. He's still insistent that he's going to study part-time so that he can work to support us. As much as I hate that he's having to put his future on hold for us, I've learned that nothing I say is going to change his mind. He wants to do right by us, and I really can't argue with that.

"I know, me too. We're soon going to be able to say that we'll meet our baby this year."

His lips brush mine as people around us start counting down to midnight.

Our kiss deepens right as the cheer goes up around us. I forget where I am, that we're surrounded by our entire class and just hand myself over to him, showing him that I am his and that I want this for many, many years to come.

Shane rips his lips from mine right as the first of the fireworks display cracks above us. He turns me in his arms, rests his hands on my belly as his chin lands on my shoulder. We look up as color explodes in the inky night sky, signaling the start of a fresh new year.

It's time to start anew, to put our past and our mistakes behind us and look forward to our future together and our new family.

Before the fireworks end, I lower my eyes and look around at all my classmates around us. I see them all differently now. I no longer need to be the center of their attention, I no longer need to be Chelsea Fierce, queen bitch, head cheerleader, and the girl no one liked. I'm now Chelsea Fierce, girlfriend, friend, and soon-to-be mother. I smile to myself, happiness washing over me once again.

My eyes land on two people in the crowd and I gasp.

"What is it?" Shane asks, noticing my reaction.

"There in the doorway."

I keep my eyes on the unlikely couple to see if Zayn's going to win his challenge tonight. He's got Poppy pinned up against the wall with his forearms caging her in.

He lowers his head, but before we get to see if his lips meet hers, the crowd moves, and our view is blocked.

"Looks like this year is going to be just as dramatic as the last one."

"That's fine as long as it doesn't involve us."

Shane turns me back around. "How about we keep our drama inside the pool house?"

"Sounds perfect. Fancy going there right now?"

"Have you all to myself to celebrate the new year? Hell yes, let's go."

He takes my hand and leads me from Zayn's house so that we can bring in the new year as we intend on spending the rest of our lives, together.

EPILOGUE

Shane
Six months later...

"Chelsea, are you okay?" I call through to the bedroom after the sound of something heavy hitting the floor rings out through the pool house. "Chelsea?" I shout again, panic starting to filter through me.

Her due date was four days ago and every weird noise she makes has me on edge.

I'm so fucking excited to finally meet our little person, but equally, I'm more terrified than I have been in my entire life.

I glance around at all the baby stuff that covers every available surface of our small home as I push from the couch to make sure she's okay.

"Chels—" My words are cut off the second I push the bedroom door open. "What the hell are you doing?" I ask, although I can't deny that the sight before me is fucking incredible.

"Please, Shane. I'm fucking dying here. I need this baby out of me," she says, looking over her shoulder, her tired eyes begging for me to do the thing she's been asking of me for the past week.

I know I should just do it. But our baby is so low now, ready to come out, it freaks me out a little just thinking about pushing myself inside her.

However, the sight of her on all fours totally bare for the taking does have my cock swelling with my need for her.

I think she thinks I've refused because I don't find her attractive like she is right now. She couldn't be farther from the truth. She's even more beautiful and sexy to me now carrying our baby. There's no doubt that I want her, it's just my fucked-up head that keeps stopping me.

"Come on. All the articles say that sex is the best way to bring on labor. Something about a chemical in sperm or something, I don't know. I just know it can help. Please. The raspberry tea, the pineapple, none of them have worked. Let's try it, please."

Unable to take her begging any longer, I drop my hand to my waistband and pop open my fly.

"Yesss," she hisses as she watches me push both my pants and boxer briefs down my legs and kick them off.

My hard cock bobs in front of me and I take it in hand as I step up to her.

Teasing her pussy with my fingers, I find her wet and ready for me.

"Oh god," she moans, spurring me on even more than I already was. Now I've decided to do this, I'm damn near desperate to slide into her.

I work her for a few more seconds, but as she starts pushing her ass higher in the air, I know she needs more.

Sweeping the head of my cock through her juices, I slowly push inside her.

My teeth clench as the familiar, yet always mind-blowing sensation consumes me until she's as full of me as she can get.

"Fucking hell, Chelsea. So good, so fucking good."

"Yes, yes," she cries as I pull slowly before thrusting back in.

My intention is to take it slow, to be gentle. But the second her heat engulfs me, I lose all control.

All too soon, her pussy is squeezing me tight, her entire body trembling as she starts to fall over the edge.

"Oh god, oh god," she chants, her fingers twisting in the sheets as pleasure washes over her.

"Fuuuuck," I groan as the tightening of her walls pushes me over the edge. I stay deep inside her long after I've come, just trying to catch my breath and give her what she wanted, something to get things moving.

Eventually, she awkwardly drops to her side, her round belly making movements hard for her.

"Fuck. I needed that," she says with a grin. "If it doesn't do the job, we're doing it again after I've had a nap."

Flipping the fabric of her skirt over her ass, she rests her hand on her bulging belly and rubs lovingly.

"You've woken him up," she says with a laugh.

I'm hardly surprised. He's probably got a headache.

We say he, but really, we have no idea what the sex is. She wanted to find out, but I liked the idea of it being a surprise. I was happy to give her what she wanted and told the sonographer—not Shelly's mom—that we wanted to know. But our baby is clearly Chelsea's child because the stubborn little thing kept its legs closed and was at such an awkward angle that the sonographer wasn't confident enough to say either way.

I thought Chelsea would be pissed, she was adamant that she wanted to know, but we found out what was really important, that everything was progressing well and that there were no concerns, so she was happy. She's since told me she's glad we didn't find out because it makes what's about to come that much more exciting.

After pulling my boxers back on, I crawl onto the bed behind her. I press my front to her back and rest my hand over hers on her belly.

"He's kicking like crazy."

She slips her hand away and allows me to feel the foot, or knee, pushing against her skin. It's the weirdest fucking feeling ever, but as much as it freaks me out to know that it's an actual person in there, it makes my heart ache. I had no idea it was possible to love someone you'd never met, but apparently it is because I love our little person something fierce.

After long silent minutes, Chelsea's breathing evens out and she relaxes into sleep.

It's still early evening and after lying in this morning, I'm nowhere near ready to go to sleep but I don't move, I'm too content with her and our baby in my arms.

Despite not thinking I'd doze off, the next thing I know I'm jostled awake as Chelsea pushes herself up on the bad.

"Ow fuck," she moans. Assuming she's got a back or hip ache once again, I don't think much of it as I open my eyes and reach to do whatever I can to help her but then she says my name and her voice is like I've never heard it before.

It has me sitting up faster than I knew possible before I look up to her wide, terrified eyes.

"Chels?"

"I... uh... I think it's time."

"Oh fuck. Fuck. Fuck," I chant, trying like hell to remember what we're supposed to do right now.

I scramble so I'm sitting between her legs and place my hands beside hers on her belly.

"Did you have a contraction?"

"I think so. I mean, I have no idea what they're meant to feel like but it was like a period pain on steroids."

"Okay. So we need to wait for the next one and see how much time is between them."

"Yeah, okay. We can do that."

She rests her head back against the wall as she keeps her breathing slow.

"Shane?" she asks.

"Yeah, baby?"

"I'm really fucking scared."

"It's okay. I'm right here. I'm not leaving your side." She nods, but I have no idea how much comfort my words give her.

The silence stretches out between us for long, excruciating minutes. I'm just starting to think that maybe it was a false alarm when Chelsea's entire body tenses. She lifts her head from the wall, the fear in her eyes stronger than ever.

"Another one?"

It takes her a few seconds to respond, but eventually, she nods her head.

"Can you call up to the house, let them know this is happening."

"Yes, I'm on it."

"Get the bags out of the closet, I double checked everything yesterday so everything should be ready." There's a quiver in her voice that I don't like, but I know that other than being beside her and holding her hand right now, there's nothing I can do.

The next four hours of my life are like a whirlwind. Despite being told that a first labor can take a very long time, Chelsea's contractions come closer and closer faster than we're expecting.

In only two hours they were down to four minutes apart and with the help of Honey at the other side of her, we make our way to the hospital.

Chelsea had already expressed her wish to have a water birth and thankfully, when we arrive at the maternity ward, there's a room and a pool free for us.

Once the midwife has done all her initial checks, I hold Chelsea's hand as she climbs into the pool.

She sighs in relief the second the warm water surrounds her and I sit there beside her, with her hand in mine throughout the rest of her labor.

Watching her in agonizing pain is possibly the worst experience of my life. In those couple of hours, I'd give anything to take her pain away, to experience it for her.

But then, a little over two hours after we first arrive, the most incredible thing happens.

Chelsea gives birth to our utterly perfect daughter.

I watch every moment of it and I'm crying long before the midwife lifts her tiny body from the water and places her on Chelsea's chest for her first cuddle with her little girl.

"Oh my god," she sobs as she stares down at a full head of dark hair. "Oh my god, I did it."

"You did, baby, and she's perfect."

"She's a she?" Chelsea asks, sounding shocked, as if she missed the midwife's announcement only a few moments ago.

"Yeah. We have a little girl. You've got yourself a little cheerleader."

"Oh my god," she repeats, breaking down as she holds our baby to her chest.

After a few minutes, the midwife gently lifts our little person from Chelsea and places her in a crib to the side of us so they can check her over.

"Dad, would you like to come and stand with her while we sort Mom out?"

I look between the two of them, totally torn for which one needs me the most right now.

"I'm fine. Go and be with her, she might be scared." That's the only encouragement I need. After dropping a kiss to Chelsea's lips and telling her how fucking incredible she is, I walk over to our baby.

I run my eyes over every inch of her. From her dark hair and equally dark eyes, just like her mommy's, all the way down her little body.

The midwife weighs her, measures her, before putting a tiny diaper on her and taking the outfit we'd chosen as the first she'd wear from the side.

She makes quick work of putting her in it and slipping a hat on her head, she does a much better job than I'm sure I'll do when they allow me to do it.

"Are you ready for your first cuddle, Daddy?"

My heart constricts as she calls me that.

I'm a fucking dad.

I knew it was coming. I've had six months to get used to the idea, but fuck, I feel totally unprepared in those moments as the midwife passes my daughter to me.

Walking back slowly, I lower us both down onto the small couch behind me.

"Hey, baby girl. How are you doing?"

Her wide eyes stare up at me. So innocent, so vulnerable. Tears form in my eyes as I stare at her.

"I'm your daddy," I mouth silently, unsure if I'm reminding myself that she's mine or making sure she knows who I am.

A sob has me dragging my eyes from my little girl and when I look up, I find Chelsea watching us with tears streaming down her cheeks and a wide smile on her face.

"I can't believe how perfect she is."

"I can, she's half you," Chelsea whispers.

The midwife breaks our moment, instructing Chelsea to

lie down so she can check her over. "We won't be long, sweetie, and then that gorgeous baby is all yours."

With everything as it should be with both Chelsea and our little girl, they're discharged six hours later.

I'd texted everyone to let them know that she was here and that both mother and baby were doing great, but as we requested, everyone stayed away. We wanted this moment to be just about us. We might be young, but we're doing this together, as a family. This moment is about us and is one we'll never be able to repeat.

My car is outside exactly where Honey parked it when we arrived. I click the car seat into the base and triple-check that it's secure before turning to help Chelsea into the car.

"I can't," she says, pausing before dropping down into the passenger seat.

"Why? What's wrong?" I ask in a panic.

"N-nothing. I just can't be that far away from her."

With a smile, I watch as she makes her way around the back of the car and pulls the door open. She climbs inside and immediately slides over to be right beside our daughter.

Closing the door behind her, I climb in and look at Chelsea in the rearview mirror.

"Ready to go home, Mommy?"

"I am if you are, Daddy."

"Christ, this is weird."

"I'm sure we'll get used to it."

"I'm not sure we've got a choice."

I'm not sure I've ever driven more like my granddad in my life, and I make my way across town toward our home.

After the holidays, Luca and Leon went back to college and after another couple of weeks, Mom moved back in our house.

As she said she would, she got in touch with a lawyer the second they reopened and filed for divorce from my father.

Much to all our shock, he signed the second he was served with the papers and he agreed to let her have the house. She's undecided as to whether she wants to stay there or not, but right now, she's turned it into her home.

She invited Chelsea and me to join her, but we're both more than happy in our pool house until we can afford to get a place of our own. That might not be for a few years as we find our feet as parents, college students, and part-time employees as we try to build a life for ourselves, but I have every confidence that it'll all work out in the end.

The house remains silent as we make our way around the back with our new arrival. It might barely be dawn, but I know for a fact that Honey is at a window somewhere watching us. She must be so desperate to come down and meet her grandchild, but much to her annoyance, I'm sure, she's holding back.

Chelsea walks ahead to open the door while I carry the bags and the car seat with our precious cargo.

Placing her down on the coffee table, we both take a seat on the edge of the couch, just staring at her.

"I can't believe we made her."

"She's beautiful."

The time stretches out as we both stare at our peacefully sleeping baby.

"Are you still happy with the name we picked?" I ask.

"Are you?"

"Yeah, it feels right."

"I agree."

I wrap my arm around Chelsea's shoulders and pull her to me, pressing my lips against her hair.

"You were incredible, Chels."

"I'm glad you think so. I knew it was going to hurt. But fuck, no one can prepare you for that."

I hold her tighter.

"She was worth it though. And I'd totally do it again."

I turn to stare at her. "One thing at a time, yeah?"

"Oh, I didn't mean anytime soon, I was just saying. Even only hours after, it's not put me off."

"You're something else, you know that?"

She shrugs, suddenly sitting forward when a dark pair of eyes flutter open.

"Hey, Nadine," Chelsea coos, reaching forward and hesitantly unstrapping her. In a matter of seconds, she has her in her arms and is cradling her like a pro.

Standing with her, I brush my finger over Nadine's cheek. "It really suits her."

"Welcome to the world, Nadine Dunn," Chelsea says, her voice cracking with emotion.

We haven't talked about marriage, our focus has been our baby, but Chelsea was adamant that she was going to have my last name so that one day we'd all have the same one.

We might have a million and one things going on in our lives right now, and I know the right thing to do is wait, but fuck if I don't want to get on one knee and demand that she become mine right now.

"You think she's hungry?" Chelsea asks, dragging me from my crazy thoughts.

"Only one way to find out."

Chelsea had some lessons in feeding in the hospital and she's quick to do exactly as she was told.

"I'm just going to put all this away while you do that."

I put everything in its new home while Chelsea nurses. When I come back out, Nadine is already asleep again in Chelsea's arms and Chelsea doesn't look too far behind.

"We should get some sleep while she is."

Chelsea nods, seemingly too exhausted to even speak. "Can you message everyone? Tell them we're home and let them know that we'll message again once we've had some rest so they can come and meet her. Message Greg too, he'll want to know."

Chelsea didn't mention her paternal dad again until almost the end of January when she decided that she was curious enough to reach out to him via text. Since then, they've only met twice. They're taking things slow, but she's decided that she'd like to get to know him, the him now, not the one from her childhood. I couldn't be prouder of her, fighting her demons and embracing a new family member.

"Of course."

I take Nadine from Chelsea's arms so she can get up easier. Even a few hours in, it feels natural to hold her in my arms.

I follow Chelsea through to our bedroom and lower Nadine to her bassinet next to Chelsea's side of the bed as Chelsea drops down onto it.

"I don't think I've ever been this exhausted."

"Get some sleep. I'll join you in a few minutes."

I send out a few messages as Chelsea lies watching Nadine sleep beside her, but when I come back, she's fast asleep.

I'm tired, although nowhere near as tired as Chelsea must be after going through all that, but I can't help but pull a chair over and sit and watch both of them sleep.

One reckless night that I never in a million years thought would happen changed my life forever.

It brought me the most important person in my life, and in turn, she just gave me another.

I shake my head as I try to process everything I'm feeling watching my entire world before me.

Eventually, my eyes get too heavy to sit any longer. Standing, I lean over the bassinet and drop a gentle kiss to Nadine's forehead before walking around the bed and crawling in behind Chelsea once again.

I wrap my arm around her waist like I did all those hours

ago, but this time there is no kicking baby in her belly because our little bundle is sleeping soundly beside us.

"I love you so much. You fucking blew me away today."

"Thank you," she mumbles in her sleep. "You saved me. You both did."

With emotion clogging my throat, I hold her tighter to me and close my eyes, ready to start our lives as parents when we next wake up.

Are you ready for Poppy and Zayn?
HUNTER is now live.

ACKNOWLEDGMENTS

When I first dreamed up Jake Thorn and the others a little over a year ago, I thought the Rosewood High series would just be three books. I had no idea just how much I was going to fall in love with all these guys!

I must admit, I was worried about trying to redeem Chelsea, she's lived up to her Queen Bitch title quite nicely in the past, but I couldn't get away from her and Shane screaming at me for their story. They're the most unlikely couple, but man, did they pull at my heartstrings as I wrote this book. I love them both so much, Chelsea's strength and fierceness and Shane for his big heart.

I took a chance on Thorn last year; it was different to what I'd written before and I questioned myself so many times about it but I am so glad I listened to my heart and just went for it. These guys have been such a huge part of my life and I cannot wait for it to continue. There are still plenty of books to come from this series and so many more characters to get to know, some of which you've not even met yet *rubs hands together excitedly*!

THANK YOU so much for taking a chance on this series, I'm so grateful to have you along for the ride with me.

As always, I need to say a huge thank you to my PA and alpha reader for Fierce. Sam openly admitted that she hated Chelsea before embarking on this book and I'm please to say that we broke her down to the point that she actually cried for Chelsea. I couldn't have completed this book in time without your help so thank you so much for that and everything else you do.

My beta readers, Darlene, Deanna, Michelle, Nicole, Susanne and Tracy for their quick feedback and support.

I should probably also give my daughter a huge shout out for being utterly incredible during Lockdown and allowing me to continue writing so that I didn't lose my mind as well as my deadlines!

I hope Chelsea and Shane's story was everything you hoped it would be. If you hadn't already guessed, we're heading back to Rosewood to get to know Zayn a little better, and at last, it's Poppy's turn.

Keep your eyes peeled though because I've also got a couple of short stories from this world coming soon in boxsets release this winter and you're not going to want to miss them!

Until next time,

Tracy xo

ABOUT THE AUTHOR

Tracy Lorraine is a new adult and contemporary romance author. Tracy has recently-ish turned thirty and lives in a cute Cotswold village in England with her husband, baby girl and lovable but slightly crazy dog. Having always been a bookaholic with her head stuck in her Kindle Tracy decided to try her hand at a story idea she dreamt up and hasn't looked back since.

Be the first to find out about new releases and offers. Sign up to my newsletter here.

If you want to know what I'm up to and see teasers and snippets of what I'm working on, then you need to be in my Facebook group Tracy's Angels.

Keep up to date with Tracy's books at
www.tracylorraine.com

ALSO BY TRACY LORRAINE

Falling Series

Falling for Ryan: Part One #1

Falling for Ryan: Part Two #2

Falling for Jax #3

Falling for Daniel (An Falling Series Novella)

Falling for Ruben #4

Falling for Fin #5

Falling for Lucas #6

Falling for Caleb #7

Falling for Declan #8

Falling For Liam #9

Forbidden Series

Falling for the Forbidden #1

Losing the Forbidden #2

Fighting for the Forbidden #3

Craving Redemption #4

Demanding Redemption #5

Avoiding Temptation #6

Chasing Temptation #7

Rebel Ink Series

Hate You #1

Trick You #2

Defy You #3

Play You #4

Inked (A Rebel Ink/Driven Crossover)

Rosewood High Series

Thorn #1

Paine #2

Savage #3

Fierce #4

Hunter #5

Faze (#6 Prequel)

Fury #6

Legend #7

Maddison Kings University Series

TMYM: Prequel

TRYS #1

TDYW #2

TBYS #3

TVYC #4

TDYD #5

Ruined Series

Ruined Plans #1

Ruined by Lies #2

Ruined Promises #3

Never Forget Series

Never Forget Him #1

Never Forget Us #2

Everywhere & Nowhere #3

Poppy
Three years ago...

"Zayn, your turn," Ethan says, his eyes moving around the circle until he finds Zayn's excited dark eyes.

It's his birthday, he should be excited. Unlike me, who's been forced to attend a fifteen-year-old boy's party while ignoring the fact he doesn't want me, Ruby, or his sister here.

We stand out like a sore thumb among his football friends, but for some crazy reason Jada, Zayn and Harley's mom, seemed to think it was a good idea.

I roll my eyes at her naïve plans. At least Scarlett, their older sister, had the sense to argue and has hidden herself in her room.

The tension in the room ticks up a notch as everyone stares at the empty bottle that Zayn spins in the middle of the circle we're all sitting in.

All the girls around me, bar Harley, seem to hold their

breath in the hope of getting a chance at seven seconds in heaven with Zayn.

I try to keep my breathing steady in the hope of covering up that I'd also be more than willing to lock myself in the closet with Zayn.

He's hot, and I can't deny that I haven't had a crush on him since they first arrived in Rosewood last year.

It's just a shame he's one of Jake's football buddies. They might all only be sophomores, but I only have to take one look at the varsity team to see what they're going to be like in two years. Their egos and wannabe god-like personas are already growing larger than life.

I have no interest in getting tangled up with that. I'm not a popular girl, I'm not destined for the cheer squad or one of the sport teams. I'll just hide in the shadows while doing my thing and counting down the days until I can leave for college and finally take charge of my own life.

I let out a sigh, lost in thoughts of a future without the weight of my family weighing down on me. Being fourteen shouldn't be like this. I shouldn't be worrying about everyone else more than myself, but sadly it's my reality.

The bottle slows to a stop and my heart jumps into my throat as realization dawns that it could be about to land on me. I glance to Harley at my side and smile, imagining everyone's irritation—mostly Zayn's—should it land on his sister.

It misses her though, and when the bottle comes to a stop, it's pointed directly at me.

My eyes fly up in shock as I look up at Zayn.

"No. No fucking way," Jake, my cousin barks, his eyes narrowing on Zayn.

"Calm down, man. It's just some fun. Poppy, you're up for it, right?" Ethan looks at me expectantly.

"I... um..." I hesitate as all the sophomore girls' eyes drill into me.

"Just let him spin it again," Shelly pipes up, one of the cheer wannabes. "Zayn doesn't want to kiss a freshman anyway. She probably doesn't have the first clue about what she's doing."

I part my lips to argue, but really, she has a point. My experience with kissing is limited to an awkward lip press with Christopher back in junior high during a game of kiss chase.

"No second spins," Ethan spits, reiterating the rules that he laid out at the beginning of this stupid game. "You get in the closet or you forfeit, and I'm pretty sure none of you want to do the dares that I've got running around in my head." He smiles wickedly and Shelly pales slightly. I've heard all about Ethan Savage's dares, and so has everyone else in the room looking at their faces. "So..." He waves his hand between the two of us and the closet being used for this game.

My nerves quadruple to the point I worry if I'm going to be able to actually walk over there.

I push to stand, feeling the stares of everyone around me but no more so than Harley's shock and my cousin's death stare.

I manage to take two steps to where Ethan is now holding the door open before a hand wraps around my wrist.

"If he tries anything with you, tell me and I'll lay him out."

"It's fine, Jake. It's just for fun," I tell him, but I don't meet his eyes. The last thing I need him to see are my nerves and, dare I say it, excitement about this.

"It better be. You're worth more than any of this group has to offer." I don't miss the sounds of the rest of the team ribbing Zayn for having to kiss his little sister's friend, but I zone them out and focus on Jake.

"They're your friends, Jake."

"Yeah, and you're my family. The only decent one I got. I want the best for you, Popsicle."

I roll my eyes at his overprotectiveness, although I can't help but feel loved. It's something I don't feel all that often where my family is concerned. I think Jake is the only person who actually understands, who gets me. And for that, I'll forever be grateful.

"It's all good. You've got nothing to worry about."

He releases me, allowing me to slip into the closet.

I wait in the shadows for Zayn to join me while the hoots and hollers from his friends continue.

"Make sure she gives you one hell of a present, Hunter," someone calls, making me swallow down the lump of anxiety that's climbed up my throat.

It's only a kiss. I can do that. It's no biggie.

Right?

There's no doubt in my mind that he's only doing this because it's a game. There's no way in hell he'd ever willingly kiss me. I might have imagined what it would be like a time or two, but I suspect it never so much as crossed his mind, let alone in this capacity.

The door widens, allowing a sliver of light to illuminate me before it clicks shut, bathing us both in darkness.

My heart beats so wildly I swear he must be able to hear it. My hands tremble and my temperature spikes.

Every noise he makes sounds incredibly loud despite the fact I have blood rushing in my ears faster than I'm sure is natural as he closes the space between us.

"Poppy?" he asks, his voice sounding calm, like this is just an everyday occurrence for him.

I remind myself that it probably is. Jake, Zayn, and the others have girls hanging off them wherever they go. He's probably well-practiced in this sort of thing.

"Y-yeah," I whisper, hating that my voice cracks, showing my nerves.

The heat of his body hits mine. "Do you have any idea how long I've wanted to do this?"

His words throw me off for a second and it takes me longer than it should to register them.

"Y-you want to k-kiss me?" I sound pathetic and I kick myself for not sounding more confident.

"Yeah. There was no one else I wanted that bottle to land on. This is the only birthday present I wanted."

"Oh God," I practically whimper when his fingers find mine.

He steps into my body, pressing me back into the wall. I gasp at the feeling of his hard body against mine as his fingers tickle up my bare arm before he grasps the back of my neck.

"Ready?" he asks, his voice deeper than it was only moments ago.

My head spins as I fight to remember to breathe.

"Y-yeah, I—" I don't get to finish my thought because his soft, full lips brush mine.

At just that small contact, my knees go weak. He must sense it because his other hand lands on my waist. It feels huge as his touch burns my skin, causing sensations to swell within me that I've never felt before.

His lips stay on mine, unmoving for what feels like forever but in reality, it's probably not more than a second before his tongue teases at the seam of my lips.

I have no idea what I'm doing, but it doesn't seem to matter because my body seems to know what's expected of me and my lips part, allowing him entry.

If I didn't already know he'd had experience, then I did in that moment as he took control of the kiss. His tongue sweeping against mine.

My arms stay rigid at my sides as his fingers twitch at my waist, obviously wanting to move, but he never moves.

He kisses me like I've seen on TV, but it feels nothing like I imagined. I'm not nervous. Not self-conscious. I just let myself go and allow him to sweep me away.

All too soon, he places a chaste kiss on my lips and backs away from me. I miss him almost instantly, to the point I actually reach out for him, but despite my eyes having adjusted to the darkness, I don't manage to make contact with him.

"Poppy?" he asks again, his voice husky and rough, it does things to my insides I can't explain.

"Yeah?" I ask eagerly, desperate to hear it again.

"Don't repeat a word I said to you."

Lead fills my veins at his warning. I should have known he was lying.

I'm too devastated to respond, desperately trying to fight the tears that are already burning the backs of my eyes.

I thought he really meant it. That he's been thinking about kissing me like I have him.

Stupid, stupid girl.

He pushes the door open, the sudden light makes me close my eyes as a chorus of cheers erupts from the other side.

My heart sinks into my feet as I wonder how the hell I'm supposed to walk out of here with my head held high.

You're not, a little voice in my head says. *You just totally screwed up.*

The ruckus only gets louder as a victorious Zayn steps from the closet after his few seconds in heaven.

"So..." someone prompts. "Did she give you the gift you've been dreaming of?"

Before he answers, he looks back at me. I might be back in the shadows but he sees me and our eyes connect for the briefest moment.

"Nah, she's a frigid bitch." He walks away as his friends erupt in laughter and a couple of the girls descend on him, probably offering to do everything I apparently couldn't. All the while, I pray for the ground to swallow me up while continuing to hide in the shadows.

How long can I stay in here? Will anyone even notice?

HUNTER SNEAK PEEK

CHAPTER ONE

Poppy

I rush out of the Hunter's kitchen with a drink in hand, ready to find Harley and Ruby to celebrate the New Year together.

Butterflies erupt in my stomach, despite all the crap in my life, this is an exciting moment. One year closer to finishing school. One year closer to taking control of my life. One year closer to leaving this place and everything I despise about it behind. This year we're going to become seniors, we get to start seriously thinking about our futures and what we want from life. I might not have it all figured out yet, but I know one thing. My future isn't here. There are too many memories and demons lurking in the shadows for me to ever want to stay.

But while I'm stuck here, I figure I'd better make the most of it.

I see a flash of Harley's bright red hair and I can't help but smile. At least I have a couple of good things in my life, my two best friends are definitely that. I have no idea how I'd survive this place without them.

The sound of the party around me begins to lessen as kids head outside, ready to watch the fireworks that are about to illuminate the sky.

I shouldn't have come tonight but despite my parents' obvious irritation that I was going to spend the night enjoying myself and they weren't, I packed a bag and walked straight out the front door. Most days I allow them to blackmail me into doing as they wish, tonight wasn't one of those nights.

I knew it was safe being here. It's mostly the seniors who are partying at the Hunter's, the majority of our junior class are elsewhere, thank God. It means that for once, I'm able to let my hair down and attempt to enjoy being a seventeen-year-old girl if just for a couple of hours, forget about the weight that presses down on my shoulders every other day of the year.

I'm almost at the door when a warm hand wraps around my wrist. The grip is hard, meaningful, and my heart jumps into my throat. A shiver of fear runs down my spine.

He's not here, I remind myself. *You're safe right now. He is not here.* It doesn't matter how many times I repeat those words in the millisecond I have before whoever has touched me makes themselves known, the fear threatens to swallow me whole regardless.

I kick myself for letting my guard down tonight, for allowing myself to think that I could have just one normal night. For once, just enjoy a party like everyone around me does without constantly looking over my shoulder, waiting for the devil to strike.

"You're looking hot tonight, Pops."

His deep, rough voice flows over me, and instantly my shiver returns, only this time it's not with fear.

Steeling myself, I lift my chin, ready to fight.

"Get your hands off me, Zayn."

I try to pull myself from his grip but he's holding too tightly. Before I've even had a chance to plan my next move, he's taken control and pulled me back until the cool of the wall bites into my skin.

He stares into my eyes and as always, I hate that he can see so deep.

"Why aren't you enjoying yourself like everyone else?"

"I... um... I am. See?" I lift my drink and tip it toward my mouth, only it doesn't meet my lips. Instead, it's taken from my fingers and pressed against his full lips in a heartbeat.

"That's soda," he states, his brows drawn.

"So?"

"Don't you want to let go, have a little fun? You're always so uptight."

I flinch at his words. I spend most of my life trying to cover up how I really feel, what's really going on with me. I really don't need him digging and finding the ugly things that I try to keep away from everyone else.

"Don't you want to have fun?"

"Who says I'm not?"

"Aside from the soda, your face."

My lips part to respond but I fear I have no argument.

"The others don't see it, do they?" His fingers lift and he tucks a lock of hair behind my ear, his touch burning all the way down to my toes.

"Don't see what, Zayn?" I snap. I shouldn't ask. I'm terrified to hear the answer, to know what he really thinks of me but that's the thing about my best friend's older brother. He affects me in a way that no one else ever has. It annoys the crap out of me.

"I don't know," he muses, staring deep into my eyes. "But I want to find out."

"Fuck you, Zayn," I spit.

"Now there's an idea. You think that'll help loosen you up a little?" His eyebrows wiggle in excitement as I will all of my muscles below my waist not to clench at the thought.

I told myself years ago that I wasn't ever allowed to lose myself in Zayn's smooth lines. He shattered my young heart all those years ago in that closet. I may never have forgiven him for that, but hell if I don't still dream about it. I tell myself that should the situation arise ever again that I'd tell him to go to hell, but I'm pretty sure I'm only lying to myself because even now, I can feel that kiss.

"Let me go," I damn near beg.

"Why, so you can go and pretend to be happy? Tell me how to make it better, Poppy. Tell me how to put a genuine smile on your face."

"Why do you care?" I ask, my eyes narrowing on his sparkling ones.

"I've always cared. I watch you, you know, when you're not looking."

"No," I argue, knowing that it can't be true. The thought of it being true and him discovering what I keep hidden is scarier than him admitting that he might actually care.

"These frown lines," he says, his finger gently running between my brows, smoothing them out. "I want to know what puts them there." His finger continues down over my nose until it connects with my lips.

I suck in a ragged breath as I watch his eyes follow its journey. It lingers on my bottom lip for a beat before pulling it out. His eyes darken as he sucks on his own bottom lip like he's imagining all kinds of dirty things.

I've seen the look on him before. Usually right before he makes a play for a cheer slut. But despite the fact I know that, it doesn't make me move. In fact, right now, with his scent filling my nose and the heat of his body seeping into mine, all it does is make me want to find out where he's going with this.

I don't need to look up to know we're alone right now, someone has turned the music down and all the voices that can be heard are coming from the garden.

I should push him away. Harley, or worse, Jake could see us and jump to conclusions. What I really don't need in my life right now is more drama. But as I remain locked in his stare, I'm powerless to move.

His hand wraps around the back of my neck, his fingers squeezing in the most incredible way.

"What keeps these muscles so tense, Pops? What are you hiding?"

My lips part to respond as he rests his forearm against the wall beside my head. He steps closer, completely surrounds me with his size and I feel like a little girl once again. I feel like I'm fourteen once more and about to experience everything I'd been dreaming about.

"Zayn," I warn as he slowly closes the space between us, the crowd from outside beginning their countdown to the New Year.

"Celebrate the New Year with me, Pops. Let's bring it in style."

He steps closer still. His hard, powerful body pressing mine back into the wall. His muscles meld with my softness and my knees threaten to give out.

Right as the first firework explodes, his lips connect with mine. His grip on my neck gets tighter and my lips part without any instruction from my brain.

You shouldn't be doing this, the little voice in my head screams. But I already know I don't have the strength in me to stop it. Not now that I can taste him, feel his tongue dancing with mine, feel his hardness pressing against my stomach.

Fuck, he actually wants me.

His tongue delves past my lips once more, searching mine out. This kiss is different to the previous one we shared.

There's no hesitation whatsoever. He knows what he's doing this time.

As he should, he's been with half of the senior girls according to the gossip.

"Oh God," I mumble against his lips, the realization of what I'm doing slamming into me full force.

Pressing my palms against his solid chest, I push in the hope of making him back up.

"Zayn, stop," I beg the second his lips part from mine.

Keeping my eyes on the fabric of my shirt, I fight down my need to pull him straight back to me.

I miss him already. It's crazy.

"You shouldn't have done that," I whisper, needing to at least attempt to tell him how wrong it was.

"Why?" His voice hits me exactly where I don't need it to. That combined with how ferociously his chest is heaving doesn't help my resolve at all.

"Because nothing good happens when we..."

"When we?"

I roll my eyes at myself, at the fact he needs me to say the words out loud. "When we kiss." I lift my eyes to him, needing him to know how serious I am.

"I don't have a black eye yet, do I?" he says, referring to what happened after that horrendous experience of our last kiss.

I might have wanted to hide in that closet for the rest of eternity but the second I heard Jake's angry growl and the girls start screaming, I didn't have a choice but to step into the light and watch as Jake rained hell down on Zayn's face for what he said about me.

"Give it time."

Our eyes hold, mine hold a warning whereas I swear his hold a promise, although I'm not entirely sure what he's trying to promise me. All I do know is that the tingles continue to race through me and my temperature doesn't decrease at all with his stare burning into me.

When the fireworks are over, the crowd starts to disperse and their chatter and laughter filter down to me. I know I need to move. I can't be standing here in this stare-off with Zayn when Jake or Harley emerges.

Thankfully, loud footsteps approaching us sound as I drag my eyes away from his dark and hungry stare.

I look up in time to see Justin clap his hand down on Zayn's shoulder. His eyes are wild and he sways a little on his feet. The guy's wasted.

I'm about to roll my eyes at the state of him when he says the words that rips the rug from beneath me once again.

"Sweet, man. I didn't think you were going to pull off your tag tonight. Right at the stroke of midnight, too."

My eyes widen as understanding washes through me. The team's little games aren't a secret around the girls of Rosewood High.

"What?" I ask, forcing the word out through the lump in my throat.

"Pop, it's not—"

"Don't lie to me, Zayn," I hiss back. "Tell me I wasn't a dare," I demand.

He swallows nervously but his lips remain sealed.

"Tell me," I damn near plead, not knowing how I'm going to deal with this again. The first rejection hurt like hell. But this time, it's so different.

That kiss, those few seconds of escape from reality, there's no way he can have any idea how much it meant to me, how much I needed it.

He gave me something that took me away, even if for a few seconds and now it's all crumbling around my feet once again.

"Pops, I—"

"No," I bark, shoving at his chest. "Don't *Pops* me. You're a fucking joke. You know that, right? The group of you are a fucking joke," I scream, briefly meeting Justin's eyes who doesn't so much as flinch at my volume.

Assholes.

Zayn takes a step back, his eyes still trained on me. Something akin to regret filling them but I refuse to acknowledge it.

Stepping past him, my arm collides with his, sending a pain right down to my fingers but despite my gasp, he doesn't react.

"I told you, nothing good comes from us kissing. It's time you realized that," I hiss at him before I storm past.

"And what if I don't?"

Shaking my head, I march from the kitchen and head toward the stairs.

What I really want to do is walk straight out of the Hunter's front door and leave this party and his games behind me. But where would I go?

Home?

I almost laugh to myself at the thought. I think I'd rather be Zayn's plaything, the pawn in his games, than being at home tonight.

I fly up the stairs, my legs burning as I take two at a time in my need to get away. I ignore all the doors until I get to the penultimate one and I swing it open.

The safety of Harley's room makes me sigh with relief. I slam it behind me, feeling the vibrations of the force I used before I throw myself at the bed.

I tell myself not to cry. Not to waste any more tears on that asshole, but it's not a fight I can win because the harder I try to keep them in, the more they insist on being released until I'm sobbing into Harley's pillow.

www.ingramcontent.com/pod-product-compliance
Lightning Source LLC
Chambersburg PA
CBHW030142200726
48285CB00004BC/1289